EVERYMAN, I will go with thee,
and be thy guide,
In thy most need to go by thy side

Modern Short Stories
to 1940

Edited by John Hadfield

Dent: London and Melbourne
EVERYMAN'S LIBRARY

© Introduction and selection, J. M. Dent & Sons Ltd, 1984
All rights reserved

Phototypeset in 10/11½ pt VIP Sabon by
Inforum Ltd, Portsmouth
Made in Great Britain by
The Guernsey Press Co. Ltd, Guernsey, C.I.
for
J. M. Dent & Sons Ltd
Aldine House, 33 Welbeck Street, London W1M 8LX
First published in Everyman's Library in 1939
Reset edition, with additions, reprinted as an Everyman Classic in 1984

No 1954 Paperback ISBN 0 460 11954 0

CONTENTS

INTRODUCTION

The short story as a distinctive literary form did not establish itself in English literature until the twentieth century. It probably originated, in rudimentary form, as an anecdote told round the primitive camp fire, when hunters described, with unconscious art and imaginative emphasis, their deeds of the day. Later it was expanded into myth and legend, and given formal expression in the classical fables.

However, once literature became, in its literal sense, something written down, the short story became one of its minor elements, yielding pride of place to history, the epic, the drama and poetry.

In Elizabethan England poetry and plays absorbed almost all the imaginative talents. The short story was only to be found in occasional collections in the tradition of *The Decameron* such as William Painter's *Palace of Pleasure*. The ascendancy of drama and poetry was maintained throughout the seventeenth century, and it was not until the appearance of Defoe and Swift that prose storytellers managed to get a hearing.

It was, however, the full-length novel that engaged the story-teller's attention throughout the eighteenth and into the middle years of the nineteenth century. Neither Fielding nor Richardson, Scott nor the Brontës, George Eliot nor Trollope, was attracted to the short story. Dickens admittedly took time off occasionally from full-length novel writing to provide a short piece for one of the Christmas magazines, but this – though often brilliant – was only part-time work.

It was not until the last decade of the nineteenth century that the short story made any serious impact upon the creative faculties of English writers. It was the development of the magazine that brought this about. It is significant that the first great specialist short-story writer in English, Rudyard Kipling, started his career as a journalist. He continued to write short stories until the outbreak of the First World War, but the story of his chosen for this collection germinated in Kipling's experience as a newspaper man in India, and appeared in *The Second Jungle Book*, published in 1895.

Although he was not a journalist, but a doctor, another master storyteller of the nineties, Arthur Conan Doyle, found an outlet for his Sherlock Holmes stories in a monthly magazine, *The Strand*. In the United States meanwhile the proliferation of newspapers and magazines around the turn of the century enabled William Sydney Porter, at one time a journalist on the *Houston Texas Post*, to rehabilitate himself after a prison sentence by undertaking a contract from the *New York World* to supply one story every week for a fee of a hundred dollars. Writing in much the same vein as his predecessor, Mark Twain, and his contemporary, Ambrose Bierce, he was a master of plot and the surprise ending—a kind of story represented in this collection by Somerset Maugham, Stacy Aumonier, and, surprisingly, also by Aldous Huxley and Evelyn Waugh.

The *Strand Magazine* and its many successors, British and American, in the first third of the twentieth century, being designed for quick consumption in small doses, demanded a plot, with recognizable characters, a beginning, an involvement, and a decisive end—preferably unexpected. Clearly a vast amount of what was printed was machine-made and ephemeral. But in all ages good writers as well as bad have to serve the public that is available to them.

'No form of art', wrote Somerset Maugham, 'is produced unless there is a demand for it, and if newspapers and magazines did not publish short stories they would not be written. All short stories are magazine short stories or newspaper stories. The writers must accept certain (but constantly changing) conditions; it has never been known yet that a good writer was unable to write his best owing to the conditions under which alone he could gain a public for his work.'

Today, in certain quarters, that statement might be regarded simply as self-justification, but it would certainly have been accepted by most of the earlier writers represented in this book.

Even that most idiosyncratic satirist who wrote stories under the name of Saki was a professional journalist.

Several of the writers, however, in the second half of the book, would probably prefer the statement by Tchekhov, that a story should have neither a beginning nor an end. It can present merely a study in character, or a mood, or the complexities of a situation to which there appears to be no solution.

Fantasy has become a favourite element in modern short stories, and has inevitably inspired some whimsical and undisciplined writing. It is represented here in its more restrained forms, with Saki's urbane and matter-of-fact 'Tobermory', with T. F. Powys's bucolic fable about 'Mr Pim and the Holy Crumb', and with Richard Hughes's 'The Ghost'. Fantasy also hovers over E. M. Forster's 'Story of the Siren', though this finely balanced tale never crosses the margin of the unseen.

The margin of the unseen is a phrase that comes to mind when considering the short stories of one of the modern masters of the medium, Walter de la Mare. He has written one or two ghost stories, but in general he observes the probabilities whilst hinting at something which just edges beyond belief. His chief characters – most frequently children – have their feet well on the ground, but there is nearly always another character, usually a woman 'of uncertain age', who is enigmatic, just a little unaccountable. The obvious and well-known example of this is 'Seaton's Aunt'. It might be said that the story I have chosen is not really a story at all. There is virtually no plot, there is little development, the ending is not a surprise. But it has the same haunting appeal as is expressed in so many of de la Mare's poems, for instance:

> Who is it calling by the darkened river
>   Where the moss lies smooth and deep,
> And the dark trees lean unmoving arms,
>   Silent and vague in sleep,
> And the bright-heeled constellations pass
>   In splendour through the gloom;
> Who is it calling o'er the darkened river
>   In music, 'Come!'?

Forrest Reid, in his critical study of de la Mare's work, calls 'Miss

Duveen' a masterpiece, 'using the word deliberately, to describe a thing that is completely successful and completely individual. No story by any other writer is in the least like it.'

What 'Miss Duveen' shares, however, with most of the stories in this collection is what John Galsworthy rated the essential in a short-story writer: 'the power of interesting sentence by sentence'. Unlike the novelist, the short-story writer cannot rely upon the cumulative effect of chapter after chapter. His writing must be more taut, highly charged, and rigorously controlled. Control is the most evident characteristic of Evelyn Waugh's very short story with its dead-pan ending. And V. S. Pritchett's 'Sense of Humour', for all its wildly comic development, yields to none in its tautness of narration.

The stories to which I have referred so far give some indication of the variety of theme and treatment that has characterized the blossoming of the short story in the twentieth century. Some critics complain that modern short-story writers concentrate upon the more sombre undertones of life. Certainly these are echoed in that devastating tale of futile conflict, Frank O'Connor's 'Guests of the Nation', in James Joyce's 'Clay', the slight but disturbing piece by D. H. Lawrence, and Katherine Mansfield's deeply moving story, 'The Garden Party'.

Yet tragic realism is only one of the many ingredients of the short story as it has developed in our own times. Even more significant has been the expression of what one can only call a poetic impulse. It is perhaps facile to suggest that some of the outstanding short-story writers of the mid-twentieth century have been poets *manqués*. Although the expansion of the magazine market gave them opportunities of publication that they had never had before, the pervasive influence on the way in which they wrote, and their choice of subject matter, was increasingly that of Tchekhov—an awareness of the poetic undertones, the tragi-comedy of ordinary life, much more than the development of episode and plot.

Although he became a successful novelist and a brilliant war-reporter H. E. Bates was originally and essentially a short-story writer. And he wrote, 'I have never from the first had the slightest interest in plot.' His story 'Alexander', though packed with vivid vignettes of character, is in essence just an account of a journey through a single day, in an idyllic countryside, recording the impact of the people and landscape described on the changing moods of the observer, a boy. It is totally realistic but its impulse is purely lyrical.

So too is the impulse behind many of the stories of Liam O'Flaherty, one of a school of Celtic writers who celebrated the simple lives of Irish peasants. But the extraordinary variety and richness of the modern English short story are exemplified in three other stories which to some extent are inspired by the lyrical impulse, though they are totally dissimilar in setting and manner.

A. E. Coppard's 'The Green Drake' appears to be just an exercise in rustic whimsy, but it is a little gem of craft and sophistication. It may seem absurd to bracket this with a characteristic P. G. Wodehouse story, set in the bar-parlour of Mr Mulliner's 'Anglers' Rest', but this genial anecdote, told in vintage Wodehouse prose, ends on a note which may be ludicrous but is sheerly lyrical in its humour. And the story by the youngest contributor to the collection, William Saroyan, shows how a tale that is lineally descended from the nineteenth-century Bierce and O. Henry can be developed to almost acrobatic virtuosity by a writer of the *New Yorker* school.

The selection of most of the stories contained in this collection was made as long ago as 1939, and I suppose it is a tribute both to the continuing interest in the short story as a literary form and to the merits of the stories chosen that the book has continued to be in demand for over forty years. In rereading it and expanding it slightly for a new impression I confess I was pleasantly surprised to find how well the original selection had worn. There was no story and no author in the original edition which I now felt inclined to omit. The one writer whose inclusion was at first regarded as slightly speculative, Stacy Aumonier, has now come into his own. It is gratifying to see how one or two others who were only beginning to establish their claims in 1939, such as Gerald Bullett, H. E. Bates, and Sir Victor Pritchett, have fully demonstrated their mastery of their craft in the past forty years.

And P. G. Wodehouse, once regarded as merely an adroit entertainer, has now taken his deserved place in the canon of English literature.

Because they were represented in other Everyman volumes in print at the time, and for no other reason, I omitted from my original selection Walter de la Mare and Aldous Huxley. I am very happy that now they both triumphantly take their places as masters of the short story, apart from their achievements as poet, novelist or essayist.

The omission of Evelyn Waugh from the original edition arose simply because the breadth of his talents had not yet been wholly proven. His wonderful war trilogy had still to be published; so had _Brideshead Revisited_. I am very happy to be able to represent him now amongst his peers with the sardonic little tale about Mr Loveday.

I think the chief shortcoming of the original selection, however, was its failure to represent one of the main streams of originality and imagination in the modern short story, that which came from Ireland. Both Frank O'Connor and Liam O'Flaherty ought to have found their place in the original edition, and now appear here as early representatives of a movement that is much more fully represented in Giles Gordon's selection for the period 1940–1980.

1984   John Hadfield

ACKNOWLEDGMENTS

Thanks are due to the following authors and publishers for permission to include stories:

Gerald Bullett for 'Wax' from *Twenty-Four Tales*; Jonathan Cape Ltd, for 'Alexander' from *Thirty Tales* by H. E. Bates, 'The Green Drake' from *Nixey's Harlequin* by A. E. Coppard, and 'Clay' from *Dubliners* by James Joyce; Chatto & Windus for 'The Ghost' from *A Moment of Time* by Richard Hughes, 'Mr Pim and the Holy Crumb' from *No Painted Plumage* by T. F. Powys, and 'Sense of Humour' from *You Make Your Own Life* by V. S. Pritchett; The Literary Trustees of Walter de la Mare and The Society of Authors as their representative for 'Miss Duveen'; Faber & Faber Ltd, Modern Age Books, Inc., and the author for 'Ever Fall in Love with a Midget?' from *Love, Here Is My Hat*; William Heinemann Ltd, for 'Louise' from *Cosmopolitans* by Somerset Maugham; Mrs Laura Huxley and Chatto & Windus for 'The Gioconda Smile' from *Mortal Coils* by Aldous Huxley; Herbert Jenkins Ltd, and Sir Pelham Wodehouse for 'The Fiery Wooing of Mordred' from *Young Men in Spats*; The Executors of the late D. H. Lawrence for 'Second Best' from *The Tales of D. H. Lawrence*; Macmillan & Co. Ltd, and the Executors of the late Stella Benson for 'The Desert Islander'; Macmillan & Co. Ltd, and Mrs Kipling for 'The Miracle of Purun Bhagat' from *The Second Jungle Book* by Rudyard Kipling; Liam O'Flaherty for 'The Black Mare' from *The Short Stories of Liam O'Flaherty*; A. D. Peters & Co. Ltd for 'Guests of the Nation' from *Collection Two* by Frank O'Connor; A. D. Peters & Co. Ltd for 'Mr Loveday's Little Outing' from *Work Suspended and Other Stories* by Evelyn Waugh; Sidgwick & Jackson Ltd, and E. M. Forster for 'The Story of the Siren' from *The Eternal Moment*; and The Viking Press for 'I'm a Fool' from *Horses and Men* by Sherwood Anderson.

JOSEPH CONRAD

The Lagoon

The white man, leaning with both arms over the roof of the little house in the stern of the boat, said to the steersman:

'We will pass the night in Arsat's clearing. It is late.'

The Malay only grunted, and went on looking fixedly at the river. The white man rested his chin on his crossed arms and gazed at the wake of the boat. At the end of the straight avenue of forests cut by the intense glitter of the river, the sun appeared unclouded and dazzling, poised low over the water that shone smoothly like a band of metal. The forests, sombre and dull, stood motionless and silent on each side of the broad stream. At the foot of big, towering trees, trunkless nipa palms rose from the mud of the bank, in bunches of leaves enormous and heavy, that hung un-stirring over the brown swirl of eddies. In the stillness of the air every tree, every leaf, every bough, every tendril of creeper and every petal of minute blossoms seemed to have been bewitched into an immobility perfect and final. Nothing moved on the river but the eight paddles that rose flashing regularly, dipped together with a single splash; while the steersman swept right and left with a periodic and sudden flourish of his blade describing a glinting semicircle above his head. The churned-up water frothed along-side with a confused murmur. And the white man's canoe, advancing upstream in the short-lived disturbance of its own making, seemed to enter the portals of a land from which the very memory of motion had for ever departed.

The white man, turning his back upon the setting sun, looked along the empty and broad expanse of the sea-reach. For the last three miles of its course the wandering, hesitating river, as if enticed irresistibly by the freedom of an open horizon, flows straight into the sea, flows straight to the east—to the east that harbours both light and darkness. Astern of the boat the repeated call of some bird, a cry discordant and feeble, skipped along over the smooth water and lost itself, before it could reach the other shore, in the breathless silence of the world.

The steersman dug his paddle into the stream, and held hard with stiffened arms, his body thrown forward. The water gurgled aloud; and suddenly the long straight reach seemed to pivot on its centre, the forests swung in a semicircle, and the slanting beams of sunset touched the broadside of the canoe with a fiery glow, throwing the slender and distorted shadows of its crew upon the streaked glitter of the river. The white man turned to look ahead. The course of the boat had been altered at right-angles to the stream, and the carved dragon-head of its prow was pointing now at a gap in the fringing bushes of the bank. It glided through, brushing the over-hanging twigs, and disappeared from the river like some slim and amphibious creature leaving the water for its lair in the forests.

The narrow creek was like a ditch: tortuous, fabulously deep; filled with gloom under the thin strip of pure and shining blue of the heaven. Immense trees soared up, invisible behind the festooned draperies of creepers. Here and there, near the glistening blackness of the water, a twisted root of some tall tree showed amongst the tracery of small ferns, black and dull, writhing and motionless, like an arrested snake. The short words of the paddlers reverberated loudly between the thick and sombre walls of vegetation. Darkness oozed out from between the trees, through the tangled maze of the creepers, from behind the great fantastic and unstirring leaves; the darkness, mysterious and invincible; the darkness scented and poisonous of impenetrable forests.

The men poled in the shoaling water. The creek broadened, opening out into a wide sweep of a stagnant lagoon. The forests receded from the marshy bank, leaving a level strip of bright green, reedy grass to frame the reflected blueness of the sky. A fleecy pink cloud drifted high above, trailing the delicate colouring of its image under the floating leaves and the silvery blossoms of the lotus. A little house, perched on high piles, appeared black in the distance. Near it, two tall nibong palms, that seemed to have come out of the forests in the background, leaned slightly over the ragged roof, with a suggestion of sad tenderness and care in the droop of their leafy and soaring heads.

The steersman, pointing with his paddle, said, 'Arsat is there. I see his canoe fast between the piles.'

The polers ran along the sides of the boat glancing over their shoulders at the end of the day's journey. They would have preferred to spend the night somewhere else than on this lagoon of weird aspect and ghostly reputation. Moreover, they disliked Arsat, first as a stranger, and also because he who repairs a ruined house, and dwells in it, proclaims that he is not afraid to live amongst the spirits that haunt the places abandoned by mankind. Such a man can disturb the course of fate by glances or words; while his familiar ghosts are not easy to propitiate by casual wayfarers upon whom they long to wreak the malice of their human master. White men care not for such things, being un-believers and in league with the Father of Evil, who leads them unharmed through the invisible dangers of this world. To the warnings of the righteous they oppose an offensive pretence of disbelief. What is there to be done?

So they thought, throwing their weight on the end of their long poles. The big canoe glided on swiftly, noiselessly, and smoothly, towards Arsat's clearing, till, in a great rattling of poles thrown down, and the loud murmurs of 'Allah be praised!' it came with a gentle knock against the crooked piles below the house.

The boatmen with uplifted faces shouted discordantly, 'Arsat! O Arsat!' Nobody came. The white man began to climb the rude ladder giving access to the bamboo platform before the house. The juragan of the boat said sulkily, 'We will cook in the sampan, and sleep on the water.'

'Pass my blankets and the basket,' said the white man, curtly.

He knelt on the edge of the platform to receive the bundle. Then the boat shoved off, and the white man, standing up, confronted Arsat, who had come out through the low door of his hut. He was a man young, powerful, with broad chest and muscular arms. He had nothing on but his sarong. His head was bare. His big, soft eyes stared eagerly at the white man, but his voice and demeanour were composed as he asked, without any words of greeting:

'Have you medicine, Tuan?'

'No,' said the visitor in a startled tone. 'No. Why? Is there sickness in the house?'

'Enter and see,' replied Arsat, in the same calm manner, and turning short round, passed again through the small doorway. The white man, dropping his bundles, followed.

In the dim light of the dwelling he made out on a couch of bamboos a woman stretched on her back under a broad sheet of red cotton cloth. She lay still, as if dead; but her big eyes, wide open, glittered in the gloom, staring upwards at the slender rafters, motionless and unseeing. She was in a high fever, and evidently unconscious. Her cheeks were sunk slightly, her lips were partly open, and on the young face there was the ominous and fixed expression—the absorbed, contemplating expression of the unconscious who are going to die. The two men stood looking down at her in silence.

'Has she been long ill?' asked the traveller.

'I have not slept for five nights,' answered the Malay, in a deliberate tone. 'At first she heard voices calling her from the water and struggled against me who held her. But since the sun of today rose she hears nothing—she hears not me. She sees nothing. She sees not me—me!'

He remained silent for a minute, then asked softly:

'Tuan, will she die?'

'I fear so,' said the white man, sorrowfully. He had known Arsat years ago, in a far country in times of trouble and danger, when no friendship is to be despised. And since his Malay friend had come unexpectedly to dwell in the hut on the lagoon with a strange woman, he had slept many times there, in his journeys up and down the river. He liked the man who knew how to keep faith in council and how to fight without fear by the side of his white friend. He liked him—not so much perhaps as a man likes his favourite dog—but still he liked him well enough to help and ask no questions, to think sometimes vaguely and hazily in the midst of his own pursuits, about the lonely man and the long-haired woman with audacious face and triumphant eyes, who lived together hidden by the forests—alone and feared.

The white man came out of the hut in time to see the enormous conflagration of sunset put out by the swift and stealthy shadows that, rising like a black and impalpable vapour above the tree-tops, spread over the heaven, extinguishing the crimson glow of floating clouds and the red brilliance of departing daylight. In a few moments all the stars came out above the intense blackness of the earth and the great lagoon gleaming suddenly with reflected lights resembled an oval patch of night sky flung down into the hopeless and abysmal night of the wilderness. The white man had some supper out of the basket, then collecting a few sticks that lay about the platform, made up a small fire, not for warmth, but for the sake of the smoke, which would keep off the mosquitoes. He wrapped himself in the blankets and sat with his back against the reed wall of the house, smoking thoughtfully.

Arsat came through the doorway with noiseless steps and squatted down by the fire. The white man moved his outstretched legs a little.

'She breathes,' said Arsat in a low voice, anticipating the expected question. 'She breathes and burns as if with a great fire. She speaks not; she hears not—and burns!'

He paused for a moment, then asked in a quiet, incurious tone: 'Tuan . . . will she die?'

The white man moved his shoulders uneasily and muttered in a hesitating manner:

'If such is her fate.'

'No, Tuan,' said Arsat, calmly. 'If such is my fate. I hear, I see, I wait. I remember . . . Tuan, do you remember the old days? Do you remember my brother?'

'Yes,' said the white man. The Malay rose suddenly and went in. The other, sitting still outside, could hear the voice in the hut. Arsat said: 'Hear me! Speak!' His words were succeeded by a complete silence. 'O Diamelen!' he cried, suddenly. After that cry there was a deep sigh. Arsat came out and sank down again in his old place.

They sat in silence before the fire. There was no sound within the house, there was no sound near them; but far away on the lagoon they could hear the voices of the boatmen ringing fitful and distinct on the calm water. The fire in the bows of the sampan shone faintly in the distance with a hazy red glow. Then it died out. The voices ceased. The land and the water slept invisible, unstirring and mute. It was as though there had been nothing left in the world but the glitter of stars streaming, ceaseless and vain, through the black stillness of the night.

The white man gazed straight before him into the darkness with wide-open eyes. The fear and fascination, the inspiration and the wonder of death—of death near, unavoidable, and unseen, soothed the unrest of his race and stirred the most indistinct, the most intimate of his thoughts. The ever-ready suspicion of evil, the gnawing suspicion that lurks in our hearts, flowed out into the stillness round him—into the stillness profound and dumb, and made it appear untrustworthy and infamous, like the placid and impenetrable mask of an unjustifiable violence. In that fleeting and powerful disturbance of his being the earth enfolded in the starlight peace became a shadowy country of inhuman strife, a battle-field of phantoms terrible and charming, august or ignoble, struggling ardently for the possession of our helpless hearts. An unquiet and mysterious country of inextinguishable desires and fears.

A plaintive murmur rose in the night; a murmur saddening and startling, as if the great solitudes of surrounding woods had tried to whisper into his ear the wisdom of their immense and lofty indifference. Sounds hesitating and vague floated in the air round him, shaped themselves slowly into words; and at last flowed on gently in a murmuring stream of soft and monotonous sentences. He stirred like a man waking up and changed his position slightly. Arsat, motionless and shadowy, sitting with bowed head under the stars, was speaking in a low and dreamy tone:

'. . . for where can we lay down the heaviness of our trouble but in a friend's heart? A man must speak of war and of love. You, Tuan, know what war is, and you have seen me in time of danger seek death as other men seek life! A writing may be lost; a lie may be written; but what the eye has seen is truth and remains in the mind!'

'I remember,' said the white man, quietly. Arsat went on with mournful composure:

'Therefore I shall speak to you of love. Speak in the night. Speak before both night and love are gone—and the eye of day looks upon my sorrow and my shame; upon my blackened face; upon my burnt-up heart.'

A sigh, short and faint, marked an almost imperceptible pause, and then his words flowed on, without a stir, without a gesture.

'After the time of trouble and war was over and you went away from my country in the pursuit of your desires, which we, men of the islands, cannot understand, I and my brother became again, as we had been before, the sword-bearers of the Ruler. You know we were men of family, belonging to a ruling race, and more fit than any to carry on our right shoulder the emblem of power. And in the time of prosperity Si Dendring showed us favour, as we, in time of sorrow, had showed to him the faithfulness of our courage. It was a time of peace. A time of deer-hunts and cock-fights; of idle talks and foolish squabbles between men whose bellies are full and weapons are rusty. But the sower watched the young rice-shoots grow up without fear, and the traders came and went, departed lean and returned fat into the river of peace. They brought news, too. Brought lies and truth mixed together, so that no man knew when to rejoice and when to be sorry. We heard from them about you also. They had seen you here and had seen you there. And I was glad to hear, for I remembered the stirring times, and I always remembered you, Tuan, till the time came when my eyes could see nothing in the past, because they had looked upon the one who is dying there—in the house.'

He stopped to exclaim in an intense whisper, 'O Mara bahia! O Calamity!' then went on speaking a little louder:

'There's no worse enemy and no better friend than a brother, Tuan, for one brother knows another, and in perfect knowledge is strength for good or evil. I loved my brother. I went to him and told him that I could see nothing but one face, hear nothing but one voice. He told me: "Open your heart so that she can see what is in it—and wait. Patience is wisdom. Inchi Midah may die or our Ruler may throw off his fear of a woman!" . . . I waited! . . . You remember the lady with the veiled face, Tuan, and the fear of our Ruler before her cunning and temper. And if she wanted her servant, what could I do? But I fed the hunger of my heart on short glances and stealthy words. I loitered on the path to the bath-houses in the daytime, and when the sun had fallen behind the forest I crept along the jasmine hedges of the women's courtyard. Unseeing, we spoke to one another through the scent of flowers, through the veil of leaves, through the blades of long grass that stood still before our lips; so great was our prudence, so faint was the murmur of our great longing. The time passed swiftly . . . and there were whispers amongst women—and our enemies watched— my brother was gloomy, and I began to think of killing and of a fierce death. . . . We are of a people who take what they want— like you whites. There is a time when a man should forget loyalty and respect. Might and authority are given to rulers, but to all men is given love and strength and courage. My brother said, "You shall take her from their midst. We are two who are like one." And I answered, "Let it be soon, for I find no warmth in sunlight that does not shine upon her." Our time came when the Ruler and all the great people went to the mouth of the river to fish by torchlight. There were hundreds of boats, and on the white sand, between the water and the forests, dwellings of leaves were built for the households of the Rajahs. The smoke of cooking-fires was like a blue mist of the evening, and many voices rang in it joyfully. While they were making the boats ready to beat up the fish, my brother came to me and said, "Tonight!" I looked to my weapons, and when the time came our canoe took its place in the circle of boats carrying the torches. The lights blazed on the water, but behind the boats there was darkness. When the shouting began and the excitement made them like mad we dropped out. The water swallowed our fire, and we floated back to the shore that was dark with only here and there the glimmer of embers. We could hear the talk of slave-girls amongst the sheds. Then we found a place deserted and silent. We waited there. She came. She came running along the shore, rapid and leaving no trace, like a leaf driven by the wind into the sea. My brother said gloomily, "Go and take her; carry her into our boat." I lifted her in my arms. She panted. Her heart was beating against my breast. I said, "I take you from those people. You came to the cry of my heart, but my arms take you into my boat against the will of the great!" "It is right," said my brother. "We are men who take what we want and can hold it against many. We should have taken her in daylight." I said, "Let us be off"; for since she was in my boat I began to think of our Ruler's many men. "Yes. Let us be off," said my brother. "We are cast out and this boat is our country now—and the sea is our refuge." He lingered with his foot on the shore, and I entreated him to hasten, for I remembered the strokes of her heart against my breast and thought that two men cannot withstand a hundred. We left, paddling down-stream close to the bank; and as we passed by the creek where they were fishing, the great shouting had ceased, but the murmur of voices was loud like the humming of insects flying at noonday. The boats floated, clustered together, in the red light of torches, under a black roof of smoke; and men talked of their sport. Men that boasted, and praised, and jeered—men that would have been our friends in the morning, but on that night were already our enemies. We paddled swiftly past. We had no more friends in the country of our birth. She sat in the middle of the canoe with covered face; silent as she is now; unseeing as she is now—and I had no regret at what I was leaving because I could hear her breathing close to me—as I can hear her now.'

He paused, listened with his ear turned to the doorway, then shook his head and went on:

'My brother wanted to shout the cry of challenge—one cry only—to let the people know we were freeborn robbers who trusted our arms and the great sea. And again I begged him in the name of our love to be silent. Could I not hear her breathing close to me? I knew the pursuit would come quick enough. My brother loved me. He dipped his paddle without a splash. He only said, "There is half a man in you now—the other half is in that woman. I can wait. When you are a whole man again, you will come back with me here to shout defiance. We are sons of the same mother." I made no answer. All my strength and all my spirit were in my hands that held the paddle—for I longed to be with her in a safe place beyond the reach of men's anger and of women's spite. My love was so great, that I thought it could guide me to a country where death was unknown, if I could only escape from Inchi Midah's fury and from our Ruler's sword. We paddled with haste, breathing through our teeth. The blades bit deep into the smooth water. We passed out of the river; we flew in clear channels amongst the shallows. We skirted the black coast; we skirted the sand beaches where the sea speaks in whispers to the land; and the gleam of white sand flashed back past our boat, so swiftly she ran upon the water. We spoke not. Only once I said, "Sleep,

Diamelen, for soon you may want all your strength." I heard the
sweetness of her voice, but I never turned my head. The sun rose
and still we went on. Water fell from my face like rain from a
cloud. We flew in the light and heat. I never looked back, but I
knew that my brother's eyes, behind me, were looking steadily
ahead, for the boat went as straight as a bushman's dart, when it
leaves the end of the sumpitan. There was no better paddler, no
better steersman than my brother. Many times, together, we had
won races in that canoe. But we never had put out our strength as
we did then—then, when for the last time we paddled together!
There was no braver or stronger man in our country than my
brother. I could not spare the strength to turn my head and look at
him, but every moment I heard the hiss of his breath getting louder
behind me. Still he did not speak. The sun was high. The heat
clung to my back like a flame of fire. My ribs were ready to burst,
but I could no longer get enough air into my chest. And then I felt I
must cry out with my last breath, "Let us rest!" . . . "Good!" he
answered; and his voice was firm. He was strong. He was brave.
He knew not fear and no fatigue . . . My brother!'

A murmur powerful and gentle, a murmur vast and faint; the
murmur of trembling leaves, of stirring boughs, ran through the
tangled depths of the forests, ran over the starry smoothness of the
lagoon, and the water between the piles lapped the slimy timber
once with a sudden splash. A breath of warm air touched the two
men's faces and passed on with a mournful sound—a breath loud
and short like an uneasy sigh of the dreaming earth.

Arsat went on in an even, low voice.

'We ran our canoe on the white beach of a little bay close to a
long tongue of land that seemed to bar our road; a long wooded
cape going far into the sea. My brother knew that place. Beyond
the cape a river has its entrance, and through the jungle of that
land there is a narrow path. We made a fire and cooked rice. Then
we lay down to sleep on the soft sand in the shade of our canoe,
while she watched. No sooner had I closed my eyes than I heard
her cry of alarm. We leaped up. The sun was half-way down the
sky already, and coming in sight in the opening of the bay we saw
a prau manned by many paddlers. We knew it at once; it was one
of our Rajah's praus. They were watching the shore, and saw us.

They beat the gong, and turned the head of the prau into the bay. I felt my heart become weak within my breast. Diamelen sat on the sand and covered her face. There was no escape by sea. My brother laughed. He had the gun you had given him, Tuan, before you went away, but there was only a handful of powder. He spoke to me quickly: "Run with her along the path. I shall keep them back, for they have no firearms, and landing in the face of a man with a gun is certain death for some. Run with her. On the other side of that wood there is a fisherman's house—and a canoe. When I have fired all the shots I will follow. I am a great runner, and before they can come up we shall be gone. I will hold out as long as I can, for she is but a woman—that can neither run nor fight, but she has your heart in her weak hands." He dropped behind the canoe. The prau was coming. She and I ran, and as we rushed along the path I heard shots. My brother fired—once—twice—and the booming of the gong ceased. There was silence behind us. That neck of land is narrow. Before I heard my brother fire the third shot I saw the shelving shore, and I saw the water again; the mouth of a broad river. We crossed a grassy glade. We ran down to the water. I saw a low hut above the black mud, and a small canoe hauled up. I heard another shot behind me. I thought, "That is his last charge." We rushed down to the canoe; a man came running from the hut, but I leaped on him, and we rolled together in the mud. Then I got up, and he lay still at my feet. I don't know whether I had killed him or not. I and Diamelen pushed the canoe afloat. I heard yells behind me, and I saw my brother run across the glade. Many men were bounding after him; I took her in my arms and threw her into the boat, then leaped in myself. When I looked back I saw that my brother had fallen. He fell and was up again, but the men were closing round him. He shouted, "I am coming!" The men were close to him. I looked. Many men. Then I looked at her. Tuan, I pushed the canoe! I pushed it into deep water. She was kneeling forward looking at me, and I said, "Take your paddle," while I struck the water with mine. Tuan, I heard him cry. I heard him cry my name twice; and I heard voices shouting, "Kill! Strike!" I never turned back. I heard him calling my name again with a great shriek, as when life is going out together with the voice—and I never turned my head.

My own name! My brother! Three times he called—but I was not afraid of life. Was she not there in that canoe? And could I not with her find a country where death is forgotten—where death is unknown!'

The white man sat up. Arsat rose and stood, an indistinct and silent figure above the dying embers of the fire. Over the lagoon a mist drifting and low had crept, erasing slowly the glittering images of the stars. And now a great expanse of white vapour covered the land: it flowed cold and grey in the darkness, eddied in noiseless whirls round the tree-trunks and about the platform of the house, which seemed to float upon a restless and impalpable illusion of a sea. Only far away the tops of the trees stood outlined on the twinkle of heaven, like a sombre and forbidding shore—a coast deceptive, pitiless and black.

Arsat's voice vibrated loudly in the profound peace.

'I had her there! I had her! To get her I would have faced all mankind. But I had her—and——'

His words went out ringing into the empty distances. He paused, and seemed to listen to them dying away very far—beyond help and beyond recall. Then he said quietly:

'Tuan, I loved my brother.'

A breath of wind made him shiver. High above his head, high above the silent sea of mist, the drooping leaves of the palms rattled together with a mournful and expiring sound. The white man stretched his legs. His chin rested on his chest, and he murmured sadly without lifting his head:

'We all love our brothers.'

Arsat burst out with an intense whispering violence:

'What did I care who died? I wanted peace in my own heart.'

He seemed to hear a stir in the house—listened—then stepped in noiselessly. The white man stood up. A breeze was coming in fitful puffs. The stars shone paler as if they had retreated into the frozen depths of immense space. After a chill gust of wind there were a few seconds of perfect calm and absolute silence. Then from behind the black and wavy line of the forests a column of golden light shot up into the heavens and spread over the semicircle of the eastern horizon. The sun had risen. The mist lifted, broke into drifting patches, vanished into thin flying wreaths; and the unveiled lagoon lay, polished and black, in the heavy shadows at the foot of the wall of trees. A white eagle rose over it with a slanting and ponderous flight, reached the clear sunshine and appeared dazzlingly brilliant for a moment, then soaring higher, became a dark and motionless speck before it vanished into the blue as if it had left the earth for ever. The white man, standing gazing upwards before the doorway, heard in the hut a confused and broken murmur of distracted words ending with a loud groan. Suddenly Arsat stumbled out with outstretched hands, shivered, and stood still for some time with fixed eyes. Then he said:

'She burns no more.'

Before his face the sun showed its edge above the tree-tops, rising steadily. The breeze freshened; a great brilliance burst upon the lagoon, sparkled on the rippling water. The forests came out of the clear shadows of the morning, became distinct, as if they had rushed nearer—to stop short in a great stir of leaves, of nodding boughs, of swaying branches. In the merciless sunshine the whisper of unconscious life grew louder, speaking in an incomprehensible voice round the dumb darkness of that human sorrow. Arsat's eyes wandered slowly, then stared at the rising sun.

'I can see nothing,' he said half aloud to himself.

'There is nothing,' said the white man, moving to the edge of the platform and waving his hand to his boat. A shout came faintly over the lagoon and the sampan began to glide towards the abode of the friend of ghosts.

'If you want to come with me, I will wait all the morning,' said the white man, looking away upon the water.

'No, Tuan,' said Arsat, softly. 'I shall not eat or sleep in this house, but I must first see my road. Now I can see nothing—see nothing! There is no light and no peace in the world; but there is death—death for many. We were sons of the same mother—and I left him in the midst of enemies; but I am going back now.'

He drew a long breath and went on in a dreamy tone:

'In a little while I shall see clear enough to strike—to strike. But she has died, and . . . now . . . darkness.'

He flung his arms wide open, let them fall along his body, then stood still with unmoved face and stony eyes, staring at the sun.

The white man got down into his canoe. The polers ran smartly along the sides of the boat, looking over their shoulders at the beginning of a weary journey. High in the stern, his head muffled up in white rags, the juragan sat moody, letting his paddle trail in the water. The white man, leaning with both arms over the grass roof of the little cabin, looked back at the shining ripple of the boat's wake. Before the sampan passed out of the lagoon into the creek he lifted his eyes. Arsat had not moved. He stood lonely in the searching sunshine; and he looked beyond the great light of a cloudless day into the darkness of a world of illusions.

O. HENRY (WILLIAM SYDNEY PORTER)

Jeff Peters as a Personal Magnet

Jeff Peters has been engaged in as many schemes for making money as there are recipes for cooking rice in Charleston, S.C.

Best of all I like to hear him tell of his earlier days when he sold liniments and cough cures on street corners, living hand to mouth, heart to heart, with the people, throwing heads or tails with fortune for his last coin.

'I struck Fisher Hill, Arkansaw,' said he, 'in a buckskin suit, moccasins, long hair, and a thirty-carat diamond ring that I got from an actor in Texarkana. I don't know what he ever did with the pocket-knife I swapped him for it.

'I was Dr Waugh-hoo, the celebrated Indian medicine man. I carried only one best bet just then, and that was Resurrection Bitters. It was made of life-giving plants and herbs accidentally discovered by Ta-qua-la, the beautiful wife of the chief of the Choctaw Nation, while gathering truck to garnish a platter of boiled dog for the annual corn dance.

'Business hadn't been good at the last town, so I only had five dollars. I went to the Fisher Hill druggist and he credited me for half a gross of eight-ounce bottles and corks. I had the labels and ingredients in my valise, left over from the last town. Life began to look rosy again after I got in my hotel room with the water running from the tap, and the Resurrection Bitters lining up on the table by the dozen.

'Fake? No, sir. There was two dollars' worth of fluid extract of cinchona and a dime's worth of aniline in that half-gross of bitters. I've gone through towns years afterwards and had folks ask for 'em again.

'I hired a wagon that night and commenced selling the bitters on Main Street. Fisher Hill was a low, malarial town; and a compound hypothetical pneumocardiac anti-scorbutic tonic was just what I diagnosed the crowd as needing. The bitters started off like sweetbreads-on-toast at a vegetarian dinner. I had sold two dozen at fifty cents apiece when I felt somebody pull my coat tail. I knew what that meant; so I climbed down and sneaked a five-dollar bill into the hand of a man with a German silver star on his lapel.

' "Constable," says I, "it's a fine night."

' "Have you got a city licence," he asks, "to sell this illegitimate essence of spooju that you flatter by the name of medicine?"

' "I have not," says I. "I didn't know you had a city. If I can find it tomorrow I'll take one out if it's necessary."

' "I'll have to close you up till you do," says the constable.

'I quit selling and went back to the hotel. I was talking to the landlord about it.

' "Oh, you won't stand no show in Fisher Hill," says he. "Dr Hoskins, the only doctor here, is a brother-in-law of the Mayor, and they won't allow no fake doctor to practise in town."

' "I don't practise medicine," says I, "I've got a State pedlar's licence, and I take out a city one wherever they demand it."

'I went to the Mayor's office the next morning and they told me he hadn't showed up yet. They didn't know when he'd be down. So Doc Waugh-hoo hunches down again in a hotel chair and lights a jimpson-weed regalia, and waits.

'By and by a young man in a blue neck-tie slips into the chair next to me and asks the time.

' "Half-past ten," says I, "and you are Andy Tucker. I've seen you work. Wasn't it you that put up the Great Cupid Combination package on the Southern States? Let's see, it was a Chilian diamond engagement ring, a wedding-ring, a potato masher, a bottle of soothing syrup, and Dorothy Vernon—all for fifty cents."

'Andy was pleased to hear that I remembered him. He was a good street man; and he was more than that—he respected his profession, and he was satisfied with 300 per cent profit. He had plenty of offers to go into the illegitimate drug and garden seed business; but he was never to be tempted off of the straight path.

'I wanted a partner; so Andy and me agreed to go out together. I told him about the situation in Fisher Hill and how finances was low on account of the local mixture of politics and jalap. Andy had just got in on the train that morning. He was pretty low himself, and was going to canvass the town for a few dollars to build a new battleship by popular subscription at Eureka Springs. So we went out and sat on the porch and talked it over.

'The next morning at eleven o'clock, when I was sitting there alone, an Uncle Tom shuffles into the hotel and asked for the doctor to come and see Judge Banks, who, it seems, was the mayor and a mighty sick man.

' "I'm no doctor," says I. "Why don't you go and get the doctor?"

' "Boss," says he, "Doc Hoskins am done gone twenty miles in de country to see some sick persons. He's de only doctor in de town, and Massa Banks am powerful bad off. He sent me to ax you to please, suh, come."

' "As man to man," says I, "I'll go and look him over." So I put a bottle of Resurrection Bitters in my pocket and goes up on the hill to the Mayor's mansion, the finest house in town, with a mansard roof and two cast-iron dogs on the lawn.

'This Mayor Banks was in bed all but his whiskers and feet. He was making internal noises that would have had everybody in San Francisco hiking for the parks. A young man was standing by the bed holding a cup of water.

' "Doc," says the Mayor, "I'm awful sick. I'm about to die. Can't you do nothing for me?"

' "Mr Mayor," says I, "I'm not a regular pre-ordained disciple of S.Q. Lapius. I never took a course in a medical college," says I, "I've just come as a fellow-man to see if I could be of assistance."

' "I'm deeply obliged," says he. "Doc Waugh-hoo, this is my nephew, Mr Biddle. He has tried to alleviate my distress, but without success. Oh, Lordy! Ow-ow-ow!!" he sings out.

'I nods at Mr Biddle and sets down by the bed and feels the Mayor's pulse. "Let me see your liver—your tongue, I mean," says I. Then I turns up the lids of his eyes and looks close at the pupils of 'em.

' "How long have you been sick?" I asked.

'I was taken down—ow-ouch—last night," says the Mayor. "Gimme something for it, doc, won't you?"

' "Mr Fiddle," says I, "raise the window shade a bit, will you?"

' "Biddle," says the young man. "Do you feel like you could eat some ham and eggs, Uncle James?"

' "Mr Mayor," says I, after laying my ear to his right shoulder-blade and listening, "you've got a bad attack of super-inflammation of the right clavicle of the harpsichord!"

' "Good Lord!" says he, with a groan. "Can't you rub something on it, or set it or anything?"

'I picks up my hat and starts for the door.

' "You ain't going, doc?" says the Mayor with a howl. "You ain't going away and leave me to die with this—superfluity of the clapboards, are you?"

' "Common humanity, Dr Whoa-ha," says Mr Biddle, "ought to prevent your deserting a fellow-human in distress."

' "Dr Waugh-hoo, when you get through ploughing," says I. And then I walks back to the bed and throws back my long hair.

' "Mr Mayor," says I, "there is only one hope for you. Drugs will do you no good. But there is another power higher yet, although drugs are high enough," says I.

' "And what is that?" says he.

' "Scientific demonstrations," says I. "The triumph of mind over sarsaparilla. The belief that there is no pain and sickness except what is produced when we ain't feeling well. Declare yourself in arrears. Demonstrate."

' "What is this paraphernalia you speak of, doc?" says the Mayor. "You ain't a Socialist, are you?"

' "I am speaking," says I, "of the great doctrine of psychic financiering—of the enlightened school of long-distance, sub-conscientious treatment of fallacies and meningitis—of that wonderful indoor sport known as personal magnetism."

' "Can you work it, doc?" asks the Mayor.

' "I'm one of the Sole Sanhedrims and Ostensible Hooplas of the Inner Pulpit," says I. "The lame talk and the blind rubber whenever I make a pass at 'em. I am a medium, a coloratura hypnotist and a spirituous control. It was only through me at the recent séances at Ann Arbor that the late president of the Vinegar Bitters Company could revisit the earth to communicate with his sister Jane. You see me peddling medicine on the streets," says I, "to the poor. I don't practise personal magnetism on them. I do not drag it in the dust," says I, "because they haven't got the dust."

' "Will you treat my case?" asks the Mayor.

' "Listen," says I. "I've had a good deal of trouble with medical societies everywhere I've been. I don't practise medicine. But, to save your life, I'll give you the pyschic treatment if you'll agree as mayor not to push the licence question."

' "Of course I will," says he. "And now get to work, doc, for them pains are coming on again."

' "My fee will be $250.00, cure guaranteed in two treatments," says I.

' "All right," says the Mayor. "I'll pay it. I guess my life's worth that much."

'I sat down by the bed and looked him straight in the eye.

' "Now," says I, "get your mind off the disease. You ain't sick. You haven't got a heart or a clavicle or a funny-bone or brains or anything. You haven't got any pain. Declare error. Now you feel the pain that you didn't have leaving, don't you?"

' "I do feel some little better, doc," says the Mayor, "darned if I don't. Now state a few lies about my not having this swelling in my left side, and I think I could be propped up and have some sausage and buckwheat cakes."

'I made a few passes with my hands.

' "Now," says I, "the inflammation's gone. The right lobe of the perihelion has subsided. You're getting sleepy. You can't hold your eyes open any longer. For the present the disease is checked. Now, you are asleep."

'The Mayor shut his eyes slowly and began to snore.

' "You observe, Mr Tiddle," says I, "the wonders of modern science."

' "Biddle," says he. "When will you give uncle the rest of the treatment, Dr Pooh-pooh?"

' "Waugh-hoo," says I. "I'll come back at eleven tomorrow. When he wakes up give him eight drops of turpentine and three pounds of steak. Good morning."

'The next morning I went back on time. "Well, Mr Riddle," says I, when he opened the bedroom door, "and how is uncle this morning?"

' "He seems much better," says the young man.

'The Mayor's colour and pulse was fine. I gave him another treatment, and he said the last of the pain left him.

' "Now," says I, "you'd better stay in bed for a day or two, and you'll be all right. It's a good thing I happened to be in Fisher Hill, Mr Mayor," says I, "for all the remedies in the cornucopia that the regular schools of medicine use couldn't have saved you. And now that error has flew and pain proved a perjurer, let's allude to a cheerfuller subject—say the fee of $250. No cheques, please; I hate to write my name on the back of a cheque almost as bad as I do on the front."

' "I've got the cash here," says the Mayor, pulling a pocket-book from under his pillow.

'He counts out five fifty-dollar notes and holds 'em in his hand.

' "Bring the receipt," he says to Biddle.

'I signed the receipt and the Mayor handed me the money. I put it in my inside pocket careful.

' "Now do your duty, officer," says the Mayor, grinning much unlike a sick man.

'Mr Biddle lays his hand on my arm.

' "You're under arrest, Dr Waugh-hoo, alias Peters," says he, "for practising medicine without authority under the State law."

' "Who are you?" I asks.

' "I'll tell you who he is," says Mr Mayor, sitting up in bed. "He's a detective employed by the State Medical Society. He's been following you over five counties. He came to me yesterday and we fixed up this scheme to catch you. I guess you won't do any more doctoring around these parts, Mr Faker. What was it you said I had, doc?" the Mayor laughs, "compound—well it wasn't softening of the brain, I guess, anyway."

' "A detective," says I.

' "Correct," says Biddle. "I'll have to turn you over to the sheriff."

' "Let's see you do it," says I, and I grabs Biddle by the throat and half throws him out of the window, but he pulls a gun and sticks it under my chin, and I stand still. Then he puts handcuffs on me, and takes the money out of my pocket.

' "I witness," says he, "that they're the same bills that you and I marked, Judge Banks. I'll turn them over to the sheriff when we get to his office, and he'll send you a receipt. They'll have to be used as evidence in the case."

' "All right, Mr Biddle," says the Mayor. "And now, Doc Waugh-hoo," he goes on, "why don't you demonstrate? Can't you pull the cork out of your magnetism with your teeth and hocus-pocus them handcuffs off?"

' "Come on, officer," says I, dignified. "I may as well make the best of it." And then I turns to old Banks and rattles my chains.

' "Mr Mayor," says I, "the time will come soon when you'll believe that personal magnetism is a success. And you'll be sure that it succeeded in this case, too."

'And I guess it did.

'When we got nearly to the gate, I says: "We might meet somebody now, Andy. I reckon you better take 'em off, and——" Hey? Why, of course it was Andy Tucker. That was his scheme; and that's how we got the capital to go into business together.'

RUDYARD KIPLING

The Miracle of Purun Bhagat

The night we felt the earth would move
    We stole and plucked him by the hand,
Because we loved him with the love
    That knows but cannot understand.

And when the roaring hillside broke,
    And all our world fell down in rain,
We saved him, we the Little Folk;
    But lo! he does not come again!

Mourn now, we saved him for the sake
    Of such poor love as wild ones may.
Mourn ye! Our brother will not wake,
    And his own kind drive us away!

        Dirge of the Langurs

There was once a man in India who was Prime Minister of one of the semi-independent native States in the north-western part of the country. He was a Brahmin, so high-caste that caste ceased to have any particular meaning for him; and his father had been an important official in the gay-coloured tag-rag and bobtail of an old-fashioned Hindu Court. But as Purun Dass grew up he felt that the old order of things was changing, and that if any one wished to get on in the world he must stand well with the English, and imitate all that the English believed to be good. At the same time a native official must keep his own master's favour. This was a difficult game, but the quiet, close-mouthed young Brahmin, helped by a good English education at a Bombay University, played it coolly, and rose, step by step, to be Prime Minister of the kingdom. That is to say, he held more real power than his master the Maharajah.

When the old king—who was suspicious of the English, their railways and telegraphs—died, Purun Dass stood high with his young successor, who had been tutored by an Englishman; and between them, though he always took care that his master should have the credit, they established schools for little girls, made roads, and started State dispensaries and shows of agricultural implements, and published a yearly blue-book on the 'Moral and Material Progress of the State,' and the Foreign Office and the Government of India were delighted. Very few native States take up English progress altogether, for they will not believe, as Purun Dass showed he did, that what was good for the Englishman must be twice as good for the Asiatic. The Prime Minister became the honoured friend of Viceroys, and Governors, and Lieutenant-Governors, and medical missionaries, and common missionaries, and hard-riding English officers who came to shoot in the State preserves, as well as of whole hosts of tourists who travelled up and down India in the cold weather, showing how things ought to be managed. In his spare time he would endow scholarships for the study of medicine and manufactures on strictly English lines, and write letters to the *Pioneer*, the greatest Indian daily paper, explaining his master's aims and objects.

At last he went to England on a visit, and had to pay enormous sums to the priests when he came back; for even so high-caste a Brahmin as Purun Dass lost caste by crossing the black sea. In London he met and talked with every one worth knowing—men whose names go all over the world—and saw a great deal more than he said. He was given honorary degrees by learned universities, and he made speeches and talked of Hindu social reform to English ladies in evening dress, till all London cried, 'This is the most fascinating man we have ever met at dinner since cloths were first laid.'

When he returned to India there was a blaze of glory, for the Viceroy himself made a special visit to confer upon the Maharajah the Grand Cross of the Star of India—all diamonds and ribbons and enamel; and at the same ceremony, while the cannon boomed, Purun Dass was made a Knight Commander of the

Order of the Indian Empire; so that his name stood Sir Purun Dass, K.C.I.E.

That evening, at dinner in the big Viceregal tent, he stood up with the badge and the collar of the Order on his breast, and replying to the toast of his master's health, made a speech few Englishmen could have bettered.

Next month, when the city had returned to its sun-baked quiet, he did a thing no Englishman would have dreamed of doing; for, so far as the world's affairs went, he died. The jewelled order of his knighthood went back to the Indian Government, and a new Prime Minister was appointed to the charge of affairs, and a great game of General Post began in all the subordinate appointments. The priests knew what had happened, and the people guessed; but India is the one place in the world where a man can do as he pleases and nobody asks why; and the fact that Dewan Sir Purun Dass, K.C.I.E., had resigned position, palace, and power, and taken up the begging-bowl and ochre-coloured dress of a Sunnyasi, or holy man, was considered nothing extraordinary. He had been, as the Old Law recommends, twenty years a youth, twenty years a fighter—though he had never carried a weapon in his life—and twenty years head of a household. He had used his wealth and his power for what he knew both to be worth; he had taken honour when it came his way; he had seen men and cities far and near, and men and cities had stood up and honoured him. Now he would let those things go, as a man drops the cloak he no longer needs.

Behind him, as he walked through the city gates, an antelope skin and brass-handled crutch under his arm, and a begging-bowl of polished brown *coco-de-mer* in his hand, barefoot, alone, with eyes cast on the ground—behind him they were firing salutes from the bastions in honour of his happy successor. Purun Dass nodded. All that life was ended; and he bore it no more ill-will or good-will than a man bears to a colourless dream of the night. He was a Sunnyasi—a houseless, wandering mendicant, depending on his neighbours for his daily bread; and so long as there is a morsel to divide in India, neither priest nor beggar starves. He had never in his life tasted meat, and very seldom eaten even fish. A five-pound note would have covered his personal expenses for food through any one of the many years in which he had been absolute master of millions of money. Even when he was being lionized in London he had held before him his dream of peace and quiet—the long, white, dusty Indian road, printed all over with bare feet, the incessant, slow-moving traffic, and the sharp-smelling wood smoke curling up under the fig-trees in the twilight, where the wayfarers sit at their evening meal.

When the time came to make that dream true the Prime Minister took the proper steps, and in three days you might more easily have found a bubble in the trough of the long Atlantic seas than Purun Dass among the roving, gathering, separating millions of India.

At night his antelope skin was spread where the darkness overtook him—sometimes in a Sunnyasi monastery by the road-side; sometimes by a mud-pillar shrine of Kala Pir, where the Jogis, who are another misty division of holy men, would receive him as they do those who know what castes and divisions are worth; sometimes on the outskirts of a little Hindu village, where the children would steal up with the food their parents had prepared; and sometimes on the pitch of the bare grazing-grounds, where the flame of his stick fire waked the drowsy camels. It was all one to Purun Dass—or Purun Bhagat, as he called himself now. Earth, people, and food were all one. But unconsciously his feet drew him away northward and eastward; from the south to Rohtak; from Rohtak to Kurnool; from Kurnool to ruined Samanah, and then up-stream along the dried bed of the Gugger river that fills only when the rain falls in the hills, till one day he saw the far line of the great Himalayas.

Then Purun Bhagat smiled, for he remembered that his mother was of Rajput Brahmin birth, from Kulu way—a Hill-woman, always home-sick for the snows—and that the least touch of Hill blood draws a man in the end back to where he belongs.

'Yonder,' said Purun Bhagat, breasting the lower slopes of the Sewaliks, where the cacti stand up like seven-branched candle-sticks—'yonder I shall sit down and get knowledge'; and the cool wind of the Himalayas whistled about his ears as he trod the road that led to Simla.

The last time he had come that way it had been in state, with a clattering cavalry escort, to visit the gentlest and most affable of Viceroys; and the two had talked for an hour together about mutual friends in London, and what the Indian common folk really thought of things. This time Purun Bhagat paid no calls, but leaned on the rail of the Mall, watching that glorious view of the Plains spread out forty miles below, till a native Mohammedan policeman told him he was obstructing traffic; and Purun Bhagat salaamed reverently to the Law, because he knew the value of it, and was seeking for a Law of his own. Then he moved on, and slept that night in an empty hut at Chota Simla, which looks like the very last end of the earth, but it was only the beginning of his journey.

He followed the Himalaya–Thibet road, the little ten-foot track that is blasted out of solid rock, or strutted out on timbers over gulfs a thousand feet deep; that dips into warm, wet, shut-in valleys, and climbs out across bare, grassy hill-shoulders where the sun strikes like a burning-glass; or turns through dripping, dark forests where the tree-ferns dress the trunks from head to heel, and the pheasant calls to his mate. And he met Thibetan herdsmen with their dogs and flocks of sheep, each sheep with a little bag of borax on his back, and wandering wood-cutters, and cloaked and blanketed Lamas from Thibet, coming into India on pilgrimage, and envoys of little solitary Hill-states, posting furiously on ring-streaked and piebald ponies, or the cavalcade of a Rajah paying a visit; or else for a long, clear day he would see nothing more than a black bear grunting and rooting below in the valley. When he first started, the roar of the world he had left still rang in his ears, as the roar of a tunnel rings long after the train has passed through; but when he had put the Mutteeanee Pass behind him that was all done, and Purun Bhagat was alone with himself, walking, wondering, and thinking, his eyes on the ground, and his thoughts with the clouds.

One evening he crossed the highest pass he had met till then—it had been a two-days' climb—and came out on a line of snow-peaks that banded all the horizon—mountains from fifteen to twenty thousand feet high, looking almost near enough to hit with a stone, though they were fifty or sixty miles away. The pass was crowned with dense, dark forest—deodar, walnut, wild cherry,

wild olive, and wild pear, but mostly deodar, which is the Himalayan cedar; and under the shadow of the deodars stood a
deserted shrine to Kali—who is Durga, who is Sitala, who is
sometimes worshipped against the smallpox.

Purun Dass swept the stone floor clean, smiled at the grinning
statue, made himself a little mud fireplace at the back of the
shrine, spread his antelope skin on a bed of fresh pine-needles,
tucked his *bairagi*—his brass-handled crutch—under his armpit,
and sat down to rest.

Immediately below him the hillside fell away, clean and cleared
for fifteen hundred feet, where a little village of stone-walled
houses, with roofs of beaten earth, clung to the steep tilt. All
round it the tiny terraced fields lay out like aprons of patchwork
on the knees of the mountain, and cows no bigger than beetles
grazed between the smooth stone circles of the threshing-floors.
Looking across the valley, the eye was deceived by the size of
things, and could not at first realize that what seemed to be low
scrub, on the opposite mountain-flank, was in truth a forest of
hundred-foot pines. Purun Bhagat saw an eagle swoop across the
gigantic hollow, but the great bird dwindled to a dot ere it was
half-way over. A few bands of scattered clouds strung up and
down the valley, catching on a shoulder of the hills, or rising up
and dying out when they were level with the head of the pass. And
'Here shall I find peace,' said Purun Bhagat.

Now, a Hill-man makes nothing of a few hundred feet up or
down, and as soon as the villagers saw the smoke in the deserted
shrine, the village priest climbed up the terraced hillside to
welcome the stranger.

When he met Purun Bhagat's eyes—the eyes of a man used to
control thousands—he bowed to the earth, took the begging-bowl
without a word, and returned to the village, saying, 'We have at
last a holy man. Never have I seen such a man. He is of the
Plains—but pale-coloured—a Brahmin of the Brahmins.' Then all
the housewives of the village said, 'Think you he will stay with
us?' and each did her best to cook the most savoury meal for the
Bhagat. Hill-food is very simple, but with buckwheat and Indian
corn, and rice and red pepper, and little fish out of the stream in
the valley, and honey from the flue-like hives built in the stone

walls, and dried apricots, and turmeric, and wild ginger, and bannocks of flour, a devout woman can make good things, and it was a full bowl that the priest carried to the Bhagat. Was he going to stay? asked the priest. Would he need a *chela*—a disciple—to beg for him? Had he a blanket against the cold weather? Was the food good?

Purun Bhagat ate, and thanked the giver. It was in his mind to stay. That was sufficient, said the priest. Let the begging-bowl be placed outside the shrine, in the hollow made by those two twisted roots, and daily should the Bhagat be fed; for the village felt honoured that such a man—he looked timidly into the Bhagat's face—should tarry among them.

That day saw the end of Purun Bhagat's wanderings. He had come to the place appointed for him—the silence and the space. After this, time stopped, and he, sitting at the mouth of the shrine, could not tell whether he were alive or dead; a man with control of his limbs, or a part of the hills, and the clouds, and the shifting rain and sunlight. He would repeat a Name softly to himself a hundred hundred times, till, at each repetition, he seemed to move more and more out of his body, sweeping up to the doors of some tremendous discovery; but, just as the door was opening, his body would drag him back, and, with grief, he felt he was locked up again in the flesh and bones of Purun Bhagat.

Every morning the filled begging-bowl was laid silently in the crutch of the roots outside the shrine. Sometimes the priest brought it; sometimes a Ladakhi trader, lodging in the village, and anxious to get merit, trudged up the path; but, more often, it was the woman who had cooked the meal overnight; and she would murmur, hardly above her breath: 'Speak for me before the gods, Bhagat. Speak for such a one, the wife of so-and-so!' Now and then some bold child would be allowed the honour, and Purun Bhagat would hear him drop the bowl and run as fast as his little legs could carry him, but the Bhagat never came down to the village. It was laid out like a map at his feet. He could see the evening gatherings, held on the circle of the threshing-floors, because that was the only level ground; could see the wonderful unnamed green of the young rice, the indigo blues of the Indian corn, the dock-like patches of buckwheat, and, in its season, the red bloom of the amaranth, whose tiny seeds, being neither grain nor pulse, make a food that can be lawfully eaten by Hindus in time of fasts.

When the year turned, the roofs of the huts were all little squares of purest gold, for it was on the roofs that they laid out their cobs of the corn to dry. Hiving and harvest, rice-sowing and husking, passed before his eyes, all embroidered down there on the many-sided plots of fields, and he thought of them all, and wondered what they all led to at the long last.

Even in populated India a man cannot a day sit still before the wild things run over him as though he were a rock; and in that wilderness very soon the wild things, who knew Kali's shrine well, came back to look at the intruder. The *langurs*, the big grey-whiskered monkeys of the Himalayas, were, naturally, the first, for they are alive with curiosity; and when they had upset the begging-bowl, and rolled it round the floor, and tried their teeth on the brass-handled crutch, and made faces at the antelope skin, they decided that the human being who sat so still was harmless. At evening, they would leap down from the pines, and beg with their hands for things to eat, and then swing off in graceful curves. They liked the warmth of the fire, too, and huddled round it till Purun Bhagat had to push them aside to throw on more fuel; and in the morning, as often as not, he would find a furry ape sharing his blanket. All day long, one or other of the tribe would sit by his side, staring out at the snows, crooning and looking unspeakably wise and sorrowful.

After the monkeys came the *barasingh*, that big deer which is like our red deer, but stronger. He wished to rub off the velvet of his horns against the cold stones of Kali's statue, and stamped his feet when he saw the man at the shrine. But Purun Bhagat never moved, and, little by little, the royal stag edged up and nuzzled his shoulder. Purun Bhagat slid one cool hand along the hot antlers, and the touch soothed the fretted beast, who bowed his head, and Purun Bhagat very softly rubbed and ravelled off the velvet. Afterward, the *barasingh* brought his doe and fawn— gentle things that mumbled on the holy man's blanket—or would come alone at night, his eyes green in the fire-flicker, to take his share of fresh walnuts. At last, the musk-deer, the shyest and almost the smallest of the deerlets, came, too, her big rabbity ears erect; even brindled, silent *mushick-nabha* must needs find out what the light in the shrine meant, and drop her moose-like nose into Purun Bhagat's lap, coming and going with the shadows of the fire. Purun Bhagat called them all 'my brothers,' and his low call of '*Bhai! Bhai!*' would draw them from the forest at noon if they were within earshot. The Himalayan black bear, moody and suspicious—Sona, who has the V-shaped white mark under his chin—passed that way more than once; and since the Bhagat showed no fear, Sona showed no anger, but watched him, and came closer, and begged a share of the caresses, and a dole of bread or wild berries. Often, in the still dawns, when the Bhagat would climb to the very crest of the pass to watch the red day walking along the peaks of the snows, he would find Sona shuffling and grunting at his heels, thrusting a curious fore-paw under fallen trunks, and bringing it away with a *whoof* of impatience; or his early steps would wake Sona where he lay curled up, and the great brute, rising erect, would think to fight, till he heard the Bhagat's voice and knew his best friend.

Nearly all hermits and holy men who live apart from the big cities have the reputation of being able to work miracles with the wild things, but all the miracle lies in keeping still, in never making a hasty movement, and, for a long time, at least, in never looking directly at a visitor. The villagers saw the outline of the *barasingh* stalking like a shadow through the dark forest behind the shrine; saw the *minaul*, the Himalayan pheasant, blazing in her best colours before Kali's statue; and the *langurs* on their haunches, inside, playing with the walnut shells. Some of the children, too, had heard Sona singing to himself, bear-fashion, behind the fallen rocks, and the Bhagat's reputation as miracle-worker stood firm.

Yet nothing was farther from his mind than miracles. He believed that all things were one big Miracle, and when a man knows that much he knows something to go upon. He knew for a certainty that there was nothing great and nothing little in this world: and day and night he strove to think out his way into the heart of things, back to the place whence his soul had come.

So thinking, his untrimmed hair fell down about his shoulders, the stone slab at the side of the antelope skin was dented into a little hole by the foot of his brass-handled crutch, and the place between the tree-trunks, where the begging-bowl rested day after day, sunk and wore into a hollow almost as smooth as the brown shell itself; and each beast knew his exact place at the fire. The fields changed their colours with the seasons; the threshing-floors filled and emptied, and filled again and again; and again and again, when winter came, the *langurs* frisked among the branches feathered with light snow, till the mother-monkeys brought their sad-eyed little babies up from the warmer valleys with the spring. There were few changes in the village. The priest was older, and many of the little children who used to come with the begging-dish sent their own children now; and when you asked of the villagers how long their holy man had lived in Kali's Shrine at the head of the pass, they answered, 'Always'.

Then came such summer rains as had not been known in the Hills for many seasons. Through three good months the valley was wrapped in cloud and soaking mist—steady, unrelenting downfall, breaking off into thunder-shower after thunder-shower. Kali's Shrine stood above the clouds, for the most part, and there was a whole month in which the Bhagat never caught a glimpse of his village. It was packed away under a white floor of cloud that swayed and shifted and rolled on itself and bulged upward, but never broke from its piers—the streaming flanks of the valley.

All that time he heard nothing but the sound of a million little waters, overhead from the trees, and underfoot along the ground, soaking through the pine-needles, dripping from the tongues of draggled fern, and spouting in newly-torn muddy channels down the slopes. Then the sun came out, and drew forth the good incense of the deodars and the rhododendrons, and that far-off, clean smell which the Hill people call 'the smell of the snows'. The hot sunshine lasted for a week, and then the rains gathered together for their last downpour, and the water fell in sheets that flayed off the skin of the ground and leaped back in mud. Purun Bhagat heaped his fire high that night, for he was sure his brothers would need warmth; but never a beast came to the shrine, though he called and called till he dropped asleep, wondering what had happened in the woods.

It was in the black heart of the night, the rain drumming like a thousand drums, that he was roused by a plucking at his blanket, and, stretching out, felt the little hand of a *langur*. 'It is better here than in the trees,' he said sleepily, loosening a fold of blanket; 'take it and be warm.' The monkey caught his hand and pulled hard. 'Is it food, then?' said Purun Bhagat. 'Wait awhile, and I will prepare some.' As he kneeled to throw fuel on the fire the *langur* ran to the door of the shrine, crooned and ran back again, plucking at the man's knee.

'What is it? What is thy trouble, Brother?' said Purun Bhagat, for the *langur*'s eyes were full of things that he could not tell. 'Unless one of thy caste be in a trap—and none set traps here—I will not go into that weather. Look, Brother, even the *barasingh* comes for shelter!'

The deer's antlers clashed as he strode into the shrine, clashed against the grinning statue of Kali. He lowered them into Purun Bhagat's direction and stamped uneasily, hissing through his half-shut nostrils.

'Hai! Hai! Hai!' said the Bhagat, snapping his fingers. 'Is *this* payment for a night's lodging?' But the deer pushed him toward the door, and as he did so Purun Bhagat heard the sound of something opening with a sigh, and saw two slabs of the floor draw away from each other, while the sticky earth below smacked its lips.

'Now I see,' said Purun Bhagat. 'No blame to my brothers that they did not sit by the fire tonight. The mountain is falling. And yet—why should I go?' His eye fell on the empty begging-bowl, and his face changed. 'They have given me good food daily since—since I came, and, if I am not swift, tomorrow there will not be one mouth in the valley. Indeed, I must go and warn them below. Back there, Brother! Let me get to the fire.'

The *barasingh* backed unwillingly as Purun Bhagat drove a pine torch deep into the flame, twirling it till it was well lit. 'Ah! ye came to warn me,' he said, rising. 'Better than that we shall do; better than that. Out, now, and lend me thy neck, Brother, for I have but two feet.'

He clutched the bristling withers of the *barasingh* with his right hand, held the torch away with his left, and stepped out of the shrine into the desperate night. There was no breath of wind, but the rain nearly drowned the flare as the great deer hurried down the slope, sliding on his haunches. As soon as they were clear of the forest more of the Bhagat's brothers joined them. He heard, though he could not see, the *langurs* pressing about him, and behind them the *uhh! uhh!* of Sona. The rain matted his long white hair into ropes; the water splashed beneath his bare feet, and his yellow robe clung to his frail old body, but he stepped down steadily, leaning against the *barasingh*. He was no longer a holy man, but Sir Purun Dass, K.C.I.E., Prime Minister of no small State, a man accustomed to command, going out to save life. Down the steep, plashy path they poured all together, the Bhagat and his brothers, down and down till the deer's feet clicked and stumbled on the wall of a threshing-floor, and he snorted because he smelt Man. Now they were at the head of the one crooked village street, and the Bhagat beat with his crutch on the barred windows of the blacksmith's house, as his torch blazed up in the shelter of the eaves. 'Up and out!' cried Purun Bhagat; and he did not know his own voice, for it was years since he had spoken aloud to a man. 'The hill falls! The hill is falling! Up and out, oh, you within!'

'It is our Bhagat,' cried the blacksmith's wife. 'He stands among his beasts. Gather the little ones and give the call.'

It ran from house to house, while the beasts, cramped in the narrow way, surged and huddled round the Bhagat, and Sona puffed impatiently.

The people hurried into the street—they were no more than seventy souls all told—and in the glare of the torches they saw their Bhagat holding back the terrified *barasingh*, while the monkeys plucked piteously at his skirts, and Sona sat on his haunches and roared.

'Across the valley and up the next hill!' shouted Purun Bhagat. 'Leave none behind! We follow!'

Then the people ran as only Hill folk can run, for they knew that in a landslip you must climb for the highest ground across the valley. They fled, splashing through the little river at the bottom, and panted up the terraced fields on the far side, while the Bhagat and his brethren followed. Up and up the opposite mountain they climbed, calling to each other by name—the roll-call of the village—and at their heels toiled the big *barasingh*, weighted by the failing strength of Purun Bhagat. At last the deer stopped in the shadow of a deep pine-wood, five hundred feet up the hillside. His instinct, that had warned him of the coming slide, told him he would be safe here.

Purun Bhagat dropped fainting by his side, for the chill of the rain and that fierce climb were killing him; but first he called to the scattered torches ahead, 'Stay and count your numbers'; then, whispering to the deer as he saw the lights gather in a cluster: 'Stay with me, Brother. Stay—till—I—go!'

There was a sigh in the air that grew to a mutter, and a mutter that grew to a roar, and a roar that passed all sense of hearing, and the hillside on which the villagers stood was hit in the darkness, and rocked to the blow. Then a note as steady, deep, and true as the deep C of the organ drowned everything for perhaps five minutes, while the very roots of the pines quivered to it. It died away, and the sound of the rain falling on miles of hard ground and grass changed to the muffled drum of water on soft earth. That told its own tale.

Never a villager—not even the priest—was bold enough to speak to the Bhagat who had saved their lives. They crouched under the pines and waited till the day. When it came they looked across the valley and saw that what had been forest, and terraced fields, and track-threaded grazing-ground was one raw, red, fan-shaped smear, with a few trees flung head-down on the scarp. That red ran high up the hill of their refuge, damming back the little river, which had begun to spread into a brick-coloured lake. Of the village, of the road to the shrine itself, and the forest behind, there was no trace. For one mile in width and two thousand feet in sheer depth the mountain-side had come away bodily, planed clean from head to heel.

And the villagers, one by one, crept through the wood to pray before their Bhagat. They saw the *barasingh* standing over him, who fled when they came near, and they heard the *langurs* wailing in the branches, and Sona moaning up the hill; but their Bhagat was dead, sitting cross-legged, his back against a tree, his crutch under his armpit, and his face turned to the north-east.

The priest said: 'Behold a miracle after a miracle, for in this very attitude must all Sunnyasis be buried! Therefore where he now is we will build the temple to our holy man.'

They built the temple before a year was ended—a little stone-and-earth shrine—and they called the hill the Bhagat's hill, and they worship there with lights and flowers and offerings to this day. But they do not know that the saint of their worship is the late Sir Purun Dass, K.C.I.E., D.C.L., Ph.D., etc., once Prime Minister of the progressive and enlightened State of Mohiniwala, and honorary or corresponding member of more learned and scientific societies than will ever do any good in this world or the next.

SAKI (H. H. MUNRO)

Tobermory

It was a chill, rain-washed afternoon of a late August day, that indefinite season when partridges are still in security or cold storage, and there is nothing to hunt—unless one is bounded on the north by the Bristol Channel, in which case one may lawfully gallop after fat red stags. Lady Blemley's house-party was not bounded on the north by the Bristol Channel, hence there was a full gathering of her guests round the tea-table on this particular afternoon. And, in spite of the blankness of the season and the triteness of the occasion, there was no trace in the company of that fatigued restlessness which means a dread of the pianola and a subdued hankering for auction bridge. The undisguised, open-mouthed attention of the entire party was fixed on the homely negative personality of Mr Cornelius Appin. Of all her guests, he was the one who had come to Lady Blemley with the vaguest reputation. Someone had said he was 'clever', and he had got his invitation in the moderate expectation, on the part of his hostess, that some portion at least of his cleverness would be contributed to the general entertainment. Until tea-time that day she had been unable to discover in what direction, if any, his cleverness lay. He was neither a wit nor a croquet champion, a hypnotic force nor a begetter of amateur theatricals. Neither did his exterior suggest the sort of man in whom women are willing to pardon a generous measure of mental deficiency. He had subsided into mere Mr Appin, and the Cornelius seemed a piece of transparent baptismal bluff. And now he was claiming to have launched on the world a discovery beside which the invention of gunpowder, of the print-ing-press, and of steam locomotion were inconsiderable trifles. Science had made bewildering strides in many directions during recent decades, but this thing seemed to belong to the domain of miracle rather than to scientific achievement.

'And do you really ask us to believe,' Sir Wilfrid was saying, 'that you have discovered a means for instructing animals in the art of human speech, and that dear old Tobermory has proved your first successful pupil?'

'It is a problem at which I have worked for the last seventeen years,' said Mr Appin, 'but only during the last eight or nine months have I been rewarded with glimmerings of success. Of course I have experimented with thousands of animals, but latterly only with cats, those wonderful creatures which have assimilated themselves so marvellously with our civilization while retaining all their highly developed feral instincts. Here and there among cats one comes across an outstanding superior intellect, just as one does among the ruck of human beings, and when I made the acquaintance of Tobermory a week ago I saw at once that I was in contact with a "Beyond-cat" of extraordinary intelligence. I had gone far along the road to success in recent experiments; with Tobermory, as you call him, I have reached the goal.'

Mr Appin concluded his remarkable statement in a voice which he strove to divest of a triumphant inflection. No one said 'Rats,' though Clovis's lips moved in a monosyllabic contortion which probably invoked those rodents of disbelief.

'And do you mean to say,' asked Miss Resker, after a slight pause, 'that you have taught Tobermory to say and understand easy sentences of one syllable?'

'My dear Miss Resker,' said the wonder-worker patiently, 'one teaches little children and savages and backward adults in that piecemeal fashion; when one has once solved the problem of making a beginning with an animal of highly developed intelligence one has no need for those halting methods. Tobermory can speak our language with perfect correctness.'

This time Clovis very distinctly said, 'Beyond-rats!' Sir Wilfrid was more polite, but equally sceptical.

'Hadn't we better have the cat in and judge for ourselves?' suggested Lady Blemley.

Sir Wilfrid went in search of the animal, and the company settled themselves down to the languid expectation of witnessing some more or less adroit drawing-room ventriloquism.

In a minute Sir Wilfrid was back in the room, his face white beneath its tan and his eyes dilated with excitement.

'By Gad, it's true!'

His agitation was unmistakably genuine, and his hearers started forward in a thrill of awakened interest.

Collapsing into an armchair he continued breathlessly: 'I found him dozing in the smoking-room, and called out to him to come for his tea. He blinked at me in his usual way, and I said, "Come on, Toby; don't keep us waiting"; and, by Gad! he drawled out in a most horribly natural voice that he'd come when he dashed well pleased! I nearly jumped out of my skin!'

Appin had preached to absolutely incredulous hearers; Sir Wilfrid's statement carried instant conviction. A Babel-like chorus of startled exclamation arose, amid which the scientist sat mutely enjoying the first fruit of his stupendous discovery.

In the midst of the clamour Tobermory entered the room and made his way with velvet tread and studied unconcern across to the group seated round the tea-table.

A sudden hush of awkwardness and constraint fell on the company. Somehow there seemed an element of embarrassment in addressing on equal terms a domestic cat of acknowledged dental ability.

'Will you have some milk, Tobermory?' asked Lady Blemley in a rather strained voice.

'I don't mind if I do,' was the response, couched in a tone of even indifference. A shiver of suppressed excitement went through the listeners, and Lady Blemley might be excused for pouring out the saucerful of milk rather unsteadily.

'I'm afraid I've spilt a good deal of it,' she said apologetically.

'After all, it's not my Axminster,' was Tobermory's rejoinder.

Another silence fell on the group, and then Miss Resker, in her best district-visitor manner, asked if the human language had been difficult to learn. Tobermory looked squarely at her for a moment and then fixed his gaze serenely on the middle distance. It was obvious that boring questions lay outside his scheme of life.

'What do you think of human intelligence?' asked Mavis Pellington lamely.

'Of whose intelligence in particular?' asked Tobermory coldly.

'Oh, well, mine, for instance,' said Mavis, with a feeble laugh.

'You put me in an embarrassing position,' said Tobermory, whose tone and attitude certainly did not suggest a shred of embarrassment. 'When your inclusion in this house-party was suggested Sir Wilfrid protested that you were the most brainless woman of his acquaintance, and that there was a wide distinction between hospitality and the care of the feeble-minded. Lady Blemley replied that your lack of brain-power was the precise quality which had earned you your invitation, as you were the only person she could think of who might be idiotic enough to buy their old car. You know, the one they call "The Envy of Sisyphus," because it goes quite nicely up-hill if you push it.'

Lady Blemley's protestations would have had greater effect if she had not casually suggested to Mavis only that morning that the car in question would be just the thing for her down at her Devonshire home.

Major Barfield plunged in heavily to effect a diversion.

'How about your carryings-on with the tortoiseshell puss up at the stables, eh?'

The moment he had said it every one realized the blunder.

'One does not usually discuss these matters in public,' said Tobermory frigidly. 'From a slight observation of your ways since you've been in this house I should imagine you'd find it inconvenient if I were to shift the conversation on to your own little affairs.'

The panic which ensued was not confined to the Major.

'Would you like to go and see if cook has got your dinner ready?' suggested Lady Blemley hurriedly, affecting to ignore the fact that it wanted at least two hours to Tobermory's dinner-time.

'Thanks,' said Tobermory, 'not quite so soon after my tea. I don't want to die of indigestion.'

'Cats have nine lives, you know,' said Sir Wilfrid heartily.

'Possibly,' answered Tobermory; 'but only one liver.'

'Adelaide!' said Mrs Cornett, 'do you mean to encourage that cat to go out and gossip about us in the servants' hall?'

The panic had indeed become general. A narrow ornamental balustrade ran in front of most of the bedroom windows at the Towers, and it was recalled with dismay that this had formed a favourite promenade for Tobermory at all hours, whence he could watch the pigeons—and heaven knew what else besides. If he intended to become reminiscent in his present outspoken strain the effect would be something more than disconcerting. Mrs Cornett, who spent much time at her toilet table, and whose complexion was reputed to be of a nomadic though punctual disposition, looked as ill at ease as the Major. Miss Scrawen, who wrote fiercely sensuous poetry and led a blameless life, merely displayed irritation; if you are methodical and virtuous in private you don't necessarily want every one to know it. Bertie van Tahn, who was so depraved at seventeen that he had long ago given up trying to be any worse, turned a dull shade of gardenia white, but he did not commit the error of dashing out of the room like Odo Finsberry, a young gentleman who was understood to be reading for the Church and who was possibly disturbed at the thought of scandals he might hear concerning other people. Clovis had the presence of mind to maintain a composed exterior; privately he was calculating how long it would take to procure a box of fancy mice through the agency of the *Exchange and Mart* as a species of hush-money.

Even in a delicate situation like the present, Agnes Resker could not endure to remain too long in the background.

'Why did I ever come down here?' she asked dramatically.

Tobermory immediately accepted the opening.

'Judging by what you said to Mrs Cornett on the croquet-lawn yesterday, you were out for food. You described the Blemleys as the dullest people to stay with that you knew, but said they were clever enough to employ a first-rate cook; otherwise they'd find it difficult to get any one to come down a second time.'

'There's not a word of truth in it! I appeal to Mrs Cornett——' exclaimed the discomfited Agnes.

'Mrs Cornett repeated your remark afterwards to Bertie van Tahn,' continued Tobermory, 'and said, "That woman is a regular Hunger Marcher; she'd go anywhere for four square meals a day," and Bertie van Tahn said——'

At this point the chronicle mercifully ceased. Tobermory had caught a glimpse of the big yellow Tom from the Rectory working his way through the shrubbery towards the stable wing.

In a flash he had vanished through the open French window.

With the disappearance of his too brilliant pupil Cornelius Appin found himself beset by a hurricane of bitter upbraiding, anxious inquiry, and frightened entreaty. The responsibility for the situation lay with him, and he must prevent matters from becoming worse. Could Tobermory impart his dangerous gift to other cats? was the first question he had to answer. It was possible, he replied, that he might have initiated his intimate friend the stable puss into his new accomplishment, but it was unlikely that his teaching could have taken a wider range as yet.

'Then,' said Mrs Cornett, 'Tobermory may be a valuable cat and a great pet; but I'm sure you'll agree, Adelaide, that he and the stable cat must be done away with without delay.'

'You don't suppose I've enjoyed the last quarter of an hour, do you?' said Lady Blemley bitterly. 'My husband and I are very fond of Tobermory—at least, we were before this horrible accomplishment was infused into him; but now, of course, the only thing is to have him destroyed as soon as possible.'

'We can put some strychnine in the scraps he always gets at dinner-time,' said Sir Wilfrid, 'and I will go and drown the stable cat myself. The coachman will be very sore at losing his pet, but I'll say a very catching form of mange has broken out in both cats and we're afraid of it spreading to the kennels.'

'But my great discovery!' expostulated Mr Appin; 'after all my years of research and experiment——'

'You can go and experiment on the shorthorns at the farm, who are under proper control,' said Mrs Cornett, 'or the elephants at the Zoological Gardens. They're said to be highly intelligent, and they have this recommendation, that they don't come creeping about our bedrooms and under chairs, and so forth.'

An archangel ecstatically proclaiming the Millennium, and then finding that it clashed unpardonably with Henley and would have to be definitely postponed, could hardly have felt more crestfallen than Cornelius Appin at the reception of his wonderful achievement. Public opinion, however, was against him—in fact, had the general voice been consulted on the subject it is probable that a strong minority vote would have been in favour of including him in the strychnine diet.

Defective train arrangements and a nervous desire to see matters brought to a finish prevented an immediate dispersal of the party, but dinner that evening was not a social success. Sir Wilfrid had had rather a trying time with the stable cat and subsequently with the coachman. Agnes Resker ostentatiously limited her repast to a morsel of dry toast, which she bit as though it were a personal enemy; while Mavis Pellington maintained a vindictive silence throughout the meal. Lady Blemley kept up a flow of what she hoped was conversation, but her attention was fixed on the doorway. A plateful of carefully dosed fish scraps was in readiness on the sideboard, but sweets and savoury and dessert went their way, and no Tobermory appeared either in the dining-room or kitchen.

The sepulchral dinner was cheerful compared with the subsequent vigil in the smoking-room. Eating and drinking had at least supplied a distraction and cloak to the prevailing embarrassment. Bridge was out of the question in the general tension of nerves and tempers, and after Odo Finsberry had given a lugubrious rendering of *Mélisande in the Wood* to a frigid audience, music was tacitly avoided. At eleven the servants went to bed, announcing that the small window in the pantry had been left open as usual for Tobermory's private use. The guests read steadily through the current batch of magazines, and fell back gradually on the 'Badminton Library' and bound volumes of *Punch*. Lady Blemley made periodic visits to the pantry, returning each time with an expression of listless depression which forestalled questioning.

At two o'clock Clovis broke the dominating silence.

'He won't turn up tonight. He's probably in the local newspaper office at the present moment, dictating the first instalment of his reminiscences. Lady What's-her-name's book won't be in it. It will be the event of the day.'

Having made this contribution to the general cheerfulness, Clovis went to bed. At long intervals the various members of the house-party followed his example.

The servants taking round the early tea made a uniform announcement in reply to a uniform question. Tobermory had not returned.

Breakfast was, if anything, a more unpleasant function than

dinner had been, but before its conclusion the situation was relieved. Tobermory's corpse was brought in from the shrubbery, where a gardener had just discovered it. From the bites on his throat and the yellow fur which coated his claws it was evident that he had fallen in unequal combat with the big Tom from the Rectory.

By midday most of the guests had quitted The Towers, and after lunch Lady Blemley had sufficiently recovered her spirits to write an extremely nasty letter to the Rectory about the loss of her valuable pet.

Tobermory had been Appin's one successful pupil, and he was destined to have no successor. A few weeks later an elephant in the Dresden Zoological Garden, which had shown no previous signs of irritability, broke loose and killed an Englishman who had apparently been teasing it. The victim's name was variously reported in the papers as Oppin and Eppelin, but his front name was faithfully rendered Cornelius.

'If he was trying German irregular verbs on the poor beast,' said Clovis, 'he deserved all he got.'

WALTER DE LA MARE

Miss Duveen

I seldom had the company of children in my grandmother's house beside the river Wandle. The house was old and ugly. But its river was lovely and youthful though it had flowed for ever, it seemed, between its green banks of osier and alder. So it was no great misfortune perhaps that I heard more talking of its waters than of any human tongue. For my grandmother found no particular pleasure in my company. How should she? My father and mother had married (and died) against her will, and there was nothing in me of those charms which, in fiction at any rate, swiftly soften a superannuated heart.

Nor did I pine for her company either. I kept out of it as much as possible.

It so happened that she was accustomed to sit with her back to the window of the room which she usually occupied, her grey old indifferent face looking inwards. Whenever necessary, I would steal close up under it, and if I could see there her large faded amethyst velvet cap I knew I was safe from interruption. Sometimes I would take a slice or two of currant bread or (if I could get it) a jam tart or a cheese cake, and eat it under a twisted old damson tree or beside the running water. And if I conversed with anybody, it would be with myself or with my small victims of the chase.

Not that I was an exceptionally cruel boy; though if I had lived on for many years in this primitive and companionless fashion, I should surely have become an idiot. As a matter of fact, I was unaware even that I was ridiculously old-fashioned—manners, clothes, notions, everything. My grandmother never troubled to tell me so, nor did she care. And the servants were a race apart. So I was left pretty much to my own devices. What wonder, then, if I at first accepted with genuine avidity the acquaintanceship of our remarkable neighbour, Miss Duveen?

It had been, indeed, quite an advent in our uneventful routine when that somewhat dubious household moved into Willowlea, a brown brick edifice, even uglier than our own, which had been long vacant, and whose sloping garden confronted ours across the Wandle. My grandmother, on her part, at once discovered that any kind of intimacy with its inmates was not much to be desired. While I, on mine, was compelled to resign myself to the loss of the Willowlea garden as a kind of No Man's Land or Tom Tiddler's ground.

I got to know Miss Duveen by sight long before we actually became friends. I used frequently to watch her wandering in her long garden. And even then I noticed how odd were her methods of gardening. She would dig up a root or carry off a potted plant from one to another overgrown bed with an almost animal-like resolution; and a few minutes afterwards I would see her restoring it to the place from which it had come. Now and again she would stand perfectly still, like a scarecrow, as if she had completely forgotten what she was at.

Miss Coppin, too, I descried sometimes. But I never more than glanced at her, for fear that even at that distance the too fixed attention of my eyes might bring hers to bear upon me. She was a smallish woman, inclined to be fat, and with a peculiar waddling gait. She invariably appeared to be angry with Miss Duveen, and would talk to her as one might talk to a post. I did not know, indeed, until one day Miss Duveen waved her handkerchief in my direction that I had been observed from Willowlea at all. Once or twice after that, I fancied, she called me; at least her lips moved; but I could not distinguish what she said. And I was naturally a little backward in making new friends. Still I grew accustomed to looking out for her and remember distinctly how first we met.

It was raining, the raindrops falling softly into the unrippled water, making their great circles, and tapping on the motionless leaves above my head where I sat in shelter on the bank. But the sun was shining whitely from behind a thin fleece of cloud, when Miss Duveen suddenly peeped in at me out of the greenery, the thin silver light upon her face, and eyed me sitting there, for all the world as if she were a blackbird and I a snail. I scrambled up hastily with the intention of retreating into my own domain, but the peculiar grimace she made at me fixed me where I was.

'Ah,' she said, with a little masculine laugh, 'So this is the young gentleman, the bold, gallant young gentleman. And what might be his name?'

I replied rather distantly that my name was Arthur.

'Arthur, to be sure!' she repeated with extraordinary geniality, and again, 'Arthur,' as if in the strictest confidence.

'I know you, Arthur, very well indeed. I have looked, I have watched; and now, please God, we need never be estranged.' And she tapped her brow and breast, making the Sign of the Cross with her lean, bluish forefinger.

'What is a little brawling brook,' she went on, 'to friends like you and me?' She gathered up her tiny countenance once more into an incredible grimace of friendliness; and I smiled as amicably as I could in return. There was a pause in this one-sided conversation. She seemed to be listening, and her lips moved, though I caught no sound. In my uneasiness I was just about to turn stealthily away, when she poked forward again.

'Yes, yes, I know you quite intimately, Arthur. We have met *here*.' She tapped her rounded forehead. 'You might not suppose it, too; but I have eyes like a lynx. It is no exaggeration, I assure you—I assure everybody. And now what friends we will be! At times,' she stepped out of her hiding-place and stood in curious dignity beside the water, her hands folded in front of her on her black pleated silk apron—'at times, dear child, I long for company—earthly company.' She glanced furtively about her. 'But I must restrain my longings; and you will, of course, understand that I do not complain. *He* knows best. And my dear cousin, Miss Coppin—she too knows best. She does not consider too much companionship expedient for me.' She glanced in some perplexity into the smoothly swirling water.

'I, you know,' she said suddenly, raising her little piercing eyes to mine, 'I am Miss Duveen, that's not, they say, quite the thing here.' She tapped her small forehead again beneath its two sleek curves of greying hair, and made a long narrow mouth at me. 'Though, of course,' she added, 'we do not tell *her* so. No!'

And I, too, nodded my head in instinctive and absorbed

imitation. Miss Duveen laughed gaily. 'He understands, he understands!' she cried, as if to many listeners. 'Oh, what a joy it is in this world, Arthur, to be understood. Now tell me,' she continued with immense nicety, 'tell me, how's your dear mamma?'

I shook my head.

'Ah,' she cried, 'I see, I see; Arthur has no mamma. We will not refer to it. No father, either?'

I shook my head again and, standing perfectly still, stared at my new acquaintance with vacuous curiosity. She gazed at me with equal concentration, as if she were endeavouring to keep the very thought of my presence in her mind.

'It is sad to have no father,' she continued rapidly, half closing her eyes; 'no head, no guide, no stay, no stronghold; but we have, O yes, we have another father, dear child, another father—eh? . . . Where . . . Where?'

She very softly raised her finger. 'On high,' she whispered, with extraordinary intensity.

'But just now,' she added cheerfully, hugging her mittened hands together, 'we are not talking of Him; we are talking of ourselves, just you and me, *so* cosy; so *secret*! And it's a grandmother? I thought so, I thought so, a grandmother! O yes, I can peep between the curtains, though they do lock the door. A grandmother—I thought so; that very droll old lady! *Such* fine clothes! Such a presence, oh yes! A grandmother.' She poked out her chin and laughed confidentially.

'And the long, bony creature, all rub and double'—she jogged briskly with her elbows, 'who's that?'

'Mrs Pridgett,' I said.

'There, there,' she whispered breathlessly, gazing widely about her. 'Think of that! *He* knows; *He* understands. How firm, how manly, how undaunted! . . . *One* t?'

I shook my head dubiously.

'Why should he?' she cried scornfully. 'But between ourselves, Arthur, that is a thing we *must* learn, and never mind the headache. We cannot, of course, know everything. Even Miss Coppin does not know everything—' she leaned forward with intense earnestness—'though I don't tell her so. We must try to learn all we can; and at once. One thing, dear child, you may be astonished to hear, I learned only yesterday, and that is how exceedingly *sad* life is.'

She leaned her chin upon her narrow bosom pursing her lips. 'And yet you know they say very little about it. . . . They don't *mention* it. Every moment, every hour, every day, every year— one, two, three, four, five, seven, ten,' she paused, frowned, 'and so on. Sadder and sadder. Why? why? It's strange, but oh, so true. You really can have no notion, child, how very sad I am myself at times. In the evening, when they all gather together, in their white raiment, up and up and up, I sit on the garden seat, on Miss Coppin's garden seat, and precisely in the middle (you'll be kind enough to remember that?) and my *thoughts* make me sad.' She narrowed her eyes and shoulders. 'Yes and frightened, my child! Why must I be so guarded? One angel—the greatest *fool* could see the wisdom of that. But billions!—with their fixed eyes shining, so very boldly, on me. I never prayed for so many, dear friend. And we pray for a good many odd things, you and I, I'll be bound. But, there, you see, poor Miss Duveen's on her theology again— scamper, scamper, scamper. In the congregations of the wicked we must be cautious! . . . Mrs Partridge and grandmamma, so nice, *so* nice; but even that, too, a *little* sad, eh?' She leaned her head questioningly, like a starving bird in the snow.

I smiled, not knowing what else she expected of me; and her face became instantly grave and set.

'He's right; perfectly right. We must speak evil of *no*-one. *No*-one. We must shut our mouths. We——' She stopped suddenly and, taking a step leaned over the water towards me, with eyebrows raised high above her tiny face. 'S—sh!' she whispered, laying a long forefinger on her lips. 'Eavesdroppers!' she smoothed her skirts, straightened her cap, and left me; only a moment after to poke out her head at me again from between the leafy bushes. 'An assignation, no!' she said firmly, then gathered her poor, cheerful, forlorn, crooked, lovable face into a most wonderful contraction at me, that assuredly meant—'But, *yes*!'

Indeed it was an assignation, the first of how many, and how few. Sometimes Miss Duveen would sit beside me, apparently so lost in thought that I was clean forgotten. And yet I half fancied it was often nothing but feigning. Once she stared me blankly out of countenance when I ventured to take the initiative and to call out Good-morning to her across the water. On this occasion she completed my consternation with a sudden, angry grimace— contempt, jealousy, outrage.

But often we met like old friends and talked. It was a novel but not always welcome diversion for me in the long shady garden that was my privy universe. Where our alders met, mingling their branches across the flowing water, and the kingfisher might be seen—there was our usual tryst. But, occasionally, at her invitation, I would venture across the stepping-stones into her demesne; and occasionally, but very seldom indeed, she would venture into mine. How plainly I see her, tip-toeing from stone to stone, in an extraordinary concentration of mind—her mulberry petticoats, her white stockings, her loose spring-side boots. And when at last she stood beside me, her mittened hand on her breast, she would laugh on in a kind of paroxysm until the tears stood in her eyes, and she grew faint with breathlessness.

'In all danger,' she told me once, 'I hold my breath and shut my eyes. And if I could tell you of every danger, I think, perhaps, you would understand——dear Miss Coppin . . .' I did not, and yet, perhaps, very vaguely I did see the connection in this rambling statement.

Like most children, I liked best to hear Miss Duveen talk about her own childhood. I contrived somehow to discover that if we sat near flowers or under boughs in blossom, her talk would generally steal round to that. Then she would chatter on and on: of the white sunny rambling house, somewhere, nowhere—it saddened and confused her if I asked where—in which she had spent her first happy years; where her father used to ride on a black horse; and her mother to walk with her in the garden in a crinolined gown and a locket with the painted miniature of a 'divine' nobleman inside it. How very far away these pictures seemed!

It was as if she herself had shrunken back into this distant past, and was babbling on like a child again, already a little isolated by her tiny infirmity.

'That was before——' she would begin to explain precisely, and then a crisscross many-wrinkled frown would net her rounded forehead, and cloud her eyes. Time might baffle her, but then, time often baffled me too. Any talk about her mother usually reminded her of an elder sister, Caroline. 'My sister, Caroline,' she would repeat as if by rote, 'you may not be aware, Arthur, was afterwards Mrs Bute. *So* charming, *so* exquisite, *so* accomplished. And Colonel Bute—an officer and a gentleman, I grant. And yet . . . But no! My dear sister was *not* happy. And so it was no doubt a blessing in disguise that by an unfortunate accident she was found *drowned*. In a lake, you will understand, not a mere shallow noisy brook. This is one of my private sorrows, which, of course, your grandmamma would be horrified to hear—horrified; and which, of course, Partridge has not the privilege of birth even to be informed of—*our* secret, dear child—with all her beautiful hair, and her elegant feet, and her eyes no more ajar than this; but blue, blue as the forget-me-not. When the time comes, Miss Coppin will close my own eyes, I hope and trust. Death, dear, dear child, I know they *say* is only sleeping. Yet I hope and trust *that*. To be sleeping wide awake; oh no!' She abruptly turned her small untidy head away.

'But didn't they shut *hers*?' I inquired.

Miss Duveen ignored the question. 'I am not uttering one word of blame,' she went on rapidly; 'I am perfectly aware that such things confuse me. Miss Coppin tells me not to think. She tells me that I can have no opinions worth the mention. She says, "Shut up your mouth." I must keep silence then. All that I am merely trying to express to you, Arthur, knowing you will regard it as sacred between us—all I am expressing is that my dear sister, Caroline, was a gifted and beautiful creature with not a shadow or vestige or tinge or taint of confusion in her mind. *Nothing*. And yet, when they dragged her out of the water and laid her there on the bank, looking—' She stooped herself double in a sudden dreadful fit of gasping, and I feared for an instant she was about to die.

'No, no, no,' she cried, rocking herself to and fro, 'you shall *not* paint such a picture in his young, innocent mind. You *shall* not.'

I sat on my stone, watching her, feeling excessively uncomfortable. 'But what *did* she look like, Miss Duveen?' I pressed forward to ask at last.

'No, no, no,' she cried again. 'Cast him out, cast him out. *Retro Sathanas!* We must not even *ask* to understand. My father and my dear mother, I do not doubt, have spoken for Caroline. Even I, if I must be called on, will strive to collect my thoughts. And that is precisely where a friend, you, Arthur, would be so precious; to know that you too, in your innocence, will be helping me to collect my thoughts on that day, to save our dear Caroline from Everlasting Anger. That, that! Oh dear: oh dear!' She turned on me a face I should scarcely have recognized, lifted herself trembling to her feet, and hurried away.

Sometimes it was not Miss Duveen that was a child again, but I that had grown up. 'Had now you been your handsome father— and I see him, O, so plainly, dear child—had you been your father, then I must, of course, have kept to the house . . . I must have; it is a rule of conduct, and everything depends on them. Where would Society be *else*?' she cried, with an unanswerable blaze of intelligence. 'I find, too, dear Arthur, that they increase—the rules increase. I try to remember them. My dear cousin, Miss Coppin, knows them all. But I—I think sometime one's *memory* is a little treacherous. And then it must vex people.'

She gazed penetratingly at me for an answer that did not come. Mute as a fish though I might be, I suppose it was something of a comfort to her to talk to me.

And to suppose that is *my* one small crumb of comfort when I reflect on the kind of friendship I managed to bestow.

I actually met Miss Coppin once; but we did not speak. I had, in fact, gone to tea with Miss Duveen. The project had been discussed as 'quite, quite impossible, dear child' for weeks. 'You must never mention it again.' As a matter of fact I had never mentioned it at all. But one day—possibly when their charge had been less difficult and exacting, one day Miss Coppin and her gaunt maid-servant and companion really did go out together, leaving Miss Duveen alone in Willowlea. It was the crowning opportunity of our friendship. The moment I espied her issuing from the house, I guessed her errand. She came hastening down to the waterside, attired in clothes of a colour and fashion I had never seen her wearing before, her dark eyes shining in her head, her hands trembling with excitement.

It was a still, warm afternoon, with Sweet Williams and linden and stocks scenting the air, when, with some little trepidation, I must confess, I followed her in formal dignity up the unfamiliar path towards the house. I know not which of our hearts beat the quicker, whose eyes cast the most furtive glances about us. My friend's cheeks were brightest mauve. She wore a large silver locket on a ribbon; and I followed her up the faded green stairs, beneath the dark pictures, to her small, stuffy bedroom under the roof. We humans, they say, are enveloped in a kind of aura; to which the vast majority of us are certainly entirely insensitive. Nevertheless, there was an air, an atmosphere as of the smell of pears in this small attic room—well, every bird, I suppose, haunts with its presence its customary cage.

'This,' she said, acknowledging the bed, the looking-glass, the deal washstand, 'this, dear child, you will pardon; in fact, you will not see. How could we sit, friends as we are, in the congregation of strangers?'

I hardly know why, but that favourite word of Miss Duveen's, 'congregation', brought up before me with extreme aversion all the hostile hardness and suspicion concentrated in Miss Coppin and Ann. I stared at the queer tea things in a vain effort not to be aware of the rest of Miss Duveen's private belongings.

Somehow or other she had managed to procure for me a bun—a saffron bun. There was a dish of a gray pudding and a plate of raspberries that I could not help suspecting (and, I am ashamed to say, with aggrieved astonishment), she must have herself gathered that morning from my grandmother's canes. We did not talk very much. Her heart gave her pain. And her face showed how hot and absorbed and dismayed she was over her foolhardy entertainment. But I sipped my milk and water, sitting on a black bandbox, and she on an old cane chair. And we were almost formal and distant to one another, with little smiles and curtseys over our cups, and polished agreement about the weather.

'And you'll strive not to be sick, dear child,' she implored me suddenly, while I was nibbling my way slowly through the bun. But it was not until rumours of the tremendous fact of Miss Coppin's early and unforeseen return had been borne in on us that Miss Duveen lost all presence of mind. She burst into tears; seized and kissed repeatedly my sticky hands; implored me to be discreet; implored me to be gone; implored me to retain her in my affections, 'as you love your poor dear mother, Arthur,' and I left her on her knees, her locket pressed to her bosom.

Miss Coppin was, I think, unusually astonished to see a small strange boy walk softly past her bedroom door, within which she sat, with purple face, her hat strings dangling, taking off her boots. Ann, I am thankful to say, I did not encounter. But when I was safely out in the garden in the afternoon sunshine, the boldness and the romance of this sally completely deserted me. I ran like a hare down the alien path, leapt from stone to stone across the river; nor paused in my flight until I was safe in my own bedroom, and had—how odd is childhood!—washed my face and entirely changed my clothes.

My grandmother, when I appeared at her tea-table, glanced at me now and again rather profoundly and inquisitively, but the actual question hovering in her mind remained unuttered.

It was many days before we met again, my friend and I. She had, I gathered from many mysterious nods and shrugs, been more or less confined to her bedroom ever since our escapade, and looked dulled and anxious; her small face was even a little more vacant in repose than usual. Even this meeting, too, was full of alarms; for in the midst of our talk, by mere chance or caprice, my grandmother took a walk in the garden that afternoon, and discovered us under our damson tree. She bowed in her dignified, aged way. And Miss Duveen, with cheeks and forehead the colour of her petticoat, elaborately curtseyed.

'Beautiful, very beautiful weather,' said my grandmother.

'It is, indeed,' said my friend, fixedly.

'I trust you are keeping pretty well?'

'As far, Ma'am, as God and a little weakness of the heart permit,' said Miss Duveen. 'He knows all,' she added firmly.

My grandmother stood silent a moment.

'Indeed he does,' she replied politely.

'And that's the difficulty,' ventured Miss Duveen, in her odd, furtive, friendly fashion.

My grandmother opened her eyes, smiled pleasantly, paused, glanced remotely at me, and, with another exchange of courtesies, Miss Duveen and I were left alone once more. But it was a grave and saddened friend I now sat beside.

'You see, Arthur, all bad things, we know, are best for us. Motives included. That comforts me. But my heart is sadly fluttered. Not that I fear or would shun society; but perhaps your grandmother . . . I never had the power to treat my fellow-creatures as if they were stocks and stones. And the effort not to notice it distresses me. A little hartshorn might relieve the *palpitation*, of course; but Miss Coppin keeps all keys. It is this shouting that makes civility such a task.'

'This shouting'—very faintly then I caught her meaning, but I was in no mood to sympathize. My grandmother's one round-eyed expressionless glance at me had been singularly disconcerting. And it was only apprehension of her questions that kept me from beating a retreat. So we sat on, Miss Duveen and I, in the shade, the day drawing towards evening, and presently we walked down to the water-side, and under the colours of sunset I flung in my crumbs to the minnows, as she talked ceaselessly on.

'And yet,' she concluded, after how involved a monologue, 'and yet, Arthur, I feel it is for your forgiveness I should be pleading. So much to do; such an arch of beautiful things might have been my gift to you. It is here,' she said, touching her forehead. 'I do not think, perhaps, that all I might say would be for your good. I must be silent and discreet about much. I must not provoke'—she lifted her mittened finger, and raised her eyes—'Them,' she said gravely. 'I am tempted, terrified, persecuted. Whispering, wrangling, shouting: the flesh is a grievous burden, Arthur; I long for peace. Only to flee away and be at rest! But,' she nodded, and glanced over her shoulder, 'about much—great trials, sad entanglements, about much the Others say, I must keep silence. It would only alarm your innocence. And that I will never, *never* do. Your father, a noble, gallant gentleman of the world, would have understood my difficulties. But he is dead . . . Whatever that may mean. I have repeated it so often when Miss Coppin thought that I was not—dead, dead, dead, dead—but I don't think that even now I grasp the meaning of the word. Of you, dear child, I will never say it. You have been life itself to me.'

How generously, how tenderly she smiled on me from her perplexed, sorrowful eyes.

'You have all the world before you, all the world. How splendid it is to be a Man. For my part I have sometimes thought, though they do not of course intend to injure me, yet I fancy, sometimes, they have grudged me *my* part in it a little. Though God forbid but Heaven's best.'

She raised that peering, dark, remote gaze to my face, and her head was trembling again. 'They are saying now to one another—"*Where is she? where is she? It's nearly dark, m'm, where is she?*" O, Arthur, but there shall be no night *there*. We must believe it, we must—in spite, dear friend, of a weak horror of glare. My cousin, Miss Coppin, does not approve of my wishes. Gas, gas, gas, all over the house, and when it is not singing, it roars. You would suppose I might be trusted with but just my own one bracket. But no—Ann, I think—indeed I fear, sometimes, has no——' She started violently and shook her tiny head. 'When I am gone,' she continued disjointedly, 'you will be prudent, cautious, dear child? Consult only your heart about me. Older you must be . . . Yes, certainly, he must be older,' she repeated vaguely. 'Everything goes on and on—and round!' She seemed astonished, as if at a sudden radiance cast on an old and protracted perplexity.

'About your soul, dear child,' she said to me once, touching my hand, 'I have never spoken. Perhaps it was one of my first duties to keep on speaking to you about your soul. I mention it now in case they should rebuke me when I make my appearance there. It is a burden; and I have so many burdens, as well as pain. And at times I cannot think very far. I *see* the thought; but it won't alter. It comes back, just like a sheep—"*Ba-aa-ah*", like that!' She burst out laughing, twisting her head to look at me the while. 'Miss Coppin, of course, has no difficulty; gentlemen have no difficulty. And this shall be the occasion of another of our little confidences. We are discreet?' She bent her head and scanned my face. 'Here,' she tapped her bosom, 'I bear his image. My only dear one's. And if you would kindly turn your head, dear child, perhaps I could pull him out.'

It was the miniature of a young, languid, fastidious-looking officer which she showed me—threaded on dingy tape, in its tarnished locket.

'Miss Coppin, in great generosity, has left me this,' she said, polishing the glass on her knee, 'though I am forbidden to wear it.

For you see, Arthur, it is a duty not to brood on the past, and even perhaps, indelicate. Some day, it may be, you, too, will love a gentle girl. I beseech you, keep your heart pure and true. This one could not. Not a single word of blame escapes me. I own to my Maker, *never* to anyone else, it has not eased my little difficulty. But it is not for us to judge. Whose office is that, eh?' And again, that lean small forefinger, beneath an indescribable grimace, pointed gently, deliberately, from her lap upward. 'Pray', pray,' she added, very violently, 'pray, till the blood streams down your face! Pray, but rebuke not. They all whisper about it. Among themselves,' she added, peering out beneath and between the interlacing branches. 'But I simulate inattention. I simulate . . .' The very phrase seemed to have hopelessly confused her. Again, as so often now, that glassy fear came into her eyes; her foot tapped on the gravel.

'Arthur,' she cried suddenly, taking my hand tightly in her lap, 'you have been my refuge in a time of trouble. You will never know it, child. My refuge, and my peace. We shall seldom meet now. All are opposed. They repeat it in their looks. The Autumn will divide us; and then, Winter; but, I think, no Spring. It is so, Arthur, there is a stir; and then they will hunt me out.' Her eyes gleamed again, far and small and black in the dusky pallor of her face.

It was indeed already Autumn; the air golden and still. The leaves were beginning to fall. The late fruits were well-nigh over. Robins and tits seemed our only birds now. Rain came in floods. The Wandle took sound and volume, sweeping deep above our stepping stones. Very seldom after this I even so much as saw our neighbour. I chanced on her one still afternoon, standing fixedly by the brawling stream, in a rusty-looking old-fashioned cloak, her scanty hair pushed high up on her forehead.

She stared at me for a moment or two, and then, with a scared look over her shoulder, threw me a little letter shaped like a cock-hat, and weighted with a pebble stone, across the stream. She whispered earnestly and rapidly at me over the water. But I could not catch a single word she said, and failed to decipher her close spidery handwriting. No doubt I was too shy, or too ashamed, or in a vague fashion too loyal, to show it to my grandmother. It is not now a flattering keepsake. I called out loudly I must go in; and still see her gazing after me, with a puzzled, mournful expression on the face peering out of the cloak.

Even after that we sometimes waved to one another across the water, but never if by hiding myself I could evade her in time. The distance seemed to confuse her, and quite silenced me. I began to see we were ridiculous friends, especially as she came now in even dingier and absurder clothes. She even looked hungry, and not quite clean, as well as ill; and she talked more to her phantoms than to me when once we met.

The first ice was in the garden. The trees stood bare beneath a pale blue sunny sky, and I was standing at the window, looking out at the hoar-frost, when my grandmother told me that it was unlikely that I should ever see our neighbour again.

I stood where I was, without turning round, staring out of the window at the motionless ghostly trees, and the few birds in forlorn unease.

'Is she dead, then?' I inquired.

'I am told,' was the reply, 'that her friends have been compelled to have her put away. No doubt, it was the proper course. It should have been done earlier. But it is not our affair, you are to understand. And, poor creature, perhaps death would have been a happier, a more merciful release. She was sadly afflicted.'

I said nothing, and continued to stare out of the window.

But I know now that the news, in spite of a vague sorrow, greatly relieved me. I should be at ease in the garden again, came the thought—no longer fear to look ridiculous, and grow hot when our neighbour was mentioned, or be saddled with her company beside the stream.

W. SOMERSET MAUGHAM

Louise

I could never understand why Louise bothered with me. She disliked me and I knew that behind my back, in that gentle way of hers, she seldom lost the opportunity of saying a disagreeable thing about me. She had too much delicacy ever to make a direct statement, but with a hint and a sigh and a little flutter of her beautiful hands she was able to make her meaning plain. She was a mistress of cold praise. It was true that we had known one another almost intimately, for five-and-twenty years, but it was impossible for me to believe that she could be affected by the claims of old association. She thought me a coarse, brutal, cynical, and vulgar fellow. I was puzzled at her not taking the obvious course and dropping me. She did nothing of the kind; indeed, she would not leave me alone; she was constantly asking me to lunch and dine with her and once or twice a year invited me to spend a week-end at her house in the country. At last I thought that I had discovered her motive. She had an uneasy suspicion that I did not believe in her; and if that was why she did not like me, it was also why she sought my acquaintance: it galled her that I alone should look upon her as a comic figure and she could not rest till I acknowledged myself mistaken and defeated. Perhaps she had an inkling that I saw the face behind the mask and because I alone held out was determined that sooner or later I too should take the mask for the face. I was never quite certain that she was a complete humbug. I wondered whether she fooled herself as thoroughly as she fooled the world or whether there was some spark of humour at the bottom of her heart. If there was it might be that she was attracted to me, as a pair of crooks might be attracted to one another, by the knowledge that we shared a secret that was hidden from everybody else.

I knew Louise before she married. She was then a frail, delicate girl with large and melancholy eyes. Her father and mother worshipped her with an anxious adoration, for some illness, scarlet fever I think, left her with a weak heart and she had to take the greatest care of herself. When Tom Maitland proposed to her they were dismayed, for they were convinced that she was much too delicate for the strenuous state of marriage. But they were not too well off and Tom Maitland was rich. He promised to do everything in the world for Louise and finally they entrusted her to him as a sacred charge. Tom Maitland was a big, husky fellow, very good-looking, and a fine athlete. He doted on Louise. With her weak heart he could not hope to keep her with him long and he made up his mind to do everything he could to make her few years on earth happy. He gave up the games he excelled in, not because she wished him to, she was glad that he should play golf and hunt, but because by a coincidence she had a heart attack whenever he proposed to leave her for a day. If they had a difference of opinion she gave in to him at once, for she was the most submissive wife a man could have, but her heart failed her and she would be laid up, sweet and uncomplaining, for a week. He could not be such a brute as to cross her. Then they would have a quiet little tussle about which should yield and it was only with difficulty that at last he persuaded her to have her own way. On one occasion seeing her walk eight miles on an expedition that she particularly wanted to make, I suggested to Tom Maitland that she was stronger than one would have thought. He shook his head and sighed.

'No, no, she's dreadfully delicate. She's been to all the best heart specialists in the world, and they all say that her life hangs on a thread. But she has an unconquerable spirit.'

He told her that I had remarked on her endurance.

'I shall pay for it tomorrow,' she said to me in her plaintive way. 'I shall be at death's door.'

'I sometimes think that you're quite strong enough to do the things you want to,' I murmured.

I had noticed that if a party was amusing she could dance till five in the morning, but if it was dull she felt very poorly and Tom had to take her home early. I am afraid she did not like my reply, for though she gave me a pathetic little smile I saw no amusement in her large blue eyes.

'You can't very well expect me to fall down dead just to please you,' she answered.

Louise outlived her husband. He caught his death of cold one day when they were sailing and Louise needed all the rugs there were to keep her warm. He left her a comfortable fortune and a daughter. Louise was inconsolable. It was wonderful that she managed to survive the shock. Her friends expected her speedily to follow poor Tom Maitland to the grave. Indeed they already felt dreadfully sorry for Iris, her daughter, who would be left an orphan. They redoubled their attentions towards Louise. They would not let her stir a finger; they insisted on doing everything in the world to save her trouble. They had to, because if she was called upon to do anything tiresome or inconvenient her heart went back on her and there she was at death's door. She was entirely lost without a man to take care of her, she said, and she did not know how, with her delicate health, she was going to bring up her dear Iris. Her friends asked why she did not marry again. Oh, with her heart it was out of the question, though of course she knew that dear Tom would have wished her to, and perhaps it would be the best thing for Iris if she did; but who would want to be bothered with a wretched invalid like herself? Oddly enough more than one young man showed himself quite ready to undertake the charge and a year after Tom's death she allowed George Hobhouse to lead her to the altar. He was a fine, upstanding fellow, and he was not at all badly off. I never saw any one so grateful as he for the privilege of being allowed to take care of this frail little thing.

'I shan't live to trouble you long,' she said.

He was a soldier and an ambitious one, but he resigned his commission. Louise's health forced her to spend the winter at Monte Carlo and the summer at Deauville. He hesitated a little at throwing up his career, and Louise at first would not hear of it; but at last she yielded as she always yielded, and he prepared to make his wife's last few years as happy as might be.

'It can't be very long now,' she said. 'I'll try not to be trouble-some.'

For the next two or three years Louise managed, notwithstanding her weak heart, to go beautifully dressed to all the most lively parties, to gamble very heavily, to dance and even to flirt with tall, slim young men. But George Hobhouse had not the stamina of Louise's first husband and he had to brace himself now and then with a stiff drink for his day's work as Louise's second husband. It is possible that the habit would have grown on him, which Louise would not have liked at all, but very fortunately (for her) the war broke out. He rejoined his regiment and three months later was killed. It was a great shock to Louise. She felt, however, that in such a crisis she must not give way to a private grief; and if she had a heart attack nobody heard of it. In order to distract her mind, she turned her villa at Monte Carlo into a hospital for convalescent officers. Her friends told her that she would never survive the strain.

'Of course it will kill me,' she said, 'I know that. But what does it matter? I must do my bit.'

It didn't kill her. She had the time of her life. There was no convalescent home in France that was more popular. I met her by chance in Paris. She was lunching at the Ritz with a tall and very handsome Frenchman. She explained that she was there on business connected with the hospital. She told me that the officers were too charming to her. They knew how delicate she was and they wouldn't let her do a single thing. They took care of her, well—as though they were all her husbands. She sighed.

'Poor George, who would ever have thought that I, with my heart, should survive him?'

'And poor Tom!' I said.

I don't know why she didn't like my saying that. She gave me her plaintive smile and her beautiful eyes filled with tears.

'You always speak as though you grudged me the few years that I can expect to live.'

'By the way, your heart's much better, isn't it?'

'It'll never be better. I saw a specialist this morning and he said I must be prepared for the worst.'

'Oh, well, you've been prepared for that for nearly twenty years now, haven't you?'

When the war came to an end Louise settled in London. She was now a woman of over forty, thin and frail still, with large eyes and pale cheeks, but she did not look a day more than twenty-five. Iris, who had been at school and was now grown up, came to live with her.

'She'll take care of me,' said Louise. 'Of course it'll be hard on her to live with such a great invalid as I am, but it can only be for such a little while, I'm sure she won't mind.'

Iris was a nice girl. She had been brought up with the knowledge that her mother's health was precarious. As a child she had never been allowed to make a noise. She had always realized that her mother must on no account be upset. And though Louise told her now that she would not hear of her sacrificing herself for a tiresome old woman the girl simply would not listen. It wasn't a question of sacrificing herself, it was a happiness to do what she could for her poor dear mother. With a sigh her mother let her do a great deal.

'It pleases the child to think she's making herself useful,' she said.

'Don't you think she ought to go out and about more?' I asked.

'That's what I'm always telling her. I can't get her to enjoy herself. Heaven knows, I never want any one to put themselves out on my account.'

And Iris, when I remonstrated with her, said: 'Poor dear mother, she wants me to go and stay with friends and go to parties, but the moment I start off anywhere she has one of her heart attacks, so I much prefer to stay at home.'

But presently she fell in love. A young friend of mine, a very good lad, asked her to marry him and she consented. I liked the child and was glad that she was to be given the chance to lead a life of her own. She had never seemed to suspect that such a thing was possible. But one day the young man came to me in great distress and told me that his marriage was indefinitely postponed. Iris felt that she could not desert her mother. Of course it was really no business of mine, but I made the opportunity to go and see Louise. She was always glad to receive her friends at tea-time and now that she was older she cultivated the society of painters and writers.

'Well, I hear that Iris isn't going to be married,' I said after a while.

'I don't know about that. She's not going to be married quite as soon as I could have wished. I've begged her on my bended knees not to consider me, but she absolutely refuses to leave me.'

'Don't you think it's rather hard on her?'

'Dreadfully. Of course it can only be for a few months, but I hate the thought of any one sacrificing themselves for me.'

'My dear Louise, you've buried two husbands, I can't see the least reason why you shouldn't bury at least two more.'

'Do you think that's funny?' she asked me in a tone that she made as offensive as she could.

'I suppose it's never struck you as strange that you're always strong enough to do anything you want to and that your weak heart only prevents you from doing things that bore you?'

'Oh, I know, I know what you've always thought of me. You've never believed that I had anything the matter with me, have you?'

I looked at her full and square.

'Never. I think you've carried out for twenty-five years a stupendous bluff. I think you're the most selfish and monstrous woman I have ever known. You ruined the lives of those two wretched men you married and now you're going to ruin the life of your daughter.'

I should not have been surprised if Louise had had a heart attack then. I fully expected her to fly into a passion. She merely gave me a gentle smile.

'My poor friend, one of these days you'll be so dreadfully sorry you said this to me.'

'Have you quite determined that Iris shall not marry this boy?'

'I've begged her to marry him. I know it'll kill me, but I don't mind. Nobody cares for me. I'm just a burden to everybody.'

'Did you tell her it would kill you?'

'She made me.'

'As if any one ever made you do anything that you were not yourself quite determined to do.'

'She can marry her young man tomorrow if she likes. If it kills me, it kills me.'

'Well, let's risk it, shall we?'

'Haven't you got any compassion for me?'

'One can't pity any one who amuses one as much as you amuse me,' I answered.

A faint spot of colour appeared on Louise's pale cheeks and though she smiled still her eyes were hard and angry.

'Iris shall marry in a month's time,' she said, 'and if anything happens to me I hope you and she will be able to forgive yourselves.'

Louise was as good as her word. A date was fixed, a trousseau of great magnificence was ordered, and invitations were issued. Iris and the very good lad were radiant. On the wedding-day, at ten o'clock in the morning, Louise, that devilish woman, had one of her heart attacks—and died. She died gently forgiving Iris for having killed her.

T. F. POWYS

Mr Pim and the Holy Crumb

The Holy Communion was about to be celebrated one winter's morning at the church of St Nicholas in the village of Madder.

The event was of very little importance to any one, save perhaps to the clergyman, to Pim the church clerk, and to a little mouse who lived under the altar.

Pim was obliged to rise early when the celebration was to take place, and to use his best endeavour to light the church fire, leaving his own bed at an hour when he liked most to remain in it. What the ceremony really meant, Pim had never had the least idea.

Though clerk of the church, he had never yet received the sacrament, for it had ever been his habit, after collecting the alms, to take his cap from his pew and retire on tiptoe from the church.

But this Christmas morning was to prove an exception, for Mr Thomas Tucker, the clergyman, had caught Pim at a disadvantage, got him into a corner of the vestry, and compelled his attention. Then it was that Mr Tucker told to Pim so strange a tale of the holy feast that the clerk, having an inquisitive mind, promised his master that this once he would partake of the elements.

When Mr Tucker had explained to him the meaning of the rite, Pim made the necessary preparations. He found the church cold, for the fire he had lit earlier with so many pains was gone out, and Pim was glad to exercise himself a little by returning to the vestry and pulling at the bell-rope.

After ringing himself warm, Pim, while Mr Tucker rested upon a chair, stepped out of the church to see what was doing abroad. The heavy tranquil weather, with its still silence, informed Pim as he looked around him that it was going to snow. He looked this way and that, with his hands placed behind his coat-tails, and as if in answer to his thoughts a large snowflake fluttered down, remained upon the path for a moment, and then melted into water.

Pim, looking up from the vanished flake, beheld Miss Jarrett and Mrs Patch, two old women who chattered like crows, coming his way. He was full of the strange story that Mr Tucker had told him in the vestry, for, shake his head as he might, he could not rid himself of it. The snowflake that he had thought to confer with had gone too soon, but the two old women appeared more likely to remain and listen.

Pim was not the man to keep anything to himself. If he heard any surprising news he would always tell it to the first person he met, whether the news was a maiden ill-treated, a nest of eggs stolen from Farmer Told, or a fire in London.

'Mr Tucker do tell I,' said Pim, addressing himself to Miss Jarrett, 'that the Lord God, the Creator of the world, who be named Christ by drunken folk when pub do close, do change 'Isself into they scrimpy bites of Mr Johnson's bread that thee do take and eat up at church railings.'

Miss Jarrett hurriedly placed her muff before her mouth to stop her laughter, while Mrs Patch winked expressively as if she knew all about such wonderful doings, though her repeated winks told Pim that the particular moment wasn't a proper one for her to explain them.

Miss Jarrett, who could hardly contain her mirth, now put her finger to her lips and passed by the clerk together with Mrs Patch, bidding him in a whisper to beware what he said, for Miss Pettifer was coming.

Pim stood to one side as the lady from the Manor walked by with her little silver bag. He touched his hat respectfully and informed Miss Pettifer that he believed it would snow before the night came.

'Can't you see,' said Miss Pettifer, a little rudely, 'that it snows now, Pim?'

Pim looked in another direction, for he once had a friend whose name was John Toole. It had always been the custom of these two, when John was alive, to meet of an evening by the village green, exchange remarks about the weather, and then walk slowly and thoughtfully to the inn. Once there, but having little money to spend, they would share a pot of beer so that their order might sound large.

John Toole hanged himself, and now Pim shook his head at his grave.

As Miss Pettifer, however late she came, had always to be allowed time to adjust her veil, sprinkle a little scent upon her handkerchief, and kneel down, Pim had no need to hurry back to the church. With his hands still behind his back, he bent over the grave.

'John,' said Pim, 'I've a-heard something that must make 'ee laugh—'tis that God Almighty in our little church do change 'Isself into a bite of stale bread.'

'That be a tale,' replied a muffled voice from the ground; 'but what be weather doing up above?'

'There be snowflakes a-falling as large as feathers,' replied Pim, showing no surprise because his friend spoke so lowlily, 'as large as feathers, but they do melt on ground.'

'So I did fancy,' replied the buried John; 'but now I've somewhat to ask of 'ee that bain't about the weather.'

'Ask away, Johnnie,' replied Pim.

'If 'ee do happen,' said the muffled voice, 'to get a word wi' thik crumb of bread that be the Lord on High, ask 'E to be kind enough to look over Johnnie Toole at the last day, for I be well content to bide where I be now. There bain't no work to do here and all be ease and comfort, and many a merry story do we bones tell together.'

Pim sighed. He nodded twice at the grave, turned, and walked to the church. Mr Tucker was standing ready robed in the vestry, Miss Pettifer was kneeling with her black fur stole covering her shoulders.

Pim solemnly tolled the last bell; he proceeded to the back pew and knelt down. The wonderful story that he had heard of—the transformation of God into the Holy Bread—made him fearful, but yet he wished to ask John Toole's question.

Another matter troubled him too. He remembered that only the evening before his wife Jane had blamed Mr Johnson's bread for giving her a pain in her chest. What if God should pain him too? Pim looked gloomy.

When his turn came Pim knelt at the altar rail next to Mrs Patch. He trembled exceedingly. He was so fearful of the consequences of the act of eating, that when he was going to put the bread into his mouth he let a large crumb fall upon the floor.

As soon as the service was over and Mr Tucker was gone out, Pim returned in a slow and fearful manner to the altar again. To have eaten so much of Mr Johnson's bread, as well as so much of his Maker, seemed a dreadful thing, but to have dropped a crumb of Him upon the floor seemed a worse.

After he had eaten God, Pim wondered what God was like. He supposed that God would very much resemble the landlord at the village inn. Mr Hookes, the landlord, looked like a judge, and indeed he might well have been the creator of all men.

' 'E did draw I out of 'Is great barrel into a little cup,' said Pim aloud, 'and when I die 'E do but empty I again into the dirt from whence I came. They be 'Is notions. But if I do eat 'E, between meals, and become as lordly as 'Isself, all me happiness be gone.

'And 'tis likely,' continued Pim, eyeing in a cautious manner the crumb upon the floor, ' 'E won't be pleased wi' Pim for dropping 'E upon church carpet so carelessly. 'Tain't proper for a Holy Crumb to be so fallen. And what be I? Only a small worm of the earth, while 'E it were who did make the round world, the seas, and wold Madder hill. 'Twouldn't do for Pim to go to heaven no more than for Johnnie Toole. Maybe 'E'll let we bide a merry family. Some do fall of a sudden, some bent and tottering like wold Barker do tarry long, but all do go to dust.

'I be sorry,' said Pim, addressing himself to the crumb, 'that I did swallow t'other half of 'Ee.'

'Mr Pim!'

The clerk of St Nicholas looked into the pulpit, he looked down the church aisle, but could see no one.

'Mr Pim!'

His name was spoken very near to him.

'If thik little crumb be changed into God, mayhap 'tis 'E who do speak,' observed Pim.

'And why not?' said the Holy Crumb; 'surely I have as good a right to speak as any other person.'

'Why, so Thee have,' exclaimed Pim, 'and now that I've found

'Ee so talkative, perhaps Thee'll listen to what I do say and maybe Thee'll grant Johnnie and I our one desire.'

'Speak on,' said the Crumb.

'John Toole and I,' remarked Pim, '—'tis 'e who do lie along by yew tree where no sun don't shine—do ask Thee to let we two bide in ground at last day.'

'But you're not dead yet.'

'I do owe God a death,' said the clerk. The Crumb smiled. 'A well-dug grave be good and a coffin be pretty, but I haven't a fancy for neither heaven nor hell. I've a mind to bide where I be put same as Johnnie, while above, in village, days will pass and be gone, will return again and be gone. Thik grey stone that do bide out in field will still be there, and maybe Mr Told's barn will bide about too. Johnnie and I don't want to go to no new place, we'd sooner be dry bones in Madder—for 'tis our home—than lords in heaven.'

'Alas!' said the Crumb.

'Thee do know for a truth,' continued Pim, 'that I bain't a proper companion for the risen gentry; they'd only laugh at me.'

'Why, so they would,' answered the Crumb, 'of course they would.'

'I bain't dissatisfied with the world,' observed Pim. 'My life has pleased me well. Before I were clerk to church and rabbit-trapper, I were ploughman to Mr Told. I do like to sit down at night-time and talk of folk that be gone. Soon I will go too, and I don't want, no more than Johnnie, to be disturbed by no trumpet.'

'But every one else wants to rise again,' remarked the Crumb, 'even the clergy.'

'Clergymen,' observed Pim, 'bain't easily satisfied. They do keep servants, and often a little dog. They do eat mutton and rice pudding, stretch out their legs before the fire, and listen to music being played.'

'Say,' inquired the Crumb, 'do people ever talk about me here? Do they name me at all?'

'Thee's name be useful,' murmured Pim.

'For what?' asked the Crumb.

'Shepherd do shout Thee's name to 'is dog, Carter Beer do damn wold Boxer wi' Thee, and Mr Tucker do say Thee bain't no liar.'

'And yet I made the green grass, Mr Pim!'

' 'Tis plain Pim with the clergy,' remarked the clerk.

'Mr Pim!'

'Yes, Holy Crumb.'

'Mr Pim, I am disappointed with you. I hoped you would have wished to dwell with me, for, to tell you a truth, I made heaven glorious for you and for John Toole.'

'But Thee made the earth too, and the sweet mould for our bed, and Thee'll have Miss Pettifer in heaven, who be a lady.'

'But you, Mr Pim, who have never eaten of the tree of knowledge: I had a mind to be happy with you for all eternity.'

'Ha! ha! ha!' laughed Pim. 'I do see the fix Thee be in, but bain't 'Ee God?'

'Yes, alas so!'

'Then do 'Ee come and be a rotted bone by John and I. But allsame Thee needn't hurry I there. I have a mind to eat a spring cabbage at Easter.'

'Mr Pim, Mr Pim, you are exactly what I meant myself to be. When I consider the troubles I have caused,' said the Holy Crumb in a low voice, 'I almost wish I had entered into a mouse instead of a man.'

'Hist! hist!' whispered Pim, 'Thee may do thik now, for a mouse do live under altar table, who do creep out when all's quiet.'

Pim moved to the front pew, winked at the Crumb and remained silent. A little mouse, with a pert, prying look, crept out from under the altar and devoured the Holy Crumb.

SHERWOOD ANDERSON

I'm a Fool

It was a hard jolt for me, one of the bitterest I ever had to face. And it all came about through my own foolishness, too. Even yet sometimes, when I think of it, I want to cry or swear or kick myself. Perhaps, even now, after all this time, there will be a kind of satisfaction in making myself look cheap by telling of it.

It began at three o'clock one October afternoon as I sat in the grand-stand at the fall trotting-and-pacing meet at Sandusky, Ohio.

To tell the truth, I felt a little foolish that I should be sitting in the grand-stand at all. During the summer before I had left my home town with Harry Whitehead and, with a nigger named Burt, had taken a job as swipe with one of the two horses Harry was campaigning through the fall race-meets that year. Mother cried and my sister Mildred, who wanted to get a job as a school-teacher in our town that fall, stormed and scolded about the house all during the week before I left. They both thought it something disgraceful that one of our family should take a place as a swipe with race-horses. I've an idea Mildred thought my taking the place would stand in the way of her getting the job she'd been working so long for.

But after all I had to work, and there was no other work to be got. A big lumbering fellow of nineteen couldn't just hang around the house and I had got too big to mow people's lawns and sell newspapers. Little chaps who could get next to people's sympathies by their sizes were always getting jobs away from me. There was one fellow who kept saying to every one who wanted a lawn mowed or a cistern cleaned, that he was saving money to work his way through college, and I used to lay awake nights thinking up ways to injure him without being found out. I kept thinking of wagons running over him and bricks falling on his head as he walked along the street. But never mind him.

I got the place with Harry and I liked Burt fine. We got along splendid together. He was a big nigger with a lazy sprawling body and soft, kind eyes, and when it came to a fight he could hit like Jack Johnson. He had Bucephalus, a big black pacing stallion that could do 2.09 or 2.10, if he had to, and I had a little gelding named Doctor Fritz that never lost a race all fall when Harry wanted him to win.

We set out from home late in July in a box car with the two horses, and after that, until late November, we kept moving along to the race-meets and the fairs. It was a peachy time for me, I'll say that. Sometimes now I think that boys who are raised regular in houses, and never have a fine nigger like Burt for best friend, and go to high schools and college, and never steal anything, or get drunk a little, or learn to swear from fellows who know how, or come walking up in front of a grand-stand in their shirt sleeves and with dirty horsy pants on when the races are going on and the grand-stand is full of people all dressed up—— What's the use of talking about it? Such fellows don't know nothing at all. They've never had no opportunity.

But I did. Burt taught me how to rub down a horse and put the bandages on after a race and steam a horse out and a lot of valuable things for any man to know. He could wrap a bandage on a horse's leg so smooth that if it had been the same colour you would think it was his skin, and I guess he'd have been a big driver, too, and got to the top like Murphy and Walter Cox and the others if he hadn't been black.

Gee whizz! it was fun. You got to a county seat town, maybe say on a Saturday or Sunday, and the fair began the next Tuesday and lasted until Friday afternoon. Doctor Fritz would be, say in the 2.25 trot on Tuesday afternoon, and on Thursday afternoon Bucephalus would knock 'em cold in the 'free-for-all' pace. It left you a lot of time to hang around and listen to horse talk, and see Burt knock some yap cold that got too gay, and you'd find out about horses and men and pick up a lot of stuff you could use all the rest of your life, if you had some sense and salted down what you heard and felt and saw.

And then at the end of the week when the race-meet was over, and Harry had run home to tend up to his livery-stables business, you and Burt hitched the two horses to carts and drove slow and steady across country, to the place for the next meeting, so as to not overheat the horses, etc., etc., you know.

Gee whizz! Gosh a'mighty! the nice hickory-nut and beech-nut and oaks and other kinds of trees along the roads, all brown and red, and the good smells, and Burt singing a song that was called *Deep River*, and the country girls at the windows of houses and everything. You can stick your colleges up your nose for all me. I guess I know where I got my education.

Why, one of those little burgs of towns you come to on the way, say now on a Saturday afternoon, and Burt says, 'Let's lay up here.' And you did.

And you took the horses to a livery stable and fed them, and you got your good clothes out of a box and put them on.

And the town was full of farmers gaping, because they could see you were race-horse people, and the kids maybe never see a nigger before and was afraid and run away when the two of us walked down their main street.

And that was before prohibition and all that foolishness, and so you went into a saloon, the two of you, and all the yaps come and stood around, and there was always someone pretended he was horsy and knew things and spoke up and began asking questions, and all you did was to lie and lie all you could about what horses you had, and I said I owned them, and then some fellow said 'Will you have a drink of whisky?' and Burt knocked his eye out the way he could say, off-hand like, 'Oh well, all right, I'm agreeable to a little nip. I'll split a quart with you.' Gee whizz!

But that isn't what I want to tell my story about. We got home late in November and I promised mother I'd quit the race-horses for good. There's a lot of things you've got to promise a mother because she don't know any better.

And so, there not being any work in our town any more than when I left there to go to the races, I went on to Sandusky and got a pretty good place taking care of horses for a man who owned a teaming and delivery and storage and coal and real-estate business there. It was a pretty good place with good eats, and a day off each week, and sleeping on a cot in a big barn, and mostly just shovelling in hay and oats to a lot of big good-enough skates of horses, that couldn't have trotted a race with a toad. I wasn't dissatisfied and I could send money home.

And then, as I started to tell you, the fall races come to Sandusky and I got the day off and I went. I left the job at noon and had on my good clothes and my new brown derby hat, I'd just bought the Saturday before, and a stand-up collar.

First of all I went down town and walked about with the dudes. I've always thought to myself, 'Put up a good front,' and so I did it. I had forty dollars in my pocket, and so I went into the West House, a big hotel, and walked up to the cigar-stand. 'Give me three twenty-five-cent cigars,' I said. There was a lot of horsemen and strangers and dressed-up people from other towns standing around in the lobby and in the bar, and I mingled amongst them. In the bar there was a fellow with a cane and a Windsor tie on, that it made me sick to look at him. I like a man to be a man and dress up, but not to go put on that kind of airs. So I pushed him aside, kind of rough, and had me a drink of whisky. And then he looked at me, as though he thought maybe he'd get gay, but he changed his mind and didn't say anything. And then I had another drink of whisky, just to show him something, and went out and had a hack out to the races, all to myself, and when I got there I bought myself the best seat I could get up in the grand-stand, but didn't go in for any of these boxes. That's putting on too many airs.

And so there I was, sitting up in the grand-stand as gay as you please and looking down on the swipes coming out with their horses, and with their dirty horsy pants on and the horse blankets swung over their shoulders, same as I had been doing all the year before. I liked one thing about the same as the other, sitting up there and feeling grand and being down there and looking up at the yaps and feeling grander and more important, too. One thing's about as good as another, if you take it just right. I've often said that.

Well, right in front of me, in the grand-stand that day, there was a fellow with a couple of girls and they was about my age. The young fellow was a nice guy all right. He was the kind maybe that goes to college and then comes to be a lawyer or maybe a newspaper editor or something like that, but he wasn't struck on himself. There are some of that kind are all right and he was one of the ones.

He had his sister with him and another girl and the sister looked around over his shoulder, accidental at first, not intending to start anything—she wasn't that kind—and her eyes and mine happened to meet.

You know how it is. Gee, she was a peach! She had on a soft dress, kind of a blue stuff and it looked carelessly made, but was well sewed and made and everything. I knew that much. I blushed when she looked right at me and so did she. She was the nicest girl I've ever seen in my life. She wasn't struck on herself and she could talk proper grammar without being like a school-teacher or something like that. What I mean is, she was O.K. I think maybe her father was well-to-do, but not rich to make her chesty because she was his daughter, as some are. Maybe he owned a drugstore or a dry-goods store in their home town, or something like that. She never told me and I never asked.

My own people are all O.K., too, when you come to that. My grandfather was Welsh and over in the old country, in Wales he was—— But never mind that.

The first heat of the first race come off and the young fellow sitting there with the two girls left them and went down to make a bet. I knew what he was up to, but he didn't talk big and noisy and let every one around know he was a sport, as some do. He wasn't that kind. Well, he come back and I heard him tell the two girls what horse he'd bet on, and when the heat was trotted they all half got their feet and acted in the excited, sweaty way people do when they've got money down on a race, and the horse they bet on is up there pretty close at the end, and they think maybe he'll come on with a rush, but he never does because he hasn't got the old juice in him, come right down to it.

And then, pretty soon, the horses came out for the 2.18 pace and there was a horse in it I knew. He was a horse Bob French had in his string, but Bob didn't own him. He was a horse owned by a Mr Mathers down at Marietta, Ohio.

This Mr Mathers had a lot of money and owned some coal mines or something, and he had a swell place out in the country, and he was struck on race-horses, but was a Presbyterian or something, and I think more than likely his wife was one, too, maybe a stiffer one than himself. So he never raced his horses hisself, and the story round the Ohio race-tracks was that when one of his horses got ready to go to the races he turned him over to Bob French and pretended to his wife he was sold.

So Bob had the horses and he did pretty much as he pleased and you can't blame Bob, at least, I never did. Sometimes he was out to win and sometimes he wasn't. I never cared much about that when I was swiping a horse. What I did want to know was that my horse had the speed and could go out in front, if you wanted him to.

And, as I'm telling you, there was Bob in this race with one of Mr Mathers's horses, which was named 'About Ben Ahem' or something like that, and was fast as a streak. He was a gelding and had a mark of 2.21, but could step in ·08 or ·09.

Because when Burt and I were out, as I've told you, the year before, there was a nigger, Burt knew, worked for Mr Mathers and we went out there one day when we didn't have no race on at the Marietta Fair and our boss Harry was gone home.

And so every one was gone to the fair but just this one nigger and he took us all through Mr Mathers's swell house and he and Burt tapped a bottle of wine Mr Mathers had hid in his bedroom, back in a closet, without his wife knowing, and he showed us this Ahem horse. Burt was always struck on being a driver but didn't have much chance to get to the top, being a nigger, and he and the other nigger gulped that whole bottle of wine and Burt got a little lit up.

So the nigger let Burt take this About Ben Ahem and step him a mile in a track Mr Mathers had all to himself, right there on the farm. And Mr Mathers had one child, a daughter, kinda sick and not very good looking, and she came home and we had to hustle and get About Ben Ahem stuck back in the barn.

I'm only telling you to get everything straight. At Sandusky, that afternoon I was at the fair, this young fellow with the two girls was fussed, being with the girls and losing his bet. You know how a fellow is that way. One of them was his girl and the other his sister. I had figured that out.

'Gee whizz!' I says to myself, 'I'm going to give him the dope.'

He was mighty nice when I touched him on the shoulder. He and the girls were nice to me right from the start and clear to the end. I'm not blaming them.

And so he leaned back and I give him the dope on About Ben Ahem. 'Don't bet a cent on this first heat because he'll go like an oxen hitched to a plough, but when the first heat is over go right down and lay on your pile.' That's what I told him.

Well, I never saw a fellow treat any one sweller. There was a fat man sitting beside the little girl, that had looked at me twice by this time, and I at her, and both blushing, and what did he do but have the nerve to turn back and ask the fat man to get up and change places with me so I could sit with his crowd.

Gee whizz, craps a'mighty! There I was. What a chump I was to go and get gay up there in the West House bar, and just because that dude was standing there with a cane and that kind of a necktie on, to go and get all balled up and drink that whisky, just to show off.

Of course she would know, me sitting right beside her and letting her smell of my breath. I could have kicked myself right down out of that grand-stand and all around that race-track and made a faster record than most of the skates of horses they had there that year.

Because that girl wasn't any mutt of a girl. What wouldn't I have give right then for a stick of chewing-gum to chew, or a lozenger, or some liquorice, or most anything. I was glad I had those twenty-five-cent cigars in my pocket and right away I give that fellow one and lit one myself. Then that fat man got up and we changed places and there I was, plunked right down beside her.

They introduced themselves and the fellow's best girl, he had with him, was named Miss Elinor Woodbury, and her father was a manufacturer of barrels from a place called Tiffin, Ohio. And the fellow himself was named Wilbur Wessen and his sister was Miss Lucy Wessen.

I suppose it was their having such swell names got me off my trolly. A fellow, just because he has been a swipe with a race-horse, and works taking care of horses for a man in the teaming, delivery, and storage business, isn't any better or worse than any one else. I've often thought that, and said it, too.

But you know how a fellow is. There's something in that kind of nice clothes, and the kind of nice eyes she had, and the way she had looked at me, awhile before, over her brother's shoulder, and me looking back at her, and both of us blushing.

I couldn't show her up for a boob, could I?

I made a fool of myself, that's what I did. I said my name was Walter Mathers from Marietta, Ohio, and then I told all three of them the smashingest lie you ever heard. What I said was that my father owned the horse About Ben Ahem and that he had let him out to this Bob French for racing purposes, because our family was proud and had never gone into racing that way, in our own name, I mean. Then I had got started and they were all leaning over and listening, and Miss Lucy Wessen's eyes were shining, and I went the whole hog.

I told about our place down at Marietta, and about the big stables and the grand brick house we had on a hill, up above the Ohio River, but I knew enough not to do it in no bragging way. What I did was to start things and then let them drag the rest out of me. I acted just as reluctant to tell as I could. Our family hasn't got any barrel factory, and, since I've known us, we've always been pretty poor, but not asking anything of any one at that, and my grandfather, over in Wales—— But never mind that.

We sat there talking like we had known each other for years and years, and I went and told them that my father had been expecting maybe this Bob French wasn't on the square, and had sent me up to Sandusky on the sly to find out what I could.

And I bluffed it through I had found out all about the 2.18 pace, in which About Ben Ahem was to start.

I said he would lose the first heat by pacing like a lame cow and then he would come back and skin 'em alive after that. And to back up what I said I took thirty dollars out of my pocket and handed it to Mr Wilbur Wessen and asked him, would he mind, after the first heat, to go down and place it on About Ben Ahem for whatever odds he could get. What I said was that I didn't want Bob French to see me and none of the swipes.

Sure enough the first heat come off and About Ben Ahem went off his stride, up the back stretch, and looked like a wooden horse or a sick one, and come in to be last. Then this Wilbur Wessen went down to the betting-place under the grand-stand and there I was with the two girls, and when that Miss Woodbury was looking the other way once, Lucy Wessen kinda, with her shoulder you know, kinda touched me. Not just tucking down, I don't mean. You know how a woman can do. They get close, but not getting gay either. You know what they do. Gee whizz!

And then they give me a jolt. What they had done, when I didn't know, was to get together, and they had decided Wilbur Wessen would bet fifty dollars, and the two girls had gone and put in ten dollars each, of their own money, too. I was sick then, but I was sicker later.

About the gelding, About Ben Ahem, and their winning their money, I wasn't worried a lot about that. It come out O.K. Ahem stepped the next three heats like a bushel of spoiled eggs going to market before they could be found out, and Wilbur Wessen had got nine to two for the money. There was something else eating at me.

Because Wilbur come back, after he had bet the money, and after that he spent most of his time talking to that Miss Woodbury, and Lucy Wessen and I was left alone together like on a desert island. Gee, if I'd only been on the square, or if there had been any way of getting myself on the square. There ain't any Walter Mathers, like I said to her and them, and there hasn't ever been one, but if there was I bet I'd go to Marietta, Ohio, and shoot him tomorrow.

There I was, big boob that I am. Pretty soon the race was over, and Wilbur had gone down and collected our money, and we had a hack down-town, and he stood us a swell supper at the West House, and a bottle of champagne beside.

And I was with that girl and she wasn't saying much, and I wasn't saying much either. One thing I know. She wasn't struck on me because of the lie about my father being rich and all that. There's a way you know. . . . Craps a'mighty! There's a kind of girl, you see just once in your life, and if you don't get busy and make hay, then you're gone for good and all, and might as well go jump off a bridge. They give you a look from inside of them somewhere, and it ain't no vamping, and what it means is—you want that girl to be your wife, and you want nice things around her like flowers and swell clothes, and you want her to have the kids you're going to have, and you want good music played and no ragtime. Gee whizz!

There's a place over near Sandusky, across a kind of bay, and it's called Cedar Point. And after we had supper we went over to it in a launch, all by ourselves. Wilbur and Miss Lucy and that Miss Woodbury had to catch a ten o'clock train back to Tiffin, Ohio, because, when you're out with girls like that, you can't get careless and miss any trains and stay out all night, like you can with some kinds of Janes.

And Wilbur blowed himself to the launch, and it cost him fifteen cold plunks, but I wouldn't never have knew if I hadn't listened. He wasn't no tin-horn kind of a sport.

Over at the Cedar Point place, we didn't stay around where there was a gang of common kind of cattle at all.

There was big dance-halls and dining-places for yaps, and there was a beach you could walk along and get where it was dark, and we went there.

She didn't talk hardly at all and neither did I, and I was thinking how glad I was my mother was all right, and always made us kids learn to eat with a fork at table, and not swill soup, and not be noisy and rough like a gang you see around a race-track that way.

Then Wilbur and his girl went away up the beach and Lucy and I sat down in a dark place, where there was some roots of old trees the water had washed up, and after that the time, till we had to go back in the launch and they had to catch their trains, wasn't nothing at all. It went like winking your eye.

Here's how it was. The place we were sitting in was dark, like I said, and there was the roots from that old stump sticking up like arms, and there was a watery smell and the night was like—as if you could put your hand out and feel it—so warm and soft and dark and sweet like an orange.

I 'most cried and I 'most swore and I 'most jumped up and danced, I was so mad and happy and sad.

When Wilbur come back from being alone with his girl, and she saw him coming, Lucy she says, 'We got to go to the train now,' and she was 'most crying, too, but she never knew nothing I knew, and she couldn't be so all busted up. And then, before Wilbur and Miss Woodbury got up to where we was, she put her face up and kissed me quick and put her head up against me and she was all quivering and—— Gee whizz!

Sometimes I hope I have cancer and die. I guess you know what I mean. We went in the launch across the bay to the train like that, and it was dark, too. She whispered and said it was like she and I could get out of the boat and walk on the water, and it sounded foolish, but I knew what she meant.

And then quick we were right at the depot, and there was a big gang of yaps, the kind that goes to the fairs, and crowded and milling around like cattle, and how could I tell her? 'It won't be long because you'll write and I'll write to you.' That's all she said.

I got a chance like a hay-barn afire. A swell chance I got.

And maybe she would write me, down at Marietta that way, and the letter would come back, and stamped on the front of it by the U.S.A., 'There ain't any such guy,' or something like that, whatever they stamp on a letter that way.

And me trying to pass myself off for a big bug and a swell—to her, as decent a little body as God ever made. Craps a'mighty—a swell chance I got!

And then the train come in, and she got on it, and Wilbur Wessen he come and shook hands with me, and that Miss Woodbury was nice, too, and bowed to me, and I at her, and the train went and I busted out and cried like a kid.

Gee, I could have run after that train and made Dan Patch look like a freight train after a wreck but, socks a'mighty, what was the use? Did you ever see such a fool?

I'll bet you what—if I had an arm broke right now or a train had run over my foot—I wouldn't go to no doctor at all. I'd go sit down and let her hurt and hurt—that's what I'd do.

I'll bet you what—if I hadn't a drunk that booze I'd a never been such a boob as to go tell such a lie—that couldn't never be made straight to a lady like her.

I wish I had that fellow right here that had on a Windsor tie and carried a cane. I'd smash him for fair. Gosh darn his eyes. He's a big fool—that's what he is.

And if I'm not another you just go find me one and I'll quit working and be a bum and give him my job. I don't care nothing for working, and earning money, and saving it for no such boob as myself.

A. E. COPPARD

The Green Drake

In the village of So-and-so lived an old woman, Rebecca Cracknell, who had a dog with an odd eye and the name of Jack, a kitten with an odd tail and the name of Jack, and a green drake with odd ambitions that was called Jack. The old woman's only son was young Jack, and her husband, long since dead, had been known as old Jack. They began by having different names, every one of them, but the forces of habit were so strong in the good old woman that she always called everything and everybody by that one name. The drake was a middle-aged duck, cooped up in a yard as dry as the deserts of Egypt. Sometimes it tried to go sporting out into the great wet world of gutters and puddles and pools, but Rebecca could not bear to see it behaving so untidily so she confined it, and there in the dry yard it pined and lived.

One day her son Jack tucked the drake under his arm.

'Jacky, my lad, I do believe today is your birthday!' And off he went with the drake under his arm for a mile or more until he came to a field with a barn in it and a pond beside, whose grassy banks so moist and green sloped gently into the water. The water itself was only a dark bronze liquid that stank, but there were three or four chestnut trees close by just casting their pure blooms into it. How bright the day! And how the wind blew!

Into this pond the young man Jack threw Jack the drake, and the drake became demented with joy. It heaved the water up with its beak and cast it over its back. It trod and danced, or flew skimming the pond from shore to shore. It tried to bury itself in the waters, to burst down through them into that duck paradise that lies at the bottom of all ponds, but half of him—and the worst half—always remained quivering in the common world above.

The lad Jack said he would leave him there to enjoy himself, because it was his birthday, and he would come again and fetch

him before nightfall. So the drake was left alone on the pond, and
swam about quacking incessantly in his pride and excitement.
How bright the day and how the wind blew, dashing among the
chestnut trees until their heavy foliage seemed a burden to them
and they snowed their white petals upon the bosom of the pond! A
crow came chattering in the trees, to scoff at the buffoonery and
bad manners of the drake. Intoxicated it was!

Later on a man in the prime of life with a brown face and a
weather-coloured hat came passing by. He'd a moleskin suit on
with the breeches belted below the knees, and a wicker bag slung
across his shoulder. He had drunk ale in the sweetness of the
morning. One hand rested in the broad belt round his belly, with
the other he took out his pipe—and spat fulsomely.

'Hey, my cocky!' he cried when he saw the drake, and he stood
viewing its antics with meditative eyes.

The drake replied, 'Quack.'

'Quack to me!' cried the man in surly tones. 'Where's your
manners?'

So the drake knew he was not conversing with a common
creature, but one who might be a god or a gentleman, and he
answered him then with care and addressed him with respect.

'Hey, my hearty!' the man exclaimed, 'you's as fine a young
feller of a duck as ever I see.'

It was—the drake informed him—his birthday.

'Hi up!' cried the man, and at once he squatted down upon a
hump on the bank of the pond, a great castle of a place that some
ants had built—ants are such ambitious creatures.

'Hi up!' repeated the man, and he said it was his birthday too.
'Allecapantho!' Now wasn't that curious?

'So I stops me at home this morning,' he continued, 'but my old
woman kept growling and groaning until I had to ask her, very
civil-like: Whatever's come over you?—I asks her— on my birthday? You're like a dog with a sore nose—I says—and I can't do
with you and I can't stand your company, not on my birthday.
You're naught but a bag o' mutton—I says—you go and pick the
fleas out of your tail—I told her—and I went off to my allotment
and cultivated a few chain of the earth. And now my neck's as stiff
as a crust of beeswax. Cold winds and sweat, I suppose. Misfor-

tune was ever following me, I tell you. Misfortune was my down-fall, and so it is, I can tell you. If you wants to know my history I can tell you: I was born honest, so I shall die poor.'

The drake snoozed upon the water, blinking with affability and deep enjoyment. Never had anybody taken so much notice of him before, or flattered him with so much kindly attention. And here he was now! The man sat on the ant-hill dividing his attention in three parts: by puffing at a cold pipe, by trying to light it again, by talking genially to the duck on the pond.

'You's as pretty a little duck as ever I seed, I couldn't say no fairer if I'd a mind to.'

'But,' the drake sorrowfully sighed, 'I am only an orphan.'

'Pooh! What about it? Any one can be an orphan if they like. Any one. 'Cept royalty. You mustn't run away with any funny notions, young feller,' the bluff man declared. 'What part are you from?'

The drake told him that he came from the village of So-and-so.

The man knew the place very well. 'Hi up! yes,' he said, 'but there's not a mortal thing in that village to attract a sunny soul, neither bliss nor blessing. There's not a man of that sort nor a woman of that sort; there's not a house of that sort, nor an inn of that sort, not a child, pony, hog, dog or hen of that sort. All poor bred-uns they be.'

The drake confessed that life there was very dull, yes; often it had desired to change its habitation.

'Dull!' roared the other. 'Why, I could not bear to live in that hole, not if the streets was paved with crystal and there was gold on every floor. No, I live in a better place nor that.'

'Pardon me, sir,' said the polite little drake. 'I do not know your name, or where you dwell.'

'Ha, ha! Allecapantho!' returned the man. 'Appercrampus! You would like to know my pedigree? There's a touch of Muscovy about you, I should say, with a brush of Indian blood. Oh, I can see it, you're a good bred-un. So am I; there's few can trace their ancestors back to history like me, not straight forward they can't. That's sound truth, speak it or be shamed. Two stones in Barclay Buttle churchyard—d'ye know it? No! Two stones in Shimp churchyard—d'ye know it? No! There used to be four in

Shimp but two on 'em fell over (or was pushed over, if truth be known), and Fiddler Kinch stole 'em for his hog-pen, but he never had no more luck with a pig till the day he died after it. Bolted his food, he did. It's true; every one can tell you truth as knows it, but if it ain't known it can't be revealed. Two stones in Shimp, two stones in Barclay Buttle, brass plate with a skull's head on it in Tooby chancel. What's amiss in that for pedigree? Tooby, Shimp and Barclay Buttle? Came over with the king of the Busbys and we're still hereabouts. William Busby.' Here the man smote his bosom with pride, and thus the duck learned that his friend's name was W. Busby, and not allecapantho or appercrampus.

'When Fiddler died the reverend Saxby discovered they stones where they were—course he'd known all along. Parson took 'em up in the dead a night and transferred them. If you want to see they stones you just lift up the cloth and you'll see 'em on top of the altar in Shimp church, all fixed and fast and consecrated upside down. What's amiss with our tribe? You never hear nothing against the family of Busby—not as a family. I could show you the stone now, if you had the time, of the Busby twins, Hezekiah and Joseph, who met untimely ends (just what it says) from the sting of a viper coming from church after being confirmed, 1766. Hi up! God bless us, I remember my old great-grandfather as used to tell me about William the Conqueror, all about that man he told me, every word. The Busbys are a great nation of chaps, they're everywhere, high up and well-breeched, please God. I heard a one up in the county of Nottinghamshire as owns a row of houses with a shaving-shop at one end and a coastguard station at the other! And all belongs, all belongs—a master man, ye know. He used to stuff birds and fishes and one thing and another, could stuff 'em well, life-like. Used to stuff for the Duke of What-ever's-the-name-of-the-feller, and for royalty. Years and years—rows of houses—till his eyes give out and he got old and his spirits sunk. Kidneys, I shouldn't wonder; I be troubled the same myself. Master man! They've got it up here.'

With his finger Busby indicated a position in the middle of his forehead, and then appeared to swallow something. 'Apper-crampus!' he added mystically.

The little drake smiled, and quacked his delight at the conversation of Mr Busby who now stood up, surveyed the surrounding field with deliberation, and then sat down upon the ant-hill again, drawing a tobacco-box from his pocket. A pipe was filled and ignited, and for a while Mr Busby puffed and gazed dreamily at the pond and the drake, and listened to the wind threshing in the chestnut trees. Ah, a lovely day!

'Who do you live with in So-and-so?' the man inquired.

'I live with Jack Cracknell,' answered the gentle duck; 'do you know him?'

'Know him! Allecapantho! I knew his father; we were at school together. He always said he was younger than me, but I can't understand how that could be because he left school afore I did and went and drove plough for the sleepy girl's husband. I kept on at school for another six months, and then I became a thatcher. All the Busbys be master men. They got it up here.' The man took his pipe from his mouth and pointed with it to his forehead again, and then spat richly over his shoulder to defeat the play of the wind.

The drake asked him another question: 'Who was the sleepy girl?'

'Eli Sadler's daughter,' continued Busby. 'She dropped off to sleep one day and she slept so's they couldn't rouse her no more. There were two girls and Eli and their mother. Of course Eli died, and there was Mary and there was this Annie. Mary was in service at the squire's, but Annie went to sleep and didn't wake up for seven years. She lay in her bed for seven unconscious years, and she didn't wake up and she didn't die. People came from all parts of the world to look at her and stick pins in her—dukes and schoolmasters and members of Parliament—but they could not wake her up, nobody couldn't. Seven years is a long time, ye know. Mystery. Her mother made a fortune a money out a that girl, a fortune. Sacks of it. But of course the mother died, and every one said to Mary: 'Mary, you'll have to come home and look arter your sleepy sister.' Mary said no, she wouldn't have that caper. 'Why not?' they says to her, 'she's your sister,' they says, 'helpless and dependent on your care.' 'Because,' says Mary, 'I shall damn soon wake her up.' And that's what she did do— woke her up! And Annie went and got married and had ten children in next to no time. Never went to sleep no more. Sleeping beauty, they called her. Huh. She was the biggest fraud as ever stepped on England's ground, the biggest fraud within forty thousand miles. And old Jack Cracknell began work for the sleepy girl's husband. Well, upon my soul, there's all sorts a dodges for getting a living, and if you wants a thing in this world you must get it by force or by fudge. Force and fudge rule this sinful world, my cocky; everything's for someone's selfish pleasure—never your own. D'ye know what my advice is to you? My advice to you, sir, is this: if your pleasure brings more harm to another than it brings in joy to you—and it very often will—then you must do the best you can with your pleasure. If'—Busby pointed with his pipe straight at the attentive little duck—'if so be you are the sort as don't stop to think, you won't know of the harm you do, and you won't pause, and you won't care. Mind you, if you are of the other sort, the sort that *do* care as man to man, my advice would be wasted—for of course you wouldn't follow it, you could not. Such is human nature,' Busby said, applying yet another match to his pipe, 'and such is life.'

'Yes, that is very true,' sighed the happy drake.

'And another thing,' continued the philosophizing thatcher. 'We may not get all we asks for, but you may lay your life we'll get all that's coming to us, and I shan't be far away from my own funeral. Nor will you, my cocky. Force and fudge, I tell you, rule this sinful world. If you can tell the tale, grief will never be your master. Take Jack Cracknell, as worked for sleepy girl's husband: I never did trust that man Cracknell. For one thing, he'd talk the skin off your nostrils! I never trusted any one from the village of So-and-so, I never liked 'em; poor bred-uns, all. Young Jack's the same. And my advice to you is: don't return there any more, preserve your independence now you've got it, and don't own him, don't listen to him, don't follow him. Never let misfortune be your downfall. My lad, I like you, I will be your friend for life. There's my hand on it.'

Busby stood up, surveyed the landscape with care, spat a good spit, rubbed his right hand upon his haunch, and went to the water's edge. So the little drake swam in to accept of his friendship.

'Hey, my cocky!' The man's hand closed tightly round the duck's neck, and the bird was snatched from the water. In a few moments its neck was limp; it fluttered no more, it spake no more, it lived no more.

'Nice li'l bird,' commented Busby, feeling its breast and back, 'beautiful bird.' And putting the body in his bag he slung the bag over his shoulder again.

'Appercrampus!' he joyously murmured as he walked away. 'Allecapantho!'

E. M. FORSTER

The Story of the Siren

Few things could have been more beautiful than my notebook on the Deist Controversy as it fell downward through the waters of the Mediterranean. It dived, like a piece of black slate, but opened soon, disclosing leaves of pale green, which quivered into blue. Now it had vanished, now it was a piece of magical india-rubber stretching out to infinity, now it was a book again, but bigger than the book of all knowledge. It grew more fantastic as it reached the bottom, where a puff of sand welcomed it and obscured it from view. But it reappeared, quite sane though a little tremulous, lying decently open on its back, while unseen fingers fidgeted among its leaves.

'It is such pity,' said my aunt, 'that you will not finish your work in the hotel. Then you would be free to enjoy yourself and this would never have happened.'

'Nothing of it but will change into something rich and strange,' warbled the chaplain, while his sister said, 'Why, it's gone in the water!' As for the boatmen, one of them laughed, while the other, without a word of warning, stood up and began to take his clothes off.

'Holy Moses!' cried the Colonel. 'Is the fellow mad?'

'Yes, thank him, dear,' said my aunt: 'that is to say, tell him he is very kind, but perhaps another time.'

'All the same I do want my book back,' I complained. 'It's for my Fellowship Dissertation. There won't be much of it left by another time.'

'I have an idea,' said some woman or other through her parasol. 'Let us leave this child of nature to dive for the book while we go on to the other grotto. We can land him either on this rock or on the ledge inside, and he will be ready when we return.'

The idea seemed good; and I improved it by saying I would be left behind too, to lighten the boat. So the two of us were deposited outside the little grotto on a great sunlit rock that guarded the harmonies within. Let us call them blue, though they suggest rather the spirit of what is clean—cleanliness passed from the domestic to the sublime, the cleanliness of all the sea gathered together and radiating light. The Blue Grotto at Capri contains only more blue water, not bluer water. That colour and that spirit is the heritage of every cave in the Mediterranean into which the sun can shine and the sea flow.

As soon as the boat left I realized how imprudent I had been to trust myself on a sloping rock with an unknown Sicilian. With a jerk he became alive, seizing my arm and saying, 'Go to the end of the grotto, and I will show you something beautiful.'

He made me jump off the rock on to the ledge over a dazzling crack of sea; he drew me away from the light till I was standing on the tiny beach of sand which emerged like powdered turquoise at the farther end. There he left me with his clothes, and returned swiftly to the summit of the entrance rock. For a moment he stood naked in the brilliant sun, looking down at the spot where the book lay. Then he crossed himself, raised his hands above his head, and dived.

If the book was wonderful, the man is past all description. His effect was that of a silver statue, alive beneath the sea, through whom life throbbed in blue and green. Something infinitely happy, infinitely wise—but it was impossible that it should emerge from the depths sunburned and dripping, holding the notebook on the Deist Controversy between its teeth.

A gratuity is generally expected by those who bathe. Whatever I offered, he was sure to want more, and I was disinclined for an argument in a place so beautiful and also so solitary. It was a relief that he should say in conversational tones, 'In a place like this one might see the Siren.'

I was delighted with him for thus falling into the key of his surroundings. We had been left together in a magic world, apart from all the commonplaces that are called reality, a world of blue whose floor was the sea and whose walls and roof of rock trembled with the sea's reflections. Here only the fantastic would be tolerable, and it was in that spirit I echoed his words, 'One might easily see the Siren.'

He watched me curiously while he dressed. I was parting the sticky leaves of the notebook as I sat on the sand.

'Ah,' he said at last. 'You may have read the little book that was printed last year. Who would have thought that our Siren would have given the foreigners pleasure!'

(I read it afterward. Its account is, not unnaturally, incomplete, in spite of there being a woodcut of the young person, and the words of her song.)

'She comes out of this blue water, doesn't she,' I suggested, 'and sits on the rock at the entrance, combing her hair.'

I wanted to draw him out, for I was interested in his sudden gravity, and there was a suggestion of irony in his last remark that puzzled me.

'Have you ever seen her?' he asked.

'Often and often.'

'I, never.'

'But have you heard her sing?'

He put on his coat and said impatiently, 'How can she sing under the water? Who could? She sometimes tries, but nothing comes from her but great bubbles.'

'She could climb on to the rock.'

'How can she?' he cried again, quite angry. 'The priests have blessed the air, so she cannot breathe it, and blessed the rocks, so that she cannot sit on them. But the sea no man can bless, because it is too big and always changing. So she lives in the sea.'

I was silent.

At this his face took on a gentler expression. He looked at me as though something was on his mind, and going out to the entrance rock gazed at the external blue. Then returning into our twilight he said, 'As a rule only good people see the Siren.'

I made no comment. There was a pause, and he continued. 'That is a very strange thing, and the priests do not know how to account for it; for she of course is wicked. Not only those who fast and go to Mass are in danger, but even those who are merely good in daily life. No one in the village had seen her for two generations. I am not surprised. We all cross ourselves before we enter the water, but it is unnecessary. Giuseppe, we thought, was safer than most. We loved him, and many of us he loved: but that is a different thing from being good.'

I asked who Giuseppe was.

'That day—I was seventeen and my brother was twenty and a great deal stronger than I was, and it was the year when the visitors, who have brought such prosperity and so many alterations into the village, first began to come. One English lady in particular, of very high birth, came, and has written a book about the place, and it was through her that the Improvement Syndicate was formed, which is about to connect the hotels with the station by a funicular railway.'

'Don't tell me about that lady in here,' I observed.

'That day we took her and her friends to see the grottoes. As we rowed close under the cliffs I put out my hand, as one does, and caught a little crab, and having pulled off its claws offered it as a curiosity. The ladies groaned, but a gentleman was pleased, and held out money. Being inexperienced, I refused it, saying that his pleasure was sufficient reward! Giuseppe, who was rowing behind, was very angry with me and reached out his hand and hit me on the side of the mouth, so that a tooth cut my lip, and I bled. I tried to hit him back, but he always was too quick for me, and as I stretched round he kicked me under the armpit, so that for a moment I could not even row. There was a great noise among the ladies, and I heard afterwards that they were planning to take me away from my brother and train me as a waiter. That, at all events, never came to pass.

'When we reached the grotto—not here, but a larger one—the gentleman was very anxious that one of us should dive for money, and the ladies consented, as they sometimes do. Giuseppe, who had discovered how much pleasure it gives foreigners to see us in the water, refused to dive for anything but silver, and the gentleman threw in a two-lira piece.

'Just before my brother sprang off he caught sight of me holding my bruise, and crying, for I could not help it. He laughed and said, "This time, at all events, I shall not see the Siren!" and went into the water without crossing himself. But he saw her.'

He broke off and accepted a cigarette. I watched the golden entrance rock and the quivering walls and the magic water through which great bubbles constantly rose.

At last he dropped his hot ash into the ripples and turned his head away, and said, 'He came up without the coin. We pulled him into the boat, and he was so large that he seemed to fill it, and so wet that we could not dress him. I have never seen a man so wet. I and the gentleman rowed back, and we covered Giuseppe with sacking and propped him up in the stern.'

'He was drowned, then?' I murmured, supposing that to be the point.

'He was not,' he cried angrily. 'He saw the Siren. I told you.'

I was silenced again.

'We put him to bed, though he was not ill. The doctor came, and took money, and the priest came and spattered him with holy water. But it was no good. He was too big—like a piece of the sea. He kissed the thumb-bones of San Biagio and they never dried till evening.'

'What did he look like?' I ventured.

'Like any one who has seen the Siren. If you have seen her "often and often" how is it you do not know? Unhappy, unhappy because he knew everything. Every living thing made him unhappy because he knew it would die. And all he cared to do was sleep.'

I bent over my notebook.

'He did no work, he forgot to eat, he forgot whether he had his clothes on. All the work fell on me, and my sister had to go out to service. We tried to make him into a beggar, but he was too robust to inspire pity, and as for an idiot, he had not the right look in his eyes. He would stand in the street looking at people, and the more he looked at them the more unhappy he became. When a child was born he would cover his face with his hands. If any one was married—he was terrible then, and would frighten them when they came out of church. Who would have believed he would marry himself! I caused that, I. I was reading out of the paper how a girl at Ragusa had "gone mad through bathing in the sea." Giuseppe got up, and in a week he and that girl came in.

'He never told me anything, but it seems that he went straight to her house, broke into her room, and carried her off. She was the daughter of a rich mineowner, so you may imagine our peril. Her father came down, with a clever lawyer, but they could do no more than I. They argued and they threatened, but at last they had to go back and we lost nothing—that is to say, no money. We took Giuseppe and Maria to the church and had them married. Ugh! that wedding! The priest made no jokes afterwards, and coming out the children threw stones. . . . I think I would have died to make her happy; but as always happens, one could do nothing.'

'Were they unhappy together, then?'

'They loved each other, but love is not happiness. We can all get love. Love is nothing. I had two people to work for now, for she was like him in everything—one never knew which of them was speaking. I had to sell our own boat and work under the bad old man you have today. Worst of all, people began to hate us. The children first—everything begins with them—and then the women, and last of all, the men. For the cause of every misfortune was—you will not betray me?'

I promised good faith, and immediately he burst into the frantic blasphemy of one who has escaped from supervision, cursing the priests, who had ruined his life, he said. 'Thus are we tricked!' was his cry, and he stood up and kicked at the azure ripples with his feet, till he had obscured them with a cloud of sand.

I, too, was moved. The story of Giuseppe, for all its absurdity and superstition, came nearer to reality than anything I had known before. I don't know why, but it filled me with desire to help others—the greatest of all our desires, I suppose, and the most fruitless. The desire soon passed.

'She was about to have a child. That was the end of everything. People said to me, "When will your charming nephew be born? What a cheerful, attractive child he will be, with such a father and mother!" I kept my face steady and replied, "I think he may be. Out of sadness shall come gladness"—it is one of our proverbs. And my answer frightened them very much, and they told the priests, who were frightened too. Then the whisper started that the child would be Antichrist. You need not be afraid: he was never born.

'An old witch began to prophesy, and no one stopped her. Giuseppe and the girl, she said, had silent devils, who could do little harm. But the child would always be speaking and laughing and perverting, and last of all he would go into the sea and fetch up the Siren into the air and all the world would see her and hear her sing. As soon as she sang, the Seven Vials would be opened, and the Pope would die and Mongibello flame, and the veil of Santa Agata would be burned. Then the boy and the Siren would marry, and together they would rule the world, for ever and ever.

'The whole village was in tumult, and the hotel-keepers became alarmed, for the tourist season was just beginning. They met together and decided that Giuseppe and the girl must be sent inland until the child was born, and they subscribed the money. The night before they were to start there was a full moon and wind from the east, and all along the coast the sea shot up over the cliffs in silver clouds. It is a wonderful sight, and Maria said she must see it once more.

' "Do not go," I said. "I saw the priest go by, and someone with him. And the hotel-keepers do not like you to be seen, and if we displease them also we shall starve."

' "I want to go," she replied. "The sea is stormy, and I may never feel it again."

' "No, he is right," said Giuseppe. "Do not go—or let one of us go with you."

' "I want to go alone," she said; and she went alone.

'I tied up their luggage in a piece of cloth, and then I was so unhappy at thinking I should lose them that I went and sat down by my brother and put my arm round his neck, and he put his arm round me, which he had not done for more than a year, and we remained thus I don't remember how long.

'Suddenly the door flew open and moonlight and wind came in together, and a child's voice said laughing, "They have pushed her over the cliffs into the sea."

'I stepped to the drawer where I keep my knives.

' "Sit down again," said Giuseppe—Giuseppe of all people! "If she is dead, why should others die, too?"

' "I guess who it is," I cried, "and I will kill him."

'I was almost out of the door, and he tripped me up, and kneeling upon me, took hold of both my hands and sprained my wrists; first my right one, then my left. No one but Giuseppe would have thought of such a thing. It hurt more than you would suppose, and I fainted. When I woke up, he was gone, and I never saw him again.'

But Giuseppe disgusted me.

'I told you he was wicked,' he said. 'No one would have expected him to see the Siren.'

'How do you know he did see her?'

'Because he did not see her "often and often," but once.'

'Why do you love him if he is wicked?'

He laughed for the first time. That was his only reply.

'Is that the end?' I asked.

'I never killed her murderer, for by the time my wrists were well he was in America; and one cannot kill a priest. As for Giuseppe, he went all over the world, too, looking for someone who had seen the Siren—either a man, or, better still, a woman, for then the child might still have been born. At last he came to Liverpool—is the district probable?—and there he began to cough, and spat blood until he died.

'I do not suppose there is any one living now who has seen her. There has seldom been more than one in a generation, and never in my life will there be both a man and a woman from whom that child can be born, who will fetch up the Siren from the sea, and destroy silence, and save the world!'

'Save the world?' I cried. 'Did the prophecy end like that?'

He leaned back against the rock, breathing deep. Through all the blue-green reflections I saw him colour. I heard him say: 'Silence and loneliness cannot last for ever. It may be a hundred or a thousand years, but the sea lasts longer, and she shall come out of it and sing.' I would have asked him more, but at that moment the whole cave darkened, and there rode in through its narrow entrance the returning boat.

P. G. WODEHOUSE

The Fiery Wooing of Mordred

The Pint of Lager breathed heavily through his nose.

'Silly fathead!' he said. 'Ash-trays in every nook and cranny of the room—ash-trays staring you in the eye wherever you look—and he has to go and do a fool thing like that.'

He was alluding to a young gentleman with a vacant, fish-like face who, leaving the bar-parlour of the Anglers' Rest a few moments before, had thrown his cigarette into the waste-paper basket, causing it to burst into a cheerful blaze. Not one of the little company of amateur fire-fighters but was ruffled. A Small Bass with a high blood pressure had had to have his collar loosened, and the satin-clad bosom of Miss Postlethwaite, our emotional barmaid, was still heaving.

Only Mr Mulliner seemed disposed to take a tolerant view of what had occurred.

'In fairness to the lad,' he pointed out, sipping his hot Scotch and lemon, 'we must remember that our bar-parlour contains no grand piano or priceless old walnut table, which to the younger generation are the normal and natural repositories for lighted cigarette-ends. Failing these, he, of course, selected the waste-paper basket. Like Mordred.'

'Like who?' asked a Whisky and Splash.

'Whom,' corrected Miss Postlethwaite.

The Whisky and Splash apologized.

'A nephew of mine. Mordred Mulliner, the poet.'

'Mordred,' murmured Miss Postlethwaite pensively. 'A sweet name.'

'And one,' said Mr Mulliner, 'that fitted him admirably, for he was a comely lovable sensitive youth with large, fawn-like eyes, delicately chiselled features, and excellent teeth. I mention these teeth, because it was owing to them that the train of events started which I am about to describe.'

'He bit somebody?' queried Miss Postlethwaite, groping.

'No. But if he had had no teeth he would not have gone to the dentist's that day, and if he had not gone to the dentist's he would not have met Annabelle.'

'Annabelle whom?'

'Who,' corrected Miss Postlethwaite.

'Oh, shoot,' said the Whisky and Splash.

Annabelle Sprockett-Sprockett, the only daughter of Sir Murgatroyd and Lady Sprockett-Sprockett of Smattering Hall, Worcestershire. Impractical in many ways (said Mr Mulliner), Mordred never failed to visit his dentist every six months, and on the morning on which my story opens he had just seated himself in the empty waiting-room and was turning the pages of a three-months-old copy of the *Tatler* when the door opened and there entered a girl at the sight of whom—or who, if our friend here prefers it—something seemed to explode on the left side of his chest like a bomb. The *Tatler* swam before his eyes, and when it solidified again he realized that love had come to him at last.

Most of the Mulliners have fallen in love at first sight, but few with so good an excuse as Mordred. She was a singularly beautiful girl, and for a while it was this beauty of hers that enchained my nephew's attention to the exclusion of all else. It was only after he had sat gulping for some minutes like a dog with a chicken bone in its throat that he detected the sadness in her face. He could see now that her eyes, as she listlessly perused her four-months-old copy of *Punch*, were heavy with pain.

His heart ached for her, and as there is something about the atmosphere of a dentist's waiting-room which breaks down the barriers of conventional etiquette he was emboldened to speak.

'Courage!' he said. 'It may not be so bad, after all. He may just fool about with that little mirror thing of his, and decide that there is nothing that needs to be done.'

For the first time she smiled—faintly, but with sufficient breadth to give Mordred another powerful jolt.

'I'm not worrying about the dentist,' she explained. 'My trouble is that I live miles away in the country and only get a chance of coming to London about twice a year for about a couple of hours. I was hoping that I should be able to put in a long spell of window-shopping in Bond Street, but now I've got to wait goodness knows how long I don't suppose I shall have time to do a thing. My train goes at one-fifteen.'

All the chivalry in Mordred came to the surface like a leaping trout.

'If you would care to take my place——'

'Oh, I couldn't.'

'Please. I shall enjoy waiting. It will give me an opportunity of catching up with my reading.'

'Well, if you really wouldn't mind——'

Considering that Mordred by this time was in the market to tackle dragons on her behalf or to climb the loftiest peak of the Alps to supply her with edelweiss, he was able to assure her that he did not mind. So in she went, flashing at him a shy glance of gratitude which nearly doubled him up, and he lit a cigarette and fell into a reverie. And presently she came out and he sprang to his feet, courteously throwing his cigarette into the waste-paper basket.

She uttered a cry. Mordred recovered the cigarette.

'Silly of me,' he said, with a deprecating laugh. 'I'm always doing that. Absent-minded. I've burned two flats already this year.'

She caught her breath.

'Burned them to the ground?'

'Well, not to the ground. They were on the top floor.'

'But you burned them?'

'Oh, yes. I burned them.'

'Well, well!' She seemed to muse. 'Well, goodbye, Mr——'

'Mulliner. Mordred Mulliner.'

'Good-bye, Mr Mulliner, and thank you so much.'

'Not at all, Miss——'

'Sprockett-Sprockett.'

'Not at all, Miss Sprockett-Sprockett. A pleasure.'

She passed from the room, and a few minutes later he was lying back in the dentist's chair, filled with an infinite sadness. This was not due to any activity on the part of the dentist, who had just said with a rueful sigh that there didn't seem to be anything to do this time, but to the fact that his life was now a blank. He loved this beautiful girl, and he would never see her more. It was just another case of ships that pass in the waiting-room.

Conceive his astonishment, therefore, when by the afternoon post next day he received a letter which ran as follows:

> 'Smattering Hall,
> Lower Smattering-on-the-Wissel,
> Worcestershire.

> 'Dear Mr Mulliner,

> 'My little girl has told me how very kind you were to her at the dentist's today. I cannot tell you how grateful she was. She does so love to walk down Bond Street and breathe on the jewellers' windows, and but for you she would have had to go another six months without her little treat.

> 'I suppose you are a very busy man, like everybody in London, but if you can spare the time it would give my husband and myself so much pleasure if you could run down and stay with us for a few days—a long week-end, or even longer if you can manage it.

> 'With best wishes,
> Yours sincerely,
> Aurelia Sprockett-Sprockett.'

Mordred read this communication six times in a minute and a quarter and then seventeen times rather more slowly in order to savour any *nuance* of it that he might have overlooked. He took it that the girl must have got his address from the dentist's secretary on her way out, and he was doubly thrilled—first, by this evidence that one so lovely was as intelligent as she was beautiful, and secondly because the whole thing seemed to him so frightfully significant. A girl, he meant to say, does not get her mother to invite fellows to her country home for long week-ends (or even longer if they can manage it) unless such fellows have made a pretty substantial hit with her. This, he contended, stood to reason.

He hastened to the nearest post office, dispatched a telegram to Lady Sprockett-Sprockett assuring her that he would be with her on the morrow, and returned to his flat to pack his effects. His heart was singing within him. Apart from anything else, the invitation could not have come at a more fortunate moment, for what with musing on his great love while smoking cigarettes he had practically gutted his little nest on the previous evening, and while it was still habitable in a sense there was no gainsaying the fact that all those charred sofas and things struck a rather melancholy note and he would be glad to be away from it all for a few days.

It seemed to Mordred, as he travelled down on the following afternoon, that the wheels of the train, clattering over the metals, were singing 'Sprockett-Sprockett'—not 'Annabelle,' of course, for he did not yet know her name—and it was with a whispered 'Sprockett-Sprockett' on his lips that he alighted at the little station of Smattering-cum-Blimpstead-in-the-Vale, which, as his hostess's note-paper had informed him, was where you got off for the Hall. And when he perceived that the girl herself had come to meet him in a two-seater car the whisper nearly became a shout.

For perhaps three minutes, as he sat beside her, Mordred remained in this condition of ecstatic bliss. Here he was, he reflected, and here she was—here, in fact, they both were—together, and he was just about to point out how jolly this was and—if he could work it without seeming to rush things too much—to drop a hint to the effect that he could wish this state of affairs to continue through all eternity, when the girl drew up outside a tobacconist's.

'I won't be a minute,' she said. 'I promised Biffy I would bring him back some cigarettes.'

A cold hand seemed to lay itself on Mordred's heart.

'Biffy?'

'Captain Biffing, one of the men at the Hall. And Guffy wants some pipe-cleaners.'

'Guffy?'

'Jack Guffington. I expect you know his name, if you are interested in racing. He was third in last year's Grand National.'

'Is he staying at the Hall, too?'

'Yes.'

'You have a large house-party?'

'Oh, not so very. Let me see. There's Billy Biffing, Jack Guffington, Ted Prosser, Freddie Boot—he's the tennis champion of the county—Tommy Mainprice, and—oh, yes, Algy Fripp—the big-game hunter, you know.'

The hand on Mordred's heart, now definitely iced, tightened its grip. With a lover's sanguine optimism, he had supposed that this visit of his was going to be just three days of jolly sylvan solitude with Annabelle Sprockett-Sprockett. And now it appeared that the place was unwholesomely crowded with his fellow men. And what fellow men! Big-game hunters . . . Tennis champions . . . Chaps who rode in Grand Nationals . . . He could see them in his mind's eye—lean, wiry, riding-breeched and flannel-trousered young Apollos, any one of them capable of cutting out his weight in Clark Gables.

A faint hope stirred within him.

'You have also, of course, with you Mrs Biffing, Mrs Guffington, Mrs Prosser, Mrs Bott, Mrs Mainprice, and Mrs Algernon Fripp?'

'Oh, no, they aren't married.'

'None of them?'

'No.'

The faint hope coughed quietly and died.

'Ah,' said Mordred.

While the girl was in the shop, he remained brooding. The fact that not one of these blisters should be married filled him with an austere disapproval. If they had had the least spark of civic sense, he felt, they would have taken on the duties and responsibilities of matrimony years ago. But no. Intent upon their selfish pleasures, they had callously remained bachelors. It was this spirit of *laissez-faire*, Mordred considered, that was eating like a canker into the soul of England.

He was aware of Annabelle standing beside him.

'Eh?' he said, starting.

'I was saying: "Have you plenty of cigarettes?" '

'Plenty, thank you.'

'Good. And of course there will be a box in your room. Men always like to smoke in their bedrooms, don't they? As a matter of fact, two boxes—Turkish and Virginian. Father put them there specially.'

'Very kind of him,' said Mordred mechanically.

He relapsed into a moody silence, and they drove off.

It would be agreeable (said Mr Mulliner) if, having shown you my nephew so gloomy, so apprehensive, so tortured with dark forebodings at this juncture, I were able now to state that the hearty English welcome of Sir Murgatroyd and Lady Sprockett-Sprockett on his arrival at the Hall cheered him up and put new life into him. Nothing, too, would give me greater pleasure than to say that he found, on encountering the dreaded Biffies and Guffies, that they were negligible little runts with faces incapable of inspiring affection in any good woman.

But I must adhere rigidly to the facts. Genial, even effusive, though his host and hostess showed themselves, their cordiality left him cold. And, so far from his rivals being weeds, they were one and all models of manly beauty, and the spectacle of their obvious worship of Annabelle cut my nephew like a knife.

And on top of all this there was Smattering Hall itself.

Smattering Hall destroyed Mordred's last hope. It was one of those vast edifices, so common throughout the countryside of England, whose original founders seem to have budgeted for families of twenty-five or so and a domestic staff of not less than a hundred. 'Home isn't home,' one can picture them saying to themselves, 'unless you have plenty of elbow room.' And so this huge, majestic pile had come into being. Romantic persons, confronted with it, thought of knights in armour riding forth to the Crusades. More earthy individuals felt that it must cost a packet to keep up. Mordred's reaction on passing through the front door was a sort of sick sensation, a kind of settled despair.

How, he asked himself, even assuming that by some miracle he succeeded in fighting his way to her heart through all these Biffies and Guffies, could he ever dare to take Annabelle from a home like this? He had quite satisfactory private means, of course, and would be able, when married, to give up the bachelor flat and

spread himself to something on a bigger scale—possibly, if sufficiently *bijou*, even a desirable residence in the Mayfair district.
But after Smattering Hall would not Annabelle feel like a sardine
in the largest of London houses?

Such were the dark thoughts that raced through Mordred's
brain before, during and after dinner. At eleven o'clock he
pleaded fatigue after his journey, and Sir Murgatroyd accompanied him to his room, anxious, like a good host, to see that
everything was comfortable.

'Very sensible of you to turn in early,' he said, in his bluff, genial
way. 'So many young men ruin their health with late hours. Now
you, I imagine, will just get into a dressing-gown and smoke a
cigarette or two and have the light out by twelve. You have plenty
of cigarettes? I told them to see that you were well supplied. I
always think the bedroom smoke is the best one of the day.
Nobody to disturb you, and all that. If you want to write letters or
anything, there is lots of paper, and here is the waste-paper
basket, which is always so necessary. Well, good night, my boy,
good night.'

The door closed, and Mordred, as foreshadowed, got into a
dressing-gown and lit a cigarette. But though, having done this, he
made his way to the writing-table, it was not with any idea of
getting abreast of his correspondence. It was his purpose to com-
pose a poem to Annabelle Sprockett-Sprockett. He had felt it
seething within him all the evening, and sleep would be impossible
until it was out of his system.

Hitherto, I should mention, my nephew's poetry, for he belonged
to the modern fearless school, had always been stark and rhyme-
less and had dealt principally with corpses and the smell of
cooking cabbage. But now, with the moonlight silvering the
balcony outside, he found that his mind had become full of words
like 'love' and 'dove' and 'eyes' and 'summer skies'.

> *Blue eyes*, wrote Mordred . . .
> *Sweet lips*, wrote Mordred . . .
> *Oh, eyes like skies of summer blue* . . .
> *Oh, love* . . .
> *Oh, dove* . . .
> *Oh, lips* . . .

With a muttered ejaculation of chagrin he tore the sheet across
and threw it into the waste-paper basket.

> Blue eyes that burn into my soul,
>   Sweet lips that smile my heart away,
> Pom-pom, pom-pom, pom something whole (Goal?)
>   And tiddly-iddly-umpty-ay (Gay? Say? Happy day?)
>
> Blue eyes into my soul that burn,
>   Sweet lips that smile away my heart,
> Oh, something something turn or yearn
>   And something something something part.
>
> You burn into my soul, blue eyes,
>   You smile my heart away, sweet lips,
> Short long short long of summer skies
>   And something something something trips. (Hips?
>   Ships? Pips?)

He threw the sheet into the waste-paper basket and rose with a
stifled oath. The waste-paper basket was nearly full now, and still
his poet's sense told him that he had not achieved perfection. He
thought he saw the reason for this. You can't just sit in a chair and
expect inspiration to flow—you want to walk about and clutch
your hair and snap your fingers. It had been his intention to pace
the room, but the moonlight pouring in through the open window
called to him. He went out on to the balcony. It was but a short
distance to the dim, mysterious lawn. Impulsively he dropped
from the stone balustrade.

The effect was magical. Stimulated by the improved conditions,
his Muse gave quick service, and this time he saw at once that she
had rung the bell and delivered the goods. One turn up and down
the lawn, and he was reciting as follows:

TO ANNABELLE

> Oh, lips that smile! Oh, eyes that shine
>   Like summer skies, or stars above!
> Your beauty maddens me like wine,
>   Oh, umpty-pumpty-tumty love!

And he was just wondering, for he was a severe critic of his own work, whether that last line couldn't be polished up a bit, when his eye was attracted by something that shone like summer skies or stars above and, looking more closely, he perceived that his bedroom curtains were on fire.

Now, I will not pretend that my nephew Mordred was in every respect the cool-headed man of action, but this happened to be a situation with which use had familiarized him. He knew the procedure.

'Fire!' he shouted.

A head appeared in an upstairs window. He recognized it as that of Captain Biffing.

'Eh?' said Captain Biffing.

'Fire!'

'What?'

'Fire!' vociferated Mordred. 'F for Francis, I for Isabel . . .'

'Oh, fire?' said Captain Biffing. 'Right ho.'

And presently the house began to discharge its occupants.

In the proceedings which followed, Mordred, I fear, did not appear to the greatest advantage. This is an age of specialization, and if you take the specialist off his own particular ground he is at a loss. Mordred's genius, as we have seen, lay in the direction of starting fires. Putting them out called for quite different qualities, and these he did not possess. On the various occasions of holocausts at his series of flats, he had never attempted to play an active part, contenting himself with going downstairs and asking the janitor to step up and see what he could do about it. So now, though under the bright eyes of Annabelle Sprockett-Sprockett he would have given much to be able to dominate the scene, the truth is that the Biffies and Guffies simply played him off the stage.

His heart sank as he noted the hideous efficiency of these young men. They called for buckets. They formed a line. Freddie Boot leaped lissomely on to the balcony, and Algy Fripp, mounted on a wheelbarrow, handed up to him the necessary supplies. And after Mordred, trying to do his bit, had tripped up Jack Guffington and upset two buckets over Ted Prosser, he was advised in set terms to withdraw into the background and stay there.

It was a black ten minutes for the unfortunate young man. One glance at Sir Murgatroyd's twisted face as he watched the operations was enough to tell him how desperately anxious the fine old man was for the safety of his ancestral home and how bitter would be his resentment against the person who had endangered it. And the same applied to Lady Sprockett-Sprockett and Annabelle. Mordred could see the anxiety in their eyes, and the thought that ere long those eyes must be turned accusingly on him chilled him to the marrow.

Presently Freddie Boot emerged from the bedroom to announce that all was well.

'It's out,' he said, jumping lightly down. 'Anybody know whose room it was?'

Mordred felt a sickening qualm, but the splendid Mulliner courage sustained him. He stepped forward, white and tense.

'Mine,' he said.

He became the instant centre of attention. The six young men looked at him.

'Yours?'

'Oh, yours, was it?'

'What happened?'

'How did it start?'

'Yes, how did it start?'

'Must have started somehow, I mean,' said Captain Biffing, who was a clear thinker. 'I mean to say, must have, don't you know, what?'

Mordred mastered his voice.

'I was smoking, and I suppose I threw my cigarette into the waste-paper basket, and as it was full of paper . . .'

'Full of paper? Why was it full of paper?'

'I had been writing a poem.'

There was a stir of bewilderment.

'A what?' said Ted Prosser.

'Writing a what?' said Jack Guffington.

'Writing a *poem*?' asked Captain Biffing of Tommy Mainprice.

'That's how I got the story,' said Tommy Mainprice, plainly shaken.

'Chap was writing a poem,' Freddie Boot informed Algy Fripp.

'You mean the chap writes poems?'

'That's right. Poems.'

'Well, I'm dashed!'

'Well, I'm blowed!'

Their now unconcealed scorn was hard to bear. Mordred chafed beneath it. The word 'poem' was flitting from lip to lip, and it was only too evident that, had there been an 's' in the word, those present would have hissed it. Reason told him that these men were mere clods, Philistines, fatheads who would not recognize the rare and the beautiful if you handed it to them on a skewer, but that did not seem to make it any better. He knew that he should be scorning them, but it is not easy to go about scorning people in a dressing-gown, especially if you have no socks on and the night breeze is cool around the ankles. So, as I say, he chafed. And finally, when he saw the butler bend down with pursed lips to the ear of the cook, who was a little hard of hearing, and after a contemptuous glance in his direction speak into it, spacing his syllables carefully, something within him seemed to snap.

'I regret, Sir Murgatroyd,' he said, 'that urgent family business compels me to return to London immediately. I shall be obliged to take the first train in the morning.'

Without another word he went into the house.

In the matter of camping out in devastated areas my nephew had, of course, become by this time an old hand. It was rarely nowadays that a few ashes and cinders about the place disturbed him. But when he had returned to his bedroom one look was enough to assure him that nothing practical in the way of sleep was to be achieved here. Apart from the unpleasant, acrid smell of burned poetry, the apartment, thanks to the efforts of Freddie Boot, had been converted into a kind of inland sea. The carpet was awash, and on the bed only a duck could have made itself at home.

And so it came about that some ten minutes later Mordred Mulliner lay stretched upon a high-backed couch in the library, endeavouring by means of counting sheep jumping through a gap in a hedge to lull himself into unconsciousness.

But sleep refused to come. Nor in his heart had he really thought that it would. When the human soul is on the rack, it cannot just curl up and close its eyes and expect to get its eight hours as if nothing had happened. It was all very well for Mordred to count sheep, but what did this profit him when each sheep in turn assumed the features and lineaments of Annabelle Sprockett-Sprockett and, what was more, gave him a reproachful glance as it drew itself together for the spring?

Remorse gnawed him. He was tortured by a wild regret for what might have been. He was not saying that with all these Biffies and Guffies in the field he had ever had more than a hundred to eight chance of winning that lovely girl, but at least his hat had been in the ring. Now it was definitely out. Dreamy Mordred may have been—romantic—impractical—but he had enough sense to see that the very worst thing you can do when you are trying to make a favourable impression on the adored object is to set fire to her childhood home, every stick and stone of which she has no doubt worshipped since they put her into rompers.

He had reached this point in his meditations, and was about to send his two hundred and thirty-second sheep at the gap, when with a suddenness which affected him much as an explosion of gelignite would have done, the lights flashed on. For an instant, he lay quivering, then, cautiously poking his head round the corner of the couch, he looked to see who his visitors were.

It was a little party of three that had entered the room. First came Sir Murgatroyd, carrying a tray of sandwiches. He was followed by Lady Sprockett-Sprockett with a siphon and glasses. The rear was brought up by Annabelle, who was bearing a bottle of whisky and two dry ginger ales.

So evident was it that they were assembling here for purposes of a family council that, but for one circumstance, Mordred, to whom anything in the nature of eavesdropping was as repugnant as it has always been to all the Mulliners, would have sprung up with a polite 'Excuse me' and taken his blanket elsewhere. This circumstance was the fact that on lying down he had kicked his slippers under the couch, well out of reach. The soul of modesty, he could not affront Annabelle with the spectacle of his bare toes.

So he lay there in silence, and silence, broken only by the swishing of soda-water and the *whoosh* of opened ginger-ale bottles, reigned in the room beyond.

Then Sir Murgatroyd spoke.

'Well, that's that,' he said, bleakly.

There was a gurgle as Lady Sprockett-Sprockett drank ginger ale. Then her quiet, well-bred voice broke the pause.

'Yes,' she said, 'it is the end.'

'The end,' agreed Sir Murgatroyd heavily. 'No good trying to struggle on against luck like ours. Here we are and here we have got to stay, mouldering on in this blasted barrack of a place which eats up every penny of my income when, but for the fussy interference of that gang of officious, ugly nitwits, there would have been nothing left of it but a pile of ashes, with a man from the Insurance Company standing on it with his fountain-pen, writing cheques. Curse those imbeciles! Did you see that young Fripp with those buckets?'

'I did, indeed,' sighed Lady Sprockett-Sprockett.

'Annabelle,' said Sir Murgatroyd sharply.

'Yes, father?'

'It has seemed to me lately, watching you with a father's eye, that you have shown signs of being attracted by Algernon Fripp. Let me tell you that if ever you allow yourself to be ensnared by his insidious wiles, or by those of William Biffing, John Guffington, Edward Prosser, Thomas Mainprice, or Frederick Boot, you will do so over my dead body. After what occurred tonight, those young men shall never darken my door again. They and their buckets! To think that we could have gone and lived in London . . .'

'In a nice little flat . . .' said Lady Sprockett-Sprockett.

'Handy for my club . . .'

'Convenient for the shops . . .'

'Within a stone's throw of the theatres . . .'

'Seeing all our friends . . .'

'Had it not been,' said Sir Murgatroyd, summing up, 'for the pestilential activities of these Guffingtons, these Biffings, these insufferable Fripps, men who ought never to be trusted near a bucket of water when a mortgaged country-house has got nicely alight. I did think,' proceeded the stricken old man, helping himself to a sandwich, 'that when Annabelle, with a ready intelligence which I cannot over-praise, realized this young Mulliner's splendid gifts and made us ask him down here, the happy ending was in sight. What Smattering Hall has needed for generations has been a man who throws his cigarette-ends into waste-paper baskets. I was convinced that here at last was the angel of mercy we required.'

'He did his best, father.'

'No man could have done more,' agreed Sir Murgatroyd cordially. 'The way he upset those buckets and kept getting entangled in people's legs. Very shrewd. It thrilled me to see him. I don't know when I've met a young fellow I liked and respected more. And what if he is a poet? Poets are all right. Why, dash it, I'm a poet myself. At the last dinner of the Loyal Sons of Worcestershire I composed a poem which, let me tell you, was pretty generally admired. I read it out to the boys over the port, and they cheered me to the echo. It was about a young lady of Bewdley, who sometimes behaved rather rudely . . .'

'Not before mother, father.'

'Perhaps you're right. Well, I'm off to bed. Come along, Aurelia. You coming, Annabelle?'

'Not yet, father. I want to stay and think.'

'Do what?'

'Think.'

'Oh, think? Well, all right.'

'But, Murgatroyd,' said Lady Sprockett-Sprockett, 'is there no hope? After all, there are plenty of cigarettes in the house, and we could always give Mr Mulliner another waste-paper basket. . . .'

'No good. You heard him say he was leaving by the first train tomorrow. When I think that we shall never see that splendid young man again . . . Why, hullo, hullo, hullo, what's this? Crying, Annabelle?'

'Oh, mother!'

'My darling, what is it?'

A choking sob escaped the girl.

'Mother, I love him! Directly I saw him in the dentist's waiting-room, something seemed to go all over me, and I knew that there could be no other man for me. And now . . .'

'Hi!' cried Mordred, popping up over the side of the couch like a jack-in-the-box.

He had listened with growing understanding to the conversation which I have related, but had shrunk from revealing his presence because, as I say, his toes were bare. But this was too much. Toes or no toes, he felt that he must be in this.

'You love me, Annabelle?' he cried.

His sudden advent had occasioned, I need scarcely say, a certain reaction in those present. Sir Murgatroyd had leaped like a jumping bean. Lady Sprockett-Sprockett had quivered like a jelly. As for Annabelle, her lovely mouth was open to the extent of perhaps three inches, and she was staring like one who sees a vision.

'You really love me, Annabelle?'

'Yes, Mordred.'

'Sir Murgatroyd,' said Mordred formally, 'I have the honour to ask for your daughter's hand. I am only a poor poet . . .'

'How poor?' asked the other, keenly.

'I was referring to my art,' explained Mordred. 'Financially, I am nicely fixed. I could support Annabelle in modest comfort.'

'Then take her, my boy, take her. You will live, of course'—the old man winced—'in London?'

'Yes. And so shall you.'

Sir Murgatroyd shook his head.

'No, no, that dream is ended. It is true that in certain circumstances I had hoped to do so, for the insurance, I may mention, amounts to as much as a hundred thousand pounds, but I am resigned now to spending the rest of my life in this infernal family vault. I see no reprieve.'

'I understand,' said Mordred, nodding. 'You mean you have no paraffin in the house?'

Sir Murgatroyd started.

'Paraffin?'

'If,' said Mordred, and his voice was very gentle and winning, 'there had been paraffin on the premises, I think it possible that tonight's conflagration, doubtless imperfectly quenched, might have broken out again, this time with more serious results. It is often this way with fires. You pour buckets of water on them and think they are extinguished, but all the time they have been smouldering unnoticed, to break out once more in—well, in here, for example.'

'Or the billiard-room,' said Lady Sprockett-Sprockett.

'*And* the billiard-room,' corrected Sir Murgatroyd.

'And the billiard-room,' said Mordred. 'And possibly—who knows?—in the drawing-room, dining-room, kitchen, servants' hall, butler's pantry and the usual domestic offices, as well. Still, as you say you have no paraffin . . .'

'My boy,' said Sir Murgatroyd, in a shaking voice, 'what gave you the idea that we have no paraffin? How did you fall into this odd error? We have gallons of paraffin. The cellar is full of it.'

'And Annabelle will show you the way to the cellar—in case you thought of going there,' said Lady Sprockett-Sprockett. 'Won't you, dear?'

'Of course, mother. You will like the cellar, Mordred, darling. Most picturesque. Possibly, if you are interested in paraffin, you might also care to take a look at our little store of paper and shavings, too.'

'My angel,' said Mordred, tenderly, 'you think of everything.'

He found his slippers, and hand in hand they passed down the stairs. Above them, they could see the head of Sir Murgatroyd, as he leaned over the banisters. A box of matches fell at their feet like a father's benediction.

JAMES JOYCE

Clay

The matron had given her leave to go out as soon as the women's tea was over, and Maria looked forward to her evening out. The kitchen was spick and span: the cook said you could see yourself in the big copper boilers. The fire was nice and bright and on one of the side-tables were four very big barmbracks. These barmbracks seemed uncut; but if you went closer you would see that they had been cut into long thick even slices and were ready to be handed round at tea. Maria had cut them herself.

Maria was a very, very small person indeed, but she had a very long nose and a very long chin. She talked a little through her nose, always soothingly: 'Yes, my dear,' and 'No, my dear.' She was always sent for when the women quarrelled over their tubs and always succeeded in making peace. One day the matron had said to her:

'Maria, you are a veritable peace-maker!'

And the sub-matron and two of the Board ladies had heard the compliment. And Ginger Mooney was always saying what she wouldn't do to the dummy who had charge of the irons if it wasn't for Maria. Every one was so fond of Maria.

The women would have their tea at six o'clock and she would be able to get away before seven. From Ballsbridge to the Pillar, twenty minutes; from the Pillar to Drumcondra, twenty minutes; and twenty minutes to buy the things. She would be there before eight. She took out her purse with the silver clasps and read again the words 'A Present from Belfast.' She was very fond of that purse because Joe had brought it to her five years before when he and Alphy had gone to Belfast on a Whit-Monday trip. In the purse were two half-crowns and some coppers. She would have five shillings clear after paying the tram fare. What a nice evening they would have, all the children singing! Only she hoped that Joe wouldn't come in drunk. He was so different when he took any drink.

Often he had wanted her to go and live with them; but she would have felt herself in the way (though Joe's wife was ever so nice with her) and she had become accustomed to the life of the laundry. Joe was a good fellow. She had nursed him and Alphy too; and Joe used often to say:

'Mamma is mamma, but Maria is my proper mother.'

After the break-up at home the boys had got her that position in the 'Dublin by Lamplight' laundry, and she liked it. She used to have such a bad opinion of Protestants, but now she thought they were very nice people, a little quiet and serious, but still very nice people to live with. Then she had her plants in the conservatory and she liked looking after them. She had lovely ferns and wax-plants and, whenever any one came to visit her, she always gave the visitor one or two slips from her conservatory. There was one thing she didn't like and that was the tracts on the walls; but the matron was such a nice person to deal with, so genteel.

When the cook told her everything was ready she went into the women's room and began to pull the big bell. In a few minutes the women began to come in by twos and threes, wiping their steaming hands in their petticoats and pulling down the sleeves of their blouses over their red steaming arms. They settled down before their huge mugs which the cook and the dummy filled up with hot tea, already mixed with milk and sugar in huge tin cans. Maria superintended the distribution of the barmbrack and saw that every woman got her four slices. There was a great deal of laughing and joking during the meal. Lizzie Fleming said Maria was sure to get the ring and, though Fleming had said that for so many Hallow Eves, Maria had to laugh and say she didn't want any ring or man either; and when she laughed her grey-green eyes sparkled with disappointed shyness and the tip of her nose nearly met the tip of her chin. Then Ginger Mooney lifted up her mug of tea and proposed Maria's health, while all the other women clattered with their mugs on the table, and said she was sorry she hadn't a sup of porter to drink it in. And Maria laughed again till the tip of her nose nearly met the tip of her chin and till her minute body nearly shook itself asunder, because she knew that Mooney meant well, though of course she had the notions of a common woman.

But wasn't Maria glad when the women had finished their tea and the cook and the dummy had begun to clear away the tea-things! She went into her little bedroom and, remembering that the next morning was a mass morning, changed the hand of the alarm from seven to six. Then she took off her working skirt and her house-boots and laid her best skirt out on the bed and her tiny dress-boots beside the foot of the bed. She changed her blouse too and, as she stood before the mirror, she thought of how she used to dress for mass on Sunday morning when she was a young girl; and she looked with quaint affection at the diminutive body which she had so often adorned. In spite of its years she found it a nice tidy little body.

When she got outside the streets were shining with rain and she was glad of her old brown waterproof. The tram was full and she had to sit on the little stool at the end of the car, facing all the people, with her toes barely touching the floor. She arranged in her mind all she was going to do, and thought how much better it was to be independent and to have your own money in your pocket. She hoped they would have a nice evening. She was sure they would, but she could not help thinking what a pity it was Alphy and Joe were not speaking. They were always falling out now, but when they were boys together they used to be the best of friends; but such was life.

She got out of her tram at the Pillar and ferreted her way quickly among the crowds. She went into Downes's cake-shop, but the shop was so full of people that it was a long time before she could get herself attended to. She bought a dozen of mixed penny cakes, and at last came out of the shop laden with a big bag. Then she thought what else would she buy: she wanted to buy something really nice. They would be sure to have plenty of apples and nuts. It was hard to know what to buy and all she could think of was cake. She decided to buy some plumcake, but Downes's plumcake had not enough almond icing on top of it, so she went over to a shop in Henry Street. Here she was a long time in suiting herself, and the stylish young lady behind the counter, who was evidently a little annoyed by her, asked her was it wedding-cake she wanted to buy. That made Maria blush and smile at the young lady; but the young lady took it all very seriously and finally cut a thick slice of plumcake, parcelled it up, and said:

'Two-and-four, please.'

She thought she would have to stand in the Drumcondra tram because none of the young men seemed to notice her, but an elderly gentleman made room for her. He was a stout gentleman and he wore a brown hard hat; he had a square red face and a greyish moustache. Maria thought he was a colonel-looking gentleman and she reflected how much more polite he was than the young men who simply stared straight before them. The gentleman began to chat with her about Hallow Eve and the rainy weather. He supposed the bag was full of good things for the little ones and said it was only right that the youngsters should enjoy themselves while they were young. Maria agreed with him and favoured him with demure nods and hems. He was very nice with her, and when she was getting out at the Canal Bridge she thanked him and bowed, and he bowed to her and raised his hat and smiled agreeably; and while she was going up along the terrace, bending her tiny head under the rain, she thought how easy it was to know a gentleman even when he has a drop taken.

Everybody said: 'Oh, here's Maria!' when she came to Joe's house. Joe was there, having come home from business, and all the children had their Sunday dresses on. There were two big girls in from next door and games were going on. Maria gave the bag of cakes to the eldest boy, Alphy, to divide, and Mrs Donnelly said it was too good of her to bring such a big bag of cakes, and made all the children say:

'Thanks, Maria.'

But Maria said she had brought something special for papa and mamma, something they would be sure to like, and she began to look for her plumcake. She tried in Downes's bag and then in the pockets of her waterproof and then on the hallstand, but nowhere could she find it. Then she asked all the children had any of them eaten it—by mistake, of course—but the children all said no and looked as if they did not like to eat cakes if they were to be accused of stealing. Everybody had a solution for the mystery and Mrs Donnelly said it was plain that Maria had left it behind her in the tram. Maria, remembering how confused the gentleman with the greyish moustache had made her, coloured with shame and vexation and disappointment. At the thought of the failure of her little surprise and of the two and fourpence she had thrown away for nothing she nearly cried outright.

But Joe said it didn't matter and made her sit down by the fire. He was very nice with her. He told her all that went on in his office, repeating for her a smart answer which he had made to the manager. Maria did not understand why Joe laughed so much over the answer he had made, but she said that the manager must have been a very overbearing person to deal with. Joe said he wasn't so bad when you knew how to take him, that he was a decent sort so long as you didn't rub him the wrong way. Mrs Donnelly played the piano for the children and they danced and sang. Then the two next-door girls handed round the nuts. Nobody could find the nutcrackers, and Joe was nearly getting cross over it and asked how did they expect Maria to crack nuts without a nutcracker. But Maria said she didn't like nuts and that they weren't to bother about her. Then Joe asked would she take a bottle of stout, and Mrs Donnelly said there was port wine too in the house if she would prefer that. Maria said she would rather they didn't ask her to take anything: but Joe insisted.

So Maria let him have his way and they sat by the fire talking over old times and Maria thought she would put in a good word for Alphy. But Joe cried that God might strike him stone dead if ever he spoke a word to his brother again and Maria said she was sorry she had mentioned the matter. Mrs Donnelly told her husband it was a great shame for him to speak that way of his own flesh and blood, but Joe said that Alphy was no brother of his and there was nearly being a row on the head of it. But Joe said he would not lose his temper on account of the night it was, and asked his wife to open some more stout. The two next-door girls had arranged some Hallow Eve games and soon everything was merry again. Maria was delighted to see the children so merry and Joe and his wife in such good spirits. The next-door girls put some saucers on the table and then led the children up to the table, blindfold. One got the prayer-book and the other three got the water; and when one of the next-door girls got the ring Mrs

Donnelly shook her finger at the blushing girl as much as to say: 'O, I know all about it!' They insisted then on blindfolding Maria and leading her up to the table to see what she would get; and, while they were putting on the bandage, Maria laughed and laughed again till the tip of her nose nearly met the tip of her chin.

They led her up to the table amid laughing and joking, and she put her hand out in the air as she was told to do. She moved her hand about here and there in the air and descended on one of the saucers. She felt a soft wet substance with her fingers and was surprised that nobody spoke or took off her bandage. There was a pause for a few seconds; and then a great deal of scuffling and whispering. Somebody said something about the garden, and at last Mrs Donnelly said something very cross to one of the next-door girls and told her to throw it out at once: that was no play. Maria understood that it was wrong that time and so she had to do it over again: and this time she got the prayer-book.

After that Mrs Donnelly played Miss McCloud's Reel for the children, and Joe made Maria take a glass of wine. Soon they were all quite merry again, and Mrs Donnelly said Maria would enter a convent before the year was out because she had got the prayer-book. Maria had never seen Joe so nice to her as he was that night, so full of pleasant talk and reminiscences. She said they were all very good to her.

At last the children grew tired and sleepy and Joe asked Maria would she not sing some little song before she went, one of the old songs. Mrs Donnelly said 'Do, please, Maria!' and so Maria had to get up and stand beside the piano. Mrs Donnelly bade the children to be quiet and listen to Maria's song. Then she played the prelude and said 'Now, Maria!' and Maria, blushing very much, began to sing in a tiny quavering voice. She sang *I dreamt that I dwelt*, and when she came to the second verse she sang again:

I dreamt that I dwelt in marble halls
    With vassals and serfs at my side,
And of all who assembled within those walls
    That I was the hope and the pride.

I had riches too great to count, could boast
   Of a high ancestral name,
But I also dreamt, which pleased me most,
   That you loved me still the same.

But no one tried to show her her mistake; and when she had ended her song Joe was very much moved. He said that there was no time like the long ago and no music for him like poor old Balfe, whatever other people might say; and his eyes filled up so much with tears that he could not find what he was looking for and in the end he had to ask his wife to tell him where the corkscrew was.

D. H. LAWRENCE

Second Best

'Oh, I'm tired!' Frances exclaimed petulantly, and in the same instant she dropped down on the turf, near the hedge-bottom. Anne stood a moment surprised, then, accustomed to the vagaries of her beloved Frances, said:

'Well, and aren't you always likely to be tired, after travelling that blessed long way from Liverpool yesterday?' and she plumped down beside her sister. Anne was a wise young body of fourteen, very buxom, brimming with common sense. Frances was much older, about twenty-three, and whimsical, spasmodic. She was the beauty and the clever child of the family. She plucked the goose-grass buttons from her dress in a nervous, desperate fashion. Her beautiful profile, looped above with black hair, warm with the dusky-and-scarlet complexion of a pear, was calm as a mask, her thin brown hand plucked nervously.

'It's not the journey,' she said, objecting to Anne's obtuseness. Anne looked inquiringly at her darling. The young girl, in her self-confident, practical way, proceeded to reckon up this whimsical creature. But suddenly she found herself full in the eyes of Frances; felt two dark, hectic eyes flaring challenge at her, and she shrank away. Frances was peculiar for these great, exposed looks, which disconcerted people by their violence and their suddenness.

'What's a matter, poor old duck?' asked Anne, as she folded the slight, wilful form of her sister in her arms. Frances laughed shakily, and nestled down for comfort on the budding breasts of the strong girl.

'Oh, I'm only a bit tired,' she murmured, on the point of tears.

'Well, of course you are, what do you expect?' soothed Anne. It was a joke to Frances that Anne should play elder, almost mother to her. But then, Anne was in her unvexed teens; men were like big dogs to her: while Frances, at twenty-three, suffered a good deal.

The country was intensely morning-still. On the common everything shone beside its shadow, and the hill-side gave off heat in silence. The brown turf seemed in a low state of combustion, the leaves of the oaks were scorched brown. Among the blackish foliage in the distance shone the small red and orange of the village.

The willows in the brook-course at the foot of the common suddenly shook with a dazzling effect like diamonds. It was a puff of wind. Anne resumed her normal position. She spread her knees, and put in her lap a handful of hazel nuts, whity-green leafy things, whose one cheek was tanned between brown and pink. These she began to crack and eat. Frances, with bowed head, mused bitterly.

'Eh, you know Tom Smedley?' began the young girl, as she pulled a tight kernel out of its shell.

'I suppose so,' replied Frances sarcastically.

'Well, he gave me a wild rabbit what he'd caught, to keep with my tame one—and it's living.'

'That's a good thing,' said Frances, very detached and ironic.

'Well, it *is*! He reckoned he'd take me to Ollerton Feast, but he never did. Look here, he took a servant from the rectory; I saw him.'

'So he ought,' said Frances.

'No, he oughtn't! And I told him so. And I told him I should tell you—an' I have done.'

Click and snap went a nut between her teeth. She sorted out the kernel, and chewed complacently.

'It doesn't make much difference,' said Frances.

'Well, 'appen it doesn't; but I was mad with him all the same.'

'Why?'

'Because I was; he's no right to go with a servant.'

'He's a perfect right,' persisted Frances, very just and cold.

'No, he hasn't, when he'd said he'd take me.'

Frances burst into a laugh of amusement and relief.

'Oh, no; I'd forgot that,' she said, adding, 'and what did he say when you promised to tell me?'

'He laughed and said, "She won't fret her fat over that." '

'And she won't,' sniffed Frances.

There was silence. The common, with its sere, blonde-headed thistles, its heaps of silent bramble, its brown-husked gorse in the glare of sunshine, seemed visionary. Across the brook began the immense pattern of agriculture, white chequering of barley stubble, brown squares of wheat, khaki patches of pasture, red stripes of fallow, with the woodland and the tiny village dark like ornaments, leading away to the distance, right to the hills, where the check-pattern grew smaller and smaller, till, in the blackish haze of heat, far off, only the tiny white squares of barley stubble showed distinct.

'Eh, I say, here's a rabbit hole!' cried Anne suddenly. 'Should we watch if one comes out? You won't have to fidget, you know.'

The two girls sat perfectly still. Frances watched certain objects in her surroundings: they had a peculiar, unfriendly look about them: the weight of greenish elderberries on their purpling stalks; the twinkling of the yellowing crab-apples that clustered high up in the hedge, against the sky: the exhausted, limp leaves of the primroses lying flat in the hedge-bottom: all looked strange to her. Then her eyes caught a movement. A mole was moving silently over the warm, red soil, nosing, shuffling hither and thither, flat, and dark as a shadow, shifting about, and as suddenly brisk, and as silent, like a very ghost of *joie de vivre*. Frances started, from habit was about to call on Anne to kill the little pest. But, today her lethargy of unhappiness was too much for her. She watched the little brute paddling, snuffing, touching things to discover them, running in blindness, delighted to ecstasy by the sunlight and the hot, strange things that caressed its belly and its nose. She felt a keen pity for the little creature.

'Eh, our Fran, look there! It's a mole.'

Anne was on her feet, standing watching the dark, unconscious beast. Frances frowned with anxiety.

'It doesn't run off, does it?' said the young girl softly. Then she stealthily approached the creature. The mole paddled fumblingly away. In an instant Anne put her foot upon it, not too heavily. Frances could see the struggling, swimming movement of the little pink hands of the brute, the twisting and twitching of its pointed nose, as it wrestled under the sole of the boot.

'It *does* wriggle!' said the bonny girl, knitting her brows in a frown at the eerie sensation. Then she bent down to look at her trap. Frances could now see, beyond the edge of the boot-sole, the heaving of the velvet shoulders, the pitiful turning of the sightless face, the frantic rowing of the flat, pink hands.

'Kill the thing,' she said, turning away her face.

'Oh—I'm not,' laughed Anne, shrinking. 'You can, if you like.'

'I *don't* like,' said Frances with quiet intensity.

After several dabbing attempts, Anne succeeded in picking up the little animal by the scruff of its neck. It threw back its head, flung its long blind snout from side to side, the mouth open in a peculiar oblong, with tiny pinkish teeth at the edge. The blind, frantic mouth gaped and writhed. The body, heavy and clumsy, hung scarcely moving.

'Isn't it a snappy little thing?' observed Anne, twisting to avoid the teeth.

'What are you going to do with it?' asked Frances sharply.

'It's got to be killed—look at the damage they do. I s'll take it home and let dadda or somebody kill it. I'm not going to let it go.'

She swaddled the creature clumsily in her pocket-handkerchief and sat down beside her sister. There was an interval of silence, during which Anne combated the efforts of the mole.

'You've not had much to say about Jimmy this time. Did you see him often in Liverpool?' Anne asked suddenly.

'Once or twice,' replied Frances, giving no sign of how the question troubled her.

'And aren't you sweet on him any more, then?'

'I should think I'm not, seeing that he's engaged.'

'Engaged? Jimmy Barrass! Well, of all things! I never thought *he*'d get engaged.'

'Why not? he's as much right as anybody else,' snapped Frances.

Anne was fumbling with the mole.

' 'Appen so,' she said at length; 'but I never thought Jimmy would, though.'

'Why not?' snapped Frances.

'*I* don't know—this blessed mole, it'll not keep still!—who's he got engaged to?'

'How should I know?'

'I thought you'd ask him; you've known him long enough. I s'd think he thought he'd get engaged now he's a Doctor of Chemistry.'

Frances laughed in spite of herself.

'What's that got to do with it?' she asked.

'I'm sure it's got a lot. He'll want to feel *somebody* now, so he's got engaged. Hey, stop it; go in!'

But at this juncture the mole almost succeeded in wriggling clear. It wrestled and twisted frantically, waved its pointed blind head, its mouth standing like a little shaft, its big, wrinkled hands spread out.

"Go in with you!' urged Anne, poking the little creature with her forefinger, trying to get it back into the handkerchief. Suddenly the mouth turned like a spark on her finger.

'Oh!' she cried, 'he's bit me.'

She dropped him to the floor. Dazed, the blind creature fumbled round. Frances felt like shrieking. She expected him to dart away in a flash, like a mouse, and there he remained groping; she wanted to cry to him to be gone. Anne, in a sudden decision of wrath, caught up her sister's walking-cane. With one blow the mole was dead. Frances was startled and shocked. One moment the little wretch was fussing in the heat, and the next it lay like a little bag, inert and black—not a struggle, scarce a quiver.

'It is dead!' Frances said breathlessly. Anne took her finger from her mouth, looked at the tiny pinpricks, and said:

'Yes, he is, and I'm glad. They're vicious little nuisances, moles are.'

With which her wrath vanished. She picked up the dead animal.

'Hasn't it got a beautiful skin?' she mused, stroking the fur with her forefinger, then with her cheek.

'Mind,' said Frances sharply. 'You'll have the blood on your skirt!'

One ruby drop of blood hung on the small snout, ready to fall. Anne shook it off on to some harebells. Frances suddenly became calm; in that moment, grown-up.

'I suppose they have to be killed,' she said, and a certain rather dreary indifference succeeded to her grief. The twinkling crab-apples, the glitter of brilliant willows now seemed to her trifling, scarcely worth the notice. Something had died in her, so that things lost their poignancy. She was calm, indifference overlying her quiet sadness. Rising, she walked down to the brook course.

'Here, wait for me,' cried Anne, coming tumbling after.

Frances stood on the bridge, looking at the red mud trodden into pockets by the feet of cattle. There was not a drain of water left, but everything smelled green, succulent. Why did she care so little for Anne, who was so fond of her? she asked herself. Why did she care so little for any one? She did not know, but she felt a rather stubborn pride in her isolation and indifference.

They entered a field where stooks of barley stood in rows, the straight, blonde tresses of the corn streaming on to the ground. The stubble was bleached by the intense summer, so that the expanse glared white. The next field was sweet and soft with a second crop of seeds; thin, straggling clover whose little pink knobs rested prettily in the dark green. The scent was faint and sickly. The girls came up in single file, Frances leading.

Near the gate a young man was mowing with the scythe some fodder for the afternoon feed of the cattle. As he saw the girls he left off working and waited in an aimless kind of way. Frances was dressed in white muslin, and she walked with dignity, detached and forgetful. Her lack of agitation, her simple, unheeding advance made him nervous. She had loved the far-off Jimmy for five years, having had in return his half-measures. This man only affected her slightly.

Tom was of medium stature, energetic in build. His smooth, fair-skinned face was burned red, not brown, by the sun, and this ruddiness enhanced his appearance of good humour and easiness. Being a year older than Frances, he would have courted her long ago had she been so inclined. As it was, he had gone his uneventful way amiably, chatting with many a girl, but remaining unattached, free of trouble for the most part. Only he knew he wanted a woman. He hitched his trousers just a trifle self-consciously as the girls approached. Frances was a rare, delicate kind of being, whom he realized with a queer and delicious stimulation in his veins. She gave him a slight sense of suffocation. Somehow this morning she affected him more than usual. She was dressed in white. He, however, being matter-of-fact in his mind, did not realize. His feeling had never become conscious, purposive.

Frances knew what she was about. Tom was ready to love her as soon as she would show him. Now that she could not have Jimmy, she did not poignantly care. Still, she would have something. If she could not have the best—Jimmy, whom she knew to be something of a snob—she would have the second best, Tom. She advanced rather indifferently.

'You are back, then!' said Tom. She marked the touch of uncertainty in his voice.

'No,' she laughed, 'I'm still in Liverpool,' and the undertone of intimacy made him burn.

'This isn't you, then?' he asked.

Her heart leapt up in approval. She looked in his eyes, and for a second was with him.

'Why, what do you think?' she laughed.

He lifted his hat from his head with a distracted little gesture. She liked him, his quaint ways, his humour, his ignorance, and his slow masculinity.

'Here, look here, Tom Smedley,' broke in Anne.

'A moudiwarp! Did you find it dead?' he asked.

'No, it bit me,' said Anne.

'Oh, aye! An' that got your rag out, did it?'

'No, it didn't!' Anne scolded sharply. 'Such language!'

'Oh, what's up wi' it?'

'I can't bear you to talk broad.'

'Can't you?'

He glanced at Frances.

'It isn't nice,' Frances said. She did not care, really. The vulgar speech jarred on her as a rule; Jimmy was a gentleman. But Tom's manner of speech did not matter to her.

'I like you to talk *nicely*,' she added.

'Do you,' he replied, tilting his hat, stirred.

'And generaliy you *do*, you know,' she smiled.

'I s'll have to have a try,' he said, rather tensely gallant.

'What?' she asked brightly.

'To talk nice to you,' he said. Frances coloured furiously, bent her head for a moment, then laughed gaily, as if she liked this clumsy hint.

'Eh now, you mind what you're saying,' cried Anne, giving the young man an admonitory pat.

'You wouldn't have to give yon mole many knocks like that,' he teased, relieved to get on safe ground, rubbing his arm.

'No indeed, it died in one blow,' said Frances, with a flippancy that was hateful to her.

'You're not so good at knockin' 'em?' he said, turning to her.

'I don't know, if I'm cross,' she said decisively.

'No?' he replied, with alert attentiveness.

'I could,' she added, harder, 'if it was necessary.'

He was slow to feel her difference.

'And don't you consider it *is* necessary?' he asked, with misgiving.

'W-ell—is it?' she said, looking at him steadily, coldly.

'I reckon it is,' he replied, looking away, but standing stubborn.

She laughed quickly.

'But it isn't necessary for *me*,' she said, with slight contempt.

'Yes, that's quite true,' he answered.

She laughed in a shaky fashion.

'I *know it is*,' she said; and there was an awkward pause.

'Why, would you *like* me to kill moles then?' she asked tentatively, after a while.

'They do us a lot of damage,' he said, standing firm on his own ground, angered.

'Well, I'll see the next time I come across one,' she promised, defiantly. Their eyes met, and she sank before him, her pride troubled. He felt uneasy and triumphant and baffled, as if fate had gripped him. She smiled as she departed.

'Well,' said Anne, as the sisters went through the wheat stubble; 'I don't know what you two's been jawing about, I'm sure.'

'Don't you?' laughed Frances significantly.

'No, I don't. But, at any rate, Tom Smedley's a good deal better to my thinking than Jimmy, so there—and nicer.'

'Perhaps he is,' said Frances coldly.

And the next day, after a secret, persistent hunt, she found another mole playing in the heat. She killed it, and in the evening, when Tom came to the gate to smoke his pipe after supper, she took him the dead creature.

'Here you are then!' she said.

'Did you catch it?' he replied, taking the velvet corpse into his fingers and examining it minutely. This was to hide his trepidation.

'Did you think I couldn't?' she asked, her face very near his.

'Nay, I didn't know.'

She laughed in his face, a strange little laugh that caught her breath, all agitation, and tears, and recklessness of desire. He looked frightened and upset. She put her hand to his arm.

'Shall you go out wi' me?' he asked, in a difficult, troubled tone.

She turned her face away, with a shaky laugh. The blood came up in him, strong, overmastering. He resisted it. But it drove him down, and he was carried away. Seeing the winsome, frail nape of her neck, fierce love came upon him for her, and tenderness.

'We s'll 'ave to tell your mother,' he said. And he stood, suffering, resisting his passion for her.

'Yes,' she replied, in a dead voice. But there was a thrill of pleasure in this death.

STACY AUMONIER

Miss Bracegirdle Does Her Duty

'This is the room, madame.'

'Ah, thank you . . . thank you.'

'Does it appear satisfactory to madame?'

'Oh, yes, thank you . . . quite.'

'Does madame require anything further?'

'Er—if not too late, may I have a hot bath?'

'*Parfaitement*, madame. The bathroom is at the end of the passage on the left. I will go and prepare it for madame.'

'There is one thing more. . . . I have had a very long journey. I am very tired. Will you please see that I am not disturbed in the morning until I ring.'

'Certainly, madame.'

Millicent Bracegirdle was speaking the truth—she *was* tired. In the sleepy cathedral town of Easingstoke, from which she came, it was customary for every one to speak the truth. It was customary, moreover, for every one to lead simple, self-denying lives—to give up their time to good works and elevating thoughts. One had only to glance at little Miss Bracegirdle to see that in her were epitomized all the virtues and ideals of Easingstoke. Indeed, it was the pursuit of duty which had brought her to the Hôtel de l'Ouest at Bordeaux on this summer's night. She had travelled from Easingstoke to London, then without a break to Dover, crossed that horrid stretch of sea to Calais, entrained for Paris, where she of necessity had to spend four hours—a terrifying experience—and then had come on to Bordeaux, arriving at midnight. The reason of this journey being that someone had to come to Bordeaux to meet her young sister-in-law, who was arriving the next day from South America. The sister-in-law was married to a missionary in Paraguay, but the climate not agreeing with her, she was returning to England. Her dear brother, the dean, would have come himself, but the claims on his time were so extensive, the parishioners would miss him so . . . it was clearly Millicent's duty to go.

She had never been out of England before, and she had a horror of travel, and an ingrained distrust of foreigners. She spoke a little French—sufficient for the purposes of travel and for obtaining any modest necessities, but not sufficient for carrying on any kind of conversation. She did not deplore this latter fact, for she was of opinion that French people were not the kind of people that one would naturally want to have conversation with; broadly speaking, they were not quite 'nice,' in spite of their ingratiating manners.

The dear dean had given her endless advice, warning her earnestly not to enter into conversation with strangers, to obtain all information from the police, railway officials—in fact, any one in an official uniform. He deeply regretted to say that he was afraid that France was not a country for a woman to travel about in *alone*. There were loose, bad people about, always on the look-out. . . . He really thought perhaps he ought not to let her go. It was only by the utmost persuasion, in which she rather exaggerated her knowledge of the French language and character, her courage, and indifference to discomfort, that she managed to carry the day.

She unpacked her valise, placed her things about the room, tried to thrust back the little stabs of homesickness as she visualized her darling room at the deanery. How strange and hard and unfriendly seemed these foreign hotel bedrooms—heavy and depressing, no chintz and lavender and photographs of . . . all the dear family, the dean, the nephews and nieces, the interior of the cathedral during harvest festival, no samplers and needlework or coloured reproductions of the paintings by Marcus Stone. Oh dear, how foolish she was! What did she expect?

She disrobed and donned a dressing-gown; then, armed with a sponge-bag and towel, she crept timidly down the passage to the bathroom, after closing her bedroom door and turning out the light. The gay bathroom cheered her. She wallowed luxuriously in the hot water, regarding her slim legs with quiet satisfaction. And for the first time since leaving home there came to her a pleasant moment—a sense of enjoyment in her adventure. After all, it *was* rather an adventure, and her life had been peculiarly devoid of it. What queer lives some people must live, travelling about, having experiences! How old was she? Not really old—not by any means. Forty-two? Forty-three? She had shut herself up so. She hardly ever regarded the potentialities of age. As the world went, she was a well-preserved woman for her age. A life of self-abnegation, simple living, healthy walking and fresh air, had kept her younger than these hurrying, pampered city people.

Love? yes, once when she was a young girl . . . he was a schoolmaster, a most estimable kind gentleman. They were never engaged—not actually, but it was a kind of understood thing. For three years it went on, this pleasant understanding and friendship. He was so gentle, so distinguished and considerate. She would have been happy to have continued in this strain for ever. But there was something lacking. Stephen had curious restless lapses. From the physical aspect of marriage she shrunk—yes, even with Stephen, who was gentleness and kindness itself. And then one day . . . one day he went away—vanished, and never returned. They told her he had married one of the country girls—a girl who used to work in Mrs Forbes's dairy—not a very nice girl, she feared, one of these fast, pretty, foolish women. Heigho! well, she had lived that down, destructive as the blow appeared at the time. One lives everything down in time. There is always work, living for others, faith, duty. . . . At the same time she could sympathize with people who found satisfaction in unusual experiences.

There would be lots to tell the dear dean when she wrote to him on the morrow; nearly losing her spectacles on the restaurant car; the amusing remarks of an American child on the train to Paris; the curious food everywhere, nothing simple and plain; the two English ladies at the hotel in Paris who told her about the death of their uncle—the poor man being taken ill on Friday and dying on Sunday afternoon, just before tea-time; the kindness of the hotel proprietor who had sat up for her; the prettiness of the chambermaid. Oh, yes, every one was really very kind. The French people, after all, were very nice. She had seen nothing—nothing but was quite nice and decorous. There would be lots to tell the dean tomorrow.

Her body glowed with the friction of the towel. She again donned her night attire and her thick, woollen dressing-gown. She tidied up the bathroom carefully in exactly the same way she was accustomed to do at home, then once more gripping her sponge-bag and towel, and turning out the light, she crept down the passage to her room. Entering the room she switched on the light and shut the door quickly. Then one of those ridiculous things happened—just the kind of thing you would expect to happen in a foreign hotel. The handle of the door came off in her hand.

She ejaculated a quiet 'Bother!' and sought to replace it with one hand, the other being occupied with the towel and sponge-bag. In doing this she behaved foolishly, for thrusting the knob carelessly against the steel pin—without properly securing it—she only succeeded in pushing the pin farther into the door and the knob was not adjusted. She uttered another little 'Bother!' and put her sponge-bag and towel down on the floor. She then tried to recover the pin with her left hand, but it had gone in too far.

'How very foolish!' she thought, 'I shall have to ring for the chambermaid—and perhaps the poor girl has gone to bed.'

She turned and faced the room, and suddenly the awful horror was upon her. *There was a man asleep in her bed!*

The sight of that swarthy face on the pillow, with its black tousled hair and heavy moustache, produced in her the most terrible moment of her life. Her heart nearly stopped. For some seconds she could neither think nor scream, and her first thought was: 'I mustn't scream!'

She stood there like one paralysed, staring at the man's head and the great curved hunch of his body under the clothes. When she began to think she thought very quickly, and all her thoughts worked together. The first vivid realization was that it wasn't the man's fault; it was *her* fault. *She was in the wrong room*. It was the man's room. The rooms were identical, but there were all his things about, his clothes thrown carelessly over chairs, his collar and tie on the wardrobe, his great heavy boots and the strange yellow trunk. She must get out somehow, anyhow.

She clutched once more at the door, feverishly driving her finger-nails into the hole where the elusive pin had vanished. She tried to force her fingers in the crack and open the door that way, but it was of no avail. She was to all intents and purposes locked in—locked in a bedroom in a strange hotel alone with a man . . . a foreigner . . . *a Frenchman!* She must think. She must think. . . . She switched off the light. If the light was off he might not wake up. It might give her time to think how to act. It was surprising that he had not awakened. If he did wake up, what would he do? How could she explain herself? He wouldn't believe her. No one would believe her. In an English hotel it would be difficult enough, but here where she wasn't known, where they were all foreigners and consequently antagonistic . . . merciful heavens!

She *must* get out. Should she wake the man? No, she couldn't do that. He might murder her. He might . . . Oh, it was too awful to contemplate! Should she scream? ring for the chambermaid? But no, it would be the same thing. People would come rushing. They would find her there in the strange man's bedroom after midnight—she, Millicent Bracegirdle, sister of the Dean of Easingstoke! Easingstoke!

Visions of Easingstoke flashed through her alarmed mind. Visions of the news arriving, women whispering around tea-tables: 'Have you heard, my dear? . . . Really no one would have imagined! Her poor brother! He will of course have to resign, you know, my dear. Have a little more cream, my love.'

Would they put her in prison? She might be in the room for the purpose of stealing or . . . She might be in the room for the purpose of breaking every one of the ten commandments. There was no explaining it away. She was a ruined woman, suddenly and irretrievably, unless she could open the door. The chimney? Should she climb up the chimney? But where would that lead to? And then she visualized the man pulling her down by her legs when she was already smothered in soot. Any moment he might wake up. . . .

She thought she heard the chambermaid going along the passage. If she had wanted to scream, she ought to have screamed before. The maid would know she had left the bathroom some minutes ago. Was she going to her room? Suddenly she remembered that she had told the chambermaid that she was not to be disturbed until she rang the next morning. That was something. Nobody would be going to her room to find out that she was not there.

An abrupt and desperate plan formed in her mind. It was already getting on for one o'clock. The man was probably a quite harmless commercial traveller or business man. He would probably get up about seven or eight o'clock, dress quickly, and go out. She would hide under his bed until he went. Only a matter of a few hours. Men don't look under their beds, although she made a religious practice of doing so herself. When he went he would be sure to open the door all right. The handle would be lying on the floor as though it had dropped off in the night. He would probably ring for the chambermaid or open it with a penknife. Men were so clever at those things. When he had gone she would creep out and steal back to her room, and then there would be no necessity to give any explanation to any one. But heavens! What an experience! Once under the white frill of that bed she would be safe till the morning. In daylight nothing seemed so terrifying.

With feline precaution she went down on her hands and knees and crept toward the bed. What a lucky thing there was that broad white frill! She lifted it at the foot of the bed and crept under. There was just sufficient depth to take her slim body. The floor was fortunately carpeted all over, but it seemed very close and dusty. Suppose she coughed or sneezed! Anything might happen. Of course . . . it would be much more difficult to explain her presence under the bed than to explain her presence just inside the door. She held her breath in suspense. No sound came from above, but under this frill it was difficult to hear anything. It was almost more nerve-racking than hearing everything . . . listening for signs and portents. This temporary escape in any case would give her time to regard the predicament detachedly. Up to the present she had not been able to visualize the full significance of her action. She had in truth lost her head. She had been like a wild animal, consumed with the sole idea of escape . . . a mouse or a cat would do this kind of thing—take cover and lie low. If only it hadn't all happened *abroad*! She tried to frame sentences of explanation in French, but French escaped her. And then—they talked so rapidly, these people. They didn't listen. The situation was intolerable. Would she be able to endure a night of it?

At present she was not altogether uncomfortable, only stuffy and . . . very, very frightened. But she had to face six or seven or eight hours of it—perhaps even then discovery in the end! The minutes flashed by as she turned the matter over and over in her head. There was no solution. She began to wish she had screamed or awakened the man. She saw now that that would have been the wisest and most politic thing to do; but she had allowed ten minutes or a quarter of an hour to elapse from the moment when the chambermaid would know that she had left the bathroom. They would want an explanation of what she had been doing in the man's bedroom all that time. Why hadn't she screamed before?

She lifted the frill an inch or two and listened. She thought she heard the man breathing but she couldn't be sure. In any case it gave her more air. She became a little bolder, and thrust her face partly through the frill so that she could breathe freely. She tried to steady her nerves by concentrating on the fact that—well, there it was. She had done it. She must make the best of it. Perhaps it would be all right after all.

'Of course I shan't sleep,' she kept on thinking, 'I shan't be able to. In any case it will be safer not to sleep. I must be on the watch.'

She set her teeth and waited grimly. Now that she had made up her mind to see the thing through in this manner she felt a little calmer. She almost smiled as she reflected that there would certainly be something to tell the dear dean when she wrote to him tomorrow. How would he take it? Of course he would believe it—he had never doubted a single word that she had uttered in her life—but the story would sound so . . . preposterous. In Easingstoke it would be almost impossible to envisage such an experience. She, Millicent Bracegirdle, spending a night under a strange man's bed in a foreign hotel! What would those women think? Fanny Shields and that garrulous old Mrs Rushbridger? Perhaps . . . yes, perhaps it would be advisable to tell the dear dean to let the story go no further. One could hardly expect Mrs Rushbridger to . . . not make implications . . . exaggerate.

Oh, dear! What were they all doing now? They would be all asleep, every one in Easingstoke. Her dear brother always retired at ten-fifteen. He would be sleeping calmly and placidly, the sleep of the just . . . breathing the clear sweet air of Sussex, not this—oh, it *was* stuffy! She felt a great desire to cough. She mustn't do that.

Yes, at nine-thirty all the servants summoned to the library—a short service—never more than fifteen minutes, her brother didn't believe in a great deal of ritual—then at ten o'clock cocoa for every one. At ten-fifteen bed for every one. The dear sweet bedroom with the narrow white bed, by the side of which she had knelt every night as long as she could remember—even in her dear mother's day—and said her prayers.

Prayers! Yes, that was a curious thing. This was the first night in her life's experience that she had not said her prayers on retiring. The situation was certainly very peculiar . . . exceptional, one might call it. God would understand and forgive such a lapse. And yet after all, why . . . what was to prevent her saying her prayers? Of course she couldn't kneel in the proper devotional attitude, that would be a physical impossibility; nevertheless, perhaps her prayers might be just as efficacious . . . if they came from the heart. So little Miss Bracegirdle curved her body and placed her hands in a devout attitude in front of her face and quite inaudibly murmured her prayers under the strange man's bed.

'Our Father which art in heaven, Hallowed be Thy name. Thy kingdom come. Thy will be done in earth as it is in heaven; Give us this day our daily bread. And forgive us our trespasses. . . .'

Trespasses! Yes, surely she was trespassing on this occasion, but God would understand. She had not wanted to trespass. She was an unwitting sinner. Without uttering a sound she went through her usual prayers in her heart. At the end she added fervently:

'Please God protect me from the dangers and perils of this night.'

Then she lay silent and inert, strangely soothed by the effort of praying. 'After all,' she thought, 'it isn't the attitude which matters—it is that which occurs deep down in us.'

For the first time she began to meditate—almost to question—church forms and dogma. If an attitude was not indispensable, why a building, a ritual, a church at all? Of course her dear brother couldn't be wrong, the church was so old, so very old, its root deep buried in the story of human life, it was only that . . . well, outward forms *could* be misleading. Her own present position for instance. In the eyes of the world she had, by one silly careless little action, convicted herself of being the breaker of every single one of the ten commandments.

She tried to think of one of which she could not be accused. But no—even to dishonouring her father and mother, bearing false witness, stealing, coveting her neighbour's . . . husband! That was the worst thing of all. Poor man! He might be a very pleasant honourable married gentleman with children and she—she was in a position to compromise him! Why hadn't she screamed? Too late! Too late!

It began to get very uncomfortable, stuffy, but at the same time draughty, and the floor was getting harder every minute. She changed her position stealthily and controlled her desire to cough. Her heart was beating rapidly. Over and over again recurred the vivid impression of every little incident and argument that had occurred to her from the moment she left the bathroom. This must, of course, be the room next to her own. So confusing, with perhaps twenty bedrooms all exactly alike on one side of a passage—how was one to remember whether one's number was 115 or 116?

Her mind began to wander idly off into her schooldays. She was always very bad at figures. She disliked Euclid and all those subjects about angles and equations—so unimportant, not leading anywhere. History she liked, and botany, and reading about strange foreign lands, although she had always been too timid to visit them. And the lives of great people, *most* fascinating—Oliver Cromwell, Lord Beaconsfield, Lincoln, Grace Darling—*there* was a heroine for you—General Booth, a great, good man, even if a little vulgar. She remembered dear old Miss Trimming talking about him one afternoon at the vicar of St Bride's garden party. She was so amusing. She . . . *Good heavens!*

Almost unwittingly, Millicent Bracegirdle had emitted a violent sneeze!

It was finished! For the second time that night she was conscious of her heart nearly stopping. For the second time that night she was so paralysed with fear that her mentality went to pieces. Now she would hear the man get out of bed. He would walk across to the door, switch on the light, and then lift up the frill. She could almost see that fierce moustached face glaring at her and growling something in French. Then he would thrust out an arm and drag her out. And then? O God in heaven! What then? . . .

'I shall scream before he does it. Perhaps I had better scream now. If he drags me out he will clap his hand over my mouth. Perhaps chloroform . . .'

But somehow she could not scream. She was too frightened even for that. She lifted the frill and listened. Was he moving stealthily across the carpet? She thought—no, she couldn't be sure. Anything might be happening. He might strike her from above—with one of those heavy boots perhaps. Nothing seemed to be happening, but the suspense was intolerable. She realized now that she hadn't the power to endure a night of it. Anything would be better than this—disgrace, imprisonment, even death. She would crawl out, wake the man, and try and explain as best she could.

She would switch on the light, cough, and say: '*Monsieur!*'

Then he would start up and stare at her.

Then she would say—what should she say?

'*Pardon, monsieur, mais je——*' What on earth was the French for 'I have made a mistake.'

'*J'ai tort. C'est la chambre*—er—*incorrect. Voulez-vous—er——*'

What was the French for 'door-knob,' 'let me go'?

It didn't matter. She would turn on the light, cough and trust to luck. If he got out of bed, and came toward her, she would scream the hotel down. . . .

The resolution formed, she crawled deliberately out at the foot of the bed. She scrambled hastily toward the door—a perilous journey. In a few seconds the room was flooded with light. She turned toward the bed, coughed, and cried out boldly:

'*Monsieur!*'

Then, for the third time that night, little Miss Bracegirdle's heart all but stopped. In this case the climax of the horror took longer to develop, but when it was reached, it clouded the other two experiences into insignificance.

The man on the bed was dead!

She had never beheld death before, but one does not mistake death.

She stared at him bewildered, and repeated almost in a whisper: '*Monsieur! . . . Monsieur!*'

Then she tiptoed toward the bed. The hair and moustache looked extraordinarily black in that grey, wax-like setting. The mouth was slightly open, and the face, which in life might have been vicious and sensual, looked incredibly peaceful and far away. It was as though she were regarding the features of a man across some vast passage of time, a being who had always been completely remote from mundane preoccupations.

When the full truth came home to her, little Miss Bracegirdle buried her face in her hands and murmured:

'Poor fellow . . . poor fellow!'

For the moment her own position seemed an affair of small consequence. She was in the presence of something greater and more all-pervading. Almost instinctively she knelt by the bed and prayed.

For a few moments she seemed to be possessed by an extraordinary calmness and detachment. The burden of her hotel predicament was a gossamer trouble—a silly, trivial, almost comic episode, something that could be explained away.

But this man—he had lived his life, whatever it was like, and now he was in the presence of his Maker. What kind of man had he been?

Her meditations were broken by an abrupt sound. It was that of a pair of heavy boots being thrown down by the door outside. She started, thinking at first it was someone knocking or trying to get in. She heard the 'boots,' however, stumping away down the corridor, and the realization stabbed her with the truth of her own position. She mustn't stop there. The necessity to get out was even more urgent.

To be found in a strange man's bedroom in the night is bad enough, but to be found in a dead man's bedroom was even worse. They could accuse her of murder, perhaps. Yes, that would be it—how could she possibly explain to these foreigners? Good God! they would hang her. No, guillotine her, that's what they do in France. They would chop her head off with a great steel knife. Merciful heavens! She envisaged herself standing blindfold, by a priest and an executioner in a red cap, like that man in the Dickens story—what was his name? . . . Sydney Carton, that was it, and before he went on the scaffold he said:

'It is a far, far better thing that I do than I have ever done.'

But no, she couldn't say that. It would be a far, far worse thing that she did. What about the dear dean? Her sister-in-law arriving alone from Paraguay tomorrow? All her dear people and friends in Easingstoke? Her darling Tony, the large grey tabby cat? It was her duty not to have her head chopped off if it could possibly be avoided. She could do no good in the room. She could not recall the dead to life. Her only mission was to escape. Any minute people might arrive. The chambermaid, the boots, the manager, the gendarmes. . . . Visions of gendarmes arriving armed with swords and note-books vitalized her almost exhausted energies. She was a desperate woman. Fortunately now she had not to worry about the light. She sprang once more at the door and tried to force it open with her fingers. The result hurt her and gave her pause. If she was to escape she must *think*, and think intensely. She mustn't do anything rash and silly, she must just think and plan calmly.

She examined the lock carefully. There was no keyhole, but there was a slip-bolt, so that the hotel guest could lock the door on the inside, but it couldn't be locked on the outside. Oh, why didn't this poor dear dead man lock his door last night? Then this trouble could not have happened. She could see the end of the steel pin. It was about half an inch down the hole. If any one was passing they must surely notice the handle sticking out too far the other side! She drew a hairpin out of her hair and tried to coax the pin back, but she only succeeded in pushing it a little farther in. She felt the colour leaving her face, and a strange feeling of faintness come over her.

She was fighting for her life, she mustn't give way. She darted round the room like an animal in a trap, her mind alert for the slightest crevice of escape. The window had no balcony and there was a drop of five stories to the street below. Dawn was breaking. Soon the activities of the hotel and the city would begin. The thing must be accomplished before then.

She went back once more and stared at the lock. She stared at the dead man's property, his razors, and brushes, and writing

materials, pens and pencils and rubber and sealing-wax. ...
Sealing-wax!

Necessity is truly the mother of invention. It is in any case quite
certain that Millicent Bracegirdle, who had never invented a thing
in her life, would never have evolved the ingenious little device she
did, had she not believed that her position was utterly desperate.
For in the end this is what she did. She got together a box of
matches, a candle, a bar of sealing-wax, and a hairpin. She made a
little pool of hot sealing-wax, into which she dipped the end of the
hairpin. Collecting a small blob on the end of it she thrust it into
the hole, and let it adhere to the end of the steel pin. At the seventh
attempt she got the thing to move. It took her just an hour and ten
minutes to get that steel pin back into the room, and when at
length it came far enough through for her to grip it with her
finger-nails, she burst into tears through the sheer physical tension of the strain. Very, very carefully she pulled it through, and
holding it firmly with her left hand she fixed the knob with her
right, then slowly turned it. The door opened!

The temptation to dash out into the corridor and scream with
relief was almost irresistible, but she forbore. She listened; she
peeped out. No one was about. With beating heart, she went out,
closing the door inaudibly. She crept like a little mouse to the
room next door, stole in and flung herself on her bed. Immediately
she did so it flashed through her mind that *she had left her
sponge-bag and towel in the dead man's room*!

In looking back upon her experience she always considered that
that second expedition was the worst of all. She might have left
the sponge-bag and towel there, only that the towel—she never
used hotel towels—had neatly inscribed in the corner 'M.B.'

With furtive caution she managed to retrace her steps. She
re-entered the dead man's room, reclaimed her property, and
returned to her own. When this mission was accomplished she
was indeed well nigh spent. She lay on her bed and groaned feebly.
At last she feel into a fevered sleep. ...

It was eleven o'clock when she awoke and no one had been to
disturb her. The sun was shining, and the experiences of the night
appeared a dubious nightmare. Surely she had dreamt it all?

With dread still burning in her heart she rang the bell. After a short interval of time the chambermaid appeared. The girl's eyes were bright with some uncontrollable excitement. No, she had not been dreaming. This girl had heard something.

'Will you bring me some tea, please?'

'Certainly, madame.'

The maid drew back the curtains and fussed about the room. She was under a pledge of secrecy, but she could contain herself no longer. Suddenly she approached the bed and whispered excitedly:

'Oh, madame, I have promised not to tell . . . but a terrible thing has happened. A man, a dead man, has been found in room 117—a guest. Please not to say I tell you. But they have all been there, the gendarmes, the doctors, the inspectors. Oh, it is terrible . . . terrible.'

The little lady in the bed said nothing. There was indeed nothing to say. But Marie Louise Lancret was too full of emotional excitement to spare her.

'But the terrible thing is—— Do you know who he was, madame? They say it is Boldhu, the man wanted for the murder of Jeanne Carreton in the barn at Vincennes. They say he strangled her, and then cut her up in pieces and hid her in two barrels which he threw into the river. . . . Oh, but he was a bad man, madame, a terrible bad man . . . and he died in the room next door . . . suicide, they think; or was it an attack of the heart? . . . Remorse, some shock perhaps. . . . Did you say a *café complet*, madame?'

'No, thank you, my dear . . . just a cup of tea . . . strong tea . . .'

'*Parfaitement*, madame.'

The girl retired, and a little later a waiter entered the room with a tray of tea. She could never get over her surprise at this. It seemed so—well, indecorous for a man—although only a waiter—to enter a lady's bedroom. There was no doubt a great deal in what the dear dean said. They were certainly very peculiar, these French people—they had most peculiar notions. It was not the way they behaved at Easingstoke. She got farther under the sheets, but the waiter appeared quite indifferent to the situation. He put the tray down and retired.

When he had gone she sat up and sipped her tea, which gradually warmed her. She was glad the sun was shining. She would have to get up soon. They said that her sister-in-law's boat was due to berth at one o'clock. That would give her time to dress comfortably, write to her brother, and then go down to the docks. Poor man! So he had been a murderer, a man who cut up the bodies of his victims . . . and she had spent the night in his bedroom! They were certainly a most—how could she describe it?—people. Nevertheless she felt a little glad that at the end she had been there to kneel and pray by his bedside. Probably nobody else had ever done that. It was very difficult to judge people. . . . Something at some time might have gone wrong. He might not have murdered the woman after all. People were often wrongly convicted. She herself . . . If the police had found her in that room at three o'clock that morning . . . It is that which takes place in the heart which counts. One learns and learns. Had she not learnt that one can pray just as effectively lying under a bed as kneeling beside it? . . . Poor man!

She washed and dressed herself and walked calmly down to the writing-room. There was no evidence of excitement among the other hotel guests. Probably none of them knew about the tragedy except herself. She went to a writing-table, and after profound meditation wrote as follows:

'My dear Brother,

'I arrived late last night after a very pleasant journey. Every one was very kind and attentive, the manager was sitting up for me. I nearly lost my spectacle case in the restaurant car! But a kind old gentleman found it and returned it to me. There was a most amusing American child on the train. I will tell you about her on my return. The people are very pleasant, but the food is peculiar, nothing *plain and wholesome*. I am going down to meet Annie at one o'clock. How have you been keeping, my dear? I hope you have not had any further return of the bronchial attacks.

'Please tell Lizzie that I remembered in the train on the way here that that large stone jar of marmalade that Mrs Hunt made is behind those empty tins in the top shelf of the cupboard next to the coach-house. I wonder

whether Mrs Butler was able to come to evensong after
all? This is a nice hotel, but I think Annie and I will stay
at the 'Grand' tonight, as the bedrooms here are rather
noisy. Well, my dear, nothing more till I return. Do take
care of yourself.—Your loving sister,

'Millicent.'

Yes, she couldn't tell Peter about it, neither in the letter nor
when she went back to him. It was her duty not to tell him. It
would only distress him; she felt convinced of it. In this curious
foreign atmosphere the thing appeared possible, but in Easingstoke the mere recounting of the fantastic situations would be
positively . . . indelicate. There was no escaping that broad
general fact—she had spent a night in a strange man's bedroom.
Whether he was a gentleman or a criminal, even whether he was
dead or alive, did not seem to mitigate the jar upon her sensibi-
lities, or rather it would not mitigate the jar upon the peculiarly
sensitive relationship between her brother and herself. To say that
she had been to the bathroom, the knob of the door-handle came
off in her hand, she was too frightened to awaken the sleeper or
scream, she got under the bed—well, it was all perfectly true. Peter
would believe her, but—one simply could not conceive such a
situation in Easingstoke deanery. It would create a curious little
barrier between them, as though she had been dipped in some
mysterious solution which alienated her. It was her duty not to tell.

She put on her hat, and went out to post the letter. She dis-
trusted a hotel letter-box. One never knew who handled these
letters. It was not a proper official way of treating them. She
walked to the head post office in Bordeaux.

The sun was shining. It was very pleasant walking about
amongst these queer excitable people, so foreign and different-
looking—and the cafés already crowded with chattering men and
women, and the flower stalls, and the strange odour of—what was
it? Salt? Brine? Charcoal? . . . A military band was playing in the
square . . . very gay and moving. It was all life, and movement,
and bustle . . . thrilling rather.

'I spent a night in a strange man's bedroom.'

Little Miss Bracegirdle hunched her shoulders, murmured to herself, and walked faster. She reached the post office and found the large metal plate with the slot for letters and 'R.F.' stamped above it. Something official at last! Her face was a little flushed— was it the warmth of the day or the contact of movement and life?—as she put her letter into the slot. After posting it she put her hand into the slot and flicked it round to see that there were no foreign contraptions to impede its safe delivery. No, the letter had dropped safely in. She sighed contentedly and walked off in the direction of the docks to meet her sister-in-law from Paraguay.

KATHERINE MANSFIELD

The Garden Party

And after all the weather was ideal. They could not have had a more perfect day for a garden party if they had ordered it. Windless, warm, the sky without a cloud. Only the blue was veiled with a haze of light gold, as it is sometimes in early summer.

The gardener had been up since dawn, mowing the lawns and sweeping them, until the grass and the dark flat rosettes where the daisy plants had been seemed to shine. As for the roses, you could not help feeling they understood that roses are the only flowers that impress people at garden parties; the only flowers that everybody is certain of knowing. Hundreds, yes, literally hundreds, had come out in a single night; the green bushes bowed down as though they had been visited by archangels.

Breakfast was not yet over before the men came to put up the marquee.

'Where do you want the marquee put, mother?'

'My dear child, it's no use asking me. I'm determined to leave everything to you children this year. Forget I am your mother. Treat me as an honoured guest.'

But Meg could not possibly go and supervise the men. She had washed her hair before breakfast, and she sat drinking her coffee in a green turban, with a dark wet curl stamped on each cheek. Jose, the butterfly, always came down in a silk petticoat and a kimono jacket.

'You'll have to go, Laura; you're the artistic one.'

Away Laura flew, still holding her piece of bread-and-butter. It's so delicious to have an excuse for eating out of doors, and besides, she loved having to arrange things; she always felt she could do it so much better than anybody else.

Four men in their shirt-sleeves stood grouped together on the garden path. They carried staves covered with rolls of canvas, and they had big tool-bags slung on their backs. They looked impressive. Laura wished now that she was not holding that piece of bread-and-butter, but there was nowhere to put it, and she couldn't possibly throw it away. She blushed and tried to look severe and even a little bit short-sighted as she came up to them.

'Good morning,' she said, copying her mother's voice. But that sounded so fearfully affected that she was ashamed, and stammered like a little girl, 'Oh—er—have you come—is it about the marquee?'

'That's right, miss,' said the tallest of the men, a lanky, freckled fellow, and he shifted his tool-bag, knocked back his straw hat, and smiled down at her. 'That's about it.'

His smile was so easy, so friendly, that Laura recovered. What nice eyes he had, small, but such a dark blue! And now she looked at the others, they were smiling too. 'Cheer up, we won't bite,' their smile seemed to say. How very nice workmen were! And what a beautiful morning! She mustn't mention the morning; she must be business-like. The marquee.

'Well, what about the lily-lawn? Would that do?'

And she pointed to the lily-lawn with the hand that didn't hold the bread-and-butter. They turned, they stared in the direction. A little fat chap thrust out his under-lip, and the tall fellow frowned.

'I don't fancy it,' said he. 'Not conspicuous enough. You see, with a thing like a marquee,' and he turned to Laura in his easy way, 'you want to put it somewhere where it'll give you a bang slap in the eye, if you follow me.'

Laura's upbringing made her wonder for a moment whether it was quite respectful of a workman to talk to her of bangs slap in the eye. But she did quite follow him.

'A corner of the tennis-court,' she suggested. 'But the band's going to be in one corner.'

'H'm, going to have a band, are you?' said another of the workmen. He was pale. He had a haggard look as his dark eyes scanned the tennis-court. What was he thinking?

'Only a very small band,' said Laura gently. Perhaps he wouldn't mind so much if the band was quite small. But the tall fellow interrupted.

'Look here, miss, that's the place. Against those trees. Over there. That'll do fine.'

Against the karakas. Then the karaka-trees would be hidden. And they were so lovely, with their broad, gleaming leaves, and their clusters of yellow fruit. They were like trees you imagined growing on a desert island, proud, solitary, lifting their leaves and fruits to the sun in a kind of silent splendour. Must they be hidden by a marquee?

They must. Already the men had shouldered their staves and were making for the place. Only the tall fellow was left. He bent down, pinched a sprig of lavender, put his thumb and forefinger to his nose and snuffed up the smell. When Laura saw that gesture she forgot all about the karakas in her wonder at him caring for things like that—caring for the smell of lavender. How many men that she knew would have done such a thing? Oh, how extraordinarily nice workmen were, she thought. Why couldn't she have workmen for friends rather than the silly boys she danced with and who came to Sunday night supper? She would get on much better with men like these.

It's all the fault, she decided, as the tall fellow drew something on the back of an envelope, something that was to be looped up or left to hang, of these absurd class distinctions. Well, for her part, she didn't feel them. Not a bit, not an atom. . . . And now there came the chock-chock of wooden hammers. Someone whistled, someone sang out, 'Are you right there, matey?' 'Matey!' The friendliness of it, the—the— Just to prove how happy she was, just to show the tall fellow how at home she felt, and how she despised stupid conventions, Laura took a big bite of her bread-and-butter as she stared at the little drawing. She felt just like a work-girl.

'Laura, Laura, where are you? Telephone, Laura!' a voice cried from the house.

'Coming!' Away she skimmed, over the lawn, up the path, up the steps, across the veranda, and into the porch. In the hall her father and Laurie were brushing their hats ready to go to the office.

'I say, Laura,' said Laurie very fast, 'you might just give a squiz at my coat before this afternoon. See if it wants pressing.'

'I will,' said she. Suddenly she couldn't stop herself. She ran at Laurie and gave him a small, quick squeeze. 'Oh, I do love parties, don't you?' gasped Laura.

'Rather,' said Laurie's warm, boyish voice, and he squeezed his sister too, and gave her a gentle push. 'Dash off to the telephone, old girl.'

The telephone. 'Yes, yes; oh, yes. Kitty? Good morning, dear. Come to lunch? Do, dear. Delighted of course. It will only be a very scratch meal—just the sandwich crusts and broken meringue-shells and what's left over. Yes, isn't it a perfect morning? Your white? Oh, I certainly should. One moment—hold the line. Mother's calling.' And Laura sat back. 'What, mother? Can't hear.'

Mrs Sheridan's voice floated down the stairs. 'Tell her to wear that sweet hat she had on last Sunday.'

'Mother says you're to wear that *sweet* hat you had on last Sunday. Good. One o'clock. Bye-bye.'

Laura put back the receiver, flung her arms over her head, took a deep breath, stretched and let them fall. 'Huh,' she sighed, and the moment after the sigh she sat up quickly. She was still, listening. All the doors in the house seemed to be open. The house was alive with soft, quick steps and running voices. The green baize door that led to the kitchen regions swung open and shut with a muffled thud. And now there came a long, chuckling, absurd sound. It was the heavy piano being moved on its stiff castors. But the air! If you stopped to notice, was the air always like this? Little faint winds were playing chase in at the tops of the windows, out at the doors. And there were two tiny spots of sun, one on the inkpot, one on a silver photograph frame, playing too. Darling little spots. Especially the one on the inkpot lid. It was quite warm. A warm little silver star. She could have kissed it.

The front door bell pealed, and there sounded the rustle of Sadie's print skirt on the stairs. A man's voice murmured; Sadie answered, careless, 'I'm sure I don't know. Wait. I'll ask Mrs Sheridan.'

'What is it, Sadie?' Laura came into the hall.

'It's the florist, Miss Laura.'

It was, indeed. There, just inside the door, stood a wide,

shallow tray full of pots of pink lilies. No other kind. Nothing but lilies—canna lilies, big pink flowers, wide open, radiant, almost frighteningly alive on bright crimson stems.

'O-oh, Sadie!' said Laura, and the sound was like a little moan. She crouched down as if to warm herself at that blaze of lilies; she felt they were in her fingers, on her lips, growing in her breast.

'It's some mistake,' she said faintly. 'Nobody ever ordered so many. Sadie, go and find mother.'

But at that moment Mrs Sheridan joined them.

'It's quite right,' she said calmly. 'Yes, I ordered them. Aren't they lovely?' She pressed Laura's arm. 'I was passing the shop yesterday, and I saw them in the window. And I suddenly thought for once in my life I shall have enough canna lilies. The garden-party will be a good excuse.'

'But I thought you said you didn't mean to interfere,' said Laura. Sadie had gone. The florist's man was still outside at his van. She put her arm round her mother's neck and gently, very gently, she bit her mother's ear.

'My darling child, you wouldn't like a logical mother, would you? Don't do that. Here's the man.'

He carried more lilies still, another whole tray.

'Bank them up, just inside the door, on both sides of the porch, please,' said Mrs Sheridan. 'Don't you agree, Laura?'

'Oh, I *do*, mother.'

In the drawing-room Meg, Jose, and good little Hans had at last succeeded in moving the piano.

'Now, if we put this chesterfield against the wall and move everything out of the room except the chairs, don't you think?'

'Quite.'

'Hans, move these tables into the smoking-room, and bring a sweeper to take these marks off the carpet and—one moment, Hans——' Jose loved giving orders to the servants, and they loved obeying her. She always made them feel they were taking part in some drama. 'Tell mother and Miss Laura to come here at once.'

'Very good, Miss Jose.'

She turned to Meg. 'I want to hear what the piano sounds like, just in case I'm asked to sing this afternoon. Let's try over *This Life is Weary*.'

Pom! Ta-ta-ta *Tee*-ta! The piano burst out so passionately that Jose's face changed. She clasped her hands. She looked mournfully and enigmatically at her mother and Laura as they came in.

> This Life is *Wee*-ary,
> A Tear—a Sigh.
> A Love that *Chan*-ges,
>   This Life is *Wee*-ary,
> A Tear—a Sigh.
> A Love that *Chan*-ges,
> And then . . . Good-bye!

But at the word 'Good-bye,' and although the piano sounded more desperate than ever, her face broke into a brilliant, dreadfully unsympathetic smile.

'Aren't I in good voice, mummy?' she beamed.

> This Life is *Wee*-ary,
> Hope comes to Die.
> A Dream—a *Wa*-kening.

But now Sadie interrupted them. 'What is it, Sadie?'

'If you please, m'm, cook says have you got the flags for the sandwiches?'

'The flags for the sandwiches, Sadie?' echoed Mrs Sheridan dreamily. And the children knew by her face that she hadn't got them. 'Let me see.' And she said to Sadie firmly, 'Tell cook I'll let her have them in ten minutes.'

Sadie went.

'Now, Laura,' said her mother quickly, 'come with me into the smoking-room. I've got the names somewhere on the back of an envelope. You'll have to write them out for me. Meg, go upstairs this minute and take that wet thing off your head. Jose, run and finish dressing this instant. Do you hear me, children, or shall I have to tell your father when he comes home tonight? And—and, Jose, pacify cook if you do go into the kitchen, will you? I'm terrified of her this morning.'

The envelope was found at last behind the dining-room clock, though how it had got there Mrs Sheridan could not imagine.

'One of you children must have stolen it out of my bag, because

I remember vividly—— Cream-cheese and lemon-curd. Have you done that?'

'Yes.'

'Egg and——' Mrs Sheridan held the envelope away from her. 'It looks like mice. It can't be mice, can it?'

'Olive, pet,' said Laura, looking over her shoulder.

'Yes, of course, olive. What a horrible combination it sounds. Egg and olive.'

They were finished at last, and Laura took them off to the kitchen. She found Jose there pacifying the cook, who did not look at all terrifying.

'I have never seen such exquisite sandwiches,' said Jose's rapturous voice. 'How many kinds did you say there were, cook? Fifteen?'

'Fifteen, Miss Jose.'

'Well, cook, I congratulate you.'

Cook swept up crusts with the long sandwich knife, and smiled broadly.

'Godber's has come,' announced Sadie, issuing out of the pantry. She had seen the man pass the window.

That meant the cream puffs had come. Godber's were famous for their cream puffs. Nobody ever thought of making them at home.

'Bring them in and put them on the table, my girl,' ordered cook.

Sadie brought them in and went back to the door. Of course Laura and Jose were far too grown-up to really care about such things. All the same, they couldn't help agreeing that the puffs looked very attractive. Very. Cook began arranging them, shaking off the extra icing sugar.

'Don't they carry one back to all one's parties?' said Laura.

'I suppose they do,' said practical Jose, who never liked to be carried back. 'They look beautifully light and feathery, I must say.'

'Have one each, my dears,' said cook in her comfortable voice. 'Yer ma won't know.'

Oh, impossible. Fancy cream puffs so soon after breakfast. The very idea made one shudder. All the same, two minutes later Jose and Laura were licking their fingers with that absorbed inward look that only comes from whipped cream.

'Let's go into the garden, out by the back way,' suggested Laura. 'I want to see how the men are getting on with the marquee. They're such awfully nice men.'

But the back door was blocked by cook, Sadie, Godber's man and Hans.

Something had happened.

'Tuk-tuk-tuk,' clucked cook like an agitated hen. Sadie had her hand clapped to her cheek as though she had toothache. Hans's face was screwed up in the effort to understand. Only Godber's man seemed to be enjoying himself; it was his story.

'What's the matter? What's happened?'

'There's been a horrible accident,' said cook. 'A man killed.'

'A man killed! Where? How? When?'

But Godber's man wasn't going to have his story snatched from under his very nose.

'Know those little cottages just below here, miss?'

Know them? Of course, she knew them. 'Well, there's a young chap living there, name of Scott, a carter. His horse shied at a traction-engine, corner of Hawke Street this morning, and he was thrown out on the back of his head. Killed.'

'Dead!' Laura stared at Godber's man.

'Dead when they picked him up,' said Godber's man with relish. 'They were taking the body home as I come up here.' And he said to the cook, 'He's left a wife and five little ones.'

'Jose, come here.' Laura caught hold of her sister's sleeve and dragged her through the kitchen to the other side of the green baize door. There she paused and leaned against it. 'Jose!' she said, horrified, 'however are we going to stop everything?'

'Stop everything, Laura!' cried Jose in astonishment. 'What do you mean?'

'Stop the garden party, of course.' Why did Jose pretend?

But Jose was still more amazed. 'Stop the garden party? My dear Laura, don't be so absurd. Of course we can't do anything of the kind. Nobody expects us to. Don't be so extravagant.'

'But we can't possibly have a garden party with a man dead just outside the front gate.'

That really was extravagant, for the little cottages were in a lane to themselves at the very bottom of a steep rise that led up to the house. A broad road ran between. True, they were far too near. They were the greatest possible eyesore, and they had no right to be in that neighbourhood at all. They were little mean dwellings painted a chocolate brown. In the garden patches there was nothing but cabbage stalks, sick hens and tomato cans. The very smoke coming out of their chimneys was poverty-stricken. Little rags and shreds of smoke, so unlike the great silvery plumes that uncurled from the Sheridans' chimneys. Washerwomen lived in the lane and sweeps and a cobbler, and a man whose house-front was studded all over with minute bird-cages. Children swarmed. When the Sheridans were little they were forbidden to set foot there because of the revolting language and of what they might catch. But since they were grown up, Laura and Laurie on their prowls sometimes walked through. It was disgusting and sordid. They came out with a shudder. But still one must go everywhere; one must see everything. So through they went.

'And just think of what the band would sound like to that poor woman,' said Laura.

'Oh, Laura!' Jose began to be seriously annoyed. 'If you're going to stop a band playing every time someone has an accident, you'll lead a very strenuous life. I'm every bit as sorry about it as you. I feel just as sympathetic.' Her eyes hardened. She looked at her sister just as she used to when they were little and fighting together. 'You won't bring a drunken workman back to life by being sentimental,' she said softly.

'Drunk! Who said he was drunk?' Laura turned furiously on Jose. She said just as they had used to say on those occasions, 'I'm going straight up to tell mother.'

'Do, dear,' cooed Jose.

'Mother, can I come into your room?' Laura turned the big glass door-knob.

'Of course, child. Why, what's the matter? What's given you such a colour?' And Mrs Sheridan turned round from her dressing-table. She was trying on a new hat.

'Mother, a man's been killed,' began Laura.

'*Not* in the garden?' interrupted her mother.

'No, no!'

'Oh, what a fright you gave me!' Mrs Sheridan sighed with relief, and took off the big hat and held it on her knees.

'But listen, mother,' said Laura. Breathless, half-choking, she told the dreadful story. 'Of course, we can't have our party, can we?' she pleaded. 'The band and everybody arriving. They'd hear us, mother; they're nearly neighbours!'

To Laura's astonishment her mother behaved just like Jose; it was harder to bear because she seemed amused. She refused to take Laura seriously.

'But, my dear child, use your common sense. It's only by accident we've heard of it. If someone had died there normally— and I can't understand how they keep alive in those poky little holes—we should still be having our party, shouldn't we?'

Laura had to say 'yes' to that, but she felt it was all wrong. She sat down on her mother's sofa and pinched the cushion frill.

'Mother, isn't it really terribly heartless of us?' she asked.

'Darling!' Mrs Sheridan got up and come over to her, carrying the hat. Before Laura could stop her she had popped it on. 'My child!' said her mother, 'the hat is yours. It's made for you. It's much too young for me. I have never seen you look such a picture. Look at yourself!' And she held up her hand-mirror.

'But, mother,' Laura began again. She couldn't look at herself; she turned aside.

This time Mrs Sheridan lost patience just as Jose had done.

'You are being very absurd, Laura,' she said coldly. 'People like that don't expect sacrifices from us. And it's not very sympathetic to spoil everybody's enjoyment as you're doing now.'

'I don't understand,' said Laura, and she walked quickly out of the room into her own bedroom. There, quite by chance, the first thing she saw was this charming girl in the mirror, in her black hat trimmed with gold daisies, and a long black velvet ribbon. Never had she imagined she could look like that. Is mother right? she thought. And now she hoped her mother was right. Am I being extravagant? Perhaps it was extravagant. Just for a moment she had another glimpse of that poor woman and those little children, and the body being carried into the house. But it all seemed blurred, unreal, like a picture in the newspaper. I'll remember it again after the party's over, she decided. And somehow that seemed quite the best plan. . . .

Lunch was over by half-past one. By half-past two they were all ready for the fray. The green-coated band had arrived and was established in a corner of the tennis-court.

'My dear!' trilled Kitty Maitland, 'aren't they too like frogs for words? You ought to have arranged them round the pond with the conductor in the middle on a leaf.'

Laurie arrived and hailed them on his way to dress. At the sight of him Laura remembered the accident again. She wanted to tell him. If Laurie agreed with the others, then it was bound to be all right. And she followed him into the hall.

'Laurie!'

'Hallo!' He was half-way upstairs, but when he turned round and saw Laura he suddenly puffed out his cheeks and goggled his eyes at her. 'My word, Laura! You do look stunning,' said Laurie. 'What an absolutely topping hat!'

Laura said faintly 'Is it?' and smiled up at Laurie, and didn't tell him after all.

Soon after that people began coming in streams. The band struck up; the hired waiters ran from the house to the marquee. Wherever you looked there were couples, strolling, bending to the flowers, greeting, moving on over the lawn. They were like bright birds that had alighted in the Sheridans' garden for this one afternoon, on their way to—where? Ah, what happiness it is to be with people who are all happy, to press hands, press cheeks, smile into eyes.

'Darling Laura, how well you look!'

'What a becoming hat, child!'

'Laura, you look quite Spanish. I've never seen you look so striking.'

And Laura, glowing, answered softly, 'Have you had tea? Won't you have an ice? The passion-fruit ices really are rather special.' She ran to her father and begged him. 'Daddy darling, can't the band have something to drink?'

And the perfect afternoon slowly ripened, slowly faded, slowly its petals closed.

'Never a more delightful garden party . . .' 'The greatest success . . .' 'Quite the most . . .'

Laura helped her mother with the good-byes. They stood side by side in the porch till it was all over.

'All over, all over, thank heaven,' said Mrs Sheridan. 'Round up the others, Laura. Let's go and have some fresh coffee. I'm exhausted. Yes, it's been very successful. But oh, these parties, these parties! Why will you children insist on giving parties!' And they all of them sat down in the deserted marquee.

'Have a sandwich, daddy dear. I wrote the flag.'

'Thanks.' Mr Sheridan took a bite and the sandwich was gone. He took another. 'I suppose you didn't hear of a beastly accident that happened today?' he said.

'My dear,' said Mrs Sheridan, holding up her hand, 'we did. It nearly ruined the party. Laura insisted we should put it off.'

'Oh, mother!' Laura didn't want to be teased about it.

'It was a horrible affair all the same,' said Mr Sheridan. 'The chap was married too. Lived just below in the lane, and leaves a wife and half a dozen kiddies, so they say.'

An awkward little silence fell. Mrs Sheridan fidgeted with her cup. Really, it was very tactless of father. . . .

Suddenly she looked up. There on the table were all those sandwiches, cakes, puffs, all uneaten, all going to be wasted. She had one of her brilliant ideas.

'I know,' she said. 'Let's make up a basket. Let's send that poor creature some of this perfectly good food. At any rate, it will be the greatest treat for the children. Don't you agree? And she's sure to have neighbours calling in and so on. What a point to have it all ready prepared. Laura!' She jumped up. 'Get me the big basket out of the stairs cupboard.'

'But, mother, do you really think it's a good idea?' said Laura.

Again, how curious, she seemed to be different from them all. To take scraps from their party. Would the poor woman really like that?

'Of course! What's the matter with you today? An hour or two ago you were insisting on us being sympathetic, and now——'

Oh, well! Laura ran for the basket. It was filled, it was heaped by her mother.

'Take it yourself, darling,' said she. 'Run down just as you are.

No, wait, take the arum lilies too. People of that class are so impressed by arum lilies.'

'The stems will ruin her lace frock,' said practical Jose.

So they would. Just in time. 'Only the basket, then. And, Laura!'—her mother followed her out of the marquee—'don't on any account——'

'What mother?'

No, better not put such ideas into the child's head! 'Nothing! Run along.'

It was just growing dusky as Laura shut their garden gates. A big dog ran by like a shadow. The road gleamed white, and down below in the hollow the little cottages were in deep shade. How quiet it seemed after the afternoon. Here she was going down the hill to somewhere where a man lay dead, and she couldn't realize it. Why couldn't she? She stopped a minute. And it seemed to her that kisses, voices, tinkling spoons, laughter, the smell of crushed grass were somehow inside her. She had no room for anything else. How strange! She looked up at the pale sky, and all she thought was, 'Yes, it was the most successful party.'

Now the broad road was crossed. The lane began, smoky and dark. Women in shawls and men's tweed caps hurried by. Men hung over the palings; the children played in the doorways. A low hum came from the mean little cottages. In some of them there was a flicker of light, and a shadow, crab-like, moved across the window. Laura bent her head and hurried on. She wished now she had put on a coat. How her frock shone! And the big hat with the velvet streamer—if only it was another hat! Were the people looking at her? They must be. It was a mistake to have come; she knew all along it was a mistake. Should she go back even now?

No, too late. This was the house. It must be. A dark knot of people stood outside. Beside the gate an old, old woman with a crutch sat in a chair, watching. She had her feet on a newspaper. The voices stopped as Laura drew near. The group parted. It was as though she was expected, as though they had known she was coming here.

Laura was terribly nervous. Tossing the velvet ribbon over her shoulder, she said to a woman standing by, 'Is this Mrs Scott's house?' and the woman, smiling queerly, said, 'It is, my lass.'

Oh, to be away from this! She actually said, 'Help me, God,' as she walked up the tiny path and knocked. To be away from those staring eyes, or to be covered up in anything, one of those women's shawls even. I'll just leave the basket and go, she decided. I shan't even wait for it to be emptied.

Then the door opened. A little woman in black showed in the gloom.

Laura said, 'Are you Mrs Scott?' But to her horror the woman answered, 'Walk in, please, miss,' and she was shut in the passage.

'No,' said Laura, 'I don't want to come in. I only want to leave this basket. Mother sent——'

The little woman in the gloomy passage seemed not to have heard her. 'Step this way, please, miss,' she said in an oily voice, and Laura followed her.

She found herself in a wretched little low kitchen, lighted by a smoky lamp. There was a woman sitting before the fire.

'Em,' said the little creature who had let her in. 'Em! It's a young lady.' She turned to Laura. She said meaningly, 'I'm 'er sister, miss. You'll excuse 'er, won't you?'

'Oh, but of course!' said Laura. 'Please, please don't disturb her. I—I only want to leave——'

But at that moment the woman at the fire turned round. Her face, puffed up, red, with swollen eyes and swollen lips, looked terrible. She seemed as though she couldn't understand why Laura was there. What did it mean? Why was this stranger standing in the kitchen with a basket? What was it all about? And the poor face puckered up again.

'All right, my dear,' said the other. 'I'll thenk the young lady.'

And again she began, 'You'll excuse her, miss, I'm sure,' and her face, swollen too, tried an oily smile.

Laura only wanted to get out, to get away. She was back in the passage. The door opened. She walked straight through into the bedroom, where the dead man was lying.

'You'd like a look at 'im, wouldn't you?' said Em's sister, and she brushed past Laura over to the bed. 'Don't be afraid, my lass'—and now her voice sounded fond and sly, and fondly she drew down the sheet—' 'e looks a picture. There's nothing to show. Come along, my dear.'

Laura came.

There lay a young man, fast asleep—sleeping so soundly, so deeply, that he was far, far away from them both. Oh, so remote, so peaceful. He was dreaming. Never wake him up again. His head was sunk in the pillow, his eyes were closed; they were blind under the closed eyelids. He was given up to his dream. What did garden parties and baskets and lace frocks matter to him? He was far from all those things. He was wonderful, beautiful. While they were laughing and while the band was playing, this marvel had come to the lane. Happy . . . happy. . . . All is well, said that sleeping face. This is just as it should be. I am content.

But all the same you had to cry, and she couldn't go out of the room without saying something to him. Laura gave a loud childish sob.

'Forgive my hat,' she said.

And this time she didn't wait for Em's sister. She found her way out of the door, down the path, past all those dark people. At the corner of the lane she met Laurie.

He stepped out of the shadow. 'Is that you, Laura?'

'Yes.'

'Mother was getting anxious. Was it all right?'

'Yes, quite. Oh, Laurie!' She took his arm, she pressed up against him.

'I say, you're not crying, are you?' asked her brother.

Laura shook her head. She was.

Laurie put his arm round her shoulder. 'Don't cry,' he said in his warm, loving voice. 'Was it awful?'

'No,' sobbed Laura. 'It was simply marvellous. But, Laurie——' She stopped, she looked at her brother. 'Isn't life,' she stammered, isn't life——' But what life was she couldn't explain. No matter. He quite understood.

'*Isn't it*, darling?' said Laurie.

STELLA BENSON

The Desert Islander

Constantine hopefully followed the Chinese servant through the unknown house. He felt hopeful of success in his plan of begging this Englishman for help, for he knew that an Englishman, alone among people of a different colour (as this Englishman was alone in this South China town), treated the helping of stray white men almost as part of the White Man's Burden. But even without this claim of one lonely white man upon another, Constantine would have felt hopeful. He knew himself to be a man of compelling manner in spite of his ugly, too long face, and his ugly, too short legs.

As Constantine stumped in on his hobnailed soles, Mr White—who was evidently not a very tactful man—said, 'Oh, are you *another* deserter from the Foreign Legion?'

'I am Constantine Andreievitch Soloviev,' said Constantine, surprised. He spoke and understood English almost perfectly (his mother had been English), yet he could not remember ever having heard the word *another* applied to himself. In fact it did not—could not possibly—so apply. There was only one of him, he knew.

Of course, in a way there was some sense in what this stupid Englishman said. Constantine had certainly been a *légionnaire* in Tonkin up till last Thursday—his narrow pipe-clayed helmet, stiff khaki greatcoat, shabby drill uniform, puttees, brass buttons, and inflexible boots were all the property of the French Government. But the core—the pearl inside this vulgar, horny shell—was Constantine Andreievitch Soloviev. That made all the difference.

Constantine saw that he must take this Didymus of an Englishman in hand at once and tell him a few exciting stories about his dangerous adventures between the Tonkin border and this Chinese city. Snakes, tigers, love-crazed Chinese princesses and brigands passed rapidly through his mind, and he chose the last, because he had previously planned several impressive things to do if he should be attacked by brigands. So now, though he had not actually met a brigand, those plans would come in useful. Constantine intended to write his autobiography some day when he should have married a rich wife and settled down. Not only did his actual life seem to him a very rare one but, also, lives were so interesting to make up.

Constantine was a desert islander—a spiritual Robinson Crusoe. He made up everything himself and he wasted nothing. *Robinson Crusoe* was his favourite book—in fact, almost the only book he had ever read—and he was proud to be, like his hero, a desert islander. He actually preferred clothing his spirit in the skins of wild thoughts that had been the prey of his wits and sheltering it from the world's weather in a leaky hut of his brain's own contriving, to enjoying the good tailoring and housing that dwellers on the mainland call experience and education. He enjoyed being barbarous, he enjoyed living alone on his island, accepting nothing, imitating nothing, believing nothing, adapting himself to nothing—implacably home-made. Even his tangible possessions were those of a marooned man rather than of a civilized citizen of this well-furnished world. At this moment his only luggage was a balalaika that he had made himself out of cigar-boxes, and to this he sang songs of his own composition— very imperfect songs. He would not have claimed that either his songs or his instrument were better than the songs and instruments made by song-makers and balalaika-makers; they were, however, much more rapturously *his* than any acquired music could have been and, indeed, in this as in almost all things, it simply never occurred to him to *take* rather than *make*. There was no mainland on the horizon of his desert island.

'I am not a beggar,' said Constantine. 'Until yesterday I had sixty piastres which I had saved by many sacrifices during my service in the Legion. But yesterday, passing through a dark forest of pines in the twilight, about twenty versts from here, I met——'

'You met a band of brigands,' said Mr White. 'Yes, I know . . . you all say that.'

Constantine stared at him. He had not lived, a desert islander, in a crowded and over-civilized world without meeting many rebuffs, so this one did not surprise him—did not even offend him. On the contrary, for a minute he almost loved the uncompromising Mr White, as a sportsman almost loves the chamois on a peculiarly inaccessible crag. This was a friend worth a good deal of trouble to secure, Constantine saw. He realized at once that the desert islander's line here was to discard the brigands and to discard noble independence.

'Very well then,' said Constantine. 'I did *not* meet brigands. I *am* a beggar. I started without a penny and I still have no penny. I hope you will give me something. That is why I have come.' He paused, drawing long pleased breaths through his large nose. This, he felt, was a distinctly self-made line of talk; it set him apart from all previous deserting *légionnaires*.

Mr White evidently thought so too. He gave a short grunting laugh. 'That's better,' he said.

'These English,' thought Constantine lovingly. 'They are the next best thing to *being* originals, for they *admire* originals.' 'I like you,' he added extravagantly, aloud. 'I like the English. I am so glad I found an Englishman to beg of instead of an American— though an American would have been much richer than you are, I expect. Still, to a beggar a little is enough. I dislike Americans; I dislike their women's wet finger-nails.'

'Wet finger-nails?' exclaimed Mr White. 'Oh, you mean their manicure polishes. Yes . . . they *do* always have wet finger-nails . . . ha, ha . . . so they do. I should never have thought of that myself.'

'Of course not,' said Constantine, genuinely surprised. '*I* thought of it. Why should *you* have thought of it?' After a moment he added, 'I am not a gramophone.'

Mr White thought that he had said, 'Have you got a gramophone?' and replied at once with some pleasure, 'Yes, I have—it is a very precious companion. Are you musical? But of course you are, being Russian. I should be very lonely without my daily ration of Chopin. Would you like some music while the servants are getting you something to eat?'

'I should like some music,' said Constantine, 'but I should not like to hear a gramophone. I will play you some music—some unique and only music on a unique and only instrument.'

'Thank you very much,' said Mr White, peering doubtfully through his glasses at the cigar-box balalaika. 'What good English you speak,' he added, trying to divert his guest's attention from his musical purpose. 'But all Russians, of course, are wonderful linguists.'

'I will play you my music,' said Constantine. 'But first I must tell you that I do not like you to say to me, "Being Russian you are musical" or "All Russians speak good English." To me it seems so stupid to see me as one of many.'

'Each one of us is one of many,' sighed Mr White patiently.

'*You*, perhaps—but *I*, not,' said Constantine. 'When you notice my English words instead of my thoughts it seems to me that you are listening wrongly—you are listening to sounds only, in the same way as you listen to your senseless gramophone——'

'But you haven't heard my gramophone,' interrupted Mr White, stung on his darling's behalf.

'What does it matter what sounds a man makes—what words he uses? Words are common to all men; thoughts belong to one man only.'

Mr White considered telling his guest to go to hell, but he said instead, 'You're quite a philosopher, aren't you?'

'I am not *quite an* anything,' said Constantine abruptly. 'I am me. All people who like Chopin also say, "You're quite a philosopher".'

'Now you're generalizing, yourself,' said Mr White, clinging to his good temper. 'Exactly what you've just complained of my doing.'

'Some people *are* general,' said Constantine. 'Now I will play you my music, and you will admit that it is not one of many musics.'

He sang a song with Russian words which Mr White did not understand. As a matter of fact, such was Constantine's horror of imitating that the words of his song were just a list of the names of the diseases of horses, learned while Constantine was a veterinary surgeon in the Ukraine. His voice was certainly peculiar to himself; it was hoarse—so hoarse that one felt as if a light cough or a discreet blowing of that long nose would clear the hoarseness away; it was veiled, as though heard from behind an intervening stillness; yet with all its hoarseness and insonorousness, it was flexible, alive, and exciting. His instrument had the same quality of quiet ugliness and oddity; it was almost enchanting. It was as if an animal—say, a goat—had found a way to control its voice into a crude goblin concord.

'That's my music,' said Constantine. 'Do you like it?'

'Frankly,' said Mr White, 'I prefer Chopin.'

'On the gramophone?'

'On the gramophone.'

'Yet one is a thing you never heard before and will never hear again—and the other is a machine that makes the same sound for millions.'

'I don't care.'

Constantine chewed his upper lip for a minute, thinking this over. Then he shook himself. 'Nevertheless, I like you,' he said insolently. 'You are almost a person. Would you like me to tell you about my life, or would you rather I explained to you my idea about Zigzags?'

'I would rather see you eat a good meal,' said Mr White, roused to a certain cordiality—as almost all Anglo-Saxons are—by the opportunity of dispensing food and drink.

'I can tell you my Zigzag idea while I eat,' said Constantine, leading the way towards the table at the other end of the room. 'Are you not eating too?'

'I'm not in the habit of eating a meat meal at ten o'clock at night.'

'Is "not being in the habit" a reason for not doing it now?'

'To me it is.'

'Oh—oh—*oh*—I wish I were like you,' said Constantine vehemently. 'It is so tiring being me—having no guide. I *do* like you.'

'Help yourself to spinach,' said Mr White crossly.

'Now shall I tell you my Zigzag idea?'

'If you can eat as well as talk.'

Constantine was exceedingly hungry; he bent low over his plate, though he sat sideways to the table, facing Mr White, ready to launch a frontal attack of talk. His mouth was too full for a moment to allow him to begin to speak, but quick, agonized glances out of his black eyes implored his host to be silent till his lips should be ready. 'You know,' he said, swallowing hurriedly, 'I always think of a zigzag as going *downwards*. I draw it in the air, *so* . . . a straight honest line, then—see—a diagonal subtle line cuts the air away from under it—so . . . Do you see what I mean? I will call the *zig* a *to*, and the *zag* a *from*. Now——'

'Why is one of your legs fatter than the other?' asked Mr White.

'It is bandaged. Now, I think of this zigzag as a diagram of human minds. Always human minds are *zigs* or *zags*—a *to* or a *from*—the brave *zig* is straight, *so* . . . the cleverer, crueller *zag* cuts away below. So are men's——'

'But why is it bandaged?'

'It was kicked by a horse. Well, so are men's understandings. Here I draw the simple, faithful understanding—and here—*zag*—the easy, clever understanding that sees through the simple faith. Now below that—see—*zig* once more—the wise, the serene, and now a *zag* contradicts once more; this is the cynic who knows all answers to serenity. Then below, once more——'

'May I see your leg?' asked Mr White. 'I was in an ambulance unit during the war.'

'Oh, what is this talk of legs?' cried Constantine. 'Legs are all the same; they belong to millions. All legs are made of blood and bone and muscle—all vulgar things. Your ambulance cuts off legs, mends legs, fits bones together, corks up blood. It treats men like bundles of bones and blood. This is so dull. Bodies are so dull. Minds are the only onliness in men.'

'Yes,' said Mr White. 'But minds have to have legs to walk about on. Let me see your leg.'

'Very well, then, let us talk of legs. We have at least legs in common, you and I.'

'Hadn't you got more sense than to put such a dirty rag round an open wound?'

'It is not dirty; it is simply of a grey colour. I washed it in a rice field.' Constantine spoke in a muffled voice from somewhere near his knee-cap, for he was now bent double, wholeheartedly interested in his leg. 'I washed the wound too, and three boils which are behind my knee. This blackness is not dirt; it is a blackness belonging to the injury.'

Mr White said nothing, but he rose to his feet as though he had heard a call. Constantine, leaving his puttee in limp coils about his foot like a dead snake, went on eating. He began to talk again about the zigzag while he stuffed food into his mouth, but he stopped talking soon, for Mr White was walking up and down the long room and not pretending to listen. Constantine, watching his host restively pacing the far end of the room, imagined that he himself perhaps smelled disagreeable, for this was a constant fear of his—that his body should play his rare personality this horrid trick. 'What is the matter?' he asked anxiously, with a shamed look. 'Why are you so far?'

Mr White's lazy, mild manner was quite changed. His voice seemed to burst out of seething irritation. 'It's a damn nuisance just now. It couldn't happen at a worse time. I've a great deal of work to do—and this fighting all over the province makes a journey so damn——'

'What is so damn?' asked Constantine, his bewilderment affecting his English.

'I'll tell you what,' said Mr White, standing in front of Constantine with his feet wide apart and speaking in an angry voice. 'You're going to bed now in my attic, and tomorrow at daylight you're going to be waked up and driven down in my car, by me (damn it!), to Lao-chow, to the hospital—a two days' drive—three hundred miles—over the worst roads you ever saw.'

Constantine's heart gave a sickening lurch. 'Why to hospital? You think my leg is dangerous?'

'If I know anything of legs,' said Mr White rather brutally, 'the doctor won't let you keep that one an hour longer than he has to.'

Constantine's mouth began instantly to tremble so much that he could scarcely speak. He thought, 'I shall die—I shall die like this—of a stupid black leg—this valuable lonely me will die.' He glared at Mr White, hungry for consolation. 'He isn't valuable—he's one of many . . . of course he could easily be brave.'

Mr White, once more indolent and indifferent, led the little Russian to the attic and left him there. As soon as Constantine saw the white sheets neatly folded back, the pleasant blue rugs squarely set upon the floor, the open wardrobe fringed with hangers, he doubted whether, after all, he did value himself so much. For in this neat room he felt betrayed by this body of his—this unwashed, unshaven, tired body, encased in coarse dirty clothes, propped on an offensive, festering leg. He decided to take all his clothes off, even though he had no other garment with him to put on; he would feel more appropriate to the shiny linen in his own shiny skin, he thought. He would have washed, but his attention was diverted as he pulled his clothes off by the wound on his leg. Though it was not very painful, it made him nearly sick with disgust now. Every nerve in his body seemed to tiptoe, alert to feel agony, as he studied the wound. He saw that a new sore place was beginning, well above the knee. With only his shirt on, he rushed downstairs, and in at the only lighted doorway. 'Look— look,' he cried. 'A new sore place. . . . Does this mean the danger is greater even than we thought?'

Mr White, in neat blue-and-white pyjamas, was carefully pressing a tie in a tie-press. Constantine had never felt so far away from a human being in his life as he felt on seeing the tie-press, those pyjamas, those monogrammed silver brushes, that elastic apparatus for reducing exercises that hung upon the door.

'Oh, go to bed,' said Mr White irascibly. 'For God's sake, show a little sense.'

Constantine was back in his attic before he thought, 'I ought to have said, "For God's sake, show a little *non*sense yourself." Sense is so vulgar.'

Sense, however, was to drive him three hundred miles to safety, next day.

All night the exhausted Constantine, sleeping only for a few minutes at a time, dreamed trivial, broken dreams about establishing his own superiority, finding, for instance, that he had after all managed to bring with him a suit-case full of clean, fashionable clothes, or noticing that his host was wearing a filthy bandage round his neck instead of a tie.

Constantine was asleep when Mr White, fully dressed, woke him next morning. A clear, steely light was slanting in at the window. Constantine was always fully conscious at the second of waking, and he was immediately horrified to see Mr White looking expressionlessly at the disorderly heap of dirty clothes that he had thrown in disgust on the floor the night before. Trying to divert his host's attention, Constantine put on a merry and courageous manner. 'Well, how is the weather for our motor car jaunt?'

'It could hardly be worse,' said Mr White placidly. 'Sheets of rain. God knows what the roads will be like.'

'Well, we are lucky to have roads at all, in this benighted China.'

'I don't know about that. If there weren't any roads we shouldn't be setting off on this beastly trip.'

'I shall be ready in two jiffies,' said Constantine, springing naked out of bed and shuffling his dreadful clothes out of Mr White's sight. 'But just tell me,' he added as his host went through the door, 'why do you drive three hundred miles on a horrible wet day just to take a perfect stranger—a beggar too—to hospital?' (He thought, 'Now he *must* say something showing that he recognizes my value.')

'Because I can't cut off your leg myself,' said Mr White gloomily. Constantine did not press his question because this new reference to the cutting off of legs set his nerves jangling again; his hands trembled so that he could scarcely button his clothes. Service in the Foreign Legion, though it was certainly no suitable adventure for a rare and sensitive man, had never obliged him to face anything more frightening than non-appreciation, coarse food, and stupid treatment. None of these things could humiliate him—on the contrary, all confirmed him in his persuasion of his own value. Only the thought of being at the mercy of his body could humiliate the excited and glowing spirit of Constantine. Death was the final, most loathsome triumph of the body; death meant dumbness and decay—yet even death he could have faced courageously could he have been flattered to its very brink.

The car, a ramshackle Ford, stood in the rain on the bald gravel of the compound, as Constantine, white with excitement, limped out through the front door. His limp, though not consciously assumed, had developed only since last night. His whole leg now felt dangerous, its skin shrinking and tingling. Constantine looked into the car. In the back seat sat Mr White's coolie, clasping a conspicuously neat little white canvas kit-bag with leather straps. The kit-bag held Constantine's eye and attacked his self-respect as the tie-press had attacked and haunted him the night before. Every one of his host's possessions was like a perfectly well-balanced, indisputable statement in a world of fevered conjecture. 'And a camp-bed—so nicely rolled,' said Constantine, leaning into the car, fascinated and humiliated. 'But only one. . . .'

'I have only one,' said Mr White.

'And you are bringing it—for me?' said Constantine, looking at him ardently, overjoyed at this tribute.

'I am bringing it for myself,' said Mr White with his unamused and short-sighted smile. 'I am assuming that a *légionnaire* is used to sleeping rough. I'm not. I'm rather fixed in my habits and I have a horror of the arrangements in Chinese inns.'

'He is morally brave,' thought Constantine, though, for the first time, it occurred to him how satisfactory it would be to slap his host's face. 'A man less brave would have changed his plans about the camp-bed at once and said, "For you, my dear man, of course—why not?" ' Constantine chattered nervously as he took his seat in the car next to his host, the driver. 'I feel such admiration for a man who can drive a motor car. I adore the machine when it does not—like the gramophone—trespass on matters outside its sphere. The machine's sphere is space, you see—it controls space—and that is so admirable—even when the machine is so very unimpressive as this one. Mr White, your motor car is *very* unimpressive indeed. Are you sure it will run three hundred miles?'

'It always seems to,' said Mr White. 'I never do anything to it except pour petrol, oil, and water into the proper openings. I am completely unmechanical.'

'You cannot be if you work a gramophone.'

'You seem to have my gramophone on your mind. To me it doesn't answer the purpose of a machine—it simply *is* Chopin, to me.'

Constantine stamped his foot in almost delighted irritation, for this made him feel a god beside this groundling. After a few minutes of self-satisfaction, however, a terrible thought invaded him. He became obsessed with an idea that he had left fleas in his bed in Mr White's attic. That smug, immaculate Chinese servant would see them when he made the bed, and on Mr White's return would say, 'That foreign soldier left fleas in our attic bed.' How bitterly did Constantine wish that he had examined the bed carefully before leaving the room, or alternatively, that he could invent some elaborate lie that would prevent Mr White from believing this revolting accusation. Constantine's mind, already racked with the fear of pain and death and with the agony of his impotence to impress his companion, became overcast with the hopelessness and remorselessness of everything. Everything despairing seemed a fact beyond dispute; everything hopeful, a mere dream. His growing certainty about the fleas, the persistence of the rain, combined with the leakiness of the car's side-curtains, the skiddiness of the road, the festering of his leg, the thought of the surgeon's saw, the perfection of that complacent kit-bag in the back seat, with the poor cigar-box balalaika tinkling beside it, the over-stability and over-rightness of his friend in need—there was not one sweet or flattering thought to which his poor trapped mind could turn.

The absurdly inadequate bullock-trail only just served the purpose of a road for the Ford. The wheels slid about, wrenching themselves from groove to groove. Constantine's comment on the difficulties of the road was silenced by a polite request on the part of Mr White. 'I can't talk while I'm driving, if you don't mind. I'm not a good driver, and I need all my attention, especially on such a bad road.'

'I will talk and you need not answer. That is my ideal plan of conversation. I will tell you why I joined the Foreign Legion. You must have been wondering about this. It will be a relief for me from my misfortunes, to talk.'

'I'd rather not, if you don't mind,' said his host serenely.

'Mean old horse,' thought Constantine passionately, his heart contracting with offence. 'It is so English to give away nothing but the bare, bald, stony fact of help—no decorations of graciousnesses and smilings. A Russian would be a much poorer helper, but a how much better friend.'

The car ground on. Constantine turned over again and again in his mind the matter of the fleas. The wet ochre-and-green country of South China streamed unevenly past, the neat, complex shapes of rice fields altering, disintegrating and re-forming, like groups in a country dance. Abrupt horns of rock began piercing through the flat rain-striped valley, and these, it seemed, were the heralds of a mountain range that barred the path of the travellers, for soon cliffs towered above the road. A village which clung to a slope at the mouth of a gorge was occupied by soldiers. 'This is where our troubles begin,' said Mr White peacefully. The soldiers were indolent, shabby, ineffectual-looking creatures, scarcely distinguishable from coolies, but their machine-guns, straddling mosquito-like about the forlorn village street, looked disagreeably wide awake and keen. Constantine felt as if his precious heart were the cynosure of all the machine-guns' waspish glances, as the car splashed between them. 'Is this safe?' he asked. 'Motoring through a Chinese war?'

'Not particularly,' smiled Mr White. 'But it's safer than neglecting that leg of yours.'

Constantine uttered a small, shrill, nervous exclamation—half a curse. 'Is a man nothing more than a leg to you?'

As he spoke, from one side of the gorge along which they were now driving, a rifle shot cracked, like the breaking of a taut wire. Its echoes were overtaken by the sputtering of more shots from a higher crag. Constantine had been tensely held for just such an attack on his courage as this—and yet he was not ready for it. His body moved instantly by itself, without consulting his self-respect; it flung its arms round Mr White. The car, thus immobilized at its source of energy, swerved, skidded, and stood still askew upon the trail. Constantine, sweating violently, recalled his pride and reassembled his sprawling arms. Mr White said nothing, but he looked with a cold benevolence into Constantine's face and shook his head slightly. Then he started the car again and drove on in silence. There was no more firing.

'Oh, *oh*, I do *wish* you had been a little bit frightened too,' said Constantine, clenching his fists. He was too much of a desert islander to deny his own fright, as a citizen of the tradition-ruled mainland might have denied it. Brave or afraid, Constantine was his own creation; he had made himself, he would stand or fall by this self that he had made. It was indeed, in a way, more interesting to have been afraid than to have been brave. Only, unfortunately, this exasperating benefactor of his did not think so.

The noon-light was scarcely brighter than the light of early morning. The unremitting rain slanted across the grey air. Trees, skies, valleys, mountains, seen through the rain-spotted wind-shield, were like a distorted, stippled landscape painted by a beginner who has not yet learned to wring living colour from his palette. However, sun or no sun, noontime it was at last, and Mr White, drawing his car conscientiously to the side of the bullock trail, as if a procession of Rolls-Royces might be expected to pass, unpacked a neat jigsaw puzzle of a sandwich-box.

'I brought a few caviare sandwiches for you,' he said gently. 'I know Russians like caviare.'

'Are your sandwiches then made of Old England's Rosbif?' asked Constantine crossly, for it seemed to him that this man used nothing but collective nouns.

'No; of bloater paste.'

They said nothing more but munched in a rather sullen silence. Constantine had lost his desire to tell Mr White why he had joined the Foreign Legion—or to tell him anything else, for that matter. There was something about Mr White that destroyed the excite-ment of telling ingenious lies—or even the common truth; and this *something* Constantine resented more and more, though he was uncertain how to define it. Mr White leaned over the steering-wheel and covered his eyes with his hands, for driving tired him. The caviare, and his host's evident weariness, irritated Constan-tine more and more; these things seemed like a crude insistence on his increasing obligation. 'I suppose you are tired of the very sight of me,' he felt impelled to say bitterly.

'No, no,' said Mr White politely but indifferently. 'Don't worry about me. It'll all be the same a hundred years hence.'

'Whether my leg is off or on—whether I die in agony or live—it will all be the same a hundred years hence, I suppose you would say,' said Constantine, morbidly goading his companion into repeating this insult to the priceless mystery of personality.

'My good man, I can't do more than I *am* doing about your leg, can I?' said Mr White irritably, as he restarted the car.

'A million times more—a million times more,' thought Constantine hysterically, but with an effort he said nothing.

As the wet evening light smouldered to an ashen twilight, they drove into Mo-ming, which was to be their night's stopping-place. Outside the city wall they were stopped by soldiers; for Mo-ming was being defended against the enemy's advance. After twenty minutes' talk in the clanking Cantonese tongue, the two white men were allowed to go through the city gate on foot, leaving the Ford in a shed outside, in the care of Mr White's coolie. Mr White carried his beautiful little kit-bag and expected Constantine to carry the camp-bed.

'What—and leave my balalaika in the car?' protested Constantine childishly.

'I think it would be safe,' said Mr White, only faintly ironic. 'Hurry up. I must go at once and call on the general in charge here. I don't want to have my car commandeered.'

Constantine limped along behind him, the camp-bed on one shoulder, the balalaika faintly tinkling under his arm. They found the inn in the centre of a tangle of looped, frayed, untidy streets—a boxlike gaunt house, one corner of which was partly ruined, for the city had been bombarded that day. The inn, which could never have been a comfortable place, was wholly disorganized by its recent misfortune; most of the servants had fled, and the inn-keeper was entirely engrossed in counting and piling up on the veranda his rescued possessions from the wrecked rooms. An impudent little boy, naked down to the waist—the only remaining servant—showed Mr White and Constantine to the only room the inn could offer.

'One room between us?' cried Constantine, thinking of his shameful, possibly verminous, clothes and his unwashed body. He felt unable to bear the idea of unbuttoning even the greasy collar of his tunic within sight of that virgin-new kit-bag. Its luminous whiteness would seem in the night like triumphant civilization's eye fixed upon the barbarian—like the smug beam of a lighthouse glowing from the mainland upon that uncouth obstruction, a desert island. 'I'm not consistent,' thought Constantine. 'That's my trouble. I ought to be proud of being dirty. At least that is a home-made condition.'

'Yes—one room between us,' said Mr White tartly. 'We must do the best we can. You look after things here, will you, while I go and see the general and make the car safe.'

Left alone, Constantine decided not to take off any clothes at all—even his coarse greatcoat—but to say that he had fever and needed all the warmth he could get. No sooner had he come to this decision than he felt convinced that he actually was feverish; his head and his injured leg ached and throbbed as though all the hot blood in his body had concentrated in those two regions, while ice seemed to settle round his heart and loins. The room was dreary and very sparsely furnished with an ugly, too high table and rigid chairs to match. The beds were simply recesses in the wall, draped with dirty mud-brown mosquito-veils. Constantine, however, stepped more bravely into this hard, matted coffin than he had into Mr White's clean attic bed. As he lay down, his leg burned and throbbed more fiercely than ever, and he began to imagine the amputation—the blood, the yawning of the flesh, the scraping of the saw upon the bone. His imagination did not supply an anaesthetic. Fever came upon him now in good earnest; he shook so much that his body seemed to jump like a fish upon the unyielding matting, he seemed to breathe in heat, without being able to melt the ice in his bones. Yet he remained artistically conscious all the time of his plight, and even exaggerated the shivering spasms of his limbs. He was quite pleased to think that Mr White would presently return and find him in this condition, and so be obliged to be interested and compassionate. Yet as he heard Mr White's heavy step on the stair, poor Constantine's eye fell on the fastidious white kit-bag, and he suddenly remembered all his fancies and fears about vermin and smells. By the time Mr White was actually standing over him, Constantine was convinced that the deepest loathing was clearly shown on that superior, towering face.

'I can't help it—I can't help it,' cried Constantine, between his chattering teeth.

Mr White seemed to ignore the Russian's agitation. 'I think the car'll be all right now,' he said. 'I left the coolie sleeping in it, to make sure. The general was quite civil and gave me a permit to get home; but it seems it's utterly impossible for us to drive on to

Lao-chow. Fighting on the road is particularly hot, and the bridges are all destroyed. The enemy have reached the opposite side of the river, and they've been bombarding the city all day. I told the general about your case; he suggests you go by river in a sampan down to Lao-chow tomorrow. You may be fired on just as you leave the city, but nothing to matter, I dare say. After that, you'd be all right—the river makes a stiff bend south here, and gets right away from the country they're fighting over. It would take you only about eighteen hours to Lao-chow, going downstream. I've already got a sampan for you. . . . Oh, Lord, isn't this disgusting?' he added, looking round the dreadful room and wrinkling his nose. 'How I loathe this kind of thing!'

'I can't help it. I can't help it.' Constantine began at first to moan and then to cry. He was by now in great pain, and he did not try to control his distress. It passed through his mind that crying was the last thing a stupid Englishman would expect of a *légionnaire*; so far so good, therefore—he was a desert islander even in his degradation. Yet he loathed himself; all his morbid fears of being offensive were upon him, and the unaccustomed exercise of crying, combined with the fever, nauseated him. Mr White, still wearing his expression of repugnance, came to his help, loosened that greasy collar, lent a handkerchief, ordered some refreshing hot Chinese tea.

'You should have known me in Odessa,' gasped Constantine in an interval between his paroxysms. 'Three of the prettiest women in the town were madly in love with me. You know me only at my worst.'

Mr White, soaking a folded silk handkerchief in cold water, before laying it on Constantine's burning forehead, did not answer. He unrolled the pillow from his camp-bed and put it under Constantine's head. As he did so, he recoiled a little, but after a second's hesitation, he pushed the immaculate little pillow into place with a heroic firmness.

'I wore only silk next to the skin then,' snuffled Constantine. The fever rose in a wave in his brain, and he shouted curses upon his cruelly perfect friend.

Mr White lay only intermittently on his camp-bed that night. He was kept busy making use of his past experience as a member of an ambulance unit. Only at daylight he slept for an hour or so.

Constantine, awakened from a short sleep by the sound of firing outside, lay on his side and watched Mr White's relaxed, sleeping face. The fever had left Constantine, and he was now sunk in cold, limp depression and fear. Luckily, he thought, there was no need to stir, for certainly he could not be expected—a sick man—to set forth in a sampan through such dangers as the persistent firing suggested. At least in this inn he knew the worst, he thought wearily, and his companion knew the worst too. 'I will not leave him,' Constantine vowed, 'until I have somehow cured him of these frightful memories of me—somehow amputated his memory of me. . . .' He lay watching his companion's face—hating it—obscurely wishing that those eyes, which had seen the worst during this loathsome night, might remain for ever shut.

Mr White woke up quite suddenly. 'Good Lord!' he said, peering at his watch. 'Nearly seven. I told the sampan man to be at the foot of the steps at daylight.'

'Are you mad?' asked Constantine shrilly. 'Listen to the firing—quite near. Besides—I'm a very sick man, as you should know by now. I couldn't even walk—much less dodge through a crowd of Chinese assassins.'

Mr White, faintly whistling Chopin, laboriously keeping his temper, left the room, and could presently be heard hee-hawing in the Chinese language on the veranda to the hee-hawing inn-keeper.

When he came back, he said, 'The sampaneer's there, waiting—only too anxious to get away from the bombing they're expecting today. He's tied up only about a hundred yards away. You'll be beyond the reach of the firing as soon as you're round the bend. Hurry up, man; the sooner you get down to hospital, and I get off on the road home, the better for us both.'

Constantine, genuinely exhausted after his miserable night, did not speak, but lay with his eyes shut and his face obstinately turned to the wall. He certainly felt too ill to be brave or to face the crackling dangers of the battle-ridden streets, but he was conscious of no plan except a determination to be as obstructive as he could—to assert at least this ignoble power over his tyrant.

'Get up, you damn fool,' shouted Mr White, suddenly plucking

the pillow from under the sick man's head, 'or I'll drag you down
to the river by the scruff of your dirty neck.'

Dirty neck! Instantly Constantine sat up—hopeless now of
curing this man's contempt, full of an almost unendurable craving
to be far away from him—to wipe him from his horizon—to be
allowed to imagine him dead. Invigorated by this violent impulse,
he rolled out of bed and sullenly watched Mr White settle up with
the inkeeper and take a few packages out of that revoltingly
refined kit-bag.

'A small tin of water-biscuits,' said Mr White, almost apologetically, 'and the remains of the bloater paste. It's all I have with
me, but it ought to keep you alive till you get to Lao-chow
tomorrow morning. . . . I'll see you down to the river first and
then pick up these things.' He spoke as if he were trying to make
little neat plans still against this disorderly and unwonted background. He brushed his splashed coat with a silver clothes-brush,
wearing the eagerly safe expression Constantine had seen on his
face as he bent over the tie-press the night before last. The orderly
man was trying to maintain his quiet impersonal self-respect amid
surroundings that humiliated him. Even Constantine understood
vaguely that his attacker was himself being attacked. 'Well, I've
done my best,' added Mr White, straightening his back after
buckling the last strap of the kit-bag, and looking at Constantine
with an ambiguous, almost appealing look.

They left the inn. The steep street that led down to the river
between mean, barricaded shops was deserted. The air of it was
outraged by the whipping sound of rifle fire—echoes clanked
sharply from wall to wall.

'It is not safe—it is not safe,' muttered Constantine, suddenly
standing rooted, feeling that his next step must bring him into the
path of a bullet.

'It's safer than a gangrenous leg.' With his great hand, Mr
White seized the little Russian's arm and dragged him almost gaily
down the steps. Constantine was by now so hopelessly mired in
humiliation that he did not even try to disguise his terror. He hung
back like a rebellious child, but he was tweaked and twitched
along, stumbling behind his rescuer. He was pressed into the little
boat. 'Here, take the biscuits—good-bye—good luck,' shouted Mr

White, and a smile of real gaiety broke out at last upon his face. The strip of rainy air and water widened between the two friends.

'Strike him dead, God!' said Constantine.

The smile did not fade at once from the Englishman's face, as his legs curiously crumpled into a kneeling position. He seemed trying to kneel on air; he clutched at his breast with one hand while the other hand still waved good-bye; he turned his alert, smiling face towards Constantine as though he were going to say again—'Good-bye—good luck.' Then he fell, head downward, on the steps, the bald crown of his head just dipping into the water. Mud was splashed over the coat he had brushed only five minutes before.

There was a loud outcry from the sampan man and his wife. They seemed to be calling Constantine's already riveted attention to the fallen man—still only twenty yards away; they seemed uncertain whether he would now let them row yet more quickly away, as they desired, or insist on returning to the help of his friend.

'Row on—row on,' cried Constantine in Russian and, to show them what he meant, he snatched up a spare pole and tried to increase the speed of the boat as it swerved into the current. Spaces of water were broadening all about the desert islander— home on his desert island again at last. As Constantine swayed over the pole, he looked back over his shoulder and flaunted his head, afraid no more of the firing now that one blessed bullet had carried away unpardonable memory out of the brain of his friend.

GERALD BULLETT

Wax

It was understood in the Croop household that Grandpa Boydel must be put away. The hour had struck, and the family were making ready to conduct the old man to his destiny. Alice, an undersized child of eleven, bent over a basin half filled with dirty water, sister Maudie at her elbow waiting with dull-eyed patience to succeed her in the use of the greasy flannel; Charles the younger, with an arm round the shoulder of his twin-brother Alfie, stood staring at the unwitting cause of this excitement; and their mother, while giving suck to her two-year-old baby-girl, kept a sharp eye on everything that went forward. The room was bare of decoration, the walls peeling, the floor covered with odd bits of worn linoleum. It contained a large iron bedstead, which at night accommodated half the family and by day served as something to sit on; a deal table crowded with saucepans, dishes, and dirty crockery; and three rickety cane chairs. The atmosphere was pungent with humanity.

Grandpa Boydel was old, older than his age. His eyes had grown bigger, his nose sharper, his cheeks more sunken. Rheumatism had gnarled and bent him, working unseen, with subtle fingers, to make of that cunning mechanism of bone and muscle and sinew a conventional emblem of old age. But there was still eighteen months to run before he would be qualified for a state pension, and it had long been a matter of anxious calculation for his daughter, Mrs Croop, whether that 'little bit of extra' was worth so much waiting for. The phrase was a euphemism born of the fact that Liz Croop had seen better days, days when an extra ten shillings a week had been not quite the gigantic sum, the impossible affluence, that it now seemed to her. Looking back on those days, which she had owed in fact to this very father of hers, she exaggerated her former dignity, especially in conversation, until credulous neighbours might have supposed that an exiled queen had come to dwell among them. But since the day when a Covent Garden porter had got her into trouble she had not had much time for looking back, though enough for the cultivation of an habitual self-pity. 'A narder-working little woman you wouldn't find,' she told the Social Worker who called to inquire after her comfort. 'And he goes on at me something crool.' No, she had not had much time for reflection; for Charley Croop, having got her into trouble once, and married her for his sins, had been getting her into trouble (though she did not now call it that) with appalling regularity ever since. She got out of these troubles as best and as often as she could, but eight stubborn souls had contrived, nevertheless, to get themselves born of her, and five of these eight—three girls and two gaunt little boys—had survived. With these pledges of Charley's affection, with Grandpa, and with Charley himself when he was not otherwise occupied, she lived in two rooms of a large brick warren on the south side of Liberty Street in Whitechapel. Two rooms, when, but for Grandpa, they might perhaps have made do with one. There was no chance of that now, for another little Croop was kicking in her womb, and eight in one room was more than the authorities permitted. And Charley, too, was a difficulty. Charley liked room to move in. 'Too 'andy with 'is 'ands, miss,' she told the Social Worker. 'See what he done to me larse night. And all because I got a new blouse on. Take that thing orf, he says. Want to make yourself pretty, do yer, he says. And then he fetches me one on the side of the 'ead. And I'm sure,' Mrs Croop ended plaintively, 'I never done nothing to deserve it. 'Ave a bit of pity, Charley, I says. But would 'e? Not 'im. Take that bleeder orf, he says, and sharp about it. And the things he called me—I durn't tell you arf. 'Tain't for myself I mind, miss, but 'snot nice for the chooldren, miss. Is it, miss? 'Tain't what *I* bin used to, any'ow, sech foul-mouthed talk!' Mrs Croop was accused, by her prouder and less expansive neighbours, of 'sucking up to the gentry'. She was a woman who enjoyed sympathy and was ready to get what she could in exchange for interesting confidences. She did not, however, confide to any stranger her plans for the disposal of Grandpa Boydel. She had made up her mind about that; Charley agreed with her;

and it would be time enough to talk when it was all over and done with.

It was clearly no use waiting any longer for that wonderful little bit of extra. The odds were that Grandpa, the old artful, would take good care to eat his pension when he got it; more probable still he would take and die before he became entitled to draw it; and anyhow it was impossible to wait any longer. For Grandpa himself had become impossible. Liz had done her duty by him. She had looked after him with daughterly devotion ever since—three years ago—he had become incapacitated for work. She had drudged and saved, a halfpenny here and a halfpenny there, to support this extra burden; Charley, who was easygoing enough when sober, had made no protest; and the poor-house had never been so much as mentioned. She was fond of the old man, and a little in awe of him still; it was nice to have a bit of company of an evening; and, so long as he did what he was told and didn't try to interfere, she could put up with him well enough. If his uselessness got on her nerves, if his grumbling wearied her and his occasional flashes of contempt made her feel small and resentful like the child she had once been, she nevertheless bore with him patiently. But this last manifestation was too much. And now, moreover, was her chance to be rid of a nuisance. Even when eating her bread he had retained his masterful manners. He had never (she fancied) ceased to regard her as an unpromising child. And now the tables were turned. He was the child, and she was in authority. For weeks past he had sat moodily in his corner, lost in a dull dream. His large blue eyes were empty of recognition; his hands groped aimlessly in front of him; he dribbled and dropped his food, and seldom answered when spoken to, and then without intelligence. In short, Grandpa had lost his wits, declared Mrs Croop, and there was no doing anything with him. He must be put away. It was sad, but exciting; the children, in their quiet way, enjoyed the sense of crisis; and Mrs Croop thought eagerly of her coming release.

'He'll be ever so nice and comfortable where he's going,' she assured her children. 'Crysake stop that snivelling, Alfie, or I'll skin the back orf of yer!' She cuffed Alfie vigorously. 'Ever so comfortable, he will. Won't you, Grandpa? Eh? Now, Alice, my gal, be quick and get that face washed if you want to come to the orsepital to see your Grandpa orf. Don't stand there gaping, girl! J'ear me? And you, Maudie, can take and give 'im a wipe down, see? Got your boots on, Grandpa? Thass right.'

2

Muddled but not too unhappy, heedless of everything external and quite unaware of the fate in store for him, Grandpa Boydel sat quiet in his corner. For longer now than he could easily remember, his private being, the city of himself, had been strangely secluded from the outer world, walled round with quietness. All sounds were agreeably dimmed: he missed, and was glad to miss, the scraping of the children's chairs on the floor, the baby's howling, the strident voice of his daughter enjoining good behaviour. The street noises that had irked him for so long—the shouting and the rumble—were now ended. It was as if those hitherto snorting roaring vehicles were being moved by magic over a road of silk; he watched them from the window, and marvelled. Days were no longer wearisome; he had defeated weariness by surrendering to it, troubling no more to assert himself against a world insolently loud and young. Nights held no terrors; even the long hours of waking were quiet and drowsy and filled with dreams, and the snoring of Alfie and Charles, who shared his bed, could not disturb this new-found privacy. His sense of smell was also dulled—merciful dispensation to a man who must spend his last years cabined with the Croops.

At first these immunities had been unwelcome to him; their gradual approach had made him uneasy and short-tempered, and the shock of their sudden final completion had puzzled and frightened him. But he soon came to terms with the change, and learned to take a secret satisfaction in it. Deaf, that's me. Deaf as a post. When he realized the comfort of it he began to think himself rather clever to be deaf. There was no one and nothing in the world worth listening to; so why worry? But even this gleam of vanity, this glancing reference to an outer world, became, as the silent days went on, muffled out of existence; and deafness, itself forgotten, was at last no more than a screen against which the drama of memory and dream incessantly moved. He forgot the world; he withdrew into himself, which was his past; images long lost came crowding upon him, so that, in time, not only were the surrounding voices mute, but the faces of his own people were strange in his sight. When Liz approached him with mouthing gestures, he averted his eyes distastefully, asking of memory: Who is this woman, and why am I here with her? And by emptying his sight of her he made her vanish, so that she had at last, she and her children with her, no more substance than the fancies with which he peopled the hospitable silence. Once or twice he went so far as to wonder if he were dead and disembodied, and with groping fingers he questioned the air about him; but the shooting pains in his head distracted him from such theories as that, and sent him grumbling to his accustomed corner. There, when the pains subsided, he could lapse back into the odd disjointed story of himself, a panorama of which he did not stop to ask the meaning. He was lost, lost to himself: he could not have told you so much as his name. But the clock of his life had become erratic, now reversing its movement, now jerking erratically from one point to another, so that vital moments were restored to him in a series of sharp bright musical sensations: a day in the country as a child; a summer's night; the touch of a girl's hair on his face; a thrashing from his father; ecstasy, anguish, a young woman lying marbled in her coffin; and a voice that kept saying again and again, quite unmeaningly: Saturday drill.

'Whatcher say, Grandpa?' screamed Liz, with sudden impatience. Arms akimbo she bent towards him menacingly, putting her face close to his. He turned his eyes away, muttering. 'Oh lumme,' said Liz, 'you and your blasted Saturday drill!' Remembering that he was to be put away, and this very morning, she yielded to a kindlier impulse and added with jocular humour: 'Want to go for a souljer, do yer? No, it's the Loony Bin for you, pore old rudder!' Sad though it was, the prospect cheered her. Her glance flashed round the room as she made her final dispositions. 'Alfie and Charley are to stay 'ere. Now 'old yer noise, Alfie, or I'll 'it yer. Maudie comes with me. See, Maudie? And Alice'll come as fur as the tram with us and that's all. You're to come back, Alice, and give an eye to Baby. See? Thass right.'

Grandpa Boydel found himself being persuaded to stand up. The woman was shouting at him. The little girls looked excited and self-important: they were ready for the outing. The little boys could do nothing but stare. He could hear nothing of what the woman said, and cared nothing. Not troubling his head with questions and answers, he suffered himself to be led out of the room, and down the stairs, and into the sunlit squalor of Liberty.

3

It was a pleasant morning for a walk, but within five minutes of the setting-out Grandpa Boydel was wishing himself home again in his dingy corner. The crisp April air stung him into a higher degree of wakefulness than he had known for weeks, and the unaccustomed exercise quickened his slow blood. He began to be nettled by a suspicion, dimly formed, that he was being led back, against his own desire, to a life that he had been glad to leave. This shrill woman and these large-eyed hungry children, they would not let him rest, but must be for ever urging him on with impatient or coaxing gestures. They dragged at his arms; they shouted; he could see them shouting. And when he wanted to sit down in the road and forget everything, forget this new-minted morning and return to his world within, they all three pressed savagely upon him, and held him up, and the woman's face became an angry grinning mask. His bones ached. He longed to lie down and be at rest. Fixing his eyes on the woman he tried to send his thought to her across the chasm, having, in this silent world, lost the habit and power of voluntary speech. He saw her mouthing at him and was intolerably puzzled. She drew back a step: something hit him in the face, and he cowered away from it. He surrendered; he submitted; his legs were set in motion again, and after a weary treadmill dream he found himself sitting in a tram. The woman was at his side, and the elder of the two girls stared accusingly at him from the opposite seat. The woman was red-eyed; her cheeks were smeared. Pore father, I didn't ought to 'ave 'it 'im, thought Liz Croop. And she gave him a quick sidelong glance, as though fearing that he might suddenly change back into the masterful parent of whom she had once stood in awe. But she was soon herself again, and mistress of the situation. 'We want to get orf at the orsepital,' she had told the conductor. And now she rose, briskly practical. 'Kerm on, Maudie! Give us an 'and wiv Grandpa, cantcher?' She rebuked her children's offences before they were committed: it saved time afterwards. 'Now, up yer come, Grandpa! None of that nonsense this time. J'ear me?'

He did not hear her, but it was all one. He had no mind to resist her now, being busy with his thoughts. Soon, moreover, he was allowed to sit down again. A small square room it was, crowded with sick people. At intervals a young man in a white overall put his red head round the edge of the inner door and said cheerfully: 'Who's next?'

One by one the numbers diminished, and at last it was Grandpa Boydel's turn.

'Look lively!' said the red-haired young man. He was a cheerful fellow; he found life endlessly amusing. 'Bring him in here then.' Liz and her Maudie led their prisoner in to the surgery. 'Now, what's wrong with the old gentleman? Rheumatism? Pains in the head? Speak up, uncle!'

Mrs Croop intervened. 'We want to put him away, sir. He's loony, sir, pore old soul. That's 'ow it is, sir.'

'Oh, so that's it,' said the young man. He waited to hear more.

'He don't reckernize us, sir. Not none of us. And I've been a good girl to him, as Gawd's my judge. Don't answer when spoke to, and his 'abits ain't so nice either. 'Tisn't safe for my girls, that's what I say. I'm sure I done my best for 'im, but "Saturday drill" is all he'll answer when spoke to—if you ever heard of sech a thing! It don't make sense to me and I can't do wiv 'im any longer, and that's Gaw's troof. Not safe in our beds, we ain't!'

'You mean he's violent?'

'Beg pardon, sir?'

'Has he been attacking you? Misbehaving himself?'

' 'E don't answer when spoke to, sir,' said Mrs Croop, impatient of these sophistries. 'You can see for yerself he don't answer,' she whined.

'Right you are,' said the young man, with extreme cheerfulness.

'Now just step into the other room, you two. And I'll call you when I want you.'

So Grandpa Boydel was left alone with his red-headed young man, and his chance of a rest was further off than ever. This did not much distress him, for even his apathy was now in danger of defeat. He frowned, averting his eyes; but this new tormentor was not to be put off by tricks of that kind. The patient was kept very busy. He was made to sit down, made to stand up, made to sit down again. Questions were bawled at him; he shook his head. He became frightened, wondering whether this young man, like Liz, would lose patience with him and slap his face; but, except for a smart blow above the knee-cap with the edge of his hand, the young man offered him no violence. Nor did he appear to be impatient: his slight frown did not suggest anger. He approached his patient's ears with an electric torch as small as a small pencil . . . and three minutes later a second young man appeared from nowhere, a curious little dish was held against the side of Grandpa Boydel's neck, and Red Head got to work with a syringe.

The patient bleated.

'A bit too warm for you?' said the operator. 'Sorry, uncle. But we're breaking through.' He refilled his syringe, whistling with satisfaction.

Grandpa Boydel sat alone in his silence. But ruthless war was being waged on that sanctuary. The roar of water in his ears became punctuated by a tearing and a crackling; and then, suddenly, it was as if the whole earth went up in one hideous explosion. The world, with its trampling feet, its blare of trumpets, its multitudinous drums, rushed in upon him. His ears were open.

'Now for the other one,' said the young man. 'A bath wouldn't hurt you, uncle, if you keep yourself warm afterwards. I'd try one if I were you. D'you know,' he added confidentially, 'there's enough wax in these ears of yours to stock a beehive. Or was, a moment ago.'

Grandpa Boydel smiled vaguely, and shook his head. He was dazed after his long swift journey; dazed, like a man just emerged from a dark and quiet pit. The world was loud around him: it would take a little getting used to. 'How did I get here, sir?' he ventured to ask. The sound of his voice astonished him.

'Hi, you!—you can come in now,' shouted the red-headed young man, putting away his syringe. 'The old gentleman's asking for you.' A gasp, a sniff, and the two Croops came shuffling in. 'Here he is, right as a trivet,' cried the young man, greeting them boisterously. 'Undernourished, of course. But that goes without saying.' He laughed; for it was no use being mournful about it.

'Whadjer mean?' demanded Mrs Croop, with an ugly look. 'Jou mean to say——'

'He's fine. He'll do. You can take him home. That's what I mean,' said the young man. 'Very difficult case,' he added, with a wink at his assistant. 'But I've dealt with it, so off you go. Good-bye, uncle—don't forget about that bath.'

Mrs Croop stared at Grandpa Boydel, and the decision with which he returned the stare unnerved her. All too evidently a father had been restored to her. 'What, better again, Grandpa, are yer?' she said timidly. 'Fancy that now!' She glanced helplessly round the room. She was beaten: there was nothing for it but to wait for the little bit of extra. 'Well,' she concluded wearily, 'you'd better come along home then, I s'pose.'

Unsteadily but unaided, Grandpa Boydel rose to his feet. 'I'll come when I'm ready, my gal,' he answered. 'And I could do with a bite of food, too.'

In single file, Liz leading, they emerged from the hospital. Maudie Croop, perplexed in the extreme by this drastic change of plan, could no longer withhold a question.

'Muvver!'

'What is it now?'

'Ain't Grandpa going in the Loony Bin, Muvver?'

'Eh?' said Grandpa sharply.

But he had heard the question imperfectly, and it was not repeated.

ALDOUS HUXLEY

The Gioconda Smile

1

'Miss Spence will be down directly, sir.'

'Thank you,' said Mr Hutton, without turning round. Janet Spence's parlourmaid was so ugly—ugly on purpose, it always seemed to him, malignantly, criminally ugly—that he could not bear to look at her more than was necessary. The door closed. Left to himself, Mr Hutton got up and began to wander round the room, looking with meditative eyes at the familiar objects it contained.

Photographs of Greek statuary, photographs of the Roman Forum, coloured prints of Italian masterpieces, all very safe and well known. Poor, dear Janet, what a prig—what an intellectual snob! Her real taste was illustrated in that water-colour by the pavement artist, the one she had paid half a crown for (and thirty-five shillings for the frame). How often he had heard her tell the story, how often expatiate on the beauties of that skilful imitation of an oleograph! 'A real Artist in the streets,' and you could hear the capital A in Artist as she spoke the words. She made you feel that part of his glory had entered into Janet Spence when she tendered him that half-crown for the copy of the oleograph. She was implying a compliment to her own taste and penetration. A genuine Old Master for half a crown. Poor, dear Janet!

Mr Hutton came to a pause in front of a small oblong mirror. Stooping a little to get a full view of his face, he passed a white, well-manicured finger over his moustache. It was as curly, as freshly auburn as it had been twenty years ago. His hair still retained its colour, and there was no sign of baldness yet—only a certain elevation of the brow. 'Shakespearean,' thought Mr Hutton, with a smile, as he surveyed the smooth and polished expanse of his forehead.

Others abide our question, thou are free. . . . Footsteps in the sea . . . Majesty. . . . Shakespeare, thou shouldst be living at this hour. No, that was Milton, wasn't it? Milton, the Lady of Christ's. There was no lady about him. He was what the women would call a manly man. That was why they liked him—for the curly auburn moustache and the discreet redolence of tobacco. Mr Hutton smiled again; he enjoyed making fun of himself. Lady of Christ's? No, no. He was the Christ of Ladies. Very pretty, very pretty. The Christ of Ladies. Mr Hutton wished there were somebody he could tell the joke to. Poor, dear Janet wouldn't appreciate it, alas!

He straightened himself up, patted his hair, and resumed his peregrination. Damn the Roman Forum; he hated those dreary photographs.

Suddenly he became aware that Janet Spence was in the room, standing near the door. Mr Hutton started, as though he had been taken in some felonious act. To make these silent and spectral appearances was one of Janet Spence's peculiar talents. Perhaps she had been there all the time, had seen him looking at himself in the mirror. Impossible! But, still, it was disquieting.

'Oh, you gave me such a surprise,' said Mr Hutton, recovering his smile and advancing with outstretched hand to meet her.

Miss Spence was smiling too: her Gioconda smile, he had once called it in a moment of half-ironical flattery. Miss Spence had take the compliment seriously, and always tried to live up to the Leonardo standard. She smiled on in silence while Mr Hutton shook hands; that was part of the Gioconda business.

'I hope you're well,' said Mr Hutton. 'You look it.'

What a queer face she had! That small mouth pursed forward by the Gioconda expression into a little snout with a round hole in the middle as though for whistling—it was like a penholder seen from the front. Above the mouth a well-shaped nose, finely aquiline. Eyes large, lustrous, and dark, with the largeness, lustre, and darkness that seems to invite sties and an occasional blood-shot suffusion. They were fine eyes, but unchangingly grave. The penholder might do its Gioconda trick, but the eyes never altered in their earnestness. Above them, a pair of boldly arched, heavily pencilled black eyebrows lent a surprising air of power, as of a

Roman matron, to the upper portion of the face. Her hair was
dark and equally Roman; Agrippina from the brows upward.

'I thought I'd just look in on my way home,' Mr Hutton went
on. 'Ah, it's good to be back here'—he indicated with a wave of his
hand the flowers in the vases, the sunshine and greenery beyond
the windows—'it's good to be back in the country after a stuffy
day of business in town.'

Miss Spence, who had sat down, pointed to a chair at her side.

'No, really, I can't sit down,' Mr Hutton protested. 'I must get
back to see how poor Emily is. She was rather seedy this morning.'
He sat down, nevertheless. 'It's these wretched liver chills. She's
always getting them. Women——' He broke off and coughed, so
as to hide the fact that he had uttered. He was about to say that
women with weak digestions ought not to marry; but the remark
was too cruel, and he didn't really believe it. Janet Spence, moreover, was a believer in eternal flames and spiritual attachments.
'She hopes to be well enough,' he added, 'to see you at luncheon
tomorrow. Can you come? Do!' He smiled persuasively. 'It's my
invitation too, you know.'

She dropped her eyes, and Mr Hutton almost thought that he
detected a certain reddening of the cheek. It was a tribute; he
stroked his moustache.

'I should like to come if you think Emily's really well enough to
have a visitor.'

'Of course. You'll do her good. You'll do us both good. In
married life three is often better company than two.'

'Oh, you're cynical.'

Mr Hutton always had a desire to say 'Bow-wow-wow' whenever that last word was spoken. It irritated him more than any
other word in the language. But instead of barking he made haste
to protest.

'No, no. I'm only speaking a melancholy truth. Reality doesn't
always come up to the ideal, you know. But that doesn't make me
believe any the less in the ideal. Indeed, I believe in it
passionately—the ideal of a matrimony between two people in
perfect accord. I think it's realizable. I'm sure it is.'

He paused significantly and looked at her with an arch expression. A virgin of thirty-six, but still unwithered; she had her

charms. And there was something really rather enigmatic about her. Miss Spence made no reply, but continued to smile. There were times when Mr Hutton got rather bored with the Gioconda. He stood up.

'I must really be going now. Farewell, mysterious Gioconda.' The smile grew intenser, focused itself, as it were, in a narrower snout. Mr Hutton made a Cinquecento gesture, and kissed her extended hand. It was the first time he had done such a thing; the action seemed not to be resented. 'I look forward to tomorrow.'

'Do you?'

For answer Mr Hutton once more kissed her hand, then turned to go. Miss Spence accompanied him to the porch.

'Where's your car?' she asked.

'I left it at the gate of the drive.'

'I'll come and see you off.'

'No, no.' Mr Hutton was playful, but determined. 'You must do no such thing. I simply forbid you.'

'But I should like to come,' Miss Spence protested, throwing a rapid Gioconda at him.

Mr Hutton held up his hand. 'No,' he repeated, and then, with a gesture that was almost the blowing of a kiss, he started to run down the drive, lightly, on his toes, with long, bounding strides like a boy's. He was proud of that run; it was quite marvellously youthful. Still, he was glad the drive was no longer. At the last bend, before passing out of sight of the house, he halted and turned round. Miss Spence was still standing on the steps, smiling her smile. He waved his hand, and this time quite definitely and overtly wafted a kiss in her direction. Then, breaking once more into his magnificent canter, he rounded the last dark promontory of trees. Once out of sight of the house he let his high paces decline to a trot, and finally to a walk. He took out his handkerchief and began wiping his neck inside his collar. What fools, what fools! Had there ever been such an ass as poor, dear Janet Spence? Never, unless it was himself. Decidedly he was the more malignant fool, since he, at least, was aware of his folly and still persisted in it. Why did he persist? Ah, the problem that was himself, the problem that was other people . . .

He had reached the gate. A large prosperous-looking motor was standing at the side of the road.

'Home, M'Nab.' The chauffeur touched his cap. 'And stop at the cross-roads on the way, as usual,' Mr Hutton added, as he opened the door of the car. 'Well?' he said, speaking into the obscurity that lurked within.

'Oh, Teddy Bear, what an age you've been!' It was a fresh and childish voice that spoke the words. There was the faintest hint of Cockney impurity about the vowel sounds.

Mr Hutton bent his large form and darted into the car with the agility of an animal regaining its burrow.

'Have I?' he said, as he shut the door. The machine began to move. 'You must have missed me a lot if you found the time so long.' He sat back in the low seat; a cherishing warmth enveloped him.

'Teddy Bear . . .' and with a sigh of contentment a charming little head declined on to Mr Hutton's shoulder. Ravished, he looked down sideways at the round, babyish face.

'Do you know, Doris, you look like the pictures of Louise de Kérouaille.' He passed his fingers through a mass of curly hair.

'Who's Louise de Kera-whatever-it-is?' Doris spoke from remote distances.

'She was, alas! *Fuit*. We shall all be "was" one of these days. Meanwhile . . .'

Mr Hutton covered the babyish face with kisses. The car rushed smoothly along. M'Nab's back, through the front window, was stonily impressive, the back of a statue.

'Your hands,' Doris whispered. 'Oh, you mustn't touch me. They give me electric shocks.'

Mr Hutton adored her for the virgin imbecility of the words. How late in one's existence one makes the discovery of one's body!

'The electricity isn't in me, it's in you.' He kissed her again, whispering her name several times: Doris, Doris, Doris. The scientific appellation of the sea-mouse, he was thinking as he kissed the throat she offered him, white and extended like the throat of a victim awaiting the sacrificial knife. The sea-mouse was a sausage with iridescent fur: very peculiar. Or was Doris the sea-cucumber, which turns itself inside out in moments of alarm? He would really have to go to Naples again, just to see the aquarium. These sea creatures were fabulous, unbelievably fantastic.

'Oh, Teddy Bear!' (More zoology; but he was only a land animal. His poor little jokes!) 'Teddy Bear, I'm so happy.'

'So am I,' said Mr Hutton. Was it true?

'But I wish I knew if it were right. Tell me, Teddy Bear, is it right or wrong?'

'Ah, my dear, that's just what I've been wondering for the last thirty years.'

'Be serious, Teddy Bear. I want to know if this is right; if it's right that I should be here with you and that we should love one another, and that it should give me electric shocks when you touch me.'

'Right? Well, it's certainly good that you should have electric shocks rather than sexual repressions. Read Freud; repressions are the devil.'

'Oh, you don't help me. Why aren't you ever serious? If only you knew how miserable I am sometimes, thinking it's not right. Perhaps, you know, there is a hell, and all that. I don't know what to do. Sometimes I think I ought to stop loving you.'

'But could you?' asked Mr Hutton, confident in the powers of his seduction and his moustache.

'No. Teddy Bear, you know I couldn't. But I could run away, I could hide from you, I could lock myself up and force myself not to come to you.'

'Silly little thing!' He tightened his embrace.

'Oh, dear, I hope it isn't wrong. And there are times when I don't care if it is.'

Mr Hutton was touched. He had a certain protective affection for this little creature. He laid his cheek against her hair and so, interlaced, they sat in silence, while the car, swaying and pitching a little as it hastened along, seemed to draw in the white road and the dusty hedges towards it devouringly.

'Goodbye, goodbye.'

The car moved on, gathered speed, vanished round a curve, and Doris was left standing by the sign-post at the cross-roads, still dizzy and weak with the languor born of those kisses and the electrical touch of those gentle hands. She had to take a deep breath, to draw herself up deliberately, before she was strong enough to start her homeward walk. She had half a mile in which to invent the necessary lies.

Alone, Mr Hutton suddenly found himself the prey of an appalling boredom.

2

Mrs Hutton was lying on the sofa in her boudoir, playing Patience. In spite of the warmth of the July evening a wood fire was burning on the hearth. A black Pomeranian, extenuated by the heat and the fatigues of digestion, slept before the blaze.

'Phew! Isn't it rather hot in here?' Mr Hutton asked as he entered the room.

'You know I have to keep warm, dear.' The voice seemed breaking on the verge of tears. 'I get so shivery.'

'I hope you're better this evening.'

'Not much, I'm afraid.'

The conversation stagnated. Mr Hutton stood leaning his back against the mantelpiece. He looked down at the Pomeranian lying at his feet, and with the toe of his right boot he rolled the little dog over and rubbed its white-flecked chest and belly. The creature lay in an inert ecstasy. Mrs Hutton continued to play Patience. Arrived at an *impasse*, she altered the position of one card, took back another, and went on playing. Her Patiences always came out.

'Dr Libbard thinks I ought to go to Llandrindod Wells this summer.'

'Well, go, my dear—go, most certainly.'

Mr Hutton was thinking of the events of the afternoon: how they had driven, Doris and he, up to the hanging wood, had left the car to wait for them under the shade of the trees, and walked together out into the windless sunshine of the chalk down.

'I'm to drink the waters for my liver, and he thinks I ought to have massage and electric treatment, too.'

Hat in hand, Doris had stalked four blue butterflies that were dancing together round a scabious flower with a motion that was like the flickering of blue fire. The blue fire burst and scattered into whirling sparks; she had given chase, laughing and shouting like a child.

'I'm sure it will do you good, my dear.'

'I was wondering if you'd come with me, dear.'

'But you know I'm going to Scotland at the end of the month.'

Mrs Hutton looked up at him entreatingly. 'It's the journey,' she said. 'The thought of it is such a nightmare. I don't know if I can manage it. And you know I can't sleep in hotels. And then there's the luggage and all the worries. I can't go alone.'

'But you won't be alone. You'll have your maid with you.' He spoke impatiently. The sick woman was usurping the place of the healthy one. He was being dragged back from the memory of the sunlit down and the quick, laughing girl, back to this unhealthy, overheated room and its complaining occupant.

'I don't think I shall be able to go.'

'But you must, my dear, if the doctor tells you to. And, besides, a change will do you good.'

'I don't think so.'

'But Libbard thinks so, and he knows what he's talking about.'

'No, I can't face it. I'm too weak. I can't go alone.' Mrs Hutton pulled a handkerchief out of her black silk bag, and put it to her eyes.

'Nonsense, my dear, you must make the effort.'

'I had rather be left in peace to die here.' She was crying in earnest now.

'O Lord! Now do be reasonable. Listen now, please.' Mrs Hutton only sobbed more violently. 'Oh, what is one to do?' He shrugged his shoulders and walked out of the room.

Mr Hutton was aware that he had not behaved with proper patience; but he could not help it. Very early in his manhood he had discovered that not only did he not feel sympathy for the poor, the weak, the diseased, and deformed; he actually hated them. Once, as an undergraduate, he spent three days at a mission in the East End. He had returned, filled with a profound and ineradicable disgust. Instead of pitying, he loathed the unfortunate. It was not, he knew, a very comely emotion, and he had been ashamed of it at first. In the end he had decided that it was temperamental, inevitable, and had felt no further qualms. Emily had been healthy and beautiful when he married her. He had loved her then. But now—was it his fault that she was like this?

Mr Hutton dined alone. Food and drink left him more benevolent than he had been before dinner. To make amends for his show of exasperation he went up to his wife's room and offered to read to her. She was touched, gratefully accepted the offer, and Mr Hutton, who was particularly proud of his accent, suggested a little light reading in French.

'French? I am so fond of French.' Mrs Hutton spoke of the language of Racine as though it were a dish of green peas.

Mr Hutton ran down to the library and returned with a yellow volume. He began reading. The effort of pronouncing perfectly absorbed his whole attention. But how good his accent was! The fact of its goodness seemed to improve the quality of the novel he was reading.

At the end of fifteen pages an unmistakable sound aroused him. He looked up; Mrs Hutton had gone to sleep. He sat still for a little while, looking with a dispassionate curiosity at the sleeping face. Once it had been beautiful; once, long ago, the sight of it, the recollection of it, had moved him with an emotion profounder, perhaps, than any he had felt before or since. Now it was lined and cadaverous. The skin was stretched tightly over the cheek-bones, across the bridge of the sharp, bird-like nose. The closed eyes were set in profound bone-rimmed sockets. The lamplight striking on the face from the side emphasized with light and shade its cavities and projections. It was the face of a dead Christ by Morales.

> *Le squelette était invisible*
> *Au temps heureux de l'art païen.*

He shivered a little, and tiptoed out of the room.

On the following day Mrs Hutton came down to luncheon. She had had some unpleasant palpitations during the night, but she was feeling better now. Besides, she wanted to do honour to her guest. Miss Spence listened to her complaints about Llandrindod Wells, and was loud in sympathy, lavish with advice. Whatever she said was always said with intensity. She leaned forward, aimed, so to speak, like a gun, and fired her words. Bang! the charge in her soul was ignited, the words whizzed forth at the narrow barrel of her mouth. She was a machine-gun riddling her hostess with sympathy. Mr Hutton had undergone similar bombardments, mostly of a literary or philosophic character—bombardments of Maeterlinck, of Mrs Besant, of Bergson, of William James. Today the missiles were medical. She talked about insomnia, she expatiated on the virtues of harmless drugs and beneficent specialists. Under the bombardment Mrs Hutton opened out, like a flower in the sun.

Mr Hutton looked on in silence. The spectacle of Janet Spence evoked in him an unfailing curiosity. He was not romantic enough to imagine that every face masked an interior physiognomy of beauty or strangeness, that every woman's small talk was like a vapour hanging over mysterious gulfs. His wife, for example, and Doris; they were nothing more than what they seemed to be. But with Janet Spence it was somehow different. Here one could be sure that there was some kind of a queer face behind the Gioconda smile and the Roman eyebrows. The only question was: What exactly was there? Mr Hutton could never quite make out.

'But perhaps you won't have to go to Llandrindod after all,' Miss Spence was saying. 'If you get well quickly Dr Libbard will let you off.'

'I only hope so. Indeed, I do really feel rather better today.'

Mr Hutton felt ashamed. How much was it his own lack of sympathy that prevented her from feeling well every day? But he comforted himself by reflecting that it was only a case of feeling, not of being better. Sympathy does not mend a diseased liver or a weak heart.

'My dear, I wouldn't eat those red currants if I were you,' he said, suddenly solicitous. 'You know that Libbard has banned everything with skins and pips.'

'But I am so fond of them,' Mrs Hutton protested, 'and I feel so well today.'

'Don't be a tyrant,' said Miss Spence, looking first at him and then at his wife. 'Let the poor invalid have what she fancies; it will do her good.' She laid her hand on Mrs Hutton's arm and patted it affectionately two or three times.

'Thank you, my dear.' Mrs Hutton helped herself to the stewed currants.

'Well, don't blame me if they make you ill again.'

'Do I ever blame you, dear?'

'You have nothing to blame me for,' Mr Hutton answered playfully. 'I am the perfect husband.'

They sat in the garden after luncheon. From the island of shade under the old cypress tree they looked out across a flat expanse of lawn, in which the parterres of flowers shone with a metallic brilliance.

Mr Hutton took a deep breath of the warm and fragrant air. 'It's good to be alive,' he said.

'Just to be alive,' his wife echoed, stretching one pale, knot-jointed hand into the sunlight.

A maid brought the coffee; the silver pots and the little blue cups were set on a folding table near the group of chairs.

'Oh, my medicine!' exclaimed Mrs Hutton. 'Run in and fetch it, Clara, will you? The white bottle on the sideboard.'

'I'll go,' said Mr Hutton. 'I've got to go and fetch a cigar in any case.'

He ran in towards the house. On the threshold he turned round for an instant. The maid was walking back across the lawn. His wife was sitting up in her deck-chair, engaged in opening her white parasol. Miss Spence was bending over the table, pouring out the coffee. He passed into the cool obscurity of the house.

'Do you like sugar in your coffee?' Miss Spence inquired.

'Yes, please. Give me rather a lot. I'll drink it after my medicine to take the taste away.'

Mrs Hutton leaned back in her chair, lowering the sunshade over her eyes, so as to shut out from her vision the burning sky.

Behind her, Miss Spence was making a delicate clinking among the coffee-cups.

'I've given you three large spoonfuls. That ought to take the taste away. And here comes the medicine.'

Mr Hutton had reappeared, carrying a wine-glass, half full of a pale liquid.

'It smells delicious,' he said, as he handed it to his wife.

'That's only the flavouring.' She drank it off at a gulp, shuddered, and made a grimace. 'Ugh, it's so nasty. Give me my coffee.'

Miss Spence gave her the cup; she sipped at it. 'You've made it like syrup. But it's very nice, after that atrocious medicine.'

At half-past three Mrs Hutton complained that she did not feel as well as she had done, and went indoors to lie down. Her husband would have said something about the red currants, but checked himself; the triumph of an 'I told you so' was too cheaply won. Instead, he was sympathetic, and gave her his arm to the house.

'A rest will do you good,' he said. 'By the way, I shan't be back till after dinner.'

'But why? Where are you going?'

'I promised to go to Johnson's this evening. We have to discuss the war memorial, you know.'

'Oh, I wish you weren't going.' Mrs Hutton was almost in tears. 'Can't you stay? I don't like being alone in the house.'

'But, my dear, I promised—weeks ago.' It was a bother having to lie like this. 'And now I must get back and look after Miss Spence.'

He kissed her on the forehead and went out again into the garden. Miss Spence received him aimed and intense.

'Your wife is dreadfully ill,' she fired off at him.

'I thought she cheered up so much when you came.'

'That was purely nervous, purely nervous. I was watching her closely. With a heart in that condition and her digestion wrecked—yes, wrecked—anything might happen.'

'Libbard doesn't take so gloomy a view of poor Emily's health.' Mr Hutton held open the gate that led from the garden into the drive; Miss Spence's car was standing by the front door.

'Libbard is only a country doctor. You ought to see a specialist.'

He could not refrain from laughing. 'You have a macabre passion for specialists.'

Miss Spence held up her hand in protest. 'I am serious. I think poor Emily is in a very bad state. Anything might happen—at any moment.'

He handed her into the car and shut the door. The chauffeur started the engine and climbed into his place, ready to drive off.

'Shall I tell him to start?' He had no desire to continue the conversation.

Miss Spence leaned forward and shot a Gioconda in his direction. 'Remember, I expect you to come and see me again soon.'

Mechanically he grinned, made a polite noise, and, as the car moved forward, waved his hand. He was happy to be alone.

A few minutes afterwards Mr Hutton himself drove away. Doris was waiting at the cross-roads. They dined together twenty miles from home, at a roadside hotel. It was one of those bad, expensive meals which are only cooked in country hotels frequented by motorists. It revolted Mr Hutton, but Doris enjoyed it. She always enjoyed things. Mr Hutton ordered a not very good brand of champagne. He was wishing he had spent the evening in his library.

When they started homewards Doris was a little tipsy and extremely affectionate. It was very dark inside the car, but looking forward, past the motionless form of M'Nab, they could see a bright and narrow universe of forms and colours scooped out of the night by the electric head-lamps.

It was after eleven when Mr Hutton reached home. Dr Libbard met him in the hall. He was a small man with delicate hands and well-formed features that were almost feminine. His brown eyes were large and melancholy. He used to waste a great deal of time sitting at the bedside of his patients, looking sadness through those eyes and talking in a sad, low voice about nothing in particular. His person exhaled a pleasing odour, decidedly antiseptic but at the same time suave and discreetly delicious.

'Libbard?' said Mr Hutton in surprise. 'You here? Is my wife ill?'

'We tried to fetch you earlier,' the soft, melancholy voice replied. 'It was thought you were at Mr Johnson's, but they had no news of you there.'

'No, I was detained. I had a break-down,' Mr Hutton answered irritably. It was tiresome to be caught out in a lie.

'Your wife wanted to see you urgently.'

'Well, I can go now.' Mr Hutton moved towards the stairs.

Dr Libbard laid a hand on his arm. 'I am afraid it's too late.'

'Too late?' He began fumbling with his watch; it wouldn't come out of the pocket.

'Mrs Hutton passed away half an hour ago.'

The voice remained even in its softness, the melancholy of the eyes did not deepen. Dr Libbard spoke of death as he would speak of a local cricket match. All things were equally vain and equally deplorable.

Mr Hutton found himself thinking of Janet Spence's words. At any moment—at any moment. She had been extraordinarily right.

'What happened?' he asked. 'What was the cause?'

Dr Libbard explained. It was heart failure brought on by a violent attack of nausea, caused in its turn by the eating of something of an irritant nature. Red currants? Mr Hutton suggested. Very likely. It had been too much for the heart. There was chronic valvular disease: something had collapsed under the strain. It was all over; she could not have suffered much.

3

'It's a pity they should have chosen the day of the Eton and Harrow match for the funeral,' old General Grego was saying as he stood, his top hat in his hand, under the shadow of the lych gate, wiping his face with his handkerchief.

Mr Hutton overheard the remark and with difficulty restrained a desire to inflict grievous bodily pain on the General. He would have liked to hit the old brute in the middle of his big red face. Monstrous great mulberry, spotted with meal! Was there no respect for the dead? Did nobody care? In theory he didn't much care; let the dead bury their dead. But here, at the graveside, he had found himself actually sobbing. Poor Emily, they had been pretty happy once. Now she was lying at the bottom of a seven-foot hole. And here was Grego complaining that he couldn't go to the Eton and Harrow match.

Mr Hutton looked round at the groups of black figures that were drifting slowly out of the churchyard towards the fleet of cabs and motors assembled in the road outside. Against the brilliant background of the July grass and flowers and foliage, they had a horribly alien and unnatural appearance. It pleased him to think that all these people would soon be dead too.

That evening Mr Hutton sat up late in his library reading the life of Milton. There was no particular reason why he should have chosen Milton; it was the book that first came to hand, that was all. It was after midnight when he had finished. He got up from his armchair, unbolted the French windows, and stepped out on to the little paved terrace. The night was quiet and clear. Mr Hutton looked at the stars and at the holes between them, dropped his eyes to the dim lawns and hueless flowers of the garden, and let them wander over the farther landscape, black and grey under the moon.

He began to think with a kind of confused violence. There were the stars, there was Milton. A man can be somehow the peer of stars and night. Greatness, nobility. But is there seriously a difference between the noble and the ignoble? Milton, the stars, death, and himself—himself. The soul, the body; the higher and the lower nature. Perhaps there was something in it, after all. Milton had a god on his side and righteousness. What had he? Nothing, nothing whatever. There were only Doris's little breasts. What was the point of it all? Milton, the stars, death, and Emily in her grave, Doris and himself—always himself . . .

Oh, he was a futile and disgusting being. Everything convinced him of it. It was a solemn moment. He spoke aloud: 'I will, I will.' The sound of his own voice in the darkness was appalling; it seemed to him that he had sworn that infernal oath which binds even the gods: 'I will, I will.' There had been New Year's days and solemn anniversaries in the past, when he had felt the same contritions and recorded similar resolutions. They had all thinned away, these resolutions, like smoke, into nothingness. But this was a greater moment and he had pronounced a more fearful oath. In the future it was to be different. Yes, he would live by reason, he would be industrious, he would curb his appetites, he would devote his life to some good purpose. It was resolved and it would be so.

In practice he was himself spending his mornings in agricultural pursuits, riding round with the bailiff, seeing that his land was farmed in the best modern way—silos and artificial manures and continuous cropping, and all that. The remainder of the day should be devoted to serious study. There was that book he had been intending to write for so long—*The Effect of Diseases on Civilization*.

Mr Hutton went to bed humble and contrite, but with a sense that grace had entered into him. He slept for seven and a half hours, and woke to find the sun brilliantly shining. The emotions of the evening before had been transformed by a good night's rest into his customary cheerfulness. It was not until a good many seconds after his return to conscious life that he remembered his resolution, his Stygian oath. Milton and death seemed somehow different in the sunlight. As for the stars, they were not there. But the resolutions were good; even in the daytime he could see that. He had his horse saddled after breakfast, and rode round the farm with the bailiff. After luncheon he read Thucydides on the plague at Athens. In the evening he made a few notes on malaria in Southern Italy. While he was undressing he remembered that there was a good anecdote in Skelton's jest-book about the Sweating Sickness. He would have made a note of it if only he could have found a pencil.

On the sixth morning of his new life Mr Hutton found among his correspondence an envelope addressed in that peculiarly vulgar handwriting which he knew to be Doris's. He opened it, and began to read. She didn't know what to say; words were so inadequate. His wife dying like that, and so suddenly—it was too terrible. Mr Hutton sighed, but his interest revived somewhat as he read on:

> 'Death is so frightening, I never think of it when I can help it. But when something like this happens, or when I am feeling ill or depressed, then I can't help remembering it is there so close, and I think about all the wicked things I have done and about you and me, and I wonder what will happen, and I am so frightened. I am so lonely, Teddy Bear, and so unhappy, and I don't know what to do. I can't get rid of the idea of dying, I am so wretched and helpless without you. I didn't mean to write to you; I meant to wait till you were out of mourning and could come and see me again, but I was so lonely and miserable, Teddy Bear, I had to write. I couldn't help it.

Forgive me, I want you so much; I have nobody in the world but you. You are so good and gentle and understanding; there is nobody like you. I shall never forget how good and kind you have been to me, and you are so clever and know so much, I can't understand how you ever came to pay any attention to me, I am so dull and stupid, much less like me and love me, because you do love me a little, don't you, Teddy Bear?'

Mr Hutton was touched with shame and remorse. To be thanked like this, worshipped for having seduced the girl—it was too much. It had just been a piece of imbecile wantonness. Imbecile, idiotic: there was no other way to describe it. For, when all was said, he had derived very little pleasure from it. Taking all things together, he had probably been more bored than amused. Once upon a time he had believed himself to be a hedonist. But to be a hedonist implies a certain process of reasoning, a deliberate choice of known pleasures, a rejection of known pains. This had been done without reason, against it. For he knew beforehand—so well, so well—that there was no interest or pleasure to be derived from these wretched affairs. And yet each time the vague itch came upon him he succumbed, involving himself once more in the old stupidity. There had been Maggie, his wife's maid, and Edith, the girl on the farm, and Mrs Pringle, and the waitress in London, and others—there seemed to be dozens of them. It had all been so stale and boring. He knew it would be; he always knew. And yet, and yet . . . Experience doesn't teach.

Poor little Doris! He would write to her kindly, comfortingly, but he wouldn't see her again. A servant came to tell him that his horse was saddled and waiting. He mounted and rode off. That morning the old bailiff was more irritating than usual.

Five days later Doris and Mr Hutton were sitting together on the pier at Southend; Doris, in white muslin with pink garnishings, radiated happiness; Mr Hutton, legs outstretched and chair tilted, had pushed the panama back from his forehead, and was trying to feel like a tripper. That night, when Doris was asleep, breathing and warm by his side, he recaptured, in this moment of darkness and physical fatigue, the rather cosmic emotion which had possessed him that evening, not a fortnight ago, when he had made his great resolution. And so his solemn oath had already gone the way of so many other resolutions. Unreason had triumphed; at the first itch of desire he had given way. He was hopeless, hopeless.

For a long time he lay with closed eyes, ruminating his humiliation. The girl stirred in her sleep. Mr Hutton turned over and looked in her direction. Enough faint light crept in between the half-drawn curtains to show her bare arm and shoulder, her neck, and the dark tangle of hair on the pillow. She was beautiful, desirable. Why did he lie there moaning over his sins? What did it matter? If he were hopeless, then so be it; he would make the best of his hopelessness. A glorious sense of irresponsibility suddenly filled him. He was free, magnificently free. In a kind of exaltation he drew the girl towards him. She woke, bewildered, almost frightened under his rough kisses.

The storm of his desire subsided into a kind of serene merriment. The whole atmosphere seemed to be quivering with enormous silent laughter.

'Could anyone love you as much as I do, Teddy Bear?' The question came faintly from distant worlds of love.

'I think I know somebody who does,' Mr Hutton replied. The submarine laughter was swelling, rising, ready to break the surface of silence and resound.

'Who? Tell me. What do you mean?' The voice had come very close; charged with suspicion, anguish, indignation, it belonged to this immediate world.

'A—ah!'

'Who?'

'You'll never guess.' Mr Hutton kept up the joke until it began to grow tedious, and then pronounced the name: 'Janet Spence.'

Doris was incredulous. 'Miss Spence of the Manor? That old woman?' It was too ridiculous. Mr Hutton laughed too.

'But it's quite true,' he said. 'She adores me.' Oh, the vast joke! He would go and see her as soon as he returned—see and conquer. 'I believe she wants to marry me,' he added.

'But you wouldn't . . . you don't intend . . .'

The air was fairly crepitating with humour. Mr Hutton laughed aloud. 'I intend to marry you,' he said. It seemed to him the best joke he had ever made in his life.

When Mr Hutton left Southend he was once more a married man. It was agreed that, for the time being, the fact should be kept secret. In the autumn they would go abroad together, and the world should be informed. Meanwhile he was to go back to his own house and Doris to hers.

The day after his return he walked over in the afternoon to see Miss Spence. She received him with the old Gioconda.

'I was expecting you to come.'

'I couldn't keep away,' Mr Hutton gallantly replied.

They sat in the summer-house. It was a pleasant place—a little old stucco temple bowered among dense bushes of evergreen. Miss Spence had left her mark on it by hanging up over the seat a blue-and-white Della Robbia plaque.

'I am thinking of going to Italy this autumn,' said Mr Hutton. He felt like a ginger-beer bottle, ready to pop with bubbling humorous excitement.

'Italy. . . .' Miss Spence closed her eyes ecstatically. 'I feel drawn there too.'

'Why not let yourself be drawn?'

'I don't know. One somehow hasn't the energy and initiative to set out alone.'

'Alone. . . .' Ah, sound of guitars and throaty singing! 'Yes, travelling alone isn't much fun.'

Miss Spence lay back in her chair without speaking. Her eyes were still closed. Mr Hutton stroked his moustache. The silence prolonged itself for what seemed a very long time.

Pressed to stay to dinner, Mr Hutton did not refuse. The fun had hardly started. The table was laid in the loggia. Through its arches they looked out on to the sloping garden, to the valley below and the farther hills. Light ebbed away; the heat and silence were oppressive. A huge cloud was mounting up the sky, and there were distant breathings of thunder. The thunder drew nearer, a wind began to blow, and the first drops of rain fell. The table was cleared. Miss Spence and Mr Hutton sat on in the growing darkness.

Miss Spence broke a long silence by saying meditatively:

'I think everyone has a right to a certain amount of happiness, don't you?'

'Most certainly.' But what was she leading up to? Nobody makes generalizations about life unless they mean to talk about themselves. Happiness: he looked back on his own life, and saw a cheerful, placid existence disturbed by no great griefs or discomforts or alarms. He had always had money and freedom; he had been able to do very much as he wanted. Yes, he supposed he had been happy—happier than most men. And now he was not merely happy; he had discovered in irresponsibility the secret of gaiety. He was about to say something about his happiness when Miss Spence went on speaking.

'People like you and me have a right to be happy some time in our lives.'

'Me?' said Mr Hutton, surprised.

'Poor Henry! Fate hasn't treated either of us very well.'

'Oh, well, it might have treated me worse.'

'You're being cheerful. That's brave of you. But don't think I can't see behind the mask.'

Miss Spence spoke louder and louder as the rain came down more and more heavily. Periodically the thunder cut across her utterances. She talked on, shouting against the noise.

'I have understood you so well and for so long.'

A flash revealed her, aimed and intent, leaning towards him. Her eyes were two profound and menacing gun-barrels. The darkness re-engulfed her.

'You were a lonely soul seeking a companion soul. I could sympathize with you in your solitude. Your marriage . . .'

The thunder cut short the sentence. Miss Spence's voice became audible once more with the words:

'. . . could offer no companionship to a man of your stamp. You needed a soul mate.'

A soul mate—he! a soul mate. It was incredibly fantastic. 'Georgette Leblanc, the ex-soul mate of Maurice Maeterlinck.' He had seen that in the paper a few days ago. So it was thus that Janet Spence had painted him in her imagination—as a soul-mater. And for Doris he was a picture of goodness and the

cleverest man in the world. And actually, really, he was what?—
Who knows?

'My heart went out to you. I could understand; I was lonely,
too.' Miss Spence laid her hand on his knee. 'You were so patient.'
Another flash. She was still aimed, dangerously. 'You never complained. But I could guess—I could guess.'

'How wonderful of you!' So he was an *âme incomprise*. 'Only a
woman's intuition . . .'

The thunder crashed and rumbled, died away, and only the
sound of the rain was left. The thunder was his laughter, magni-
fied, externalized. Flash and crash, there it was again, right on top
of them.

'Don't you feel that you have within you something that is
akin to this storm?' He could imagine her leaning forward as
she uttered the words. 'Passion makes one the equal of the
elements.'

What was his gambit now? Why, obviously, he should have
said 'Yes', and ventured on some unequivocal gesture. But Mr
Hutton suddenly took fright. The ginger beer in him had gone flat.
The woman was serious—terribly serious. He was appalled.

Passion? 'No,' he desperately answered. 'I am without passion.'

But his remark was either unheard or unheeded, for Miss
Spence went on with a growing exaltation, speaking so rapidly,
however, and in such a burningly intimate whisper that Mr
Hutton found it very difficult to distinguish what she was saying.
She was telling him, as far as he could make out, the story of her
life. The lightning was less frequent now, and there were long
intervals of darkness. But at each flash he saw her still aiming
towards him, still yearning forward with a terrifying intensity.
Darkness, the rain, and then flash! her face was there, close at
hand. A pale mask, greenish white; the large eyes, the narrow
barrel of the mouth, the heavy eyebrows. Agrippina, or wasn't it
rather—yes, wasn't it rather George Robey?

He began devising absurd plans for escaping. He might suddenly jump up, pretending he had seen a burglar—Stop thief! stop
thief!—and dash off into the night in pursuit. Or should he say
that he felt faint, a heart attack? or that he had seen a ghost—
Emily's ghost—in the garden? Absorbed in his childish plotting,

he had ceased to pay any attention to Miss Spence's words. The spasmodic clutching of her hand recalled his thoughts.

'I honoured you for that, Henry,' she was saying.

Honoured him for what?

'Marriage is a sacred tie, and your respect for it, even when the marriage was, as it was in your case, an unhappy one, made me respect you and admire you, and—shall I dare say the word?——'

Oh, the burglar, the ghost in the garden! But it was too late.

'. . . yes, love you, Henry, all the more. But we're free now, Henry.'

Free? There was a movement in the dark, and she was kneeling on the floor by his chair.

'Oh, Henry, Henry, I have been unhappy too.'

Her arms embraced him, and by the shaking of her body he could feel that she was sobbing. She might have been a suppliant crying for mercy.

'You mustn't, Janet,' he protested. Those tears were terrible, terrible. 'Not now, not now! You must be calm; you must go to bed.' He patted her shoulder, then got up, disengaging himself from her embrace. He left her still crouching on the floor beside the chair on which he had been sitting.

Groping his way into the hall, and without waiting to look for his hat, he went out of the house, taking infinite pains to close the front door noiselessly behind him. The clouds had blown over, and the moon was shining from a clear sky. There were puddles all along the road, and a noise of running water rose from the gutters and ditches. Mr Hutton splashed along, not caring if he got wet.

How heartrendingly she had sobbed! With the emotions of pity and remorse that the recollection evoked in him there was a certain resentment: why couldn't she have played the game that he was playing—the heartless, amusing game? Yes, but he had known all the time that she wouldn't, she couldn't, play that game; he had known and persisted.

What had she said about passion and the elements? Something absurdly stale, but true, true. There she was, a cloud black-bosomed and charged with thunder, and he, like some absurd little Benjamin Franklin, had sent up a kite into the heart of the menace. Now he was complaining that his toy had drawn the lightning.

She was probably still kneeling by that chair in the loggia, crying.

But why hadn't he been able to keep up the game? Why had his irresponsibility deserted him, leaving him suddenly sober in a cold world? There were no answers to any of his questions. One idea burned steady and luminous in his mind—the idea of flight. He must get away at once.

4

'What are you thinking about, Teddy Bear?'

'Nothing.'

There was a silence. Mr Hutton remained motionless, his elbows on the parapet of the terrace, his chin in his hands, looking down over Florence. He had taken a villa on one of the hilltops to the south of the city. From a little raised terrace at the end of the garden one looked down a long fertile valley on to the town and beyond it to the bleak mass of Monte Morello and, eastward of it, to the peopled hill of Fiesole, dotted with white houses. Everything was clear and luminous in the September sunshine.

'Are you worried about anything?'

'No, thank you.'

'Tell me, Teddy Bear.'

'But, my dear, there's nothing to tell.' Mr Hutton turned round, smiled, and patted the girl's hand. 'I think you'd better go in and have your siesta. It's too hot for you here.'

'Very well, Teddy Bear. Are you coming too?'

'When I've finished my cigar.'

'All right. But do hurry up and finish it, Teddy Bear.' Slowly, reluctantly, she descended the steps of the terrace and walked towards the house.

Mr Hutton continued his contemplation of Florence. He had need to be alone. It was good sometimes to escape from Doris and the restless solicitude of her passion. He had never known the pains of loving hopelessly, but he was experiencing now the pains of being loved. These last weeks had been a period of growing discomfort. Doris was always with him, like an obsession, like a guilty conscience. Yes, it was good to be alone.

He pulled an envelope out of his pocket and opened it, not without reluctance. He hated letters; they always contained something unpleasant—nowadays, since his second marriage. This was from his sister. He began skimming through the insulting home-truths of which it was composed. The words 'indecent haste', 'social suicide', 'scarcely cold in her grave', 'person of the lower classes', all occurred. They were inevitable now in any communication from a well-meaning and right-thinking relative. Impatient, he was about to tear the stupid letter to pieces when his eye fell on a sentence at the bottom of the third page. His heart beat with uncomfortable violence as he read it. It was too monstrous! Janet Spence was going about telling everyone that he had poisoned his wife in order to marry Doris. What damnable malice! Ordinarily a man of the suavest temper, Mr Hutton found himself trembling with rage. He took the childish satisfaction of calling names—he cursed the woman.

Then suddenly he saw the ridiculous side of the situation. The notion that he should have murdered anyone in order to marry Doris! If they only knew how miserably bored he was. Poor, dear Janet! She had tried to be malicious; she had only succeeded in being stupid.

A sound of footsteps aroused him; he looked round. In the garden below the little terrace the servant girl of the house was picking fruit. A Neapolitan, strayed somehow as far north as Florence, she was a specimen of the classical type—a little debased. Her profile might have been taken from a Sicilian coin of a bad period. Her features, carved floridly in the grand tradition, expressed an almost perfect stupidity. Her mouth was the most beautiful thing about her; the calligraphic hand of nature had richly curved it into an expression of mulish bad temper. . . . Under her hideous black clothes, Mr Hutton divined a powerful body, firm and massive. He had looked at her before with a vague interest and curiosity. Today the curiosity defined and focused itself into a desire. An idyll of Theocritus. Here was the woman;

he, alas, was not precisely like a goatherd on the volcanic hills. He called to her.

'Armida!'

The smile with which she answered him was so provocative, attested so easy a virtue, that Mr Hutton took fright. He was on the brink once more—on the brink. He must draw back, oh! quickly, quickly, before it was too late. The girl continued to look up at him.

'*Ha chiamato?*' she asked at last.

Stupidity or reason? Oh, there was no choice now. It was imbecility every time.

'*Scendo*,' he called back to her. Twelve steps led from the garden to the terrace. Mr Hutton counted them. Down, down, down, down. . . . He saw a vision of himself descending from one circle of the inferno to the next—from a darkness full of wind and hail to an abyss of sinking mud.

5

For a good many days the Hutton case had a place on the front page of every newspaper. There had been no more popular murder trial since George Smith had temporarily eclipsed the European War by drowning in a warm bath his seventh bride. The public imagination was stirred by this tale of a murder brought to light months after the date of the crime. Here, it was felt, was one of those incidents in human life, so notable because they are so rare, which do definitely justify the ways of God to man. A wicked man had been moved by an illicit passion to kill his wife. For months he had lived in sin and fancied security—only to be dashed at last more horribly into the pit he had prepared for himself. Murder will out, and here was a case of it. The readers of the newspapers were in a position to follow every movement of the hand of God. There had been vague, but persistent, rumours in the neighbourhood; the police had taken action at last. Then came the exhumation order, the post-mortem examination, the inquest, the evidence of the experts, the verdict of the coroner's jury, the trial, the condemnation. For once Providence had done its duty, obviously, grossly, didactically, as in a melodrama. The news-papers were right in making of the case the staple intellectual food of a whole season.

Mr Hutton's first emotion when he was summoned from Italy to give evidence at the inquest was one of indignation. It was a monstrous, a scandalous thing that the police should take such idle, malicious gossip seriously. When the inquest was over he would bring an action for malicious prosecution against the Chief Constable; he would sue the Spence woman for slander.

The inquest was opened; the astonishing evidence unrolled itself. The experts had examined the body, and had found traces of arsenic; they were of opinion that the late Mrs Hutton had died of arsenic poisoning.

Arsenic poisoning. . . . Emily had died of arsenic poisoning? After that, Mr Hutton learned with surprise that there was enough arsenicated insecticide in his greenhouses to poison an army.

It was now, quite suddenly, that he saw it: there was a case against him. Fascinated, he watched it growing, growing, like some monstrous tropical plant. It was enveloping him, surrounding him; he was lost in a tangled forest.

When was the poison administered? The experts agreed that it must have been swallowed eight or nine hours before death. About lunch-time? Yes, about lunch-time. Clara, the parlour-maid, was called. Mrs Hutton, she remembered, had asked her to go and fetch her medicine. Mr Hutton had volunteered to go instead; he had gone alone. Miss Spence—ah, the memory of the storm, the white aimed face! the horror of it all!—Miss Spence confirmed Clara's statement, and added that Mr Hutton had come back with the medicine already poured out in a wineglass, not in the bottle.

Mr Hutton's indignation evaporated. He was dismayed, fright-ened. It was all too fantastic to be taken seriously, and yet this nightmare was a fact—it was actually happening.

M'Nab had seen them kissing, often. He had taken them for a drive on the day of Mrs Hutton's death. He could see them reflected in the wind-screen, sometimes out of the tail of his eye.

The inquest was adjourned. That evening Doris went to bed

with a headache. When he went to her room after dinner, Mr Hutton found her crying.

'What's the matter?' He sat down on the edge of her bed and began to stroke her hair. For a long time she did not answer, and he went on stroking her hair mechanically, almost unconsciously; sometimes, even, he bent down and kissed her bare shoulder. He had his own affairs, however, to think about. What had happened? How was it that the stupid gossip had actually come true? Emily had died of arsenic poisoning. It was absurd, impossible. The order of things had been broken, and he was at the mercy of an irresponsibility. What had happened, what was going to happen? He was interrupted in the midst of his thoughts.

'It's my fault—it's my fault!' Doris suddenly sobbed out. 'I shouldn't have loved you; I oughtn't to have let you love me. Why was I ever born?'

Mr Hutton didn't say anything, but looked down in silence at the abject figure of misery lying on the bed.

'If they do anything to you I shall kill myself.'

She sat up, held him for a moment at arm's length, and looked at him with a kind of violence, as though she were never to see him again.

'I love you, I love you, I love you.' She drew him, inert and passive, towards her, clasped him, pressed herself against him. 'I didn't know you loved me as much as that, Teddy Bear. But why did you do it—why did you do it?'

Mr Hutton undid her clasping arms and got up. His face became very red. 'You seem to take it for granted that I murdered my wife,' he said. 'It's really too grotesque. What do you all take me for? A cinema hero?' He had begun to lose his temper. All the exasperation, all the fear and bewilderment of the day, was transformed into a violent anger against her. 'It's all such damned stupidity. Haven't you any conception of a civilized man's mentality? Do I look the sort of man who'd go about slaughtering people? I suppose you imagined I was so insanely in love with you that I could commit any folly. When will you women understand that one isn't insanely in love? All one asks for is a quiet life, which you won't allow one to have. I don't know what the devil ever induced me to marry you. It was all a damned stupid, practical joke. And now you go about saying I'm a murderer. I won't stand it.'

Mr Hutton stamped towards the door. He had said horrible things, he knew—odious things that he ought speedily to unsay. But he wouldn't. He closed the door behind him.

'Teddy Bear!' He turned the handle; the latch clicked into place. 'Teddy Bear!' The voice that came to him through the closed door was agonized. Should he go back? He ought to go back. He touched the handle, then withdrew his fingers and quickly walked away. When he was half-way down the stairs he halted. She might try to do something silly—throw herself out of the window or God knows what! He listened attentively; there was no sound. But he pictured her very clearly, tiptoeing across the room, lifting the sash as high as it would go, leaning out into the cold night air. It was raining a little. Under the window lay the paved terrace. How far below? Twenty-five or thirty feet? Once, when he was walking along Piccadilly, a dog had jumped out of a third-storey window of the Ritz. He had seen it fall; he had heard it strike the pavement. Should he go back? He was damned if he would; he hated her.

He sat for a long time in the library. What had happened? What was happening? He turned the question over and over in his mind and could find no answer. Suppose the nightmare dreamed itself out to its horrible conclusion. Death was waiting for him. His eyes filled with tears; he wanted so passionately to live. 'Just to be alive.' Poor Emily had wished it too, he remembered: 'Just to be alive.' There were still so many places in this astonishing world unvisited, so many queer delightful people still unknown, so many lovely women never so much as seen. The huge white oxen would still be dragging their wains along the Tuscan roads, the cypresses would still go up, straight as pillars, to the blue heaven; but he would not be there to see them. And the sweet southern wines—Tear of Christ and Blood of Judas—others would drink them, not he. Others would walk down the obscure and narrow lanes between the bookshelves in the London Library, sniffing the dusty perfume of good literature, peering at strange titles, discovering unknown names, exploring the fringes of vast domains of knowledge. He would be lying in a hole in the ground. And why, why? Confusedly he felt that some extraordinary kind of justice was being done. In the past he had been wanton and imbecile and irresponsible. Now Fate was playing as wantonly, as irresponsibly, with him. It was tit for tat, and God existed after all.

He felt that he would like to pray. Forty years ago he used to kneel by his bed every evening. The nightly formula of his childhood came to him almost unsought from some long unopened chamber of the memory. 'God bless Father and Mother, Tom and Cissie and the Baby, Mademoiselle and Nurse, and everyone that I love, and make me a good boy. Amen.' They were all dead now—all except Cissie.

His mind seemed to soften and dissolve; a great calm descended upon his spirit. He went upstairs to ask Doris's forgiveness. He found her lying on the couch at the foot of the bed. On the floor beside her stood a blue bottle of liniment, marked 'Not to be taken'; she seemed to have drunk about half of it.

'You didn't love me,' was all she said when she opened her eyes to find him bending over her.

Dr Libbard arrived in time to prevent any very serious consequences. 'You mustn't do this again,' he said, while Mr Hutton was out of the room.

'What's to prevent me?' she asked defiantly.

Dr Libbard looked at her with his large, sad eyes. 'There's nothing to prevent you,' he said. 'Only yourself and your baby. Isn't it rather bad luck on your baby, not allowing it to come into the world because you want to go out of it?'

Doris was silent for a time. 'All right,' she whispered. 'I won't.'

Mr Hutton sat by her bedside for the rest of the night. He felt himself now to be indeed a murderer. For a time he persuaded himself that he loved this pitiable child. Dozing in his chair, he woke up, stiff and cold, to find himself drained dry, as it were, of every emotion. He had become nothing but a tired and suffering carcase. At six o'clock he undressed and went to bed for a couple of hours' sleep. In the course of the same afternoon the coroner's jury brought in a verdict of 'Wilful Murder,' and Mr Hutton was committed for trial.

6

Miss Spence was not at all well. She had found her public appearances in the witness-box very trying, and when it was all over she had something that was very nearly a breakdown. She slept badly, and suffered from nervous indigestion. Dr Libbard used to call every other day. She talked to him a great deal—mostly about the Hutton case. . . . Her moral indignation was always on the boil. Wasn't it appalling to think that one had had a murderer in one's house? Wasn't it extraordinary that one could have been for so long mistaken about the man's character? (But she had had an inkling from the first.) And then the girl he had gone off with—so low class, so little better than a prostitute. The news that the second Mrs Hutton was expecting a baby—the posthumous child of a condemned and executed criminal—revolted her; the thing was shocking—an obscenity. Dr Libbard answered her gently and vaguely, and prescribed bromide.

One morning he interrupted her in the midst of her customary tirade. 'By the way,' he said in his soft, melancholy voice, 'I suppose it was really you who poisoned Mrs Hutton.'

Miss Spence stared at him for two or three seconds with enormous eyes, and then quietly said 'Yes.' After that she started to cry.

'In the coffee, I suppose.'

She seemed to nod assent. Dr Libbard took out his fountain pen, and in his neat, meticulous calligraphy wrote out a prescription for a sleeping-draught.

LIAM O'FLAHERTY

The Black Mare

I bought the mare at G—, from a red-whiskered tinker and, if the truth were only known, I believe he stole her somewhere in the south, for he parted with her for thirty shillings. Or else it was because she was so wild that there was not another man at the whole fair had the courage to cross her back with his legs and trot her down the fair green but myself, for it was not for nothing that they called me Dan of the Fury in those days. However, when I landed from the hooker at the pier at Kilmurrage and, mounting her, trotted up to the village, they all laughed at me. For she was a poor-looking animal that day, with long shaggy hair under her belly, and the flesh on her ribs was as scarce as hospitality in a priest's house. She didn't stand an inch over fourteen hands, and my legs almost touched the ground astride of her. So they laughed at me, but I paid no heed to them. I saw the fire in her eyes, and that was all I needed. You see this drop of whiskey in this glass, stranger? It is a pale, weak colour, and it would not cover an inch with wetness, but it has more fire in it than a whole teeming lake of soft water. So the mare.

I set her to pasture in a little field I had between two hills in the valley below the fort. I cared for her as a mother might care for an only child, and all that winter I never put a halter in her mouth or threw my legs across her back, but I used to watch her for hours galloping around the fields snorting, with her great black eyes spitting fire and her nostrils opened so wide that you could hide an egg in each of them. And, Virgin of the Valiant Deeds, when she shed her winter coat in spring and I combed her glossy sides, what a horse she was! As black as the sloes they pick on the slope of Coillnamhan Fort, with never a hair of red or white or yellow. Her tail swept to the ground, and when the sun shone on her sides you could see them shimmering like the jewels on a priest's vestments;

may the good God forgive me, a sinner, for the comparison. But what is nearer to God than a beautiful horse? Tell me that, stranger, who have been in many lands across the sea.

And then the day came when all the unbroken mares of Inverara were to be shod. For it was the custom then, stranger, to shoe all the young mares on the same day, and to break them before they were shod on the wide sandy beach beneath the village of Coillnamhan.

There were seven mares that day gathered together from the four villages of Inverara, and there were good horses among them, but none as good as mine. She was now a little over fifteen hands high, and you could bury a child's hand between her haunches. She was perfect in every limb, like a horse from the stable of the God Crom. I can see her yet, stranger, standing on the strand stamping with her hind leg and cocking her ears at every sound. But it's an old saying, talk of beauty today, talk of death tomorrow.

I kept her to the last, and gave her to a lad to hold while I mounted a bay mare that my cousin had brought from Kilmillick, and I broke her in three rounds of the strand, although she had thrown three strong and hardy men before I seized her halter. And then my mare was brought down, and then and there I offered three quarts of the best whiskey that could be bought for money to the man that could stay on her back for one length of the strand. One after the other they mounted her, but no sooner did they touch her back than she sent them headlong to the ground. She would gather her four legs together and jump her own height from the ground, and with each jump they flew from her back, and she would run shivering around again until they caught her. I smiled, sitting there on a rock.

Then Shemus, the son of Crooked Michael, spat on his hands, tightened his crios around his waist, and said that if the devil were hiding in her bowels and Lucifer's own step-brother riding on her mane, he would break her. He was a man I never liked, that same son of Crooked Michael, a braggart without any good in him, a man who must have come crooked from his mother's womb, and his father before him was the same dishonest son of a horse-stealing tinker. 'Be careful,' I said to him; 'that mare is used to have men about her that didn't drink their mother's milk from a teapot.' And when I saw the ugly look he gave me I knew that there was trouble coming, and so there was.

He got up on her all right, for, to give the devil his due, he was agile on his limbs and, although no horseman, there were few men in the island of Inverara that he couldn't throw with a twist of the wrist he had. But as soon as his legs rubbed her flanks she neighed and gathered herself together to spring, and just as she was that way doubled up he kicked her in the mouth with his foot. She rose to her hind legs and before she could plant her fore feet on the ground again to jump, I had rushed from the rock and with one swing of my right arm I had pulled him to the ground. I was so mad that before he could rush at me I seized him by the thigh and the back of the neck, and I would have broken every limb in his putrid body if they didn't rush in and separate us. Then the craven son of a reptile that he was, as soon as he saw himself held, he began to bellow like a young bull wanting to get at me. But I took no heed of him. My father's son was never a man to crow over a fallen enemy.

They brought the mare over to me and I looked at her. She looked at me and a shiver passed down her flank and she whinnied, pawing the sand with her hind hoof.

'Take off that halter,' said I to the men.

They did. I still kept looking at the mare and she at me. She never moved. Then coming over to her as she stood there without saddle or bridle, stepping lightly on my toes, I laid my right hand on her shoulder. 'Pruach, pruach, my beautiful girl,' I called to her, rubbing her shoulders with my left hand. Then I rose from the strand, leaning on the strength of my right hand and landed on her back as lightly as a bird landing on a rose bush. She darted forward like a flash of lightning from a darkened sky. You see that strand, stretching east from the rock to where it ends in a line of boulders at the eastern end. It is four hundred paces and it rises to the south of the boulders into a high sand bank underneath the road. Well, I turned her at the sand bank with a sudden flash of my hand across her eyes, leaning out over her mane. And then back again we came, with a column of sand rising after us and the ground rising up in front of us with the speed of our progress.

'Now,' said I to myself, 'I will show this son of Crooked Michael what Dan of the Fury can do on horseback.'

Raising myself gently with my hands on her shoulders, I put my two feet square on her haunches and stood straight, leaning against the wind, balancing myself with every motion of her body, and as she ran, stretched flat with her belly to earth, I took my blue woollen shirt off my back and was down again on her shoulders as light as a feather before we reached the western end, where the men stood gaping as if they had seen a priest performing a miracle. 'God be with a man,' they cried. And the women sitting on the hillock that overlooks the beach screamed with fear and enjoyment, and of all the beautiful women that were gathered there that day there was not one that would not have been glad to mate with me with or without marriage.

Back over the strand again we went, the black mare and I, like lightning flying from the thunder, and the wave that rose when we passed the rock in the west had not broken on the strand when we turned again at the sand bank. Then coming back again like the driven wind in winter I rose once more, standing on her haunches, and may the devil swallow me alive if I hadn't put my shirt on my back again and landed back on her shoulders before we reached the rock. There I turned her head to the sea and drove her out into it until the waves lapped her heaving belly. I brought her back to the rock as gentle as a lamb and dismounted.

Ha! My soul from the devil, but that was a day that will never be forgotten as long as there is a man left to breathe the name of Dan of the Fury. But all things have their end, and sure it's a queer day that doesn't bring the night, and the laugh is the herald of the sigh. It was two years after that I got this fractured thigh. Well I remember that four days before the races where I got this broken limb, I met red haired Mary of Kilmillick. As I was looking after her, for she had shapely hips and an enticing swing in them, my horse stumbled, and although I crossed myself three times and promised to make a journey to the Holy Well at Kilmillick, I'll swear by Crom that the spell of the Evil One was put on the mare. But that is old woman's talk. Mary promised me the morning of the races that if the black mare won I could put a ring on her finger, and as I cantered up to the starting point I swore I would win both the race and the girl if the devil himself were holding on to the black mare's tail.

Seventeen horses lined up at the starting point. I took up my position beside a bay stallion that the parish priest, Fr. John Costigan, had entered. He was a blood stallion and had won many races on the mainland, but the parish priest was allowed to enter him, for who could go against a priest. Then, as now, there was nobody in Inverara who was willing to risk being turned into a goat by making a priest obey the rules of a race. Six times they started us and six times we were forced to come back to the starting point, for that same braggart, the son of Crooked Michael, persisted in trying to get away before the appointed time. At last the parish priest knocked him off his horse with a welt of his blackthorn stick and the race started.

We were off like sixteen claps of thunder. We had to circle the field three times, that big field above the beach at Coillnamhan, and before we had circled it the second time, the bay stallion and the mare were in front with the rest nowhere. Neck to neck we ran, and no matter how I urged the mare she would not leave the stallion. Then in the third round of the field I caught a sight of Mary looking at me with a sneer on her face, as if she thought I was afraid to beat the priest's horse. That look drove me mad. I forgot myself. We were stretching towards the winning post. The stallion was reaching in front of me. Mad with rage I struck the mare a heavy blow between the ears. I had never struck her in my life and as soon as I had done it I started with fright and shame. I had struck my horse. I spoke to her gently but she just shivered from the tip of her ears to her tail and darted forward with one mighty rush that left the stallion behind.

I heard a shout from the people. I forgot the blow. I forgot the mare. I leaned forward on her mane and yelled myself. We passed the winning post, with the stallion one hundred yards or more behind us. I tried to draw rein. Her head was like a firm rock. I cursed her and drew rein again. I might have been a flea biting her back. At one bound she leapt the fence and swept down the beach. She was headed straight for the boulders. I saw them in front of me and grew terrified. Between us and the boulders was the sand bank, fifteen feet high. She snorted, raised her head and tried to stop when she saw the fall. I heard a shout from the people. Then I became limp. We rose in the air. We fell. The mare struck the rocks and I remembered no more.

They told me afterward that she was shattered to a pulp when they found us, and sure it's the good God that only gave me a broken leg.

RICHARD HUGHES

The Ghost

He killed me quite easily by crashing my head on the cobbles. *Bang!* Lord, what a fool I was! All my hate went out with that first bang: a fool to have kicked up that fuss just because I had found him with another woman. And now he was doing this to me—*bang!* That was the second one, and with it *everything* went out.

My sleek young soul must have glistened somewhat in the moonlight: for I saw him look up from the body in a fixed sort of way. That gave me an idea: I would haunt him. All my life I had been scared of ghosts: now I was one myself, I would get a bit of my own back. *He* never was: he said there weren't such things as ghosts. Oh, weren't there! I'd soon teach him. John stood up, still staring in front of him: I could see him plainly: gradually all my hate came back. I thrust my face close up against his: but he didn't seem to see it, he just stared. Then he began to walk forward, as if to walk through me: and I was afeard. Silly, for me—a spirit—to be afeard of his solid flesh: but there you are, fear doesn't act as you would expect, ever: and I gave back before him, then slipped aside to let him pass. Almost he was lost in the street-shadows before I recovered myself and followed him.

And yet I don't think he could have given me the slip: there was still something between us that drew me to him—willy-nilly, you might say, I followed him up to High Street, and down Lily Lane.

Lily Lane was all shadows: but yet I could still see him as clear as if it was daylight. Then my courage came back to me: I quickened my pace till I was ahead of him—turned round, flapping my hands and making a moaning sort of noise like the ghosts did I'd read of. He began to smile a little, in a sort of satisfied way: but yet he didn't seem properly to see me. Could it be that his hard disbelief in ghosts made him so that he *couldn't* see me? '*Hoo!*' I whistled through my small teeth. '*Hoo!*

Murderer! Murderer!'—Someone flung up a top window. 'Who's that?' she called. 'What's the matter?'—So other people could hear, at any rate. But I kept silent: I wouldn't give him away—not yet. And all the time he walked straight forward, smiling to himself. He never had any conscience, I said to myself: here he is with new murder on his mind, smiling as easy as if it was nothing. But there was a sort of hard look about him, *all* the same.

It was odd, my being a ghost so suddenly, when ten minutes ago I was a living woman: and now, walking on air, with the wind clear and wet between my shoulder-blades. Ha-ha! I gave a regular shriek and a screech of laughter, it all felt so funny . . . surely John must have heard *that*: but no, he just turned the corner into Pole Street.

All along Pole Street the plane-trees were shedding their leaves: and then I knew what I would do. I made those dead leaves rise up on their thin edges, as if the wind was doing it. All along Pole Street they followed him, pattering on the roadway with their five dry fingers. But John just stirred among them with his feet, and went on: and I followed him: for as I said, there was still some tie between us that drew me.

Once only he turned and seemed to see me: there was a sort of recognition in his face: but no fear, only triumph. 'You're glad you've killed me,' thought I, 'but I'll make you sorry!'

And then all at once the fit left me. A nice sort of Christian, I, scarcely fifteen minutes dead and still thinking of revenge, instead of preparing to meet my Lord! Some sort of voice in me seemed to say: 'Leave him, Millie, leave him alone *before it is too late*!' Too late? Surely I could leave him when I wanted to? Ghosts haunt as they like, don't they? I'd make just one more attempt at terrifying him: then I'd give it up and think about going to heaven.

He stopped, and turned, and faced me full.

I pointed at him with both my hands.

'John!' I cried. 'John! It's all very well for you to stand there, and smile, and stare with your great fish-eyes and think you've won: but you haven't! I'll do you. I'll *finish* you! I'll——'

I stopped, and laughed a little. Windows shot up. 'Who's that? What's the row?'—and so on. They had all heard: but he only turned and walked on.

'Leave him, Millie, before it is too late,' the voice said.

So that's what the voice meant: leave him before I betrayed his secret, and had the crime of revenge on my soul. Very well, I would: I'd leave him. I'd go straight to heaven before any accident happened. So I stretched up my two arms, and tried to float into the air: but at once some force seized me like a great gust, and I was swept away after him down the street. There was something stirring in me that still bound me to him.

Strange, that I should be so real to all those people that they thought me still a living woman: but he—who had most reason to fear me, why, it seemed doubtful whether he even saw me. And where was he going to, right up the desolate long length of Pole Street?—He turned into Rope Street. I saw a blue lamp: that was the police station.

'Oh, Lord,' I thought, 'I've done it! Oh, Lord, he's going to give himself up!'

'You drove him to it,' the voice said. 'You fool, did you think he didn't see you? What did you expect? Did you think he'd shriek, and gibber with fear at you? Did you think your John was a coward?—Now his death is on your head!'

'I didn't do it, I didn't!' I cried. 'I never wished him any harm, never, not *really*! I wouldn't hurt him, not for anything, I wouldn't. Oh, John, don't stare like that. There's still time . . . time!'

And all this while he stood in the door, looking at me, while the policemen came out and stood round him in a ring. He couldn't escape now.

'Oh, John,' I sobbed, 'forgive me! I didn't mean to do it! It was jealousy, John, what did it . . . because I loved you.'

Still the police took no notice of him.

'That's her,' said one of them in a husky voice. 'Done it with a hammer, she done it . . . brained him. But, Lord, isn't her face ghastly? Haunted, like.'

'Look at her 'ead, poor girl. Looks as if she tried to do herself in with the 'ammer, after.'

Then the sergeant stepped forward.

'Anything you say will be taken down as evidence against you.'

'John!' I cried softly, and held out my arms—for at last his face had softened.

'Holy Mary!' said one policeman, crossing himself. 'She's seeing him!'

'They'll not hang her,' another whispered. 'Did you notice her condition, poor girl?'

V. S. PRITCHETT

Sense of Humour

It started one Saturday. I was working new ground and I decided I'd
stay at the hotel the week-end and put in an appearance at church.

'All alone?' asked the girl in the cash desk.

It had been raining since ten o'clock.

'Mr Good has gone,' she said. 'And Mr Straker. He usually
stays with us. But he's gone.'

'That's where they make their mistake,' I said. 'They think they
know everything because they've been on the road all their lives.'

'You're a stranger here, aren't you?' she said.

'I am,' I said. 'And so are you.'

'How do you know that?'

'Obvious,' I said. 'Way you speak.'

'Let's have a light,' she said.

'So's I can see you,' I said.

That was how it started. The rain was pouring down on to the
glass roof of the office.

She'd a cup of tea steaming on the register. I said I'd have one,
too. 'What's it going to be and I'll tell them,' she said, but I said
just a cup of tea.

'I'm T.T.,' I said. 'Too many soakers on the road as it is.'

I was staying there the week-end so as to be sharp on the job on
Monday morning. What's more it pays in these small towns to
turn up at church on Sundays, Presbyterians in the morning,
Methodists in the evening. Say 'Good morning' and 'Good evening' to them. 'Ah!' they say. 'Church-goer! pleased to see that!
T.T., too.' Makes them have a second look at your lines in the
morning. 'Did you like our service, Mister—er—er?' 'Humphrey's
my name.' 'Mr Humphrey.' See? It pays.

'Come into the office, Mr Humphrey,' she said, bringing me a
cup. 'Listen to that rain.'

I went inside.

'Sugar?' she said.

'Three,' I said. We settled to a very pleasant chat. She told me all about herself, and we got on next to families.

'My father was on the railway,' she said.

' "The engine gave a squeal," ' I said. ' "The driver took out his pocket-knife and scraped him off the wheel." '

'That's it,' she said. 'And what is your father's business? You said he had a business.'

'Undertaker,' I said.

'Undertaker?' she said.

'Why not?' I said. 'Good business. Seasonable like everything else. High class undertaker,' I said.

She was looking at me all the time wondering what to say and suddenly she went into fits of laughter.

'Undertaker,' she said, covering her face with her hands and went on laughing.

'Here,' I said. 'What's up?'

'Undertaker!' she laughed and laughed. Struck me as being a pretty thin joke.

'Don't mind me,' she said. 'I'm Irish.'

'Oh, I see,' I said. 'That's it, is it? Got a sense of humour.'

Then the bell rang and a woman called out 'Muriel! Muriel!' and there was a motor bike making a row at the front door.

'All right,' the girl called out. 'Excuse me a moment, Mr Humphrey,' she said. 'Don't think me rude. That's my boy friend. He wants the bird turning up like this.'

She went out but there was her boy friend looking over the window ledge into the office. He had come in. He had a cape on, soaked with rain, and the rain was in beads in his hair. It was fair hair. It stood up on end. He'd been economizing on the brilliantine. He didn't wear a hat. He gave me a look and I gave him a look. I didn't like the look of him. And he didn't like the look of me. A smell of oil and petrol and rain and mackintosh came off him. He had a big mouth with thick lips. They were very red. I recognized him at once as the son of the man who ran the Kounty Garage. I saw this chap when I put my car away. The firm's car. A lock-up, because of the samples. Took me ten minutes to ram the idea into his head. He looked as though he'd never heard of samples. Slow—you know the way they are in the provinces. Slow on the job.

'Oh, Colin,' says she. 'What do you want?'

'Nothing,' the chap said. 'I came in to see you.'

'To see me?'

'Just to see you.'

'You came in this morning.'

'That's right,' he said. He went red. 'You was busy,' he said.

'Well, I'm busy now,' she said.

He bit his tongue, and licked his big lips over and took a look at me. Then he started grinning.

'I got the new bike, Muriel,' he said. 'I've got it outside.'

'It's just come down from the works,' he said.

'The laddie wants you to look at his bike,' I said. So she went out and had a look at it.

When she came back she had got rid of him.

'Listen to that rain,' she said.

'Lord, I'm fed up with this line,' she said.

'What line?' I said. 'The hotel line?'

'Yes,' she said. 'I'm fed right up to the back teeth with it.'

'And you've got good teeth,' I said.

'There's not the class of person there used to be in it,' she said. 'All our family have got good teeth.'

'Not the class?'

'I've been in it five years and there's not the same class at all. You never meet any fellows.'

'Well,' said I. 'If they're like that half-wit at the garage, they're nothing to be struck on. And you've met me.'

I said it to her like that.

'Oh,' says she. 'It isn't as bad as that yet.'

It was cold in the office. She used to sit all day in her overcoat. She was a smart girl with a big friendly chin and a second one coming and her forehead and nose were covered with freckles. She had copper-coloured hair too. She got her shoes through the trade from Duke's traveller and her clothes, too, off the Hollenborough mantle man. I told her I could do her better stockings than the ones she'd got on. She got a good reduction on everything.

Twenty-five or thirty-three and a third. She had her expenses cut right back. I took her to the pictures that night in the car. I made Colin get the car out for me.

'That boy wanted me to go on the back of his bike. On a night like this,' she said.

'Oh,' she said, when we got to the pictures. 'Two shillings's too much. Let's go into the one-and-sixes at the side and we can nip across into the two-shillings when the lights go down.'

'Fancy your father being an undertaker,' she said in the middle of the show. And she started laughing as she had laughed before.

She had her head screwed on all right. She said:

'Some girls have no pride once the lights go down.'

Every time I went to that town I took a box of something. Samples, mostly, they didn't cost me anything.

'Don't thank me,' I said. 'Thank the firm.'

Every time I took her out I pulled the blinds in the back seat of the car to hide the samples. That chap Colin used to give us oil and petrol. He used to give me a funny look. Fishy sort of small eyes he'd got. Always looking miserable. Then we would go off. Sunday was her free day. Not that driving's any holiday for me. And, of course, the firm paid. She used to take me down to see her family for the day. Start in the morning, and taking it you had dinner and tea there, a day's outing cost us nothing. Her father was something on the railway, retired. He had a long stocking, somewhere, but her sister, the one that was married, had had her share already.

He had a tumour after his wife died and they just played upon the old man's feelings. It wasn't right. She wouldn't go near her sister and I don't blame her, taking money like that. Just played upon the old man's feelings.

Every time I was up there Colin used to come in looking for her.

'Oh, Colin,' I used to say. 'Done my car yet?' He knew where he got off with me.

'No, now, I can't, Colin. I tell you I'm going out with Mr Humphrey,' she used to say to him. I heard her.

'He keeps on badgering me,' she said to me.

'You leave him to me,' I said.

'No, he's all right,' she said.

'You let me know if there's any trouble with Colin,' I said. 'Seems to be a harum-scarum sort of half-wit to me,' I said.

'And he spends every penny he makes,' she said.

Well, we know that sort of thing is all right while it lasts, I told her, but the trouble is that it doesn't last.

We were always meeting Colin on the road. I took no notice of it first of all and then I grew suspicious and awkward at always meeting him. He had a new motor bicycle. It was an Indian, a scarlet thing that he used to fly over the moor with, flat out. Muriel and I used to go out over the moor to Ingley Wood in the firm's Morris—I had a customer out that way.

'May as well do a bit of business while you're about it,' I said.

'About what?' she said.

'Ah ha!' I said.

'That's what Colin wants to know,' I said.

Sure enough, coming back we'd hear him popping and back-firing close behind us, and I put out my hand to stop him and keep him following us, biting our dirt.

'I see his little game,' I said. 'Following us.'

So I saw to it that he did follow. We could hear him banging away behind us and the traffic is thick on the Ingley road in the afternoon.

'Oh, let him pass,' Muriel said. 'I can't stand those dirty things banging in my ears.'

I waved him on and past he flew with his scarf flying out, blazing red, into the traffic. 'We're doing 58 ourselves,' she said, leaning across to look.

'Powerful buses those,' I said. 'Any fool can do it if he's got the power. Watch me step on it.'

But we did not catch Colin. Half an hour later he passed us coming back. Cut right in between us and a lorry—I had to brake hard. I damn nearly killed him. His ears were red with the wind. He didn't wear a hat. I got after him as soon as I could but I couldn't touch him.

Nearly every week-end I was in that town seeing my girl, that fellow was hanging around. He came into the bar on Saturday nights, he poked his head into the office on Sunday mornings. It was a sure bet that if we went out in the car he would pass us on the road. Every time we would hear that scarlet thing roar by like a horse-stinger. It didn't matter where we were. He passed us on the main road, he met us down the side roads. There was a little cliff under oak-trees at May Ponds, she said, where the view was pretty. And there, soon after we got there, was Colin on the other side of the water, watching us. Once we found him sitting on his bike, just as though he were waiting for us.

'You been here in a car?' I said.

'No, motor bike,' she said and blushed. 'Cars can't follow in these tracks.'

She knew a lot of places in that country. Some of the roads weren't roads at all and were bad for tyres and I didn't want the firm's car scratched by bushes, but you would have thought Colin could read what was in her mind. For nine times out of ten he was there. It got on my nerves. It was a red, roaring, powerful thing and he opened it full out.

'I'm going to speak to Colin,' I said. 'I won't have him annoying you.'

'He's not annoying me,' she said. 'I've got a sense of humour.'

'Here, Colin,' I said one evening when I put the car away. 'What's the idea?'

He was taking off his overalls. He pretended he did not know what I was talking about. He had a way of rolling his eyeballs, as if they had got wet and loose in his head, while he was speaking to me and you never knew if it was sweat or oil on his face. It was always pale, with high colour on his cheeks and very red lips.

'Miss MacFarlane doesn't like being followed,' I said.

He dropped his jaw and gaped at me. I could not tell whether he was being very surprised or very sly. I used to call him 'Marbles' because when he spoke he seemed to have a lot of marbles in his mouth.

Then he said he never went to the places we went to, except by accident. He wasn't following us, he said, but we were following him. We never let him alone, he said. Everywhere he went, he said, we were there. Take last Saturday, he said, we were following him for miles down the by-pass, he said. 'But you passed us first and then sat down in front,' I said. 'I went to Ingley Wood,' he said. 'And you followed me there.' 'No, we didn't,' I said, 'Miss MacFarlane decided to go there.'

He said he did not want to complain but fair was fair. 'I suppose you know,' he said, 'that you have taken my girl off me. Well, you can leave *me* alone, can't you?'

'Here,' I said. 'One minute! Not so fast! You said I've taken Miss MacFarlane from you. Well, she was never your girl. She only knew you in a friendly way.'

'She was my girl,' was all he said.

He was pouring oil into my engine. He had some cotton wool in one hand and the can in the other. He wiped up the green oil that had overflowed, screwed on the cap, pulled down the bonnet and whistled to himself.

I went back to Muriel and told her what Colin had said.

'I don't like trouble,' I said.

'Don't you worry,' she said. 'I had to have someone to go to all these places with before you came. Couldn't stick in here all day Sunday.'

'Ah,' I said. 'That's it, is it? You've been to all these places with him?'

'Yes,' she said. 'And he keeps on going to them. He's sloppy about me.'

'Good God,' I said. 'Sentimental memories.'

I felt sorry for that fellow. He knew it was hopeless, but he loved her. I suppose he couldn't help himself. Well, it takes all sorts to make a world, as my old mother used to say. If we were all alike it wouldn't do. Some men can't save money. It just runs through their fingers. He couldn't save money so he lost her. I suppose all he thought of was love.

I could have been friends with that fellow. As it was I put a lot of business his way. I didn't want him to get the wrong idea about me. We're all human after all.

We didn't have any more trouble with Colin after this until Bank Holiday. I was going to take her down to see my family. The old man's getting a bit past it now and has given up living over the shop. He's living out on the Barnum Road, beyond the tram stop. We were going down in the firm's car, as per usual, but something went wrong with the mag. and Colin had not got it right for the holiday. I was wild about this. What's the use of a garage who can't do a rush job for the holidays! What's the use of being an old customer if they're going to let you down! I went for Colin bald-headed.

'You knew I wanted it,' I said. 'It's no use trying to put me off with a tale about the stuff not coming down from the works. I've heard that one before.'

I told him he'd got to let me have another car, because he'd let me down. I told him I wouldn't pay his account. I said I'd take my business away from him. But there wasn't a car to be had in the town because of the holiday. I could have knocked the fellow down. After the way I'd sent business to him.

Then I saw through his little game. He knew Muriel and I were going to my people and he had done this to stop it. The moment I saw this I let him know that it would take more than him to stop me doing what I wanted.

I said:

'Right. I shall take the amount of Miss MacFarlane's train fare and my own from the account at the end of the month.'

I said:

'You may run a garage, but you don't run the railway service.'

I was damned angry going by train. I felt quite lost on the railway after having a car. It was crowded with trippers too. It was slow—stopping at all the stations. The people come in, they tread all over your feet, they make you squeeze up till you're crammed against the window, and the women stick out their elbows and fidget. And then the expense! A return for two runs you into just over a couple of quid. I could have murdered Colin.

We got there at last. We walked up from the tram stop. Mother was at the window and let us in.

'This is Miss MacFarlane,' I said.

And mother said:

'Oh, pleased to meet you. We've heard a lot about you.'

'Oh,' mother said to me, giving me a kiss, 'are you tired? You haven't had your tea, have you? Sit down. Have this chair, dear. It's more comfortable.'

'Well, my boy?' my father said.

'Want a wash?' my father said. 'We've got a wash basin downstairs,' he said. 'I used not to mind about washing upstairs before.

Now I couldn't do without it. Funny how your ideas change as you get older.'

'How's business?' he said.

'Mustn't grumble,' I said. 'How's yours?'

'You knew,' he said, 'we took off the horses: except for one or two of the older families we have got motors now.'

But he'd told me that the last time I was there. I'd been at him for years about motor hearses.

'You've forgotten I used to drive them,' I said.

'Bless me, so you did,' he said.

He took me up to my room. He showed me everything he had done to the house. 'Your mother likes it,' he said. 'The traffic's company for her. You know what your mother is for company.'

Then he gives me a funny look.

'Who's the girl?' he says.

My mother came in then and said:

'She's pretty, Arthur.'

'Of course she's pretty,' I said. 'She's Irish.'

'Oh,' said the old man. 'Irish! Got a sense of humour, eh?'

'She wouldn't be marrying me if she hadn't,' I said. And then I gave *them* a look.

'Marrying her, did you say?' exclaimed my father.

'Any objection?' I said.

'Now, Ernest dear,' said my mother. 'Leave the boy alone. Come down while I pop the kettle on.'

She was terribly excited.

'Miss MacFarlane,' the old man said.

'No sugar, thank you, Mrs Humphrey. I beg your pardon, Mr Humphrey?'

'The Glen Hotel at Swansea, I don't suppose you know that?' my father said.

'I wondered if you did being in the catering line.'

'It doesn't follow she knows every hotel,' my mother said.

'Forty years ago,' the old man said, 'I was staying at the Glen in Swansea and the head waiter . . .'

'Oh, no, not that one. I'm sure Miss MacFarlane doesn't want to hear that one,' my mother said.

'How's business with you, Mr Humphrey?' said Muriel. 'We passed a large cemetery near the station.'

'Dad's Ledger,' I said.

'The whole business has changed so that you wouldn't know it, in my lifetime,' said my father. 'Silver fittings have gone clean out. Every one wants simplicity nowadays. Restraint. Dignity,' my father said.

'Prices did it,' my father said.

'The war,' he said.

'You couldn't get the wood,' he said.

'Take ordinary mahogany, just an ordinary piece of mahogany. Or teak,' he said. 'Take teak. Or walnut.'

'You can certainly see the world go by in this room,' I said to my mother.

'It never stops,' she said.

Now it was all bicycles over the new concrete road from the gun factory. Then traction engines and cars. They came up over the hill where the A.A. man stands and choked up round the tram stop. It was mostly holiday traffic. Everything with a wheel on it was out.

'On this stretch,' my father told me, 'they get three accidents a week.' There was an ambulance station at the cross-roads.

We had hardly finished talking about this, in fact the old man was still saying that something ought to be done, when the telephone rang.

'Name of MacFarlane?' the voice said on the wire.

'No. Humphrey,' my father said. 'There is a Miss MacFarlane here.'

'There's a man named Colin Mitchell lying seriously injured in an accident at the Cottage Hospital, gave me the name of MacFarlane as his nearest relative.'

That was the police. On to it at once. That fellow Colin had followed us down by road.

Cry, I never heard a girl cry, as Muriel cried, when we came back from the hospital. He had died in the ambulance. Cutting in, the old game he used to play on me. Clean off the saddle and under the Birmingham bus. The blood was everywhere, they said. People were still looking at it when we went by. Head on. What a mess! Don't let's talk about it.

She wanted to see him but they said 'No.' There wasn't anything recognizable to see. She put her arms round my neck and cried 'Colin. Colin,' as if I were Colin, and clung to me. I was feeling sick myself. I held her tight and I kissed her and I thought, 'Holiday ruined.'

'Damn fool man,' I thought 'Poor devil,' I thought.

'I knew he'd do something like this.'

'There, there,' I said to her. 'Don't think about Colin.'

Didn't she love me, I said, and not Colin? Hadn't she got me? She said, yes, she had. And she loved me. But, 'Oh, Colin! Oh, Colin!' she cried. 'And Colin's mother,' she cried. 'Oh, it's terrible.' She cried and cried.

We put her to bed and I sat with her and my mother kept coming in.

'Leave her to me,' I said. 'I understand her.'

Before they went to bed they both came in and looked at her. She lay sobbing with her head in the pillow.

I could quite understand her being upset. Colin was a decent fellow. He was always doing things for her. He mended her electric lamp and he riveted the stem of a wine-glass so that you couldn't see the break. He used to make things for her. He was very good with his hands.

She lay on her side with her face burning and feverish with misery and crying, scalded by the salt, and her lips shrivelled up. I put my arm under her neck and I stroked her forehead. She groaned. Sometimes she shivered and sometimes she clung to me, crying, 'Oh, Colin! Colin!'

My arm ached with the cramp and I had a crick in my back, sitting in the awkward way I was on the bed. It was late. There was nothing to do but to ache and sit watching her and thinking. It is funny the way your mind drifts. When I was kissing her and watching her I was thinking out who I'd show our new autumn range to first. Her hand held my wrist tight and when I kissed her I got her tears on my lips. They burned and stung. Her neck and shoulders were soft and I could feel her breath hot out of her nostrils on the back of my hand. Ever noticed how hot a woman's breath gets when she's crying? I drew out my hand and lay down beside her and 'Oh, Colin, Colin,' she sobbed, turning over and clinging to me. And so I lay there, listening to the traffic, staring at the ceiling and shivering whenever the picture of Colin shooting right off that damned red thing into the bus came into my mind— until I did not hear the traffic any more, or see the ceiling any more, or think any more, but a change happened—I don't know when. This Colin thing seemed to have knocked the bottom out of everything and I had a funny feeling we were going down and down and down in a lift. And the further we went the hotter and softer she got. Perhaps it was when I found with my hands that she had very big breasts. But it was like being on the mail steamer and feeling engines start up under your feet, thumping louder and louder. You can feel it in every vein of your body. Her mouth opened and her tears dried. Her breath came through her open mouth and her voice was blind and husky. 'Colin, Colin, Colin,' she said, and her fingers were hooked into me. I got out and turned the key in the door.

In the morning I left her sleeping. It did not matter to me what my father might have heard in the night, but still I wondered. She would hardly let me touch her before that. I told her I was sorry but she shut me up. I was afraid of her. I was afraid of mentioning Colin. I wanted to go out of the house there and then and tell someone everything. Did she love Colin all the time? Did she think I was Colin? And every time I thought of that poor devil covered over with a white sheet in the hospital mortuary, a kind of picture of her and me under the sheets with love came into my mind. I couldn't separate the two things. Just as though it had all come from Colin.

I'd rather not talk any more about that. I never talked to Muriel about it. I waited for her to say something but she didn't. She didn't say a word.

The next day was a bad day. It was grey and hot and the air smelled of oil fumes from the road. There's always a mess to clear up when things like this happen. I had to see to it. I had the job of ringing up the boy's mother. But I got round that, thank God, by ringing up the garage and getting them to go round and see the old lady. My father is useless when things are like this. I was the whole morning on the phone: to the hospital, the police, the coroner—

and he stood fussing beside me, jerking up and down like a fat india-rubber ball. I found my mother washing up at the sink and she said:

'That poor boy's mother! I can't stop thinking of her.' Then my father comes in and says—just as though I was a customer:

'Of course if Mrs Mitchell desires it we can have the remains of the deceased conveyed to his house by one of our new specially sprung motor hearses and can, if necessary, make all the funeral arrangements.'

I could have hit him because Muriel came into the room when he was saying this. But she stood there as if nothing had happened.

'It's the least we can do for poor Mrs Mitchell,' she said. There were small creases of shadow under her eyes which shone with a soft strong light I had never seen before. She walked as if she were really still in that room with me, asleep. God, I loved that girl! God, I wanted to get all over this, this damned Colin business that had come right into the middle of everything like this, and I wanted to get married right away. I wanted to be alone with her. That's what Colin did for me.

'Yes,' I said. 'We must do the right thing by Colin.'

'We are sometimes asked for long-distance estimates,' my father said.

'It will be a little something,' my mother said.

'Dad and I will talk it over,' I said.

'Come into the office,' my father said. 'It occurred to me that it would be nice to do the right thing by this friend of yours.'

We talked it over. We went into the cost of it. There was the return journey to reckon. We worked it out that it would come no dearer to old Mrs Mitchell than if she took the train and buried the boy here. That is to say, my father said, if I drove it.

'It would look nice,' my father said.

'Saves money and it would look a bit friendly,' my father said. 'You've done it before.'

'Well,' I said. 'I suppose I can get a refund on my return ticket from the railway.'

But it was not as simple as it looked, because Muriel wanted to come. She wanted to drive back with me and the hearse. My mother was very worried about this. It might upset Muriel, she thought. Father thought it might not look nice to see a young girl sitting by the coffin of a grown man.

'It must be dignified,' my father said. 'You see if she was there it might look as though she were just doing it for the ride—like these young women on bakers' vans.'

My father took me out into the hall to tell me this because he did not want her to hear. But she would not have it. She wanted to come back with Colin.

'Colin loved me. It is my duty to him,' she said.

'Besides,' she said, suddenly, in her full open voice—it had seemed to be closed and carved and broken and small—'I've never been in a hearse before.'

'And it will save her fare too,' I said to my father.

That night I went again to her room. She was awake. I said I was sorry to disturb her but I would go at once only I wanted to see if she was all right. She said, in the closed voice again, that she was all right.

'Are you sure?' I said.

She did not answer. I was worried. I went over to the bed.

'What is the matter? Tell me what is the matter,' I said.

For a long time she was silent. I held her hand, I stroked her head. She was lying stiff in the bed. She would not answer. I dropped my hand to her small white shoulder. She stirred and drew up her legs and half turned and said, 'I was thinking of Colin.'

'Where is he?' she asked.

'They've brought him round. He's lying downstairs.'

'In the front room?'

'Yes, ready for the morning. Now be a sensible girl and go back by train.'

'No, no,' she said. 'I want to go with Colin. Poor Colin. He loved me and I didn't love him.' And she drew my hands down to her breasts.

'Colin loved me,' she whispered.

'Not like this,' I whispered.

It was a warm grey morning like all the others when we took Colin back. They had fixed the coffin in before Muriel came out. She came down wearing the bright blue hat she had got off Dormer's millinery man and she kissed my mother and father good-bye. They were very sorry for her. 'Look after her, Arthur,' my mother said. Muriel got in beside me without a glance behind her at the coffin. I started the engine. They smiled at us. My father raised his hat, but whether it was to Muriel and me or to Colin, or to the three of us, I do not know. He was not, you see, wearing his top hat. I'll say this for the old boy, thirty years in the trade have taught him tact.

After leaving my father's house you have to go down to the tram terminus before you get on to the by-pass. There was always one or two drivers, conductors or inspectors there, doing up their tickets, or changing over the trolley arms. When we passed I saw two of them drop their jaws, stick their pencils in their ears, and raise their hats. I was so surprised by this that I nearly raised mine in acknowledgment, forgetting that we had the coffin behind. I had not driven one of my father's hearses for years.

Hearses are funny things to drive. They are well-sprung, smooth-running cars, with quiet engines, and, if you are used to driving a smaller car, before you know where you are, you are speeding. You know you ought to go slow, say 25 to 30 maximum, and it's hard to keep it down. You can return empty at 70 if you like. It's like driving a fire engine. Go fast out and come back slow—only the other way round. Open out in the country but slow down past houses. That's what it means. My father was very particular about this.

Muriel and I didn't speak very much at first. We sat listening to the engine and the occasional jerk of the coffin behind when we went over a pot-hole. We passed the place where poor Colin—but I didn't say anything to Muriel, and she, if she noticed—which I doubt—did not say anything to me. We went through Cox Hill, Wammering and Yodley Mount, flat country, don't care for it myself. 'There's a wonderful lot of building going on,' Muriel said at last.

'You won't know these places in five years,' I said.

But my mind kept drifting away from the road and the green fields and the dullness, and back to Colin—five days before he had come down this way. I expected to see that Indian coming flying straight out of every corner. But it was all bent and bust up properly now. I saw the damned thing.

He had been up to his old game, following us, and that had put
the end to following. But not quite; he was following us now,
behind us in the coffin. Then my mind drifted off that and I
thought of those nights at my parents' house, and Muriel. You
never know what a woman is going to be like. I thought, too, that
it had put my calculations out. I mean, supposing she had a baby.
You see I had reckoned on waiting eighteen months or so. I would
have eight hundred then. But if we had to get married at once, we
shuld have to cut right down. Then I kept thinking it was funny
her saying 'Colin!' like that in the night; it was funny it made her
feel that way with me, and how it made me feel when she called me
Colin. I'd never thought of her in that way, in what you might call
the 'Colin' way.

I looked at her and she looked at me and she smiled but still we
did not say very much, but the smiles kept coming to both of us.
The light-railway bridge at Dootheby took me by surprise and I
thought the coffin gave a jump as we took it.

'Colin's still watching us,' I nearly said.

There were tears in her eyes.

'What was the matter with Colin?' I said. 'Nice chap, I thought.
Why didn't you marry him?'

'Yes,' she said. 'He was a nice boy. But he'd no sense of
humour.'

'And I wanted to get out of that town,' she said.

'I'm not going to stay there, at that hotel,' she said.

'I want to get away,' she said. 'I've had enough.'

She had a way of getting angry with the air, like that. 'You've
got to take me away,' she said. We were passing slowly into
Muster, there was a tram ahead and people thick on the narrow
pavements, dodging out into the road. But when we got into the
Market Square where they were standing around, they saw the
coffin. They began to raise their hats. Suddenly she laughed. 'It's
like being the King and Queen,' she said.

'They're raising their hats,' she said.

'Not all of them,' I said.

She squeezed my hand and I had to keep her from jumping
about like a child on the seat as we went through.

'There they go.'

'Boys always do,' I said.

'And another.'

'Let's see what the policeman does.'

She started to laugh but I shut her up. 'Keep your sense of humour to yourself,' I said.

Through all those towns that run into one another, as you might say, we caught it. We went through, as she said, like royalty. So many years since I drove a hearse, I'd forgotten what it was like.

I was proud of her, I was proud of Colin, and I was proud of myself. And, after what had happened, I mean on the last two nights, it was like a wedding. And although we knew it was for Colin, it was for us too, because Colin was with both of us. It was like this all the way.

'Look at that man there. Why doesn't he raise his hat? People ought to show respect for the dead,' she said.

FRANK O'CONNOR

Guests of the Nation

1

At dusk this big Englishman Belcher would shift his long legs out of the ashes and ask, 'Well, chums, what about it?' and Noble or me would say, 'As you please, chum' (for we had picked up some of their curious expressions), and the little Englishman 'Awkins would light the lamp and produce the cards. Sometimes Jeremiah Donovan would come up of an evening and supervise the play, and grow excited over 'Awkins's cards (which he always played badly), and shout at him as if he was one of our own, 'Ach, you divil you, why didn't you play the tray?' But, ordinarily, Jeremiah was a sober and contented poor devil like the big Englishman Belcher, and was looked up to at all only because he was a fair hand at documents, though slow enough at these, I vow. He wore a small cloth hat and big gaiters over his long pants, and seldom did I perceive his hands outside the pockets of that pants. He reddened when you talked to him, tilting from toe to heel and back and looking down all the while at his big farmer's feet. His uncommon broad accent was a great source of jest to me, I being from the town as you may recognize.

I couldn't at the time see the point of me and Noble being with Belcher and 'Awkins at all, for it was and is my fixed belief you could have planted that pair in any untended spot from this to Claregalway and they'd have stayed put and flourished like a native weed. I never seen in my short experience two men that took to the country as they did.

They were handed on to us by the Second Battalion to keep when the search for them became too hot, and Noble and myself, being young, took charge with a natural feeling of responsibility. But little 'Awkins made us look right fools when he displayed he knew the countryside as well as we did and something more. 'You're the bloke they calls Bonaparte?' he said to me. 'Well, Bonaparte, Mary Brigid Ho'Connell was arskin' abaout you and said 'ow you'd a pair of socks belonging to 'er young brother.' For it seemed, as they explained it, that the Second used to have little evenings of their own, and some of the girls of the neighbourhood would turn in, and, seeing they were such decent fellows, our lads couldn't well ignore the two Englishmen, but invited them in and were hail-fellow-well-met with them. 'Awkins told me he learned to dance 'The Walls of Limerick' and 'The Siege of Ennis' and 'The Waves of Tory' in a night or two, though naturally he could not return the compliment, because our lads at that time did not dance foreign dances on principle.

So whatever privileges and favours Belcher and 'Awkins had with the Second they duly took with us, and after the first evening we gave up all pretence of keeping a close eye on their behaviour. Not that they could have got far, for they had a notable accent and wore khaki tunics and overcoats with civilian pants and boots. But it's my belief they never had an idea of escaping and were quite contented with their lot.

Now, it was a treat to see how Belcher got off with the old woman of the house we were staying in. She was a great warrant to scold, and crotchety even with us, but before ever she had a chance of giving our guests, as I may call them, a lick of her tongue, Belcher had made her his friend for life. She was breaking sticks at the time, and Belcher, who hadn't been in the house for more than ten minutes, jumped up out of his seat and went across to her.

'Allow me, madam,' he says, smiling his queer little smile; 'please allow me,' and takes the hatchet from her hand. She was struck too parlatic to speak, and ever after Belcher would be at her heels carrying a bucket, or basket, or load of turf, as the case might be. As Noble wittily remarked, he got into looking before she lept, and hot water or any little thing she wanted Belcher would have it ready before her. For such a huge man (and though I am five foot ten myself I had to look up to him) he had an uncommon shortness—or should I say lack—of speech. It took us some time to get used to him walking in and out like a ghost, without a syllable out of him. Especially because 'Awkins talked enough for a platoon, it was strange to hear big Belcher with his toes in the ashes come out with a solitary 'Excuse me, chum,' or 'That's right, chum.' His one and only abiding passion was cards, and I will say for him he was a good card-player. He could have fleeced me and Noble many a time; only if we lost to him, 'Awkins lost to us, and 'Awkins played with the money Belcher gave him.

'Awkins lost to us because he talked too much, and I think now we lost to Belcher for the same reason. 'Awkins and Noble would spit at one another about religion into the early hours of the morning; the little Englishman as you could see worrying the soul out of young Noble (whose brother was a priest) with a string of questions that would puzzle a cardinal. And to make it worse, even in treating of these holy subjects, 'Awkins had a deplorable tongue; I never in all my career struck across a man who could mix such a variety of cursing and bad language into the simplest topic. Oh, a terrible man was little 'Awkins, and a fright to argue! He never did a stroke of work, and when he had no one else to talk to he fixed his claws into the old woman.

I am glad to say that in her he met his match, for one day when he tried to get her to complain profanely of the drought she gave him a great comedown by blaming the drought upon Jupiter Pluvius (a deity neither 'Awkins nor I had ever even heard of, though Noble said among the pagans he was held to have something to do with rain). And another day the same 'Awkins was swearing at the capitalists for starting the German war, when the old dame laid down her iron, puckered up her little crab's mouth and said, 'Mr 'Awkins, you can say what you please about the war, thinking to deceive me because I'm an ignorant old woman, but I know well what started the war. It was that Italian count that stole the heathen divinity out of the temple in Japan, for believe me, Mr 'Awkins, nothing but sorrow and want follows them that disturbs the hidden powers!' Oh, a queer old dame, as you remark!

2

So one evening we had our tea together, and 'Awkins lit the lamp and we all sat in to cards. Jeremiah Donovan came in too, and sat down and watched us for a while. Though he was a shy man and didn't speak much, it was easy to see he had no great love for the two Englishmen, and I was surprised it hadn't struck me so clearly before. Well, like that in the story, a terrible dispute blew up late in the evening between 'Awkins and Noble, about capitalists and priests and love for your own country.

'The capitalists,' says 'Awkins, with an angry gulp, 'the capitalists pays the priests to tell you all about the next world, so's you waon't notice what they do in this!'

'Nonsense, man,' says Noble, losing his temper, 'before ever a capitalist was thought of people believed in the next world.'

'Awkins stood up as if he was preaching a sermon. 'Oh, they did, did they?' he says with a sneer. 'They believed all the things you believe, that's what you mean? And you believe that God created Hadam and Hadam created Shem and Shem created Jehoshophat? You believe all the silly hold fairy-tale abaout Heve and Heden and the happle? Well, listen to me, chum. If you're entitled to 'old to a silly belief like that, I'm entitled to 'old to my own silly belief—which is, that the fust thing your God created was a bleedin' capitalist with mirality and Rolls-Royce complete. Am I right, chum?' he says then to Belcher.

'You're right, chum,' says Belcher, with his queer smile, and gets up from the table to stretch his long legs into the fire and stroke his moustache. So, seeing that Jeremiah Donovan was going, and there was no knowing when the conversation about religion would be over, I took my hat and went out with him. We strolled down towards the village together, and then he suddenly stopped, and blushing and mumbling, and shifting, as his way was, from toe to heel, he said I ought to be behind keeping guard on the prisoners. And I, having it put to me so suddenly, asked him what the hell he wanted a guard on the prisoners at all for, and said that so far as Noble and me were concerned we had talked it over and would rather be out with a column. 'What use is that pair to us?' I asked him.

He looked at me for a spell and said, 'I thought you knew we were keeping them as hostages.' 'Hostages——?' says I, not quite understanding. 'The enemy,' he says in his heavy way, 'have prisoners belong' to us, and now they talk of shooting them. If they shoot our prisoners we'll shoot theirs, and serve them right.' 'Shoot them?' said I, the possibility just beginning to dawn on me. 'Shoot them, exactly,' said he. 'Now,' said I, 'wasn't it very unforeseen of you not to tell me and Noble that?' 'How so?' he asks. 'Seeing that we were acting as guards upon them, of course.' 'And hadn't you reason enough to guess that much?' 'We had not, Jeremiah Donovan, we had not. How were we to know when the men were on our hands so long?' 'And what difference does it make? The enemy have our prisoners as long or longer, haven't they?' 'It makes a great difference,' said I. 'How so?' said he sharply; but I couldn't tell him the difference it made, for I was struck too silly to speak. 'And when may we expect to be released from this anyway?' said I. 'You may expect it tonight,' says he. 'Or tomorrow or the next day at latest. So if it's hanging round here that worries you, you'll be free soon enough.'

I cannot explain it even now, how sad I felt, but I went back to the cottage, a miserable man. When I arrived the discussion was still on, 'Awkins holding forth to all and sundry that there was no next world at all and Noble answering in his best canonical style that there was. But I saw 'Awkins was after having the best of it. 'Do you know what, chum?' he was saying, with his saucy smile, 'I think you're jest as big a bleedin' hunbeliever as I am. You say you believe in the next world and you know jest as much abaout the next world as I do, which is sweet damn-all. What's 'Eaven? You dunno. Where's 'Eaven? You dunno. Who's in 'Eaven? You dunno. You know sweet damn-all! I arsk you again, do they wear wings?'

'Very well then,' says Noble, 'they do; is that enough for you? They do wear wings.' 'Where do they get them then? Who makes them? 'Ave they a fact'ry for wings? 'Ave they a sort of store where you 'ands in your chit and tikes your bleedin' wings? Answer me that.'

'Oh, you're an impossible man to argue with,' says Noble. 'Now listen to me——'. And off the pair of them went again.

It was long after midnight when we locked up the Englishmen

and went to bed ourselves. As I blew out the candle I told Noble what Jeremiah Donovan had told me. Noble took it very quietly. After we had been in bed about an hour he asked me did I think we ought to tell the Englishmen. I having thought of the same thing myself (among many others) said no, because it was more than likely the English wouldn't shoot our men, and anyhow it wasn't to be supposed the Brigade who were always up and down with the Second Battalion and knew the Englishmen well would be likely to want them bumped off. 'I think so,' says Noble. 'It would be sort of cruelty to put the wind up them now.' 'It was very unforeseen of Jeremiah Donovan anyhow,' says I, and by Noble's silence I realized he took my meaning.

So I lay there half the night, and thought and thought, and picturing myself and young Noble trying to prevent the Brigade from shooting 'Awkins and Belcher sent a cold sweat out through me. Because there were men on the Brigade you daren't let nor hinder without a gun in your hand, and at any rate, in those days disunion between brothers seemed to me an awful crime. I knew better after.

It was next morning we found it so hard to face Belcher and 'Awkins with a smile. We went about the house all day scarcely saying a word. Belcher didn't mind us much; he was stretched into the ashes as usual with his usual look of waiting in quietness for something unforeseen to happen, but little 'Awkins gave us a bad time with his audacious gibing and questioning. He was disgusted at Noble's not answering him back. 'Why can't you tike your beating like a man, chum?' he says. 'You with your Hadam and Heve! I'm a Communist—or an Anarchist. An Anarchist, that's what I am.' And for hours he went round the house, mumbling when the fit took him 'Hadam and Heve! Hadam and Heve!'

3

I don't know clearly how we got over that day, but get over it we did, and a great relief it was when the tea-things were cleared away and Belcher said in his peaceable manner, 'Well, chums, what about it?' So we all sat round the table and 'Awkins produced the cards, and at that moment I heard Jeremiah Donovan's footsteps up the path, and a dark presentiment crossed my mind. I rose quietly from the table and laid my hand on him before he reached the door. 'What do you want?' I asked him. 'I want those two soldier friends of yours,' he says reddening. 'Is that the way it is, Jeremiah Donovan?' I ask. 'That's the way. There were four of our lads went west this morning, one of them a boy of sixteen.' 'That's bad, Jeremiah,' says I.

At that moment Noble came out, and we walked down the path together talking in whispers. Feeney, the local intelligence officer, was standing by the gate. 'What are you going to do about it?' I asked Jeremiah Donovan. 'I want you and Noble to bring them out: you can tell them they're being shifted again; that'll be the quietest way.' 'Leave me out of that,' says Noble suddenly. Jeremiah Donovan looked at him hard for a minute or two. 'All right so,' he said peaceably. 'You and Feeney collect a few tools from the shed and dig a hole by the far end of the bog. Bonaparte and I'll be after you in about twenty minutes. But whatever else you do, don't let anyone see you with the tools. No one must know but the four of ourselves.'

We saw Feeney and Noble go round to the houseen where the tools were kept, and sidled in. Everything if I can so express myself was tottering before my eyes, and I left Jeremiah Donovan to do the explaining as best he could, while I took a seat and said nothing. He told them they were to go back to the Second. 'Awkins let a mouthful of curses out of him at that, and it was plain that Belcher, though he said nothing, was duly perturbed. The old woman was for having them stay in spite of us, and she did not shut her mouth until Jeremiah Donovan lost his temper and said some nasty things to her. Within the house by this time it was pitch dark, but no one thought of lighting the lamp, and in the darkness the two Englishmen fetched their khaki top-coats and said good-bye to the woman of the house. 'Just as a man mikes a 'ome of a bleedin' place,' mumbles 'Awkins shaking her by the hand, 'some bastard at headquarters thinks you're too cushy and shunts you off.' Belcher shakes her hand very hearty. 'A thousand thanks, madam,' he says, 'a thousand thanks for everything . . .' as though he'd made it all up.

We go round to the back of the house and down towards the fatal bog. Then Jeremiah Donovan comes out with what is in his mind. 'There were four of our lads shot by your fellows this morning so now you're to be bumped off.' 'Cut that stuff out,' says 'Awkins flaring up. 'It's bad enough to be mucked about such as we are without you plying at soldiers.' 'It's true,' says Jeremiah Donovan, 'I'm sorry, 'Awkins, but 'tis true,' and comes out with the usual rigmarole about doing our duty and obeying our superiors. 'Cut it out,' says 'Awkins irritably, 'Cut it out!'

Then, when Donovan sees he is not being believed he turns to me. 'Ask Bonaparte here,' he says. 'I don't need to arsk Bonaparte. Me and Bonaparte are chums.' 'Isn't it true, Bonaparte?' says Jeremiah Donovan solemnly to me. 'It is,' I say sadly, 'it is.' 'Awkins stops. 'Now, for Christ's sike. . . .' 'I mean it, chum,' I say. 'You daon't saound as if you mean it. You knaow well you don't mean it.' 'Well, if he don't I do,' says Jeremiah Donovan. 'Why the 'ell sh'd you want to shoot me, Jeremiah Donovan?' 'Why the hell should your people take out four prisoners and shoot them in cold blood upon a barrack square?' I perceive Jeremiah Donovan is trying to encourage himself with hot words.

Anyway, he took little 'Awkins by the arm and dragged him on, but it was impossible to make him understand that we were in earnest. From which you will perceive how difficult it was for me, as I kept feeling my Smith and Wesson and thinking what I would do if they happened to put up a fight or ran for it, and wishing in my heart they would. I knew if only they ran I would never fire on them. 'Was Noble in this?' 'Awkins wanted to know, and we said yes. He laughed. But why should Noble want to shoot him? Why should we want to shoot him? What had he done to us? Weren't we chums (the word lingers painfully in my memory)? Weren't we? Didn't we understand him and didn't he understand us? Did either of us imagine for an instant that he'd shoot us for all the so-and-so brigadiers in the so-and-so British Army? By this time I began to perceive in the dusk the desolate edges of the bog that was to be their last earthly bed, and, so great a sadness overtook my mind, I could not answer him. We walked along the edge of it in the darkness, and every now and then 'Awkins would call a halt and begin again, just as if he was wound up, about us being chums, and I was in despair that nothing but the cold and open grave made ready for his presence would convince him that we meant it all. But all the same, if you can understand, I didn't want him to be bumped off.

4

At last we saw the unsteady glint of a lantern in the distance and made towards it. Noble was carrying it, and Feeney stood somewhere in the darkness behind, and somehow the picture of the two of them so silent in the boglands was like the pain of death in my heart. Belcher, on recognizing Noble, said "Allo, chum' in his usual peaceable way, but 'Awkins flew at the poor boy immediately, and the dispute began all over again, only that Noble hadn't a word to say for himself, and stood there with the swaying lantern between his gaitered legs.

It was Jeremiah Donovan who did the answering. 'Awkins asked for the twentieth time (for it seemed to haunt his mind) if anybody thought he'd shoot Noble. 'You would,' says Jeremiah Donovan shortly. 'I wouldn't, damn you!' 'You would if you knew you'd be shot for not doing it.' 'I wouldn't, not if I was to be shot twenty times over; he's my chum. And Belcher wouldn't— isn't that right, Belcher?' 'That's right, chum,' says Belcher peaceably. 'Damned if I would. Anyway, who says Noble'd be shot if I wasn't bumped off? What d'you think I'd do if I was in Noble's place and we were out in the middle of a blasted bog?' 'What would you do?' 'I'd go with him wherever he was going. I'd share my last bob with him and stick by 'im through thick and thin.'

'We've had enough of this,' says Jeremiah Donovan, cocking his revolver. 'Is there any message you want to send before I fire?' 'No, there isn't, but . . .' 'Do you want to say your prayers?' 'Awkins came out with a cold-blooded remark that shocked even me and turned to Noble again. 'Listen to me, Noble,' he said. 'You and me are chums. You won't come over to my side, so I'll come over to your side. Is that fair? Just you give me a rifle and I'll go with you wherever you want.'

Nobody answered him.

'Do you understand?' he said. 'I'm through with it all. I'm a deserter or anything else you like, but from this on I'm one of you. Does that prove to you that I mean what I say?' Noble raised his head, but as Donovan began to speak he lowered it again without answering. 'For the last time have you any messages to send?' says Donovan in a cold and excited voice.

'Ah, shut up, you, Donovan; you don't understand me, but these fellows do. They're my chums; they stand by me and I stand by them. We're not the capitalist tools you seem to think us.'

I alone of the crowd saw Donovan raise his Webley to the back of 'Awkins's neck, and as he did so I shut my eyes and tried to say a prayer. 'Awkins had begun to say something else when Donovan let fly, and, as I opened my eyes at the bang, I saw him stagger at the knees and lie out flat at Noble's feet, slowly, and as quiet as a child, with the lantern-light falling sadly upon his lean legs and bright farmer's boots. We all stood very still for a while watching him settle out in the last agony.

Then Belcher quietly takes out a handkerchief, and begins to tie it about his own eyes (for in our excitement we had forgotten to offer the same to 'Awkins), and, seeing it is not big enough, turns and asks for a loan of mine. I give it to him and as he knots the two together he points with his foot at 'Awkins. ' 'E's not quite dead,' he says, 'better give 'im another.' Sure enough 'Awkins's left knee as we see it under the lantern is rising again. I bend down and put my gun to his ear; then, recollecting myself and the company of Belcher, I stand up again with a few hasty words. Belcher understands what is in my mind. 'Give 'im 'is first,' he says. 'I don't mind. Poor bastard, we dunno what's 'appening to 'im now.' As by this time I am beyond all feeling I kneel down again and skilfully give 'Awkins the last shot so as to put him for ever out of pain.

Belcher who is fumbling a bit awkwardly with the handkerchiefs comes out with a laugh when he hears the shot. It is the first time I have heard him laugh, and it sends a shiver down my spine, coming as it does so inappropriately upon the tragic death of his old friend. 'Poor blighter,' he says quietly, 'and last night he was so curious abaout it all. It's very queer, chums, I always think. Naow, 'e knows as much abaout it as they'll ever let 'im know, and last night 'e was all in the dark.'

Donovan helps him to tie the handkerchiefs about his eyes. 'Thanks, chum,' he says. Donovan asks him if there are any messages he would like to send. 'Naow, chum,' he says, 'none for me. If any of you likes to write to 'Awkins's mother you'll find a letter from 'er in 'is pocket. But my missus left me eight years ago. Went away with another fellow and took the kid with her. I likes the feelin' of a 'ome (as you may 'ave noticed) but I couldn't start again after that.'

We stand around like fools now that he can no longer see us. Donovan looks at Noble and Noble shakes his head. Then Donovan raises his Webley again and just at that moment Belcher laughs his queer nervous laugh again. He must think we are talking of him; anyway, Donovan lowers his gun. ' 'Scuse me, chums,' says Belcher, 'I feel I'm talking the 'ell of a lot . . . and so silly . . . abaout me being so 'andy abaout a 'ouse. But this thing come on me so sudden. You'll forgive me, I'm sure.' 'You don't want to say a prayer?' asks Jeremiah Donovan. 'No, chum,' he replies, 'I don't think that'd 'elp. I'm ready if you want to get it over.' 'You understand,' says Jeremiah Donovan, 'it's not so much our doing. It's our duty, so to speak.' Belcher's head is raised like a real blind man's, so that you can only see his nose and chin in the lamplight. 'I never could make out what duty was myself,' he said, 'but I think you're all good lads, if that's what you mean. I'm not complaining.' Noble, with a look of desperation, signals to Donovan, and in a flash Donovan raises his gun and fires. The big man goes over like a sack of meal, and this time there is no need of a second shot.

I don't remember much about the burying, but that it was worse than all the rest, because we had to carry the warm corpses a few yards before we sunk them in the windy bog. It was all mad lonely, with only a bit of lantern between ourselves and the pitch-blackness, and birds hooting and screeching all round disturbed by the guns. Noble had to search 'Awkins first to get the letter from his mother. Then having smoothed all signs of the grave away, Noble and I collected our tools, said good-bye to the others, and went back along the desolate edge of the treacherous bog without a word. We put the tools in the houseen and went into the house. The kitchen was pitch-black and cold, just as we left it, and the old woman was sitting over the hearth telling her beads. We walked past her into the room, and Noble struck a match to light the lamp. Just then she rose quietly and came to the doorway, being not at all so bold or crabbed as usual.

'What did ye do with them?' she says in a sort of whisper, and Noble took such a mortal start the match quenched in his trembling hand. 'What's that?' he asks without turning round. 'I heard ye,' she said. 'What did you hear?' asks Noble, but sure he wouldn't deceive a child the way he said it. 'I heard ye. Do you think I wasn't listening to ye putting the things back in the houseen?' Noble struck another match and this time the lamp lit for him. 'Was that what ye did with them?' she said, and Noble said nothing—after all what could he say?

So then, by God, she fell on her two knees by the door, and began telling her beads, and after a minute or two Noble went on his knees by the fireplace, so I pushed my way out past her, and stood at the door, watching the stars and listening to the damned shrieking of the birds. It is so strange what you feel at such moments, and not to be written afterwards. Noble says he felt he seen everything ten times as big, perceiving nothing around him but the little patch of black bog with the two Englishmen stiffening into it; but with me it was the other way, as though the patch of bog where the two Englishmen were was a thousand miles away from me, and even Noble mumbling just behind me and the old woman and the birds and the bloody stars were all far away, and I was somehow very small and very lonely. And anything that ever happened me after I never felt the same about again.

EVELYN WAUGH

Mr Loveday's Little Outing

'You will not find your father greatly changed,' remarked Lady Moping, as the car turned into the gates of the County Asylum.

'Will he be wearing a uniform?' asked Angela.

'No, dear, of course not. He is receiving the very best attention.'

It was Angela's first visit and it was being made at her own suggestion.

Ten years had passed since the showery day in late summer when Lord Moping had been taken away; a day of confused but bitter memories for her; the day of Lady Moping's annual garden party, always bitter, confused that day by the caprice of the weather which, remaining clear and brilliant with promise until the arrival of the first guests, had suddenly blackened into a squall. There had been a scuttle for cover; the marquee had capsized; a frantic carrying of cushions and chairs; a tablecloth lifted to the boughs of the monkey-puzzler, fluttering in the rain; a bright period and the cautious emergence of guests onto the soggy lawns; another squall; another twenty minutes of sunshine. It had been an abominable afternoon, culminating at about six o'clock in her father's attempted suicide.

Lord Moping habitually threatened suicide on the occasion of the garden party; that year he had been found black in the face, hanging by his braces in the orangery; some neighbours, who were sheltering there from the rain, set him on his feet again, and before dinner a van had called for him. Since then Lady Moping had paid seasonal calls at the asylum and returned in time for tea, rather reticent of her experience.

Many of her neighbours were inclined to be critical of Lord Moping's accommodation. He was not, of course, an ordinary inmate. He lived in a separate wing of the asylum, specially devoted to the segregation of wealthier lunatics. These were given every consideration which their foibles permitted. They might choose their own clothes (many indulged in the liveliest fancies), smoke the most expensive brands of cigars and, on the anniversaries of their certification, entertain any other inmates for whom they had an attachment, to private dinner parties.

The fact remained, however, that it was far from being the most expensive kind of institution; the uncompromising address, 'COUNTY HOME FOR MENTAL DEFECTIVES' stamped across the note-paper, worked on the uniforms of their attendants, painted, even, upon a prominent hoarding at the main entrance, suggested the lowest associations. From time to time, with less or more tact, her friends attempted to bring to Lady Moping's notice particulars of seaside nursing homes, of 'qualified practitioners with large private grounds suitable for the charge of nervous or difficult cases', but she accepted them lightly; when her son came of age he might make any changes that he thought fit; meanwhile she felt no inclination to relax her economical regime; her husband had betrayed her basely on the one day in the year when she looked for loyal support, and was far better off than he deserved.

A few lonely figures in greatcoats were shuffling and loping about the park.

'Those are the lower-class lunatics,' observed Lady Moping. 'There is a very nice little flower garden for people like your father. I sent them some cuttings last year.'

They drove past the blank, yellow brick façade to the doctor's private entrance and were received by him in the 'visitors' room', set aside for interviews of this kind. The window was protected on the inside by bars and wire netting; there was no fireplace; when Angela nervously attempted to move her chair further from the radiator, she found that it was screwed to the floor.

'Lord Moping is quite ready to see you,' said the doctor.

'How is he?'

'Oh, very well, very well indeed, I'm glad to say. He had rather a nasty cold some time ago, but apart from that his condition is excellent. He spends a lot of his time in writing.'

They heard a shuffling, skipping sound approaching along the flagged passage. Outside the door a high peevish voice, which

Angela recognized as her father's, said: 'I haven't the time, I tell you. Let them come back later.'

A gentler tone, with a slight rural burr, replied, 'Now come along. It is a purely formal audience. You need stay no longer than you like.'

Then the door was pushed open (it had no lock or fastening) and Lord Moping came into the room. He was attended by an elderly little man with full white hair and an expression of great kindness.

'That is Mr Loveday who acts as Lord Moping's attendant.'

'Secretary,' said Lord Moping. He moved with a jogging gait and shook hands with his wife.

'This is Angela. You remember Angela, don't you?'

'No, I can't say that I do. What does she want?'

'We just came to see you.'

'Well, you have come at an exceedingly inconvenient time. I am very busy. Have you typed out that letter to the Pope yet, Loveday?'

'No, my lord, if you remember, you asked me to look up the figures about the Newfoundland fisheries first?'

'So I did. Well, it is fortunate, as I think the whole letter will have to be redrafted. A great deal of new information has come to light since luncheon. A great deal . . . You see, my dear, I am fully occupied.' He turned his restless, quizzical eyes upon Angela. 'I suppose you have come about the Danube. Well, you must come again later. Tell them it will be all right, quite all right, but I have not had time to give my full attention to it. Tell them that.'

'Very well, Papa.'

'Anyway,' said Lord Moping rather petulantly, 'it is a matter of secondary importance. There is the Elbe and the Amazon and the Tigris to be dealt with first, eh, Loveday? . . . *Danube* indeed. Nasty little river. I'd only call it a stream myself. Well, can't stop, nice of you to come. I would do more for you if I could, but you see how I'm fixed. Write to me about it. That's it. *Put it in black and white.*'

And with that he left the room.

'You see,' said the doctor, 'he is in excellent condition. He is putting on weight, eating and sleeping excellently. In fact, the whole tone of his system is above reproach.'

The door opened again and Loveday returned.

'Forgive my coming back, sir, but I was afraid that the young lady might be upset at his Lordship's not knowing her. You mustn't mind him, miss. Next time he'll be very pleased to see you. It's only today he's put out on account of being behindhand with his work. You see, sir, all this week I've been helping in the library and I haven't been able to get all his Lordship's reports typed out. And he's got muddled with his card index. That's all it is. He doesn't mean any harm.'

'What a nice man,' said Angela, when Loveday had gone back to his charge.

'Yes. I don't know what we should do without old Loveday. Everybody loves him, staff and patients alike.'

'I remember him well. It's a great comfort to know that you are able to get such good warders,' said Lady Moping; 'people who don't know, say such foolish things about asylums.'

'Oh, but Loveday isn't a warder,' said the doctor.

'You don't mean he's cuckoo, too?' said Angela.

The doctor corrected her.

'He is an *inmate*. It is rather an interesting case. He has been here for thirty-five years.'

'But I've never seen anyone saner,' said Angela.

'He certainly has that air,' said the doctor, 'and in the last twenty years we have treated him as such. He is the life and soul of the place. Of course he is not one of the private patients, but we allow him to mix freely with them. He plays billiards excellently, does conjuring tricks at the concert, mends their gramophones, valets them, helps them in their crossword puzzles and various— er—hobbies. We allow them to give him small tips for services rendered, and he must by now have amassed quite a little fortune. He has a way with even the most troublesome of them. An invaluable man about the place.'

'Yes, but why is he here?'

'Well, it is rather sad. When he was a very young man he killed somebody—a young woman quite unknown to him, whom he knocked off her bicycle and then throttled. He gave himself up immediately afterwards and has been here ever since.'

'But surely he is perfectly safe now. Why is he not let out?'

'Well, I suppose if it was to anyone's interest, he would be. He has no relatives except a step-sister who lives in Plymouth. She used to visit him at one time, but she hasn't been for years now. He's perfectly happy here and I can assure you *we* aren't going to take the first steps in turning him out. He's far too useful to us.'

'But it doesn't seem fair,' said Angela.

'Look at your father,' said the doctor. 'He'd be quite lost without Loveday to act as his secretary.'

'It doesn't seem fair.'

Angela left the asylum, oppressed by a sense of injustice. Her mother was unsympathetic.

'Think of being locked up in a looney bin all one's life.'

'He attempted to hang himself in the orangery,' replied Lady Moping, '*in front of the Chester-Martins.*'

'I don't mean Papa. I mean Mr Loveday.'

'I don't think I know him.'

'Yes, the looney they have put to look after papa.'

'Your father's secretary. A very decent sort of man, I thought, and eminently suited to his work.'

Angela left the question for the time, but returned to it again at luncheon on the following day.

'Mums, what does one have to do to get people out of the bin?'

'The bin? Good gracious, child, I hope that you do not anticipate your father's return *here*.'

'No. No. Mr Loveday.'

'Angela, you seem to me to be totally bemused. I see it was a mistake to take you with me on our little visit yesterday.'

After luncheon Angela disappeared to the library and was soon immersed in the lunacy laws as represented in the encyclopaedia.

She did not reopen the subject with her mother, but a fortnight later, when there was a question of taking some pheasants over to her father for his eleventh Certification Party she showed an unusual willingness to run over with them. Her mother was occupied with other interests and noticed nothing suspicious.

Angela drove her small car to the asylum, and after delivering the game, asked for Mr Loveday. He was busy at the time making a crown for one of his companions who expected hourly to be anointed Emperor of Brazil, but he left his work and enjoyed several minutes' conversation with her. They spoke about her father's health and spirits. After a time Angela remarked, 'Don't you ever want to get away?'

Mr Loveday looked at her with his gentle, blue-grey eyes. 'I've got very well used to the life, miss. I'm fond of the poor people here, and I think that several of them are quite fond of me. At least, I think they would miss me if I were to go.'

'But don't you ever think of being free again?'

'Oh yes, miss, I think of it—almost all the time I think of it.'

'What would you do if you got out? There must be *something* you would sooner do than stay here.'

The old man fidgeted uneasily. 'Well, miss, it sounds ungrateful, but I can't deny I should welcome a little outing, once, before I get too old to enjoy it. I expect we all have our secret ambitions, and there *is* one thing I often wish I could do. You mustn't ask me what. . . . It wouldn't take long. But I do feel that if I had done it, just for a day, an afternoon even, then I would die quiet. I could settle down again easier, and devote myself to the poor crazed people here with a better heart. Yes, I do feel that.'

There were tears in Angela's eyes that afternoon as she drove away. 'He *shall* have his little outing, bless him,' she said.

From that day onwards for many weeks Angela had a new purpose in life. She moved about the ordinary routine of her home with an abstracted air and an unfamiliar, reserved courtesy which greatly disconcerted Lady Moping.

'I believe the child's in love. I only pray that it isn't that uncouth Egbertson boy.'

She read a great deal in the library, she cross-examined any guests who had pretensions to legal or medical knowledge, she showed extreme good will to old Sir Roderick Lane-Foscote their Member. The names 'alienist', 'barrister' or 'governmental official' now had for her the glamour that formerly surrounded film actors and professional wrestlers. She was a woman with a cause, and before the end of the hunting season she had triumphed. Mr Loveday achieved his liberty.

The doctor at the asylum showed reluctance but no real opposition. Sir Roderick wrote to the Home Office. The necessary papers were signed, and at last the day came when Mr Loveday took leave of the home where he had spent such long and useful years.

His departure was marked by some ceremony. Angela and Sir Roderick Lane-Foscote sat with the doctors on the stage of the gymnasium. Below them was assembled everyone in the institution who was thought to be stable enough to endure the excitement.

Lord Moping, with a few suitable expressions of regret, presented Mr Loveday on behalf of the wealthier lunatics with a gold cigarette case; those who supposed themselves to be emperors showered him with decorations and titles of honour. The warders gave him a silver watch and many of the non-paying inmates were in tears on the day of the presentation.

The doctor made the main speech of the afternoon. 'Remember,' he remarked, 'that you leave behind you nothing but our warmest good wishes. You are bound to us by ties that none will forget. Time will only deepen our sense of debt to you. If at any time in the future you should grow tired of your life in the world, there will always be a welcome for you here. Your post will be open.'

A dozen or so variously afflicted lunatics hopped and skipped after him down the drive until the iron gates opened and Mr Loveday stepped into his freedom. His small trunk had already gone to the station; he elected to walk. He had been reticent about his plans, but he was well provided with money, and the general impression was that he would go to London and enjoy himself a little before visiting his step-sister in Plymouth.

It was to the surprise of all that he returned within two hours of his liberation. He was smiling whimsically, a gentle, self-regarding smile of reminiscence.

'I have come back,' he informed the doctor. 'I think that now I shall be here for good.'

'But, Loveday, what a short holiday. I'm afraid that you have hardly enjoyed yourself at all.'

'Oh yes, sir, thank you, sir, I've enjoyed myself *very much*. I'd been promising myself one little treat, all these years. It was short, sir, but *most* enjoyable. Now I shall be able to settle down again to my work here without any regrets.'

Half a mile up the road from the asylum gates, they later discovered an abandoned bicycle. It was a lady's machine of some antiquity. Quite near it in the ditch lay the strangled body of a young woman, who, riding home to her tea, had chanced to overtake Mr Loveday, as he strode along, musing on his opportunities.

Alexander

1

Early one August morning a curious black cart on low springs, drawn by a little shaggy pony with a tail that swept about its legs like a shirt, jogged steadily off from a narrow street bordering the river, climbed in a leisurely manner through the town, and began travelling slowly and almost sleepily eastward towards open country.

In the cart, half concealed by piles of creaking baskets, sat a small, fair-haired boy of eleven or twelve, with drowsy blue eyes; and by his side a fat, sunburnt man with white hair, dressed in breeches and black leggings and a red waistcoat, evidently put on with special care and worn with special pride. All the buttons of this garment resembled fishes' eyes, and a good many cunning pockets were concealed in every part of it, inside and outside, back and front. A silver watch-chain dangled across it, bearing handsome engraved medals won for fishing and shooting. Something about the waistcoat, perhaps the medals themselves, seemed to attract the boy, for he sat very still, his head to one side, gazing at it. Sometimes he looked exactly as if about to drop off to sleep, his head nodding and his eyes shutting with a kind of thankful bliss. At these moments, as if regarding this as the pleasantest, most flattering thing in all the world, the man would turn on him a gaze mild with approbation and beatitude. He crouched as he drove, flapping the reins gently on the pony's back, and from time to time would raise his head and stare across the plain at the countless cornfields and orchards stretching away to an horizon darkened by misty woods lying upon it like sleeping giants.

For a mile or more the cart drove on in this fashion, the boy still half asleep, the man meditative, the pony never changing its pace.

The sun rose up, at first like a fluffy yellow ball, then like a disk of polished brass. Trees, cornfields, farms, pastures, horses and workmen among the mown corn, all appeared instantly bathed in a soft transfiguring light. Objects a great distance off, little towers, smoking chimneys, village spires, became lightly pencilled into the scene. The sun ran swiftly over the plain, pursuing lines of black shadow. A covey of partridges scurried, screamed, then spread out like a black fan and vanished, the barley ears waving briefly and lightly where they came to earth. Slowly the woods resolved themselves; the trees stood in sharp, unbroken line; then the dew became visible in manifold, glittering drops, giving the parched grasses a look of fresh life, hanging upon the trees like ladies' ear-rings and covering each of the black and crimson berries on the hedge-side like a shell of glass. Soon everywhere was under a warm stillness; all the mist dispersed stealthily and silently, without wind, and the trees seemed to stoop with an invisible burden of heavy airs and the rich loveliness of the ripening year.

As the cart went on, a black shadow began to glide steadily by the horse's side, and a strong fresh scent, with something autumnal about it, began to blow swiftly into the nostrils of the boy, who could feel the sun growing warmer and warmer on his closed lids and on his cheeks and hands.

Presently the man took out his watch and remarked in a soft bass voice: 'Nearly nine.' The boy raised his head and yawned, but did not answer.

Little by little the nature of the country began to change. Gentle hills and a long shallow valley with a white stream appeared. Soon a vast and magnificent view unfolded like a picture.

Being long-sighted, the man would rest his eyes upon remote objects like windmills, water-towers, specks that were cattle or harvesters. All at once his eyes sparkled with eagerness and he began to nudge and pummel the boy into a state of wakefulness and attention. At last he tightened the reins and called excitedly, half standing up among the baskets:

'Alexander! Alexander! Boy, look, look! What is it? Can you see? Open your peepers, Alexander, and just look, look, look. What do you make of it?'

And the boy, excited also, sat upright.

'Herons!' the man whispered.

As the boy gazed up the word was repeated several times, more and more excitedly. Two large, beautiful birds appeared overhead, flapping their way with splendour towards the east, silently and impressively, with the sun shining golden upon them at sudden intervals. The cart had come for the first time to a standstill. The little horse stood quietly panting. Nothing else could be heard; only the strange, golden stillness seemed to ring like the dim echo of a bell over everything as they watched the birds, two diminishing shapes becoming swallowed in the depth of blue sky.

After a long interval, during which the boy emerged for the first time into unconfused wakefulness, the man flapped the reins and remarked:

'I used to know a man who stuffed birds, specially herons. If I'd had a gun just now I might have knocked that pair down for him. He was a masterpiece. For all you knew they might as lief have been alive as dead.'

The cart moved forward again. The boy, on whom the herons had made a great impression, suddenly remarked:

'You shouldn't shoot birds, not even sparrows.'

'Sparrows are pests,' said the man. 'That's law, Alexander. You can't get away from the law.'

'God might strike you, all the same,' said the boy.

'God what?' uttered the man, as if astonished or not catching the words. 'God what did you say?'

'It's been known! Ursula told me about a man who had stolen a calf from a widow woman and while he was eating it afterwards, God struck him.'

'How? Struck him?'

'I don't know how. Ursula says——'

'Never mind what Ursula says! The woman's all nonsense and popery. Never you mind what she says, the old fool. There's no truth in it.'

The boy did not speak. To all this conversation he had listened gravely, taking everything to heart. Each time he looked at the man, his uncle, he was overcome with reverence and admiration. Nevertheless, there was a warm note of affection between them.

Often something serious and mature lurked in Alexander's eyes; and frequently from the other's some child-like and naïve light shone down upon him.

The cart proceeded at the same unvarying pace as before. Now the boy sat upright. The hot morning sun began to burn him. Gradually the sky assumed a richer shade of blue and the grasses began to give off a little vapour. The boy began to take a great interest in what was going on, his mind dwelling on the day ahead—where they were going, what would take place, how much longer they must drive. He tried often to picture the great house to which he understood they were driving, the long avenues of plums and pears, the over-reaching apple-tress, the walls bearing peaches, apricots, and even quinces in great abundance, and the old, wizened, solitary creature who lived in this house surrounded by many brown-and-black dogs and a white cat which she never allowed out of sight. He pondered for a long time, but without enlightenment, on this strange creature who sold fruit to his uncle—'Because, Mr Bishop, you knew me when I was a girl and I can trust you not to break the trees and put the wrong measure in the basket for yourself,' and sometimes he pictured the garden with great success, almost smelling the warm ripeness given off by fruits and leaves.

'What time shall we be there?' he looked up and asked.

The man was lighting his pipe and to Alexander it seemed a long time before he answered:

'A little after ten if we don't stop anywhere. Are you hungry? Ursula put some cheese-cakes in the basket in case you were hungry.'

He was not hungry. In spite of this and though he considered Ursula's cheese-cakes very moderate indeed, he ate two and, while eating, loosened the collar of his shirt. The sun was hot on his face and neck. A little afterwards the road turned abruptly to the left, and from the hot stillness of the open country they passed suddenly into a cool wood of beeches, oaks, and firs, to the accompaniment of stirring leaves and branches, a fitful talking of birds, a gentle whispering of a thousand unknown mysterious voices.

'The house sits that way, on the far side of the wood,' said the man, pointing the whip.

Alexander looked into the wood, from which now and then broke strange scuffling noises. He saw nothing but a vast extent of trees with a glimpse of some fungi as large as pancakes and bright orange in colour. All the leaves, twigs, grasses were dripping with dew, setting up everywhere a kind of watery music, as if from a hidden spring. Drops fell from the overhanging branches and plopped on the cart and the baskets and even on his hands.

Something red appeared along the road. Before long it grew large and life-like and resolved into a woman in a red woollen jacket and a black skirt, carrying a basket. His uncle suddenly began whistling and gave the horse a playful flick as if he were very happy.

From that moment, until they drew level with the woman, the man stared hard at the black skirt, and when they came closer brought the little horse to a walk and tried to catch a glimpse of the woman's face, which was turned away from them. Suddenly she started violently at the sound of wheels, and turning sharply, almost, dropped her basket.

His uncle ceased whistling. 'I thought so! Annie Fell, my girl!' he shouted at once. 'It is you! Yes, it's you right enough. Thinks I, coming all along the road, that's Annie Fell's walk, it's like her father's. God bless me! You look well. Mushrooms! So you got up before you went anywhere this morning. Well, God bless me, God bless me.'

While speaking he slapped one knee in astonishment. Alexander took in the woman's fresh, plump features, her sturdy body, and the immense yellow bunch of hair, too heavy to be held up, falling like fine wool about her neck and shoulders.

'Oh! it's Eli. It's so long since we saw you.'

'Yes! Seven or eight years. At Pollyanna's wedding. Ah, how's Pollyanna?'

'Ah, she's poorly. Her legs keep swelling. She ain't good for much.'

'That's no good. A woman needs good legs. . . .' There was a pause, as if this statement had added to the sum of human knowledge or had a mysterious, subtle meaning. Alexander felt awkward and took his eyes away from the woman and was relieved when his uncle broke the silence again.

'How's your father, my girl?'

She looked up and said in a weary, disillusioned voice, 'He ain't worth a hatful of crabs, either. He's had an operation and every drop and tittle he has Cilla and I have to put down him with a spoon. We have a life with him.'

'So they cut him, did they?'

'There's cuts on him as long as a kidney bean, and a bit longer, I'll swear,' she said.

'That's no good to a man. It's all knifing and butchery with doctors. What do they care? What's the like of me and you to one of them? They want to see what's inside you, and so out comes the knife and you're half-way to Kingdom Come without a chance to say "Our Father". Ah! . . . Are you going home? Give me your basket then, and get up and we'll put you down at the house. No, I don't hold with this butchery.'

He shook his head gravely and vehemently. The woman climbed into the cart and sat between the boy and his uncle. Alexander remained silent and reserved. When they drove off he concentrated his attention on the wood, looking for jays, squirrels, and mushrooms. But often he glanced at the woman furtively, attracted by something warm about her, and the thought of the unfortunate man with cuts as long as beans on his body would trouble him strangely, until he felt that he would be glad when they were alone once more, only his uncle and himself and the little horse bearing them steadily forward into the unfamiliar, golden country.

He observed with relief, a little later, a break in the woodland and a small stone house with snug, diamond-paned windows, tucked away in the clear space. A number of hens and geese, with a white goat, were bobbing hither and thither like scraps of paper on the surrounding grass, and a warm smell of animals and burning wood reached him. Uncle Bishop brought the cart to a standstill and the woman alighted.

Alexander felt as if he had been pressed in a little box. His body seemed shrunken and he would have been thankful to have driven off without delay. But, looking up, the woman said:

'You must come in and say half a word to him——'

'I don't know about that,' said Eli, gazing at the distance. 'We've a long way to go.'

'Don't say you won't have a glass,' she went on, as if pleading. 'You haven't so far but what it might be a little farther.'

And to Alexander's disappointment and annoyance his uncle began to alight also. The boy sat still, holding the reins, glaring. His heart sank lower. And in a not very convincing tone he suddenly said:

'I'll sit here.'

'Oh! but the horse can look after itself,' said the woman.

They both looked at him. 'Make haste,' said his uncle. 'It's Fanny's boy; you know Fanny,' he explained to the woman.

'Fanny's boy! So that's Fanny's boy? Well, well, I knew your mother years ago. You tell her you saw Annie Fell.'

'Ah, that's right, there's something for you to remember.'

So he followed them across the grass, through a wicket-gate and into a garden flanked by trees. A grey sheep-dog lay like a rug across the doorstep, dozing. The door stood open. Uncle Bishop and the woman entered, but Alexander lingered behind, trying to look as if the sheep-dog interested him, though secretly he was afraid of dogs.

'Cilla! Cilla!' the woman began to call upstairs. 'Cilla, here's a visitor. Ah! you couldn't guess in a month of Sundays.'

'Let's go up,' she said.

She removed her hat, and Uncle Bishop began to follow her heavily up some narrow stairs. At their departure the sheep-dog opened his eyes, got lazily to his feet and pattered after them. Alexander began to wonder if he too ought to go, but presently feet resounded overhead and a murmur of voices floated down, and he felt that he had been forgotten.

A little time passed. The sun was hot on his face, and the wooden lintel burned against his hand. Nothing stirred. In the dense sheltered growth of the garden there was not a breath, not a petal or leaf in motion. Bees would appear and spend a little time among some yellow dahlias and then surge away.

Absolute silence seized all things. Alexander began to look for something to occupy his mind, and, turning to the house, he caught sight of a double-barrel sporting gun standing by the wall. The gun was very handsome and fascinating, and though he dare not touch it, he remained gazing at it for a long time, imagining himself taking aim. Presently, tiring of the gun, he looked about the room. It had a low, curious aspect and an appearance of being very old. Some tall geraniums, pink and milk in colour, bloomed in the window, their pretty silken petals falling on a lace-cushion, hung with bunches of bobbins, standing beneath. A chain of birds' eggs was looped over a looking-glass, and a blue enamel bowl of small dark plums stood on the floor.

Presently, as he was scrutinizing a photograph of some soldiers and wondering if they had ever fought with Zulus, a curious, rhythmical noise, like that of a purring cat, startled him. It seemed to him to issue from a door standing half-open by the stairs.

He tiptoed towards the door, stood for a moment very still, and then poked in his head. He recoiled with great haste immediately, trembling.

In the room an old woman, an incredibly astoundingly old woman, with a face like a dried lemon and scarcely any hairs on her head, sat asleep with her hands locked together in her lap, clasping a yellow comb. Her mouth opened regularly the smallest fraction, and emitted a strange half-whistling, half-purring sound. His startled mind refused to think who she might be, or what she was doing there, but retained only the awful, haunting impression that her closed eyes were staring at him through their bluish lids.

He turned and retreated hurriedly. As he reached the garden something stirred there also and the hot stillness was broken by the noise of footsteps coming. He waited, a little nervously, and then, without any other hint or warning, he found himself face to face with a young girl. He looked at her, but did not move, and again nothing seemed to take place in his mind. Only his eyes did their work, drinking in the impression of her pretty, delicate face, her soft neck, and her light hair almost the colour of barley. Each impression smote him sharply, until his breast seemed as if about to burst with its own throbbing. In a strange way, without deliberation, he idealized her at once, thinking that he must be careful how he spoke to her and how he acted before her, and he felt acutely conscious of his physical self and was filled with the impression that everything about her, her large profound blue eyes, the yellow pansy tucked in her hair, the little printed flowerets on her dress, and also the plums in her basket, were all staring at him, astonished and unflinching.

After a little silence she began to move in his direction. As she came nearer the look of dumb astonishment on her face increased.

Not knowing what to do, Alexander muttered stupidly:

'I'm waiting for someone.'

In rather a soft, drawling voice, and looking first towards the road and then at him, she said slowly in reply:

'Did you come in that cart?'

'Yes, that's our cart,' he said quickly. Then, as if to appear at ease, he added:

'You didn't notice if the horse had moved on, I expect, did you?'

'No, he hadn't moved.'

'That's all right,' he said. 'I only wondered, because he's a bit restless in summer.'

She remained silent, and feeling this silence acutely he remarked:

'They're nice plums,' not daring to look into her face, but simply gazing at the dark blue fruit instead.

'They fall off and I have to pick them up every morning,' she told him. 'Look at my hands.'

He cast a brief glance at her stained fingers and felt immediately in some way flattered because she had asked him to do so.

'They're eating plums, I suppose,' he remarked.

Suddenly, without answering, she moved past him, and thinking that he had perhaps offended her and that she was about to disappear irrevocably, he called rather timidly after her:

'I suppose I could have a look at the garden?'

She called back at once:

'Wait a moment, I'll take you down.'

Almost simultaneously with this she reappeared, now with an empty basket.

'Perhaps I'd better make certain about the horse; he won't stand in hot weather,' remarked Alexander.

He satisfied himself by staring over the wicket at the little horse grazing peacefully by the woodside. As he rejoined the girl he tried to walk slowly and naturally, without eagerness and without excitement. Nevertheless, he was conscious of being filled and overcome by a sensation which in its novelty and wonder seemed to deprive him of something with every step he took with the girl deeper into the garden. And in place of what he lost came a host of strange, unbelievable emotions of which hitherto he had suspected nothing, a sense of pleasure which filled his mind like a sweet smell.

It was a long garden, with not many flowers, but a great number of fruit-trees set very thick and close, so that they appeared to be strangling each other. White beehives stood here and there in open spaces. Under the trees the same hot, overpowering stillness as ever stifled everything. All the time Alexander longed to make some sensible or amusing remark to the girl, who walked a little ahead of him, bumping the empty basket softly on her knees at each step, but something prevented him, and he became entranced merely by watching her.

He walked behind her as if dreaming. Presently the path turned to the right, and he caught a faint, brackish odour of water and saw a small pond.

The water was shallow and dingy-looking, the surface sprinkled with countless little yellow sloe leaves and the edge fringed with coarse grasses. When the girl ran on, however, and reached the far side, it seemed to Alexander as clear as a mirror, reflecting her white figure with strange purity, and he felt an odd desire to jump across the pond in a very romantic fashion and land at her feet.

But suddenly the girl called:

'Can you climb trees?'

How best to answer this he did not know. But after a second he said:

'What trees are there to climb?'

'Only the sloe-tree!' she cried.

She ran towards a large sloe-bush overhanging the pond. Climbing trees was an accomplishment of Alexander's, but the sloe-bush seemed to him dense, prickly, and not quite assailable.

'Do you think the sloes are quite ripe?' he remarked in a hesitant voice.

'Don't you want to climb?' the girl flashed out at once.

'Yes, of course.'

'Then shall I climb first or will you?' she asked, while he hesitated.

'Oh, you first, you go,' he said.

She immediately made a light spring and climbed easily and quickly to a fork in the trunk, and, squatting there, gave the tree a sudden violent shake which brought sloes pelting down on the grass, in the pond, and on Alexander's head.

'Bite one, bite one!' she called in extreme excitement.

But Alexander only shook his head, and dropping into the grass, broke into a slow, almost diplomatic smile, without a word.

All this gave him confidence and he looked up at her light form. In these moments he forgot his uncle, the little horse and the journey which meant so much to him, and felt that his whole existence was bound up in the girl, who never ceased attracting him. Seeing her suddenly leave the tree and take a bound through the grass to his side overcame him with a strange faintness. When she sat down he tried at once to look as if interested in some object in the pond. His quick glance arrested her. She followed his gaze, a silence deepening and falling upon them immediately, a silence he found hard to endure again.

But he could say nothing. He half-closed his eyes against the brilliant sunshine. The thoughts he conceived were unbalanced and spasmodic and he could never work them out. An incredible length of time seemed to pass. . . . At last a pair of pigeons broke from just beyond the sloe-bush, and flew over the house. The girl gazed up at them. In a flash, his heart clamouring in his throat, he turned and looked at her face, upturned to the sunshine, her bright hair and her long sunburnt neck uncovered almost to the delicate bosom having its source in a little shadow. He was carried utterly away. It seemed to him that he must lie flat on his face, without speaking or moving, lest he should choke with joy.

'Pigeons . . .' Her voice floated off, tranquilly. Then in the distance rose suddenly a sound and Alexander imagined he heard voices.

They both sprang to their feet and began instinctively to walk in the direction of the house.

'I can hear my mother,' said the girl.

He felt it would be somehow nice and courteous if he said: 'Is that your mother in the red blouse?'

'Yes . . . only that's not a blouse,' she answered in a rather deprecating tone. 'Are you going a long way?'

'I don't know how far it is.'

'What are all those baskets for?'

And feeling rather important, he answered:

'They're fruit-baskets. Every one has to be filled before we come back again.'

But although he spoke in a very bold way his excitement never ceased.

When they reached the house his uncle, the girl's mother, and another woman with fair hair and a pale pink dress and a rather cheerful, pretty face, whom he had not seen before, all stood about a well, the woman peering into the well—while his uncle turned the windlass. As he approached the bucket rose, swaying and spilling water.

He stood still and watched, trying to assume a very careless appearance, as if nothing had happened and he had never moved from that spot.

Then, rather than have his presence noticed with surprise, he said:

'Are you going to start?'

The two women and his uncle turned sharply and looked at him.

'Where in thunder have you sprung from?'

'He's been after the plums . . . that's it. I'll be bound that's about the drift . . .' and such remarks came from the smiling women.

He only broke into the same slow, almost diplomatic smile as before, without a word.

When he turned the girl had vanished. He felt at once a sickening sensation and a desire, regardless of what his uncle and the women might say, to run and look for her. Uncle Bishop and the two women made off in the direction of the wicket, taking the water for the little horse. Casting hurried glances about him, but without reward, he sauntered after them.

While the horse was drinking, the woman in the pink dress, whom he rather liked, said in such a way that it was difficult to understand if she referred to him or to the horse:

'Would he like a curd tart, do you think?'

Alexander did not answer. The horse ceased drinking. Suddenly his uncle bellowed in a stentorian voice in his ear:

'Do you hear? Would you like a curd tart?'

'Please,' said Alexander at once, starting.

'Well then, fathead, listen! Go along with you.'

Alexander followed the pink dress. All the time he was conscious of a vagueness, an unreality in everything. As he stood in the kitchen waiting for the woman to return with the tart he darted glances this way and that, in pursuit of the vanished girl, and even took three steps towards the other door, thinking himself alone, in order to search further for her.

Again a sound startled him. Glancing round, he found himself for the second time face to face with the old, dried-up woman. This time her eyes, wide open, looked at him like two black balls of peppermint. They stared horribly, and all of her little black figure huddled soundlessly in the corner seemed to him sinister in its watchfulness and lack of life.

He felt hypnotized and yet revolted, and dared not move until the woman in the pink dress returned. And then he turned away quickly, eating with difficulty and conscious of a lump in his throat.

'Perhaps you'll remember me to your mother,' the woman said behind him. 'Say you saw Cilla . . . just Cilla. Then she'll know. Don't you forget.'

He made an obedient murmur, and cast a last hasty glance into the garden, hotter and stiller it seemed than ever. But nothing stirred, nothing broke the stillness there.

He climbed into the cart and sat motionless. Uncle Bishop looked at his watch and said, 'God bless me!' four or five times over, and after climbing into the cart too, he began to say farewell.

'Good day, good day,' he kept repeating. 'You ought to rub Pollyanna's legs every day with hound's-tongue ointment three or four times. Tell her they're Bishop's very words, and she knows I'm right. You can't go wrong with hound's-tongue, it's a cure-all. What? . . . Doctors? . . . They might as well be in Bedlam, with the poor thing's legs rotting off with pain. What's that? Ha, ha! God bless me, that's a fact!' he burst out, trying to give the girl's mother a playful poke with the whip. 'You're fat enough, too, and no mistake, but I remember what my mother said about you the day you were married. There's no flesh on her, she says, she's got neither bosom nor backside. They're nothing but little apples.'

The women laughed and Uncle Bishop, in great spirits, suddenly began to shout a great many indiscreet things, saying farewell over and over again, alternately flicking the little horse and reining it tight again.

They began to move off at last. Alexander tried to smile. The wheels turned, a little faster every second. He was overcome by a sensation of being dragged somewhere against his will.

Then all at once, in a most subtle way, he was aware that the girl was watching him. He felt this as certainly as if she had held her finger-tips very close to his cheek. He turned impulsively, and beheld her with her chin resting on her hands and her hands resting on the top of the little gate, staring at him. The blood rushed to his cheeks, and filled with all his former joy, he kept turning and seeing her in the same careless, lovely watchful pose, while the cart drew steadily farther and farther away.

Finally he saw her no more. The house, the goat, the hens, and at last the wood itself slipped into the distance. An unfamiliar, beautiful valley unfolded itself before his gaze. The dew had vanished and there was a hard brilliance about the sky as if it were a gem.

A clock chimed eleven. Uncle Bishop's breath smelt sweetly of wine. Alexander fixed his eyes on the distance, hardly knowing what he did, dreaming endlessly.

2

When they had driven a little longer the road made a sudden curve like a sickle, and while his thoughts were still of the girl and all that had taken place in the wood, a square stone house standing alone among dark clumps of trees came suddenly into sight. All other thoughts momentarily at an end, he gazed and asked:

'Is this where she lives?'

'Hold hard,' said his uncle. 'You'll see her if you wait a moment. Go along with you and open the gate. Hullo! the damned dogs already! Go along and don't be frightened.'

As Alexander alighted and began to push back the massive iron gates a furious chorus of barking dogs greeted him, and suddenly six or seven bitches, all of the same black-and-brown breed and each very corpulent, rushed out at him from nowhere, yelping and snapping about his heels and striking terror into him. He hated dogs, and standing stock-still, cast one despairing look at his uncle, who at once leapt up like a fat old jack-in-the-box and began wildly brandishing his whip and shouting:

'Damn the dogs, get back! Damn the dogs!'

He jerked the reins excitedly. 'Get out, you scallywags!' he shouted afresh as the cart moved forward. 'God bless me, what does a woman want with seven dogs? Get back!'

The cart drove in and the yelping bitches were scattered in all directions. Partly to protect himself, and partly to show that he was not wholly afraid, Alexander seized the little horse's bridle and led it towards the house. Green lawns and a superb orchard lay before him. His gaze fell fascinated on scores and scores of trees stretching infinitely ahead.

Suddenly his uncle whispered a little excitedly:

'There's the old tit herself, yes, there she is. Coming towards us. See her?'

And looking up, Alexander saw approaching him a small, frail woman in black, wearing a snuff-brown bonnet and carrying a silver-knobbed walking-stick in her hands. She looked as if got up to match her dogs, who all instantly ceased barking and waddled towards her in a curious apathetic way, snuffing about her skirts. She walked as though on ice, hardly progressing at all, with her head and hands quivering in agitation, as if for ever dispatching little signals of terror and distress. Behind her came a white cat and yet another dog, an aged, weary creature who moved even more slowly than its mistress.

His uncle began to hobble across the lawn to meet her, muttering again, 'The old tit, the old tit!' at every step he took.

When he reached the old lady he formed an enormous trumpet with his hands, and bellowed into her ears like thunder:

'Glad to see you. Nice weather, God bless me. Not very lucky with the dogs again, I see.'

A little plaintive voice piped out, hardly audible, in reply:

'So you've come. No, no . . . it's awful. What with the boys stealing the fruit, and then the dogs having litters all the time. . . . The boys have broken the wall again. It's dreadful. I don't know what to do, people rob me right and left. What's it coming to?'

She turned her doleful, shaking head first to the garden, then to the dogs, half of which were heavy with puppies, and lastly to Uncle Bishop.

'Damn brutes!' he began. 'Not the dogs, I've nothing against the dogs. The boys I mean. . . . Not the dogs. Why don't you do something?'

'What can I do?'

'Say your prayers . . .' muttered Uncle Bishop in an undertone. 'The old tit. Say your prayers.'

'Wha-a-at? . . . Whose boy is that?'

'My nephew; Fanny's boy. Alexander, come and shake hands. He's twelve. Strong lad, isn't he?' he bellowed.

And Alexander, trying to bear out this statement, yet afraid of hurting the old woman, shook hands, and her hand seemed to him like a piece of cold fish and her eyes seemed ready to stream with tears as she looked at him.

'Would he like a piece of cake, do you think?' she said.

Alexander, not daring to refuse, although again not hungry, at once said 'Please.'

'Please!' repeated his uncle in a staggering voice.

Nodding and quaking, the old lady turned and slowly retreated, all the dogs following her like mourners at a funeral. While she had gone Uncle Bishop gave the little horse its nose-bag and Alexander unpacked the fruit-baskets and set them on the grass.

After a long interval the procession returned. Alexander's uncle at once began a secretive whisper:

'She's rich, the old teaser. Her husband invented a patent candlestick and made a fortune, but he broke his neck on horse-back. She had a son, but he's a lunatic and no one knows where he is, and so it's all hers, all the blessed money and this orchard, everything. Fetch the piece of cake, fetch it, fetch it—be on the right side of her, my boy, go along, fetch it.'

Alexander was forced to go and take from the old lady's quivering fingers a large triangle of bright yellow cake, which looked distasteful and sickly.

'It's saffron cake,' she said to him, in a trembling little voice.

What saffron cake was he did not know, but he tried to look as if he did know and as if he were very grateful. Then his uncle and the old woman began to discuss the fruit-gathering and he was left unnoticed, feeling awkward as he lingered about with the cake he did not want.

'The little golden plums on the bank are ripe, two trees of them,' he heard her say. 'Get them . . . get them all. The boys and the wasps are after them. And then there's a tree of pearmains: that's loaded, and there'll be none left if you leave them. Pears, there's two trees of pears, the big early ones at the end of the garden, and the little sweet pears. You know where they are. There's a ladder stands by the wall. You know where everything is, don't you? It's a poor year. Some of the trees are blighted, but you do as you think fit.'

'You know you can trust us,' bellowed Uncle Bishop. 'You know that you always have trusted us.'

'Yes, I trust you.'

But while they were taking hooks and baskets and all the time they were walking down the long avenue of apples into the depths of the garden, Alexander was conscious of her eyes pursuing all their movements, as if she did not trust them. Her eyes reminded him of gooseberries, and he also felt that though she was so very deaf this deafness did not matter, since her sight was so uncanny and remarkable. And as he turned and shot a last furtive look along the avenue all the seven dogs and the white cat appeared to be watching him too.

'It's a garden, if you like, isn't it?' he old uncle kept whispering, as though the intricacy of the avenues and the never-ending branches stooping under a weight of red, yellow and green globes awed him. 'There's a peach, on the wall, and next to it's an apricot, but there's never a finger allowed on them, the old tit, not a finger. Don't you touch them, do you hear that? Eat what you like and fill your pockets, but she'll know almost if you look on that wall. God bless me if she won't.'

But Alexander, so much attracted by the garden, scarcely listened. Everywhere heavily laden trees stood, and as in the little garden in the wood, not a breath or leaf stirred itself, and the sunshine seemed to burn the stillness and came through the leaves with a soft liquid light. In odd places under the trees there were vegetable marrows, which he thought looked like fat sucking pigs asleep in the sunshine. In the distance some pigeons were cooing, and a flock of starlings flew up from an apple-tree and soared away like black dust. They walked on and on. 'Did you ever see the like?' the old man kept saying. And then suddenly they came to a point where this level, tranquil order of things changed, and the garden dipped abruptly. They halted. Before them lay a kind of oval basin which it seemed to Alexander might have been a stone-pit in some bygone time. Here the trees hung from ledges and precipices and flourished in a toy green valley. 'Cunning,' he heard his uncle say. Very cunning and very wonderful indeed he thought it also as he stood there gazing with large eyes at the little golden plums in the grass, with a sensation as if the outer world had been left aside for ever.

'Get a basket. Let's begin,' said his uncle suddenly. 'The little yellow tree first of all.'

Alexander, rather dazed, took the basket in which lay the saffron cake, and though not hungry, he longed to taste the cake and the tempting, sweet-looking plums. And so he took first a bite at the strange-coloured cake and then at the fruit. The cake he concluded at once was poisonous, but the plums were like honey, and he went on eating them, hardly filling up the basket at all. And shortly, without fuss, and with an expression of sleepy indifference, he put some of the ripest plums in his pockets and dropped the saffron cake into long grass, like a stone.

As the work went on, Uncle Bishop at times murmured in a cracked bass some old song Alexander had heard already a hundred times, but which possessed for him still the same enchantment and surprise, and at others related all he knew of some old murder, very cold-blooded and gruesome, telling it all so skilfully and with such cunning pauses that Alexander would cease all movement, and sit on a branch or stand in the grass as if paralysed, not breathing, wondering if the climax would ever come. At times they were very silent. In these pauses the boy wished only that he might lie still in the shady grass, to sleep, or to watch with sleepy eyes the rabbits feeding in the green hollow. But each time a curious sense of pride prevented his doing this. And conscientiously he went on filling and refilling his basket with plums.

When the plum-tree had been stripped the man sighed, and as if for reward, ate the first plum Alexander had seen pass his lips, and blew out his cheeks and spat the stone to an extraordinary height in the air. Then he seized his jacket and opened his watch and looked at the sun.

'Oh, Lord!' he muttered, scratching himself. 'It's nearly one. Fetch the basket.'

A sudden feeling of joy and relief filled Alexander, who felt as if he had been locked in a room and released.

When he returned with the basket Uncle Bishop was already seated under a large pear-tree, stropping a magnificent clasp-knife on his trousers-knee in readiness.

'What have they put in for us?' he kept saying. 'What? Cold pie? What sort of a pie? What ... Rabbit? Never! God bless my buttons, but it must be. It can't be pigeon. It must be the rabbit Ursula bought from the gipsy. And what else? Give me the pie. God bless me, it's heavy, it must have been a hare. What else, my son?'

'Potatoes, cold beans, bread ... cheese,' recited Alexander, 'and here's another pie, a fruit pie, yes, that's fruit, and here's something else. Bottles.'

'Bottles?'

After saying this, his mouth remained open and Alexander saw a look of sly astonishment creep into his face. Then he stretched out his hands and took the bottles from Alexander and slowly held them up to the sunshine, closing one eye deliberately. Presently he remarked:

'That's for you.'

'What is it?'

'Drink! Never mind what. Never ask what a drink is, it's not manners.'

And leaning backwards, Alexander drank slowly and deeply, scarcely tasting what he drank, but aware only of the satisfaction and coolness of drinking, until he felt as if the breath were being squeezed from his body and he could drink no longer. Suddenly, with a great burst for breath, he ceased and sat upright. His uncle was still drinking, with his head also thrown back, so that he looked to Alexander very like a man blowing a black trumpet from which no sound ever came. And as he watched, wondering how long this could last, the half-sweet, half-bitter taste of what he had drunk awoke in his mouth.

'Is yours herb beer too?' he leaned forward and asked.

His uncle did not answer, however, but suddenly smacking his lips and corking up the bottle, took his clasp-knife and cut the pie. Alexander received the leg of a rabbit, and immediately felt strangely important, as if he had been given a prize or had said something very witty and clever. He sat with his mouth open, staring.

'Eat, sonny, eat,' urged his uncle at once. 'There's beans too, and potatoes. Eat!' He waved his long arms about him to the trees and the sky. 'All the pears and the little red apples have to be gathered before we go, and it's a long journey.'

He himself cut two thick slices of bread and began to spear pieces of rabbit with the point of his knife, eating ravenously. A knife and fork had been packed up for the boy, but he felt it would be almost degrading and a little childish to use them, and rather furtively he took out a small tortoise-shell penknife and began spearing fragments of rabbit's flesh too. There was no time for conversation. And gradually everywhere grew silent. Hardly a bird spoke, and the thick wall of trees about them stood still and breathless. The sun lay directly overhead and Alexander could see the heat shimmering in waves beyond the baskets lying in squares and rings of yellow in the grass.

Soon he felt his thoughts fly back again to all that had happened in the wood. The same overbearing silence, the same heat, the same uncanny sense of utter stillness, without a quiver or breath! The picturesque little house, the old woman sitting staring like death, with a comb clasped in her hands, the pond, the sloe-tree, and most vivid of all, the flowerets on the young girl's dress reflected in the shining dark water! He ceased eating and the faint sickness and shock of unexpected joy obsessed him.

'Come, eat your leg, eat your leg, boy!'

He started and responded mechanically, lifting the rabbit-leg in his fingers, and then sank into thought again.

As he sat there, alternately eating and dreaming, he could only wonder what she was doing, where she could be.

'If you don't want the leg, don't waste it. Have a little of this pie instead. Look, see the crust.'

He took a slice of pie, which had been made with late raspberries, gooseberries, damsons, and a sprinkling of dewberries. As he ate he looked up and asked:

'That man in the little house over there, he's very ill, isn't he?'

'Yes, God bless him; he won't live, poor fellow.'

'Shall you go back to see him?'

'We might and we might not. I don't know,' he said, shaking his head, and the boy felt driven back to silence.

During the remainder of that meal he did not speak again; only his uncle's answer, 'We might and we might not,' careered repeatedly through his head, troubling him.

Not long later the man, with a sleepy 'Don't you fidget, my son,' stretched back on the grass and closed his eyes. In obedience the boy sat for some moments very still, feeling as if he were the only creature alive in the still, drowsy noonday.

He rose presently and walked idly away. ... The house appeared, its white stone exterior looking forbidding in the sunshine. He stood for some moments staring at it, and then turned abruptly down a little sloping path leading towards a group of firs. A grasshopper began chirring, and a low hum of wasps rose from the plum-trees. Suddenly Alexander stared, slackened his pace, and then, gazing still harder at the object he saw under an apple-tree just ahead, ceased walking altogether. Two small eyes like black beans returned his stare, and an intense sensation of guilt and nervousness refused to let him go forward or run away.

Before him sat a man, a very small person in a blue-striped shirt, a black cap, and stone-coloured trousers fastened with a most handsome belt of plaited and twisted leather decorated with pieces of brass. His shirt-sleeves were rolled up, and on his right fore-arm a purple dragon had been tattooed and on his left there was a crimson bird, like a swallow, designed as if it were flying towards his shoulder. Alexander could not surmise if this man were old or young. He only felt that his thin face with its sharp nose, black little eyes, and bony forehead was very, very cunning. And after a long silence, during which the eyes never flickered, he said falteringly in an apologetic voice:

'We're picking the fruit.'

'What's your name?' asked the man, with a very cunning squint and in a sharp arresting voice.

'I'm Mr Bishop's nephew.'

The man thought a minute, then asked: 'Did you come in that cart with that little nag?'

'Yes.'

'Well, that's all about of a nag, that is. I wouldn't be seen dead with a nag like that. It's a midget!' he went on derisively. 'Don't you feed it?'

Alexander, who was devoted to the little horse, was too outraged to speak, and only nodded several times, staring at the other's thin, cunning face until he detested it. And then suddenly the man remarked:

'I've got a boy about your clip. How old are you?'

'Twelve,' said Alexander.

'Yes, he's about that. Perhaps he's older, though. I don't know, it's a job to tell.' And he informed Alexander abruptly: 'I've got fourteen children; you wouldn't believe that perhaps, would you?'

'Yes,' said Alexander at once, though he felt he couldn't believe a word.

'He was the first to be born after I came home from Turkey, he was. Seven came before Turkey, and seven after, and there's no doubt the first are the strongest. There's no doubt they are. Fine, strong women and men all of them, and two with children of their own. Only yesterday my eldest came to see me. He's with a duke—yes, he's a duke's servant—a duke with a name as long as your legs. I can't pronounce his name, no more could you. And this duke says to him, "Baxter," he says, "if there's any mortal thing you want while I'm away from home, you take it. Take it!"

He was drunk—he drinks a lot, this duke—but it didn't matter,
and no sooner's his back turned than Wag—that's my son—orders
another servant to kill a turkey and gets a leg of mutton and a little
barrel of beer, besides a lot of waistcoats and a pair of gaiters—
doeskin gaiters, mark you—gentlefolk don't know what they have
got, they don't wear things out—and a pair of pants worn once
and never a second more, and shoes and God knows what besides
he didn't get—and I'll slit my throat if he didn't hire a conveyance
and bring them home and say to me, "Dad, what with having
fourteen of us and times hard, you could do with the duke's
trousers!" Oh, my God! I laughed till the tears rolled down my
cheeks. Why I laughed I don't know, but there you are, he's my
son, and he's a chip off the old block; and I'm proud of him. And
money! Before he goes he says to me, "Dad, here's a quid," and he
opens his pocket for me to look. And there they lay, hundreds of
them, hundreds and hundreds of pounds like packs of playing
cards, hundreds and hundreds. . . .'

During all this discourse Alexander grew more and more
incredulous and yet more and more fascinated. He felt all the time
that he was being told wonderful enormous lies. Everything he
could do towards believing these lies he did, yet the thought of so
much money, so many children, and the look of constant crafti-
ness on the man's face defeated him.

He stood as if spellbound.

'Haven't seen the old lady about, I suppose?' asked the man
suddenly, completely closing one eye and squinting up at Alexander with the other.

The boy shook his head.

'Good,' remarked the other, and took out a small clay pipe,
very stained and dirty. 'She's a tough customer. No smoking in
this garden—perhaps you don't believe that? Well, believe it or
not, it's true. She's afraid she'll be burnt in her bed. Her husband,
when he was alive, did nothing but experiment and experiment
with things all day and all night long. And one night he set the
house afire. . . . That's the reason. "Baxter," she says every morning, "don't you dare strike a match." ' Just at this moment the
man did strike a match and began smoking. 'She's like some little
cheese-mouse, twittering and trembling about her money. Not

like a man I worked for once. He had money. God strike me, he had some money! "Baxter," he used to say to me, "if you want a glass of beer there's a bucket." A bucket! And I used to draw a bucket of beer as you might draw a bucket of water for your little old nag. . . . But he killed himself. Money! That's what money did for that man. Money ain't no good. The old lady, what's all her money bring? What's she got? Her only son in an asylum, and nobody, not a soul, to live with her—all alone—might as well be under the ground.'

This time Alexander followed the discourse without a thought for its truth, only fascinated profoundly, and as the man went on to tell more and more fantastic episodes he crept nearer and at last sat down at his feet.

While listening he caught sight of an object lying partially concealed by the man's jacket. After some time he made out the fur, then the ears and whiskers of a dead rabbit. From its snout hung a globule of bright red.

'Did you catch that?' he asked, pointing at the dead animal.

'Not so loud. Did I catch what?' the man asked sharply, and pretended suddenly to be extremely stupid, looking everywhere except where Alexander was pointing.

'That!' repeated the boy.

'Where? What is it you're after? What you mean—"catch"? There's nothing but slugs to catch here.'

To judge from his puzzled, apathetic movements the man looked as if he had just woken up. Nothing of his slyness remained. And yet Alexander felt that under this mask of stupidity the cunning was growing deeper.

He became silent, and the man took advantage of the silence to relight his pipe, while Alexander, nonplussed by this last change of attitude, wondered if he dare ask another question. After a long silence he did ask it.

'Do you live here?' he said.

'Over yonder, by the wood,' said the man.

'What's your name?' he ventured to ask, timidly.

'Smack. . . .'

As he uttered this, his mouth snapped shut as sharply as a mouse-trap, and with a sound very like a smack. This produced a great effect on Alexander, who sat open-mouthed for some moments before daring to say:

'Were you christened that?'

'Christened? . . . Lord God, my mother ran off all of a sudden, feeling a bit of a pain in the fields one day, and delivered me under a haystack. I wasn't christened.'

'Don't you go to church, either?'

His face screwed itself up with contempt.

'Church?' he said.

Alexander was impressed by this also, and would have been glad to say how he too hated church, and that he did not understand the psalms or the sermon and could never remember the responses, and how he agreed with his Uncle Bishop that it was all popery and humbug, but suddenly the man drew out a bottle from somewhere and took an immense drink, a drink so long that it seemed to the boy that the bottle must have been emptied over and over again. When it ended the man stretched himself, licked his lips several times, and said suddenly:

'You look as if you've never seen a man drink. Why, my dad, if he were alive, poor old devil that I should ever say so, he'd tell you how he used to drink ten pints of a morning, mowing grass. . . .' He squinted and nodded with all his cunning, and then got nimbly to his feet.

Something at frequent intervals had been troubling Alexander, and now as the man prepared to leave him he felt an overwhelming desire to ask another question. And almost against his will he said:

'Do you know the people over there in the wood?'

'Which wood?' said the man.

'There's a little house,' began Alexander, and suddenly he felt a strange ache as he visualized it all, 'you can hardly see it, the trees are so thick. There's an old woman there and someone used to live there named Pollyanna, only she's married and bedridden now, because of her legs. And there's an old man—he's had an operation. It's over there, not very far. We passed it as we came this morning.'

All through this the boy's voice trembled and there lurked in his mind a picture of the young girl. Overcome by a suspicion that

every word he spoke must reveal his inner feelings he began to
stammer also. Anxiety and joy set up a conflict within him.

'In the wood, you say? The wood . . . but which wood?' said the
man. 'There's so many woods.'

'Over there,' said Alexander, almost desperately.

'No, I can't say. Lord Almighty, there's a good many people I
don't know—thousands!'

Suddenly he cocked his eyes for the last time at Alexander, and
walking very sharp like a sharp little dog down the narrow path,
passed from sight.

When Alexander returned to the high bank overlooking the
disused stone-pit his Uncle Bishop was stretching himself after his
sleep.

'Cover the plums with a sack or two,' he began saying. 'That's
it, that's it. The basket we'd better take down with us. Drink
before you put the bottle away, drink, drink!'

'Where are we going?' asked the boy after drinking some herb
beer.

'You take the baskets while I bring the ladder. Make straight
for the big pear-tree. Straight on, you couldn't miss it.'

Under an immense pear-tree, on which the fruit hung almost
like ropes of onions, the boy presently set down the baskets. A
thick, angry hum of wasps met him, and some birds flew up with
startled cries from among the branches. Half-rotted pears lay
about in the grass under the tree, bored by wasps and pecked at by
birds, and a faint odour of what he thought was like wine or balm
met him as he walked round and round the tree, crushing pears with
his boots and disturbing wasps in his anxiety to find a pear to taste.

'Try one, try one,' suddenly urged his uncle, who had come up
behind, a little breathless, with the ladder.

Gaining courage from this, Alexander snatched a fine yellow
pear from the tree and crushed his teeth into its unblemished skin.
For ever afterwards a recollection of the rare flavour, the strange,
wine-like odour and honeyed juice of this pear remained with
him. His uncle had seized a pear also and was sucking it with
quick gasps of pleasure. Even more excited than Alexander about
the fruit he kept opening his eyes extremely wide, until they shone
like blue glass marbles.

Neither the man nor the boy for some time uttered a word. At last Uncle Bishop said:

'You must put a few in a bag for yourself. Not yet, later on. And don't let the old tit see you do it.'

Alexander neither did nor said anything in answer to this, but remained spellbound for some moments under a sudden notion which had flashed into his head.

And throughout the afternoon this same idea of taking something, perhaps a plum or a pear, as a gift to the girl never ceased to attract and trouble him. Screened by the thick leaves from view, he would sometimes gather a pear, rub it to a polish on his shirt and put it aside very religiously and tenderly. If however a bruise or crack appeared, he would drop it, feeling a sense of acute loss, into the basket. The afternoon slipped by. Once as he was gathering a pear from a high branch he heard a rustling in the grass beneath him. He started and looked down to see four or five dogs snuffing about the baskets. He heard the old woman coming too. Her snail-like approach and the remembrance of her keen sight made it agonizing for him to sit in the tree without movement or sound.

Then she carried on a conversation with his uncle which seemed to him to go on and on, everlastingly.

'Oh! the wasps, you see the destruction they cause,' she wailed. 'The fruit all eaten away! If it goes on like this I shall have nothing. Dear, dear, just look at it. Just look. It drives me out of my mind to think about it. What shall I do? Come away, Pretty, come away, naughty creature. There's nothing for you. Oh, dear, dear! If it weren't for the labour I'd have all trees down, I'd have them all down tomorrow, and there'd be an end of it all.'

All her troubles and griefs had to be poured into Uncle Bishop's ear. Over and over again she complained and sighed, until Alexander felt that he must drop off the branch with exhaustion and suspense.

Worst of all, she at last looked round and asked in a quaking, suspicious voice:

'Where's the little boy?'

'Oh! he's gone off,' bellowed Uncle Bishop. 'Lord knows where, but he's not far away. Down among the rabbits, I shouldn't wonder.'

'Look after him,' she implored. 'Don't let him touch them. I wouldn't have them touched, not for anything. No one's ever killed one, and no one ever shall, I can't bear it.'

'They'll eat you out of your bed before very long!' muttered Uncle Bishop brutally, not loud enough for her to hear.

'Don't let him touch them, don't let him touch them,' was all she said.

A moment later she had begun to shuffle away, all the dogs trailing in a waddling, abject string behind her skirts. A long time elapsed before she passed out of sight and the boy had courage to move again. When he descended at last and looked about him it seemed as if the sun were already lower in the sky.

3

When evening began to come on at last, Alexander and his uncle carried back to the house all the fruit they had gathered, and under the supervision of the old lady, who stood tottering a little distance off, weighed and measured it, Alexander writing down the figures with extreme care on a sheet of paper. All the dogs and the white cat were also there, staring like wooden things or dragging themselves about the grass on their bellies, never running or barking. The little horse seemed to have grown impatient and stood restlessly stamping and frisking against the evening flies. The boy shared this impatience, fixing his mind constantly on the time when they must pass through the wood, longing desperately to depart.

'Does the little boy understand figures?' the old lady wanted to know. 'He won't make mistakes?'

'Bless you, he goes to school!' shouted Uncle Bishop, with pride and force. 'What he doesn't know isn't worth knowing. Nowadays things are different. They're taught everything, every mortal thing you can wish. Why, he learns Latin now—Latin! God bless your heart, he could write all the names of these apples and pears down for you in Latin.'

'What good would that do?'

'A good deal, you bet your life, a good deal. The boy wouldn't do it for nothing. He's got a head on him—you see for yourself.

Turn round, my boy. There, you can see now—his head's as big as a pumpkin.'

Uncle Bishop never lost an opportunity of showing how proud he was of Alexander, and to complete the force of this pride he often exaggerated and frequently told lies. And as he turned round in order to display his head, Alexander felt extremely foolish and half-scowled in vexation. He longed for his uncle to pay his accounts and ached for the sound of wheels again. But his uncle dallied a little longer, and patting the boy's head, at last said to him:

'Now, you go over and show the lady what you've written. Go along.'

Alexander held out the paper in silence.

'I see, I see,' she said, squinting and trembling more than ever. 'Good lad, he writes well.' And for a long time he had to stand at her side, writing down all the figures his uncle shouted, vexed and uneasy. During this time he discovered that a strange smell hung about her, compounded of preserved cloth, dogs, camphor, horse-beans and something dry and musty. And so much fruit had to be weighed and accounted for that he felt at last as if he had breathed this queer odour all his life.

The sun had plunged behind the largest tree before his uncle and the old woman vanished into the house to settle the accounts. All the dogs disappearing also, he was left alone and sat on a little wooden bench with great relief, wondering what time it could be and how soon a start would be made. Then shortly his face assumed an intense, meditative expression.

'Shall I get the apricot?' he thought. 'Could I go back into the garden without being seen?'

And presently, followed by the indistinct voices of his uncle and the old woman, he edged away and strolled in an indifferent manner down the path under the trees. His heart seemed to swell, beating with ponderous thumps. All things were flagged and hushed. An army of shadows advanced to meet him. His footsteps awoke echoes infinitely, making him turn round in fear, as if other footsteps were following him. Mysterious objects under the trees made him start and hasten too.

Suddenly he became aware of footsteps coming not from

behind, but before. His impulse was to turn and run, but for some strange reason he ceased walking.

Then a figure appeared. It was Smack. Approaching very slowly, he began to say as soon as he saw Alexander:

'Oh, it's you, it's you, is it? God strike me, it looked like the old woman.' The boy remained dumb, simply gazing at the sack of either apples or potatoes that the man was carrying.

'You're like my son Squint, you are,' Smack went on, 'he creeps about on hands and knees and gets atop of you before you hear a sound. Why, I've seen him drop on a hare like you might drop on a beetle. Perhaps you wouldn't believe that? Well, believe it or not, but there it is. He's a miracle. . . . "Squint," I says to him one day, "you can drop on hares, but could you drop on a fox?" He looks at me and says "Could I drop on a fox?"—just like that. That's all. He's like that. But next day there was a meet. Full cry they came across from these woods, all the pinks and the ladies thinking they would be in at the kill, and the dogs running like mad. I was there, with Squint, behind a hedge. All of a sudden there's a gallows of a row, and God bless my poor old mother, the fox walked through the hedge. Dainty! I never saw a wedding where there was anything so dainty. And there she stood. She never moved. She just looked at Squint, and Squint—what did he do? God strike me, but he dropped on her, he dropped on her. And when the hunt came up, there he stood, there stood our Squint with his arms round the fox's neck.'

And once again Alexander was carried away by the cunning of it all. Almost hypnotized by nods and winks he did not know what to say. But suddenly Smack asked him sharply:

'Where's the old woman, eh?'

'She's in the house, settling the accounts up,' stammered Alexander.

'In the house, eh?'

'They've just gone in.' And abruptly he gathered courage to ask: 'You didn't remember the name of the people in the wood, did you, after all?'

'Name of the people in the wood?'

'There's an old man, and two women . . .' began the boy.

But Smack shook his head, this time almost sorrowfully,

as if he hated not being able to conjure up some answer.

'Perhaps I know them,' he said at last. 'There's thousands of people I do know, thousands. I dare say I know them.'

'There's a girl,' persisted Alexander.

'A girl?' the other repeated. 'A girl?' And suddenly he managed to attach to that word something incredulous, cynical, mocking, and his thin lips and eyes squeezed themselves into a repellent smile.

Directly afterwards he laughed and sidled off, and Alexander found himself walking rapidly towards the wall bearing the apricot-tree, no longer afraid, but driven by a feeling of desperation and wretchedness. All his sweetest, most tender emotions felt wounded. It seemed to him monstrous that what aroused in him elation and joy should have struck Smack as contemptible and petty. He did not understand and felt that it was all horrible, that in some strange way he had betrayed a mysterious and precious trust. Only the intensity of his own beliefs comforted him.

He hurried on. He resolved suddenly to snatch the apricot quickly, and, regardless of everything, run as fast as possible back to the house again.

In the dying sunlight the apricot-trees had a rich, luxuriant, exclusive look about them. On the third tree hung a very special apricot he had noted several times. He plucked it, quickly and gently, and began to run.

He emerged from among the trees just in time to hear the voice of his uncle begin impatiently shouting:

'Where are you? Where are you? Boy! Where have you been? Here, here . . . tell us what ninety-three pence make. Ninety-three pence . . . what? Come here, you'd better come inside. Take your cap off. And remember if the old tit asks you anything shout in her ear. Shout! Now make haste, go along the passage.'

Alexander was hurried into a gloomy passage, where he noted a strong odour of damp and mice and saw several pairs of antlers branched from the walls and a stuffed white owl staring down at him. When at a furtive whisper from his uncle he entered a door on the right, he saw the old lady, now with spectacles on, sitting alone at a shining oval table. A good deal of money, with three or four dark red leather bags and heaps of bills, were strewn about.

Again the odour of damp and mice met him. All the furniture was of pale yellow wood, with faded blue damask upholstery and many cushions. Little pairs of milky green and pink glass vases stood on a white mantelpiece, like small dolls preening themselves in the large mirror behind. Something dead, old-fashioned, and sad lurked about the room, and to the boy it seemed full of memories, of the lingering presences of men and women who had once lived, talked, and perhaps sung and danced there. He noticed that the walls were covered with old portraits, every other portrait looking like a picture of the Saviour, except that all the figures were wearing bowler hats and deerstalkers and white silk neckties.

'Go in, go in,' urged his uncle, giving him little impatient punches from behind.

He advanced and stood silently before the table, staring at the heaps of money.

Suddenly his uncle began to say at the top of his voice:

'Here's the boy. He'll manage it. It'll be put right before you can wink.'

The old lady turned and searched Alexander's face with sharp squints. 'Mind you do, and don't make mistakes,' she said.

'That's all right, you trust him,' bawled his uncle. 'Now, my son, tell the lady what ninety-three pence are.'

Alexander, a little bewildered, had to think a moment before replying. 'Seven and ninepence,' he said at last.

'Shout!'

'Seven and ninepence,' he shouted.

'Seven and ninepence?' she repeated. 'Are you sure? You haven't made a mistake, have you? If you think you haven't made a mistake, write it down . . . just there . . . write it down.'

Alexander took from her shaking fingers a small black pen, with which he wrote down the figures seven and nine with laborious care in an old, dirty book. As he wrote, her stiff sleeves brushed against him and he was continually afraid that she would feel or smell or in some other way divine that he had the apricot about him. All the little tremors and starts of her body alarmed him.

'Has he written it?' she croaked suspiciously after a silence. 'I can't see.'

'Yes, he's written it!' proclaimed his uncle. 'You can trust him. What you want is a light.' Twilight was rapidly creeping through the room. 'You're not likely to see. Haven't you got some sort of a lamp?' he asked.

'Wha-a-t?'

'A lamp! You want some sort of a light on the subject or else you won't know shillings from ha'pence.'

'What does he say?' she turned and asked Alexander in a puzzled voice.

But this was never answered, for suddenly his Uncle Bishop snatched out his matches and struck a light, letting it flare up in his fingers. The old woman stood at once petrified, all her features white and stiff with horror. Then she began to struggle, as if choking, her eyes bulged, her hands waved hither and thither, she tried to stand up, her head looked as if it must totter off with rage, and then at last she croaked out in a terrible voice:

'What are you doing, what are you doing? Put it out at once! Oh, you wicked man, you wicked man! You mustn't do it, I won't have it! Put it out at once!'

Her voice was thin and rasping. 'Put it out, you wicked man! Put it out!' she kept saying in fury.

Uncle Bishop's mouth fell open, and without a word he pinched out the flame with his fingers. There was silence. The boy dared not stir.

Then the old lady began another struggle: she tried to calm herself, to sit down, to administer reprimands, but only infuriated trembling went on accompanied by a strange half-kissing, half-rattling sound. Gradually she coiled herself up, trembling less and less, like a spring, until she sank into the chair again. As she became quieter the silence seemed to become more and more intense. A little smoke wandered through the air and the pungent odour of it spread about the room. But the boy hardly dared to look or smell.

After what seemed an interminable silence, the old woman held up one finger and shook it admonishingly at Uncle Bishop for a long time. 'You must never do that,' she said. 'I never allow that—I never allow a naked light, not even in the garden, not anywhere. Did you want to frighten my life out?'

'Let me pay you what I owe. That's enough. God damn it, what next, what else?' he muttered. 'Let me pay you!'

'You might have been the death of me!' she quavered.

He did not heed, however, and began to shout with increased impatience:

'Never mind that, let's pay you and be off; we shall have dark on us.'

Still she remained unenlightened, muttering constantly about life, fire, and death, until the man mustered suddenly a thunderous shout:

'Let me pay you, do you hear, let me pay you!'

When she heard at last, there was a change in her demeanour. After an abrupt jerk of her head towards the table and a rapid fluttering of her hands about the bills and leather money-bags, an excited, almost skilful motion, as if she were working on a lace-pillow, she suddenly looked up at Alexander almost gratefully and asked him to add up a little column of figures.

'Add them carefully,' she warned him, however. 'Be very careful, your uncle's money isn't to be thrown away.'

'Never mind her. Add them up quickly,' urged his uncle. 'She's scared out of her life because we might cheat her. But it's all right, never mind, you just tell her what it amounts to.'

'Three pounds, seven and a penny,' said Alexander after a feverish interval.

'Tell her. Shout!'

Urged on by his uncle, he found something delightful in shouting, deliberately:

'Three pounds, seven shillings and a penny,' several times over.

His uncle began to count out the money, the woman nodding her head with a sort of feverish anticipation. When the three notes, the silver, and the odd penny were being passed across the table, he kept shouting:

'Are you satisfied? Are you satisfied?'

'If you are,' she said. 'I am if you are.'

'Thank God for that!'

'Shall I get the reins untied?' asked Alexander.

'Yes, off you go! I'll be there before very long!'

As he left the room and hurried along the gloomy passage he

was overcome by a sense of great relief, followed by elation. Reaching the yard, he heard a sound and turned to see all the seven fat dogs following him. He clapped his hands loudly, hastening them into retreat. He felt he was sick of dogs, money, the dark house, and the rasping voice and ever-quivering head and fingers of the old woman. He touched the apricot in his pocket repeatedly, feeling very happy. Aroused by his approach, the little horse began to show signs of joy too, stamping one foot, tossing its head and tinkling the harness. Alexander stroked the horse's nose and then untied the reins and climbed into the cart.

Five minutes later all was ready. Surrounded by the seven dogs, who crawled about like huge beetles in the approaching twilight, the old woman muttered a few departing words.

'You must come again,' she said, and it almost seemed as if she regretted their departure. 'It's a bad year, and there's no peace from the boys, but there's a few black plums, and if any one does have them it shall be you. They're very good. Shall I expect you?'

'Yes, you can expect us!' shouted the man, impatient to flick the whip.

'Here, little one,' she then said.

And into the boy's outstretched hands she reached up and put first a small apple, on which already birds had been feeding, then a piece of cake, this time made with fruit and baked very hard, and lastly a penny. Then she looked up at him softly and said:

'God bless you.'

And these words seemed to transport him into a rare, trance-like frame of mind, so that he was hardly conscious of her face, the grey house, and the seven stupid faces of the dogs slipping gradually away from him, and of the cart beginning to move forward smoothly and steadily into the summer twilight.

4

They drove forward at an even more leisurely pace than that of the morning. Frequently the little horse walked, the man not using the whip except to flick the air. The baskets creaked under their great weight and the wheels made a monotonous grinding sound. Elsewhere the same tranquil, almost sleepy hush prevailed as in the early morning and at noon, and the same summer odours remained and the same sense of rich and lovely fruitfulness; only outlines and colours were changed; everything shaped itself by degrees of shadow and not light, and it seemed as if flowers and leaves were resting after intense toil, colourless and drooping, simply releasing breaths of heavy perfume.

Ever since morning the boy had been conscious of casting his thoughts forward to this time. Now, as he began to arrive near the fulfilment of them, he felt a desire to travel as swiftly as they had done. To sit still and not surge recklessly on at the pace of thought was an agony. And before long he could not resist asking:

'Let me drive.'

'You! It's too dark. You sit still and eat the old tit's cake.'

'Shall we be long?'

'We're almost in the wood.'

There was something calm and reassuring about these words. He saw the dark belt of trees grow closer and vaster, as though it would reassure and protect him. The singing season was almost past, and owls and jays alone would call in the twilight, but there seemed to him something singing and jubilant in the silence and half-darkness, and gradually his mind filled itself with thoughts and images of a singing, dream-like quality also. And so the distance was obscured, the fading sky retreated and solitary trees standing like dark ghosts seemed to creep away or dissolve where they stood, and nothing remained but the wood standing ready to receive them into its bosom. The little horse slowed to a walk, its feet padding the dust as softly as if shod with leather. The wheels scarcely turned. Nothing called, nothing seemed to happen. . . . Alexander's hand crept to his pocket and closed about the apricot. And then, simultaneously, to the accompaniment of myriads of echoes rising like a confusion of voices, the wood closed about him, and the air he breathed became cooler, sharply sweet with a scent of damp leaves and of evening time and decay.

They drove on and on. Sounds became more numerous, and the wood seemed to be quivering with life. In the echoes of hoofs and wheels, in the stirring branches, in the rustle of invisible creatures over dead leaves, in passing moths, in the cries of birds, in his own breathing, there was something urgent and vital. Sounds seemed to run on before him, heralding his coming.

More and more, however, he became troubled by the thought that this coming might signify nothing. He was oppressed by uncertainty, and he dared not ask if they might stop in the wood.

All he dared to say, in a casual tone as if he had half-forgotten its existence, was:

'Isn't this where we stopped at a house?'

But there was no answer. He waited, and not daring to repeat his question, looked cautiously at his uncle's face, and seeing something passive and preoccupied about it, looked away quickly without a word, lapsing into a mood of half-painful, half-joyful expectancy.

He was astonished a moment later by feeling the cart suddenly come to a standstill. No house was visible, and he did not understand the reason of it all until his uncle climbed out and began striking matches for the lamps.

In order to relieve his wonder completely, he half-whispered, however:

'What's the matter?'

There was a low grunt in answer. Then, as he watched the lamplight swell into a soft circle in the surrounding darkness, he felt unresistingly borne upon him an image of the girl's young, sweet face, filling him with an exuberance of happiness mingled with pain and longing, all the sublime emotion of first ecstasy transforming him, filling his soul with something so fresh, so joyous and amazing that he felt he could not have spoken or that he could scarcely have looked at her even had she suddenly appeared in the lamplight. He felt that he would suffer deeply if he never saw her again, knowing at last, and for the first time in his life, the meaning of suffering as he already knew the meaning of joy.

He was scarcely conscious of the cart moving forward again, the lamplight floating constantly before them like a yellow cloud, the air growing cooler under the trees. His mood of ecstasy resembled a tide, flowing in upon him wave after wave, and his thoughts became tangled and he gained only an impression of trees, very dark and monarchal, endlessly passing and passing.

A light appeared in the wood at last, and startled him abruptly from this mood of entrancement. He became alert and conscious of realities, sitting upright and tense. As he saw the light approaching and enlarging, he felt himself seized with sudden courage, and he said quickly and almost sharply, as if afraid his voice would break:

'Are we going to stop here?'

'Good Lord, what should we stop for?' came the answer. 'At this time of night? God bless me, we've nothing to stop for; we've long enough to go without that. What's the matter? Eat the cake she gave you if you're hungry. Fill your belly a bit. It's a long way, my lad, out of the wood and through the valley. A long way yet.'

It seemed as if he did not listen to these words. He became aware of them instead as one becomes aware of a flock of birds flying from a horizon. The character of each word is lost in the whole as the individuality of each bird is lost in the flock; only about their meaning, as of the species of bird, there remains no doubt. And he did not answer, feeling once again that he could not trust himself to speak, and also that perhaps he would have cried if he had begun to speak. A white moth flew past, and he felt that just as swiftly and irrevocably had the light of the house flown by before he could raise a hand to catch it. A great oak stumbled towards them like a malformed creature and lurched into darkness. All things retreated or moved endlessly on and on. Only he himself, clinging to his precious thoughts, remained unmoving, not able to resist the wretchedness overpowering him.

Again the little horse fell into the same unbroken leisurely pace as in the early morning. Soon they passed out of the wood, reaching open fields under a calm deep-blue sky sown with stars. A smell of harvest would come, pass away, and be renewed, stronger and stronger.

His uncle began to murmur some old song, as he had done under the plum-trees.

His wretchedness became complete, and his thoughts raced backward to the morning. With strange sharpness he saw the sunshine begin to beautify everything again, the golden, unfamiliar countryside, the harvesters, the distant woods, the dew clinging to the leaves—and at last the house, the hot, sweet garden, the unbroken stillness into which the girl had come like a vision, silently too.

The song went on. And to the boy it seemed that nothing so beautiful or memorable had ever taken place in his life, and as he recalled the moments by the pond, under the sloe-tree, his unhappiness was mingled suddenly with an ecstatic joy. He felt that there was a strange sharp pleasure even in disappointment, even in the pain of not seeing her again.

The sleepy voice of his uncle sang drowsily on for long afterwards. Something in it alternately pained and fortified him. Then he would feel half ashamed, half foolish as he remembered all his secret thoughts, all his idealizing of the girl throughout the long day. Once he caught an image of her face, beautifully fresh and enchanting in all its detail, and filled with an agony of bliss he asked himself over and over again:

'Why didn't we stop there? Shall I ever see her again? Will she remember me?'

When this mood, like all others, had exhausted itself, he passed into a long tranquillity. Familiar fields and trees appeared in the darkness, and the horse began travelling a little faster, as if sensing home. He brooded quietly now on the day that had passed, turning it over and over in his mind like some legend almost too wonderful to believe, mingling with it strange tales he had heard, things he had treasured up in his soul long, long ago, and he thought with special pleasure of the little house, the woman whose name was Cilla, the great fruit garden, the dogs, the little sharp man who had told him wonderful lies, and the old woman saying 'God bless you' as they drove away, his mind filling moment by moment with a mysterious elation and joy.

Soon they drove into a street by the river and so into a little yard. He saw the familiar sycamore-tree, obscure sheds, low black stables, and then the house, throwing a stream of light on the tree.

At the sound of their approach a door opened, and there appeared first an old fat woman with a shawl over her head, then his aunt, a little shrewd, quick person who ran hither and thither like an ant, and lastly his mother, plump, rosy-faced, and looking rather like a kind, soft-hearted nurse.

They began to pour out a stream of arguments and questions

and to remonstrate severely with his uncle, who did not once reply.

'Where have you been, what's been happening to you? Oh, dear! keeping the boy out in that cart, I wonder you don't die of shame. What's been happening, Alexander? Aren't you cold riding in the cart? I wonder he isn't perished. Hot, did you say? Yes, in day-time I'll own, but the dews are so heavy. It's not sense—I'd be ashamed. Jump you down, my lamb. Lord, there's dew on the cart, bless me if there isn't. Jump you down and come indoors. Lord love us!'

To all this he said nothing. He felt that the three women, particularly Ursula and even his mother, were being foolish. In the cart it had been peaceful and he had dreamed. Not to relinquish this peace or these dreams seemed everything to him. He turned slowly and walked away.

Ursula hobbled after him to the house. As he reached the door and she ushered him into the light she broke out again:

'What happened, my lamb? Did you stop anywhere?'

He shook his head; a sharp feeling half of wretchedness, half of aching joy, swept over him; with difficulty he murmured: 'No, we didn't stop anywhere.'

With these words he heard the little horse walking away to its stable and the last tinkle of chains, and with the cry of an owl, with the closing of a door somewhere, with his uncle's voice asking if all were locked for the night, he felt that the strange long eventfulness of the day was closing, was being shut away from him like a book. He sat motionless, not knowing whether to laugh or cry with overwhelming happiness and pain.

And suddeny, his heart very full, he felt that everything which had filled and beautified the day had at last slipped away into the past, and lay in his mind like a clearly remembered dream.

He could only sit silent in wonder. The day had passed, the journey was at an end.

When would another begin?

WILLIAM SAROYAN

Ever Fall in Love with a Midget?

'I don't suppose you ever fell in love with a midget weighing thirty-nine pounds, did you?'

'No,' I said, 'but have another beer.'

'Down in Gallup,' he said, 'twenty years ago. Fellow by the name of Rufus Jenkins came to town with six white horses and two black ones. Said he wanted a man to break the horses for him because his left leg was wood and he couldn't do it. Had a meeting at Parker's Mercantile Store and finally came to blows, me and Henry Walpal. Bashed his head with a brass cuspidor and ran away to Mexico, but he didn't die.

'Couldn't speak a word. Took up with a cattle-breeder named Diego, educated in California. Spoke the language better than you and me. Said, "Your job, Murph, is to feed them prize bulls." I said, "Fine; what'll I feed them?" He said, "Hay, lettuce, salt, and beet." I said, "Fine; they're your bulls."

'Came to blows two days later over an accordion he claimed I stole. I borrowed it and during the fight busted it over his head; ruined one of the finest accordions I ever saw. Grabbed a horse and rode back across the border. Texas. Got to talking with a fellow who looked honest. Turned out to be a Ranger who was looking for me.'

'Yeah,' I said. 'You were saying, a thirty-nine pound midget.'

'Will I ever forget that lady?' he said. 'Will I ever get over that amazon of small proportions?'

'Will you?' I said.

'If I live to be sixty,' he said.

'Sixty?' I said. 'You look more than sixty now.'

'That's trouble showing in my face. Trouble and complications. I was fifty-six three months ago.'

'Oh.'

'Told the Texas Ranger my name was Rothstein, mining engineer from Pennsylvania, looking for something worth while. Mentioned two places in Houston. Nearly lost an eye early one morning, going down the stairs. Ran into a six-footer with an iron-claw where his right hand was supposed to be. Said, "You broke up my home." Told him I was a stranger in Houston. The girls gathered at the top of the stairs to see a fight. Seven of them. Six feet and an iron-claw. That's bad on the nerves. Kicked him in the mouth when he swung for my head with the claw. Would have lost an eye except for quick thinking. Rolled into the gutter and pulled a gun. Fired seven times, but I was back upstairs. Left the place an hour later, dressed in silk and feathers, with a hat swung around over my face. Saw him standing on the corner, waiting. Said, "Care for a wiggle?" Said he didn't. Went on down the street, left town.

'I don't suppose you ever had to put on a dress to save your skin, did you?'

'No,' I said, 'and I never fell in love with a midget weighing thirty-nine pounds. Have another beer.'

'Thanks. Ever try to herd cattle on a bicycle?'

'No,' I said.

'Left Houston with sixty cents in my pocket, gift of a girl named Lucinda. Walked fourteen miles in fourteen hours. Big house with barb-wire all around, and big dogs. One thing I never could get around. Walked past the gate, anyway, from hunger and thirst. Dogs jumped up and came for me. Walked right into them, growing older every second. Went up to the door and knocked. Big negress opened the door, closed it quick. Said, "On your way, white trash."

'Knocked again. Said, "On your way." Again. "On your way." Again. This time the old man himself opened the door, ninety if he was a day. Sawed-off shotgun too.

'Said, "I ain't looking for trouble, father. I'm hungry and thirsty, name's Cavanaugh."

'Took me in and made mint juleps for the two of us.

'Said, "Living here alone, father?"

'Said, "Drink and ask no questions; maybe I am and maybe I ain't. You saw the negress. Draw your own conclusions."

'I'd heard of that, but didn't wink out of tact.

'Called out, "Elvira, bring this gentleman sandwiches."

'Young enough for a man of seventy, probably no more than forty, and big.

'Said, "Any good at cards?" Said, "No."

'Said, "Fine, Cavanaugh, take a hand of poker."

'Played all night.

'If I told you that old Southern gentleman was my grandfather, you wouldn't believe me, would you?'

'No.'

'Well, it so happens he wasn't, although it would have been remarkable if he had been.'

'Where did you herd cattle on a bicycle?'

'Toledo, Ohio, 1918.'

'Toledo, Ohio?' I said. 'They don't herd cattle up there.'

'They don't any more. They did in 1918. One fellow did, leastways. Book-keeper named Sam Gold. Only Jewish cowboy I ever saw. Straight from the East-Side New York. Sombrero, lariats, Bull Durham, two head of cattle, and two bicycles. Called his place Gold Bar Ranch, two acres, just outside the city limits.

'That was the year of the War, you'll remember.'

'Yeah,' I said.

'Remember a picture called *Shoulder Arms*?'

'Sure. Saw it five times.'

'Remember when Charlie Chaplin thought he was washing *his* foot, and the foot turned out to be another man's?'

'Sure.'

'You may not believe me, but I was the man whose foot was washed by Chaplin in that picture.'

'It's possible,' I said, 'but how about herding them two cows on a bicycle? How'd you do it?'

'Easiest thing in the world. Rode no hands. Had to, otherwise couldn't lasso the cows. Worked for Sam Gold till the cows ran away. Bicycles scared them. They went into Toledo and we never saw hide or hair of them again. Advertised in every paper, but never got them back. Broke his heart. Sold both bikes and returned to New York.

'Took four aces from a deck of red cards and walked to town.

Poker. Fellow in the game named Chuck Collins, liked to gamble. Told him with a smile I didn't suppose he'd care to bet a hundred dollars I wouldn't hold four aces the next hand. Called it. My cards were red on the blank side. The other cards were blue. Plumb forgot all about it. Showed him four aces. Ace of spades, ace of clubs, ace of diamonds, ace of hearts. I'll remember them four cards if I live to be sixty. Would have been killed on the spot except for the hurricane that year.'

'Hurricane?'

'You haven't forgotten the Toledo hurricane of 1918, have you?'

'No,' I said. 'There was no hurricane in Toledo, in 1918, or any other year.'

'For the love of God, then, what do you suppose that commotion was? And how come I came to in Chicago? Dream-walking down State Street?'

'I guess they scared you.'

'No, that wasn't it. You go back to the papers of November 1918 and I think you'll find there was a hurricane in Toledo. I remember sitting on the roof of a two-storey house, floating north-west.'

'North-west?'

'Sure.'

'Okay, have another beer.'

'Thanks,' he said, 'thaaaaanks.'

'I don't suppose *you* ever fell in love with a midget weighing thirty-nine pounds, did you?' I said.

'Who?' he said.

'You,' I said.

'No,' he said, 'can't say I have.'

'Well,' I said, 'let *me* tell *you* about it.'

Everyman
A selection of titles

BIOGRAPHY

Bligh, William. *A Book of the 'Bounty'*
Boswell, James. *The Life of Samuel Johnson*
Byron, Lord. *Letters*
Cibber, Colley. *An Apology for the Life of Colley Cibber*
*De Quincey, Thomas. *Confessions of an English Opium-Eater*
Forster, John. *Life of Charles Dickens* (2 vols)
*Gaskell, Elizabeth. *The Life of Charlotte Brontë*
*Gilchrist, Alexander. *The Life of William Blake*
Houghton, Lord. *The Life and Letters of John Keats*
*Johnson, Samuel. *Lives of the English Poets: a selection*
Pepys, Samuel. *Diary* (3 vols)
Thomas, Dylan
    Adventures in the Skin Trade
    Portrait of the Artist as a Young Dog
Tolstoy. *Childhood, Boyhood and Youth*
*Vasari, Giorgio. *Lives of the Painters, Sculptors, and Architects*
    (4 vols)

ESSAYS AND CRITICISM

Arnold, Matthew. *On the Study of Celtic Literature*
*Bacon, Francis. *Essays*
Coleridge, Samuel Taylor
    Biographia Literaria
    Shakespearean Criticism (2 vols)
Dryden, John. *Of Dramatic Poesy and other critical essays*
    (2 vols)

*Lawrence, D.H. *Stories, Essays and Poems*
*Milton, John. *Prose Writings*
Montaigne, Michel Eyquem de. *Essays* (3 vols)
Paine, Thomas. *The Rights of Man*
Pater, Walter. *Essays on Literature and Art*
Spencer, Herbert. *Essays on Education and Kindred Subjects*

FICTION

---

*American Short Stories of the Nineteenth Century
Austen, Jane
    Emma
    Mansfield Park
    Northanger Abbey
    Persuasion
    Pride and Prejudice
    Sense and Sensibility
*Bennett, Arnold. *The Old Wives' Tale*
Boccaccio, Giovanni. *The Decameron*
Brontë, Anne
    Agnes Grey
    The Tenant of Wildfell Hall
Brontë, Charlotte
    Jane Eyre
    The Professor and *Emma* (a fragment)
    Shirley
    Villette
Brontë, Emily. *Wuthering Heights* and *Poems*
*Bunyan, John. *Pilgrim's Progress*
Butler, Samuel.
    Erewhon and *Erewhon Revisited*
    The Way of All Flesh
Collins, Wilkie
    The Moonstone
    The Woman in White
Conrad, Joseph
    The Nigger of the 'Narcissus', Typhoon, Falk and other stories
    Nostromo

HISTORY

LEGENDS AND SAGAS

*Beowulf and Its Analogues
*Chrétien de Troyes. *Arthurian Romances*
 Egils Saga
 Holinshed, Raphael. *Chronicle*
*Layamon and Wace. *Arthurian Chronicles*
*The Mabinogion
*The Saga of Gisli
*The Saga of Grettir the Strong
 Snorri Sturluson. *Heimskringla* (3 vols)
*The Story of Burnt Njal

POETRY AND DRAMA

*Anglo-Saxon Poetry
*American Verse of the Nineteenth Century
*Arnold, Matthew. *Selected Poems and Prose*
*Blake, William. *Selected Poems*
*Browning, Robert. *Men and Women and other poems*
 Chaucer, Geoffrey
    **Canterbury Tales*
    **Troilus and Criseyde*
*Clare, John. *Selected Poems*
*Coleridge, Samuel Taylor. *Poems*
*Elizabethan Sonnets
*English Moral Interludes
*Everyman and Medieval Miracle Plays
*Everyman's Book of Evergreen Verse
*Gay, John. *The Beggar's Opera and other eighteenth-century*
        plays
*The Golden Treasury of Longer Poems
 Goldsmith, Oliver. *Poems and Plays*
*Hardy, Thomas. *Selected Poems*
*Herbert, George. *The English Poems*
*Hopkins, Gerard Manley. *The Major Poems*
 Ibsen, Henrik
    **A Doll's House; The Wild Dick; The Lady from the Sea*
    **Hedda Gabler; The Master Builder; John Gabriel Borkman*

*Keats, John. *Poems*
*Langland, William. *The Vision of Piers Plowman*
  Marlowe, Christopher. *Complete Plays and Poems*
*Milton, John. *Complete Poems*
*Middleton, Thomas. *Three Plays*
*Palgrave's Golden Treasury
*Pearl, Patience, Cleanness, and Sir Gawain and the Green Knight
*Pope, Alexander. *Collected Poems*
*Restoration Plays
*The Rubáiyát of Omar Khayyám and other Persian poems
*Shelley, Percy Bysshe. *Selected Poems*
*Six Middle English Romances
*Spenser, Edmund. *The Faerie Queene: a selection*
  The Stuffed Owl
*Synge, J.M. *Plays, Poems and Prose*
*Tennyson, Alfred. *In Memoriam, Maud and other poems*
  Thomas, Dylan
      Collected Poems, 1934–1952
      Under Milk Wood
*Wilde, Oscar. *Plays, Prose Writings and Poems*
*Wordsworth, William. *Selected Poems*

RELIGION AND PHILOSOPHY

  Aristotle. *Metaphysics*
*Bacon, Francis. *The Advancement of Learning*
*Berkeley, George. *Philosophical Works including the works on
      vision*
*The Buddha's Philosophy of Man
*Chinese Philosophy in Classical Times
*Descartes, René. *A Discourse on Method*
*Hindu Scriptures
  Hume, David. *A Treatise of Human Nature*
*Kant, Immanuel. *A Critique of Pure Reason*
*The Koran
*Leibniz, Gottfried Wilhelm. *Philosophical Writings*
*Locke, John. *An Essay Concerning Human Understanding
      (abridgment)*
*Moore, Thomas. *Utopia*

Pascal, Blaise. *Pensées*
Plato. *The Trial and Death of Socrates*
*The Ramayana and Mahábhárata

SCIENCES: POLITICAL AND GENERAL

Aristotle. *Ethics*
*Castiglione, Baldassare. *The Book of the Courtier*
*Coleridge, Samuel Taylor. *On the Constitution of the Church and
    State*
*Darwin, Charles. *The Origin of Species*
George, Henry. *Progress and Poverty*
Harvey, William. *The Circulation of the Blood and other writings*
*Hobbes, Thomas. *Leviathan*
*Locke, John. *Two Treatises of Government*
*Machiavelli, Niccolò. *The Prince and other political writings*
Marx, Karl. *Capital. Volume 1*
*Mill, J.S. *Utilitarianism; On Liberty; Representative
    Government*
Owen, Robert. *A New View of Society and other writings*
*Plato. *The Republic*
*Ricardo, David. *The Principles of Political Economy and
    Taxation*
Rousseau, J.-J.
    Emile
    The Social Contract and *Discourses*
Smith, Adam. *The Wealth of Nations*
*Wollstonecraft, Mary. *A Vindication of the Rights of Woman*

TRAVEL AND TOPOGRAPHY

Boswell, James. *The Journal of a Tour to the Hebrides*
*Darwin, Charles. *The Voyage of the 'Beagle'*
Giraldus Cambrensis. *Itinerary through Wales* and *Description
    of Wales*
Stevenson, R.L. *An Inland Voyage; Travels with a Donkey; The
    Silverado Squatters*
Stow, John. *The Survey of London*
*White, Gilbert. *The Natural History of Selborne*